D1250409

The Secret Garden

a graphic novel

Mariah Marsden & Hanna Luechtefeld

Andrews McMeel
PUBLISHING®

To those tending their own secret gardens.

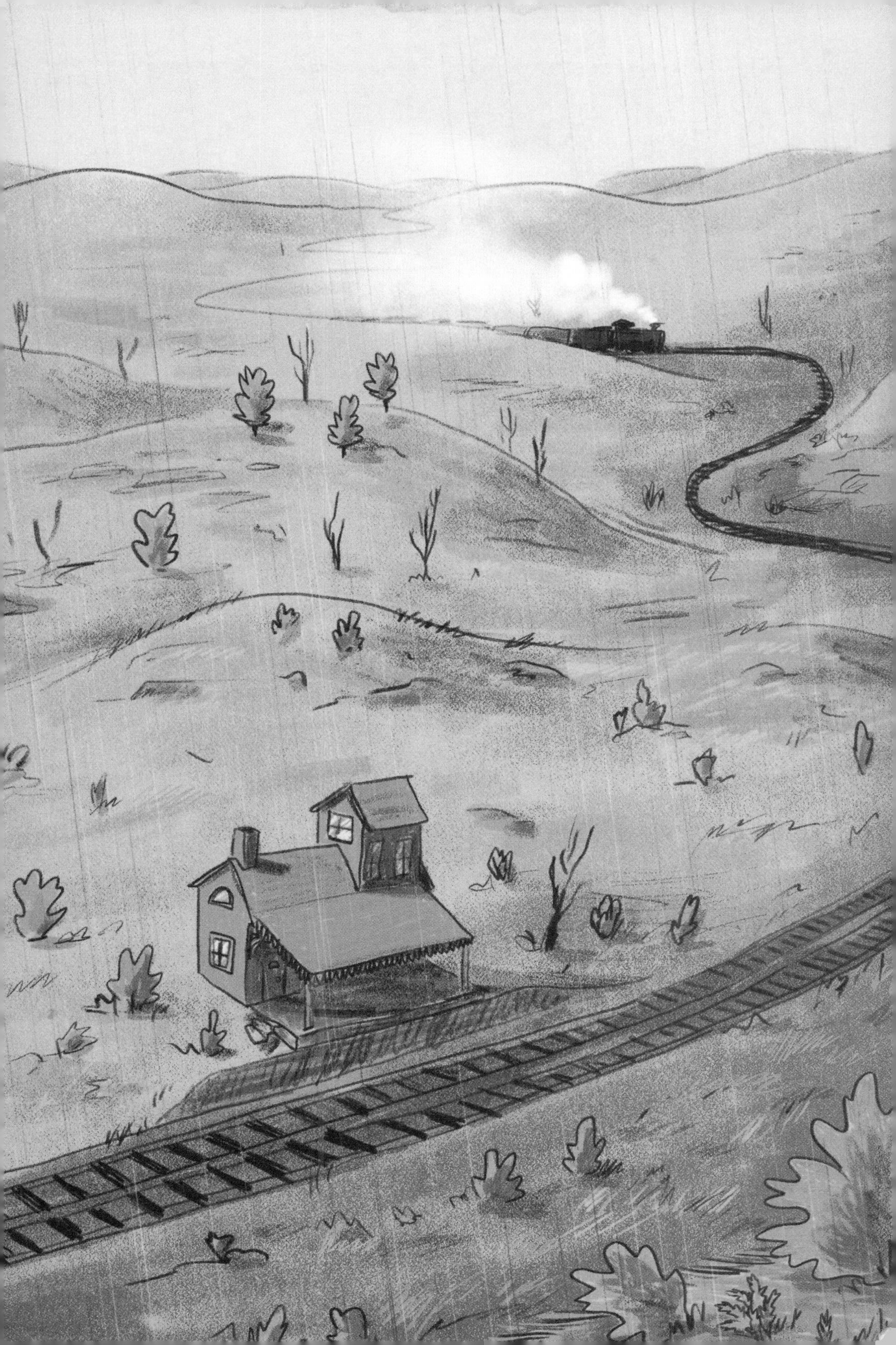

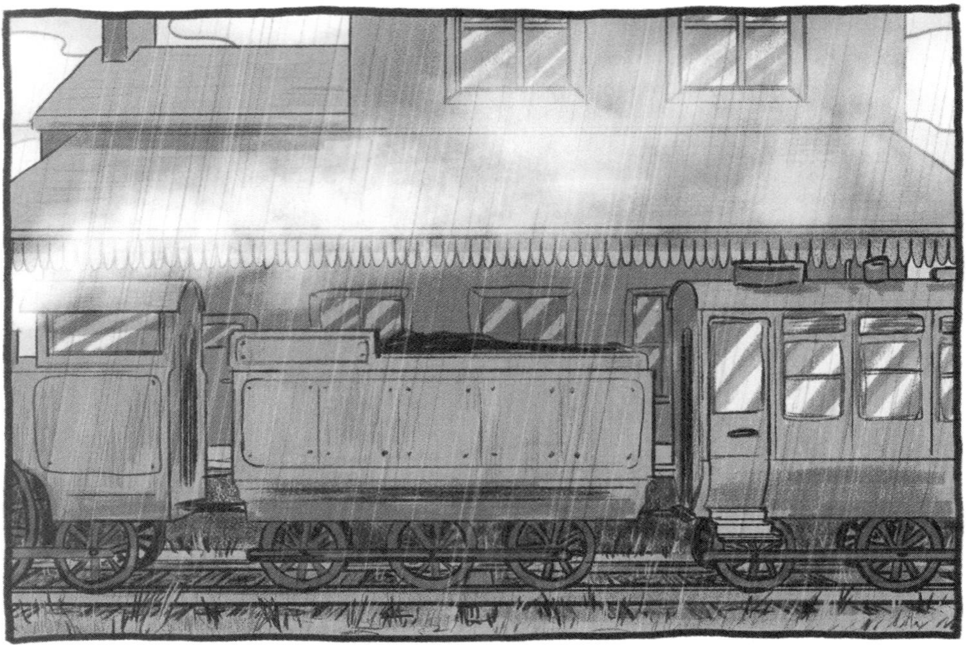

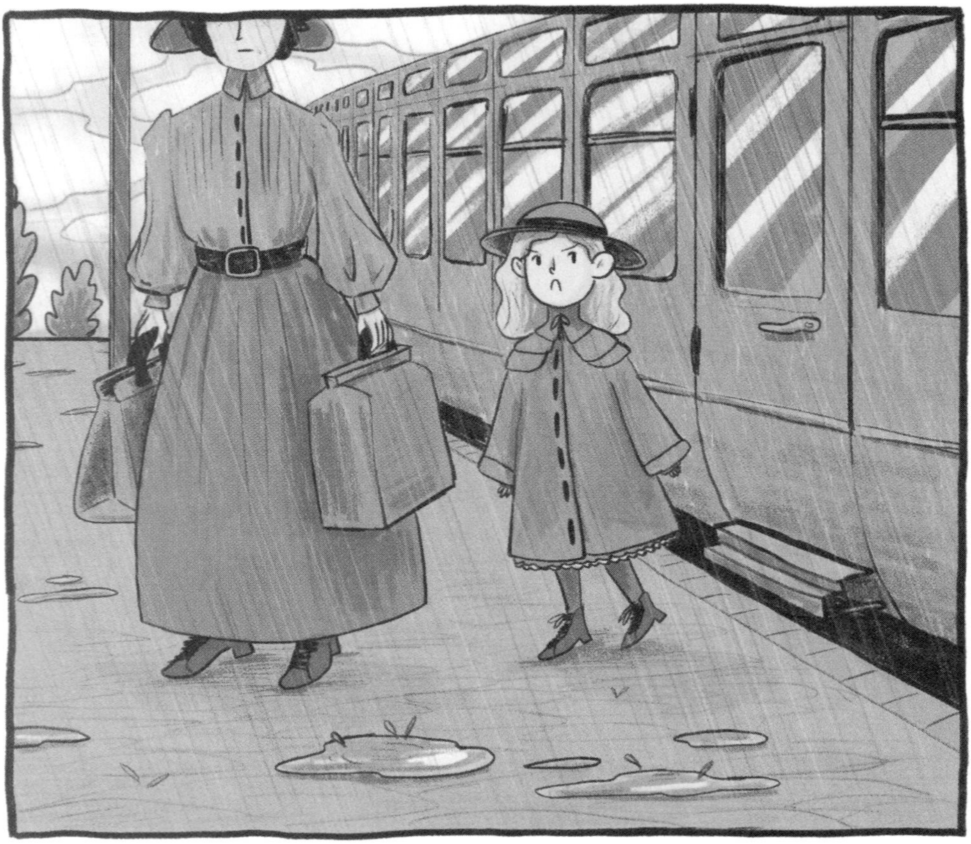

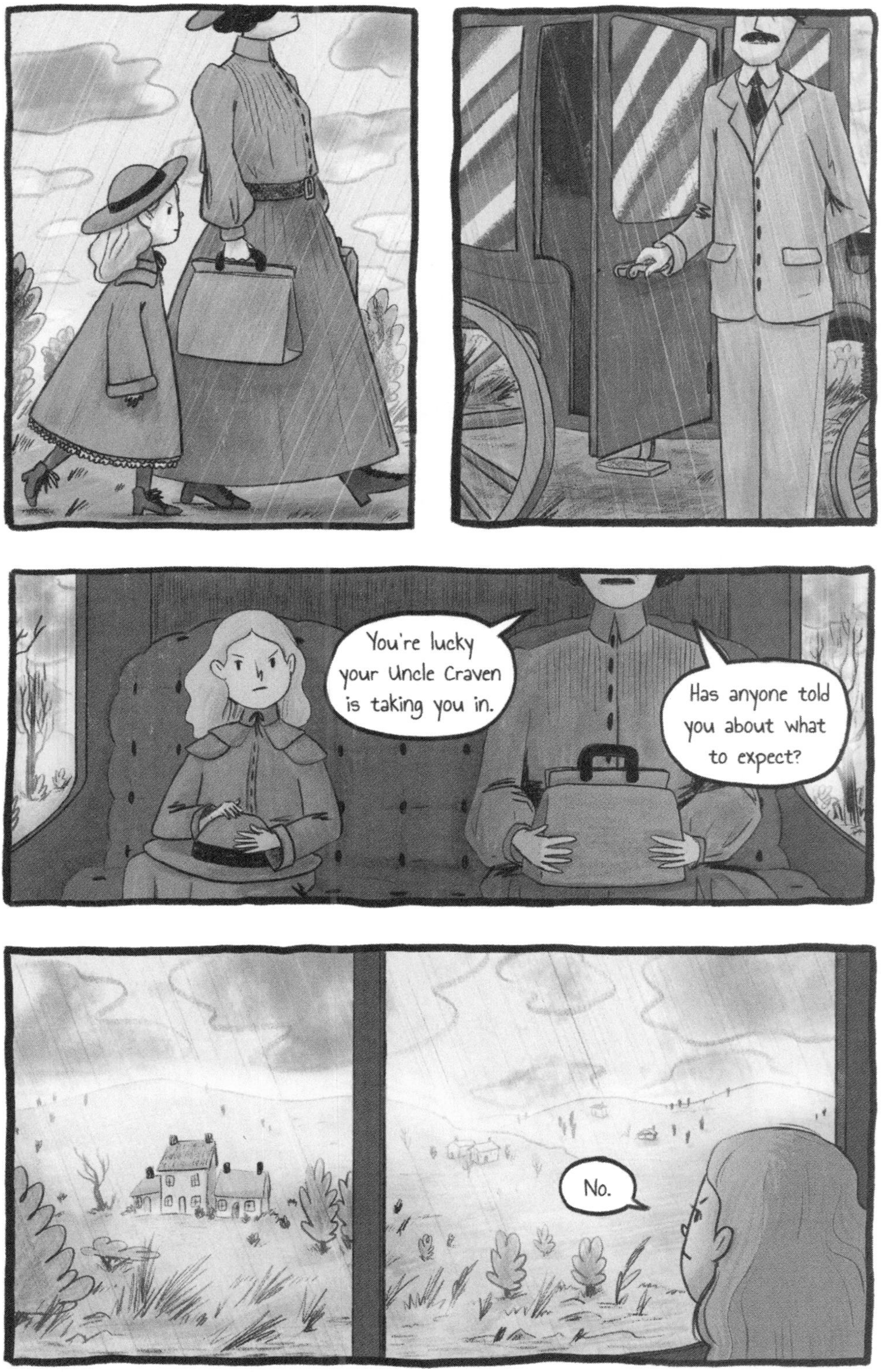
You're lucky your Uncle Craven is taking you in.
Has anyone told you about what to expect?
No.

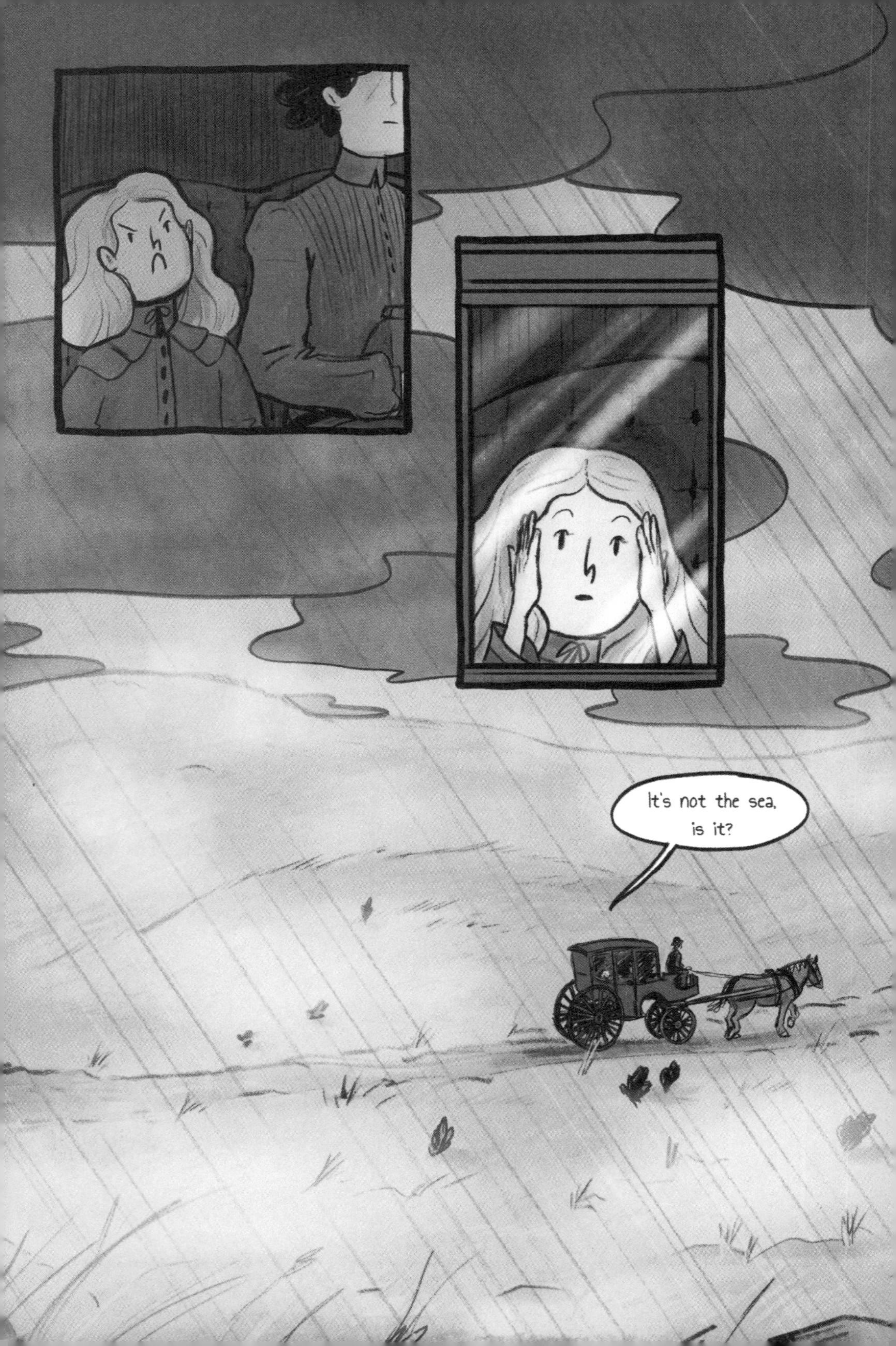
It's not the sea, is it?

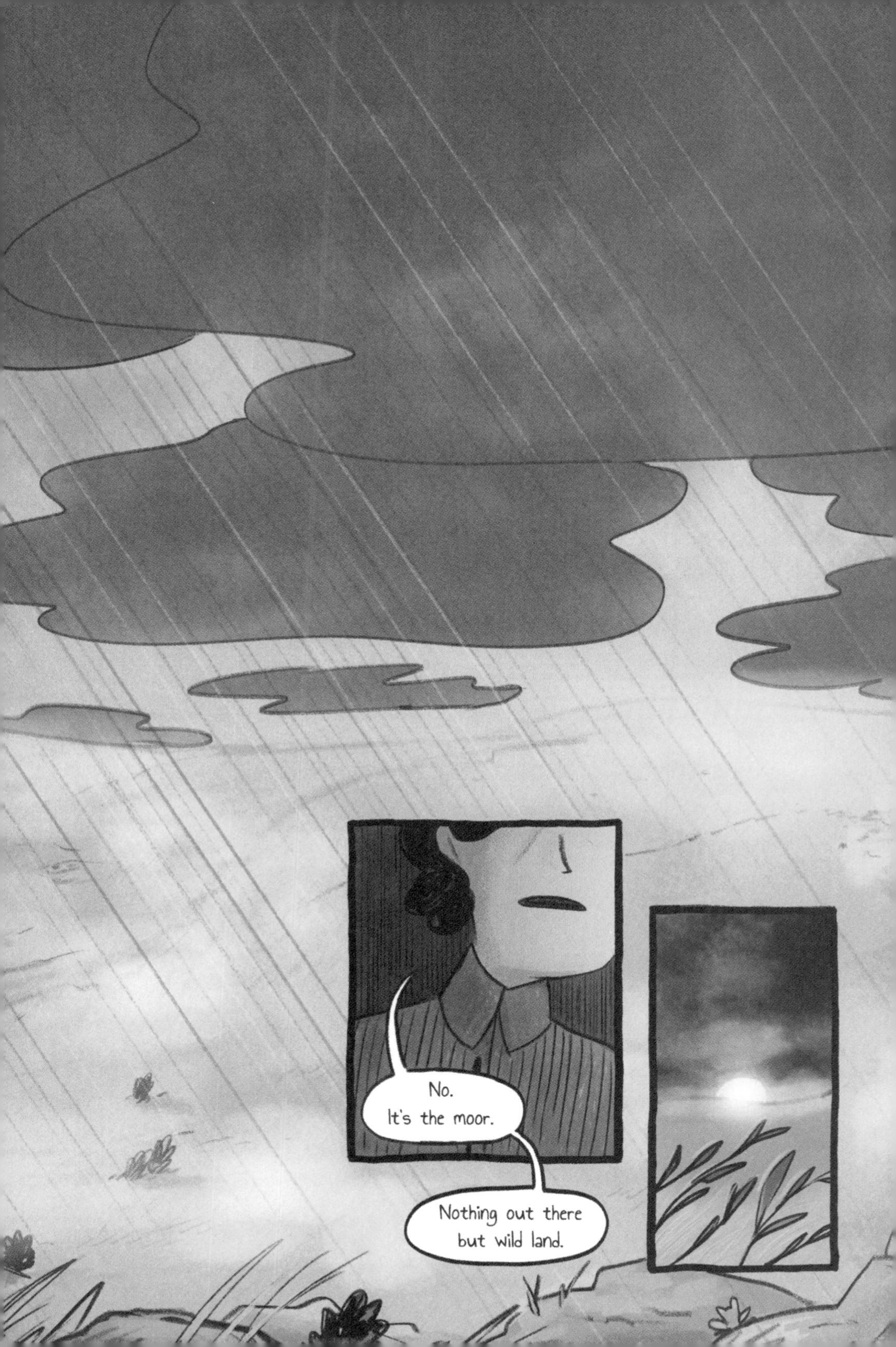
No.
It's the moor.
Nothing out there
but wild land.

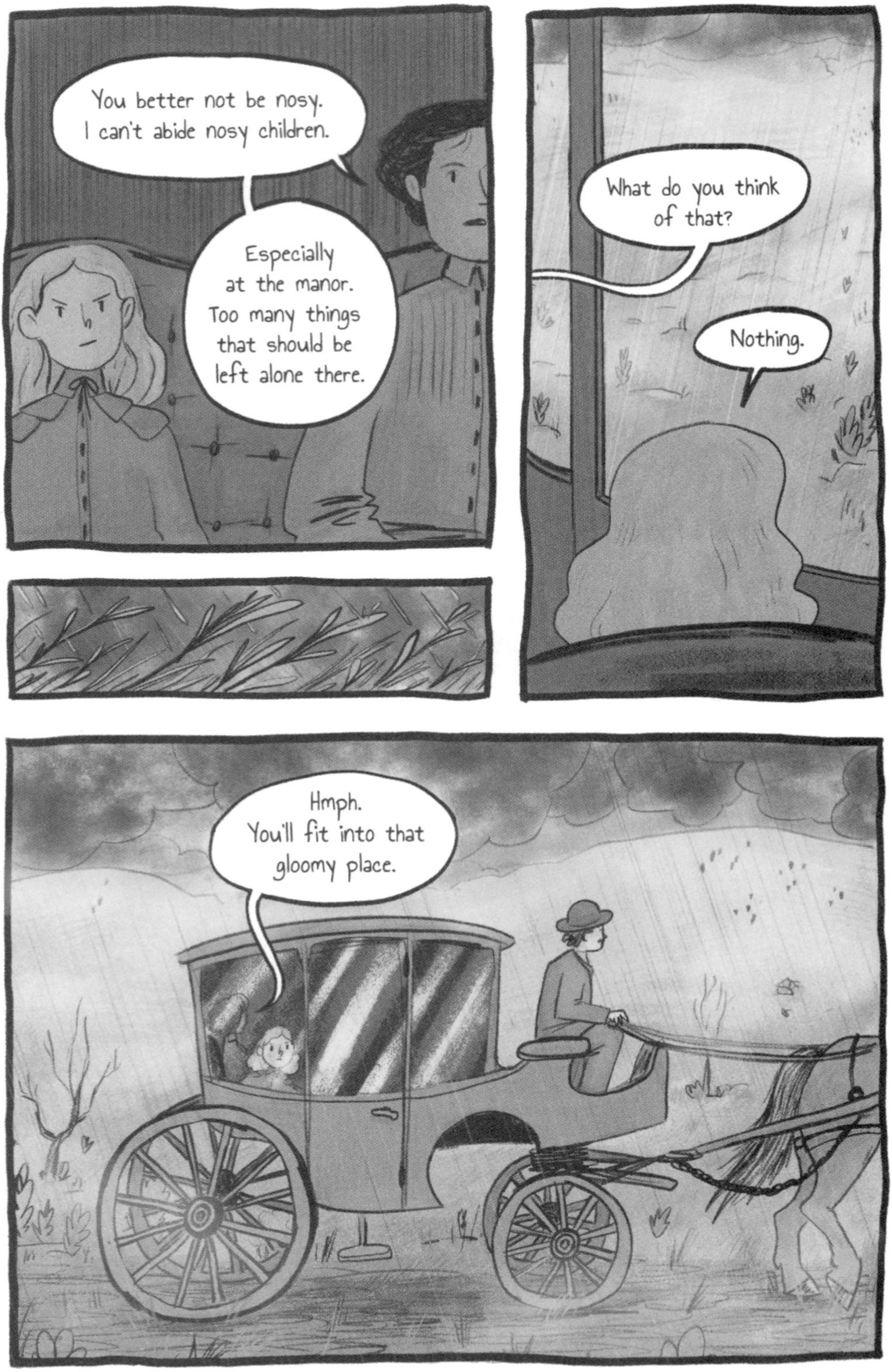
You better not be nosy. I can't abide nosy children.
Especially at the manor. Too many things that should be left alone there.
What do you think of that?
Nothing.
Hmph. You'll fit into that gloomy place.

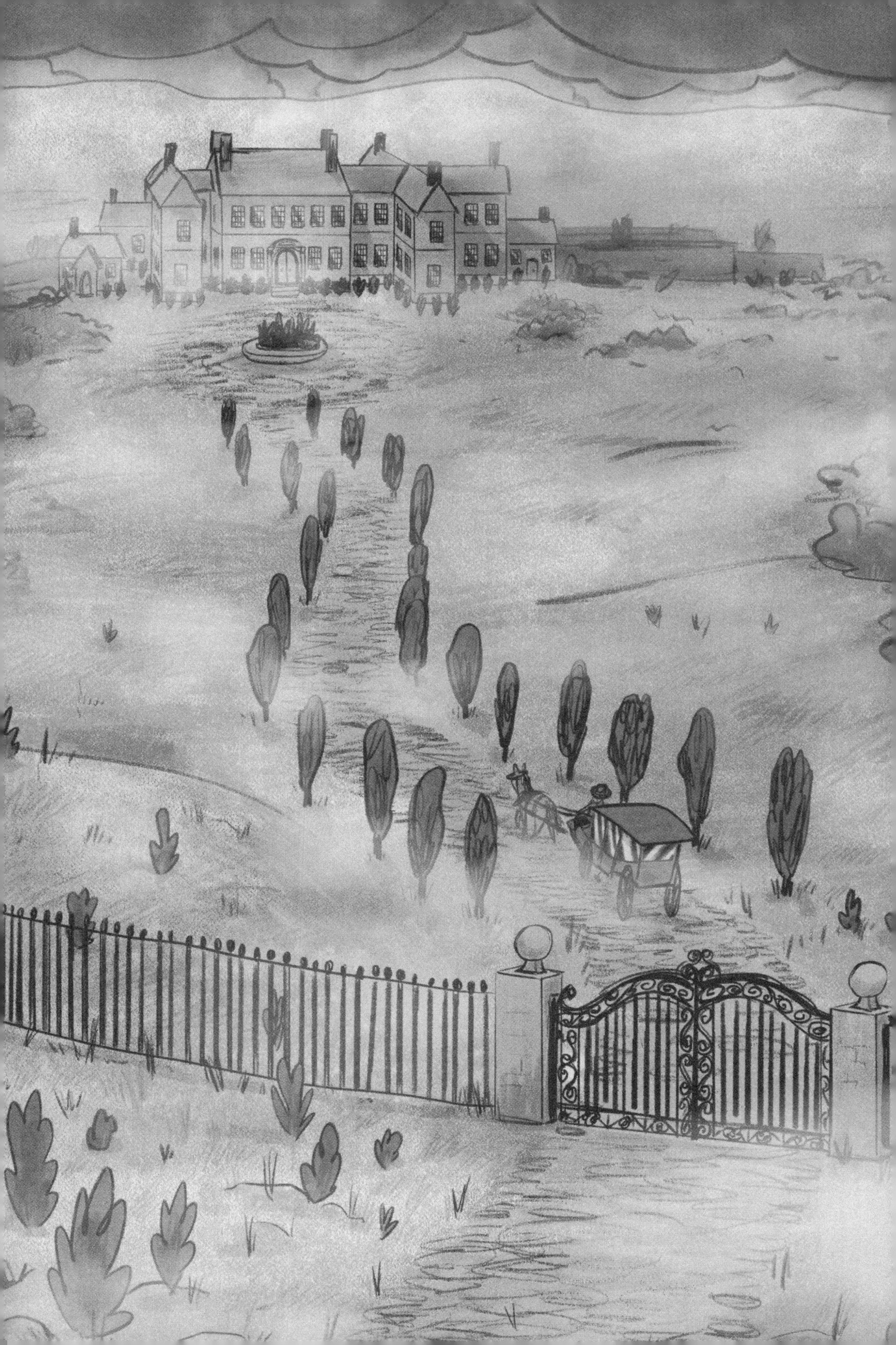

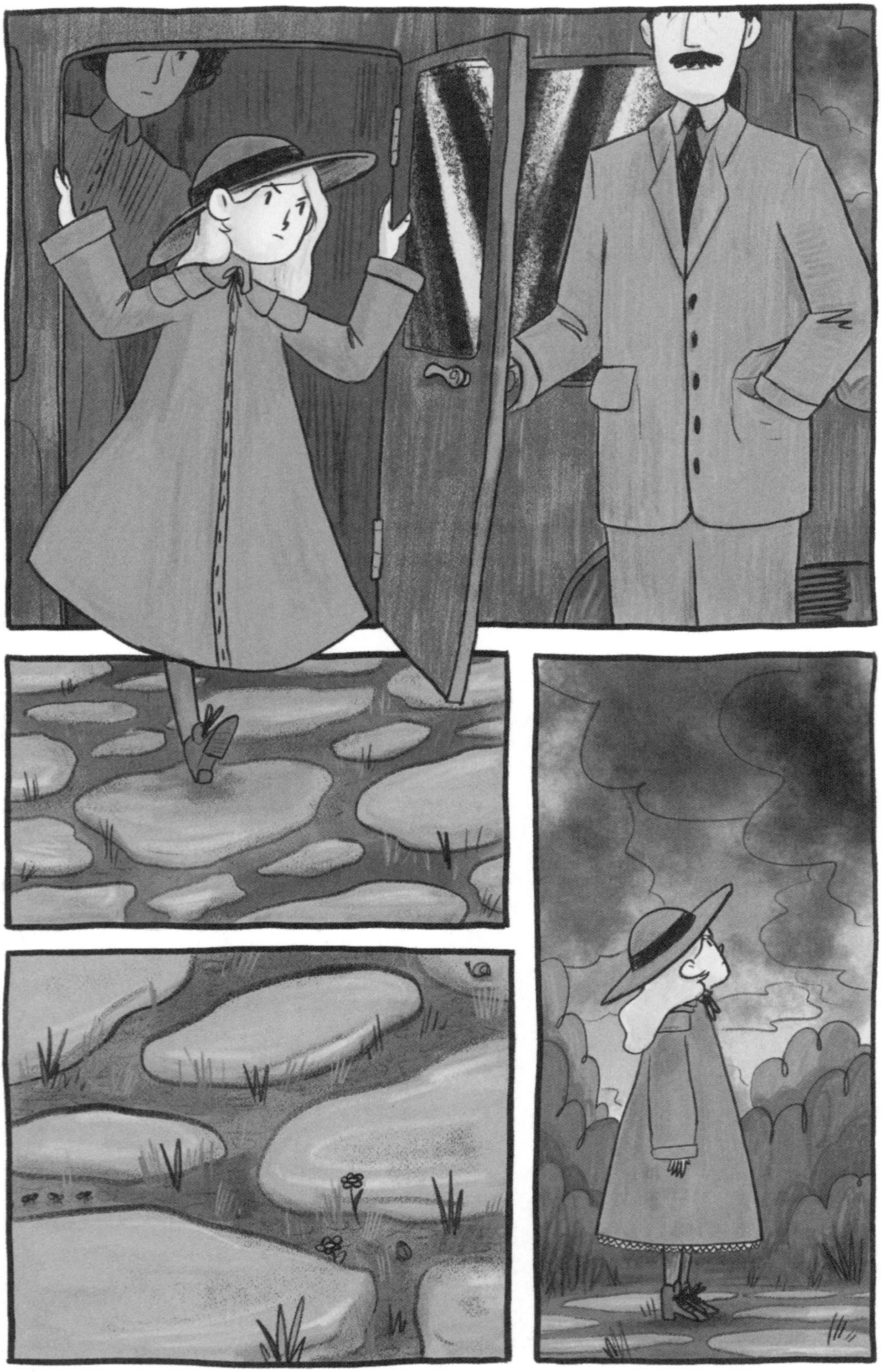

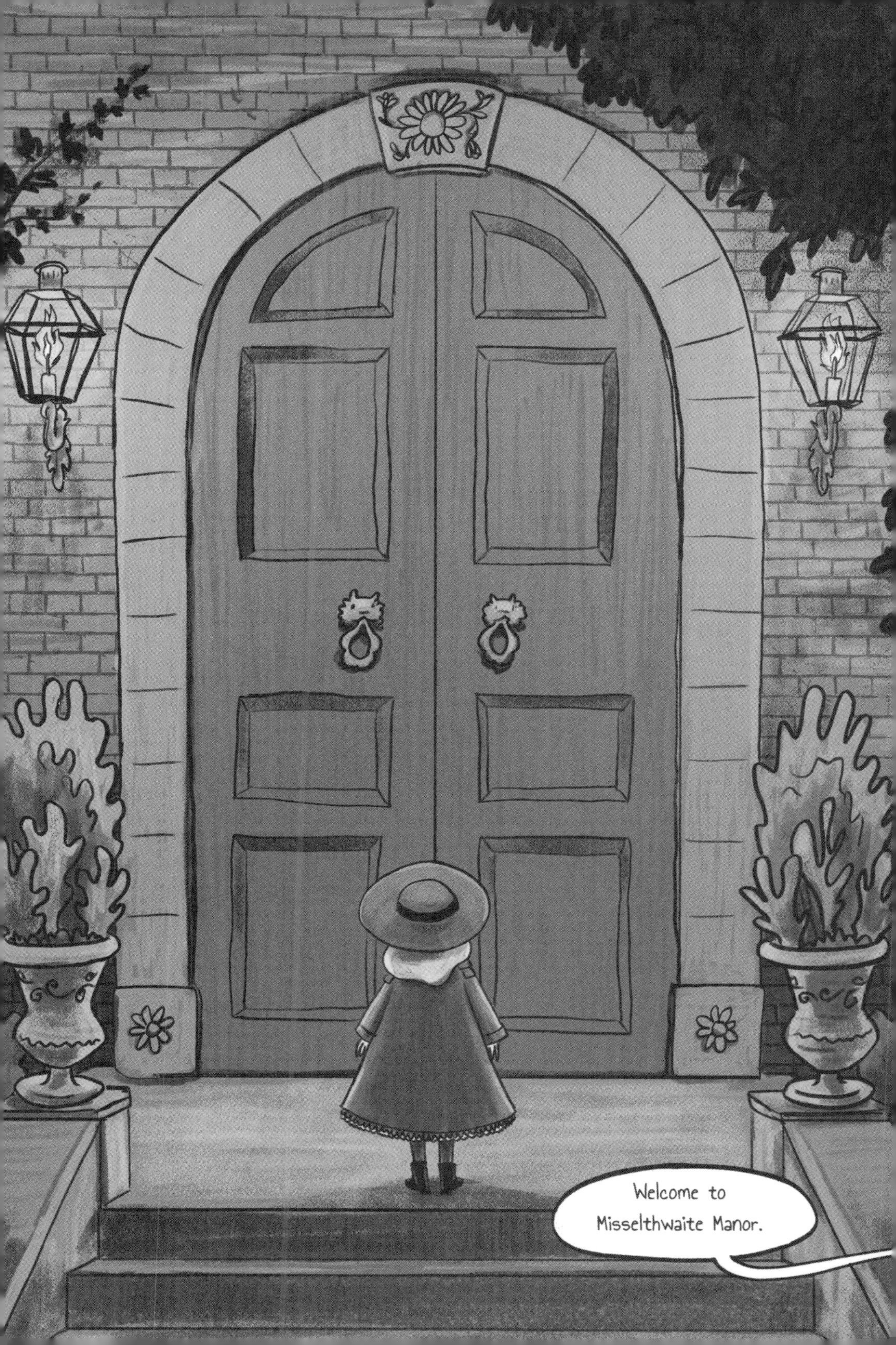
Welcome to Misselthwaite Manor.

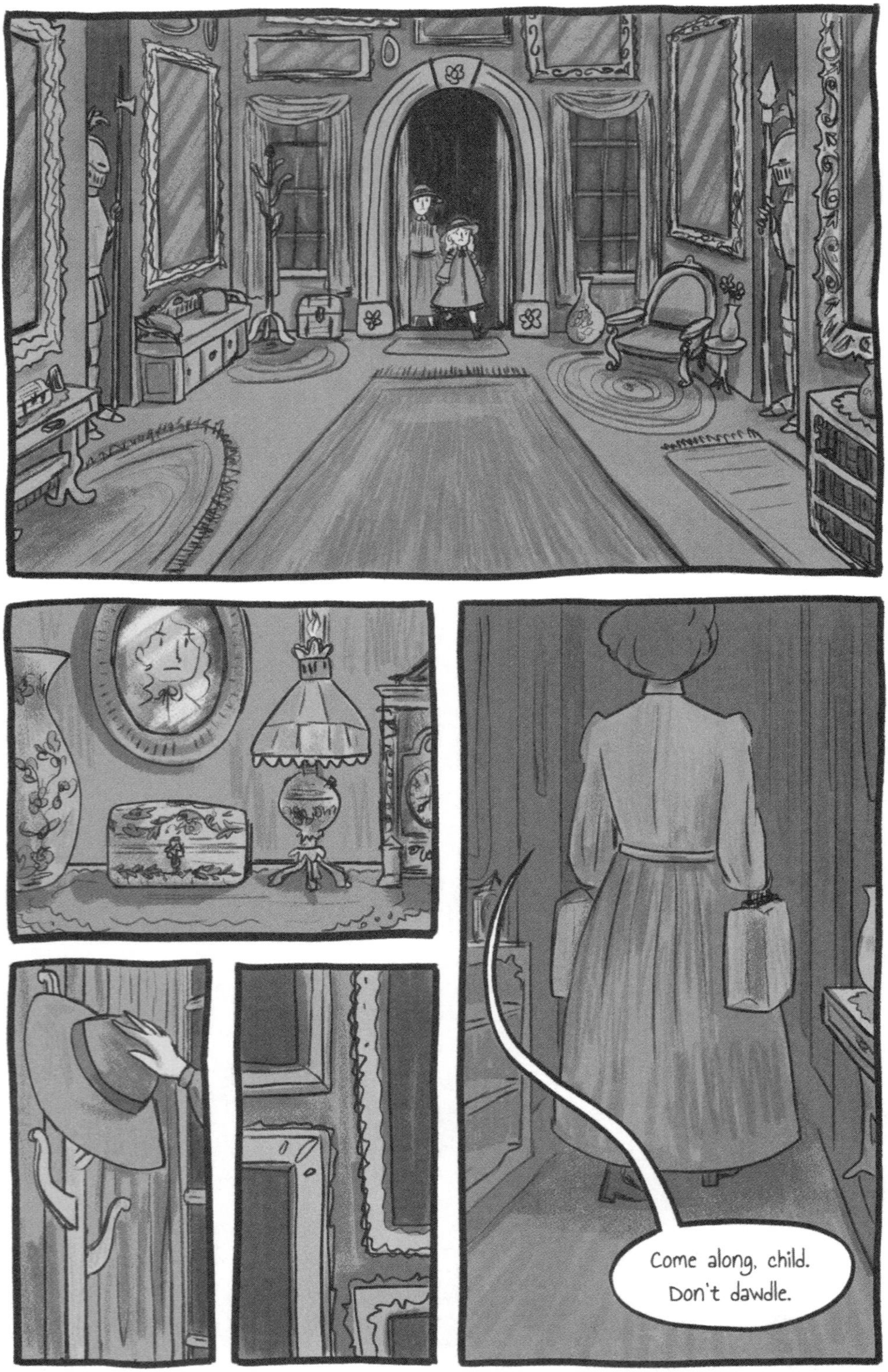
Come along, child. Don't dawdle.

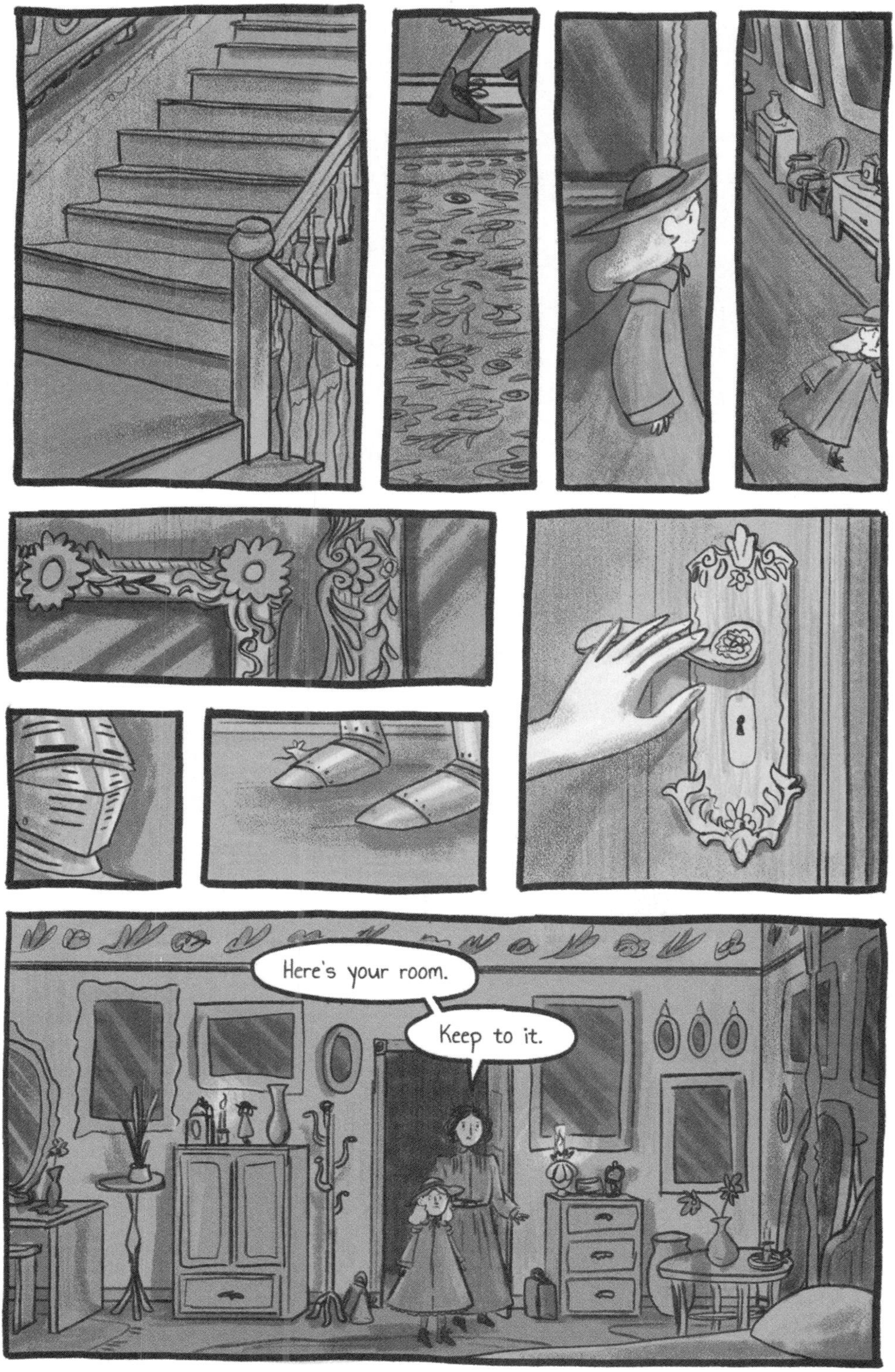
Here's your room.
Keep to it.

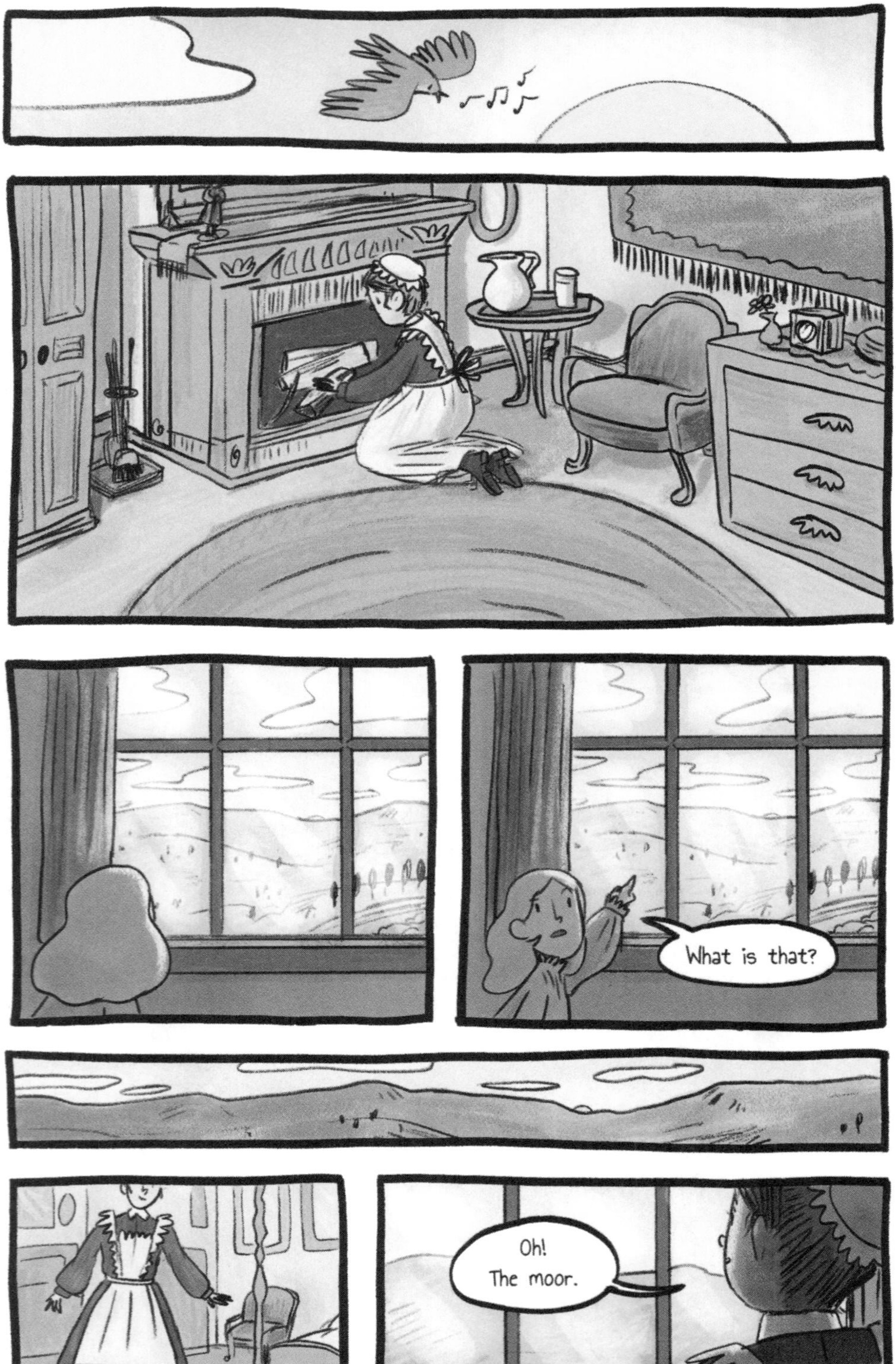
What is that?
Oh!
The moor.

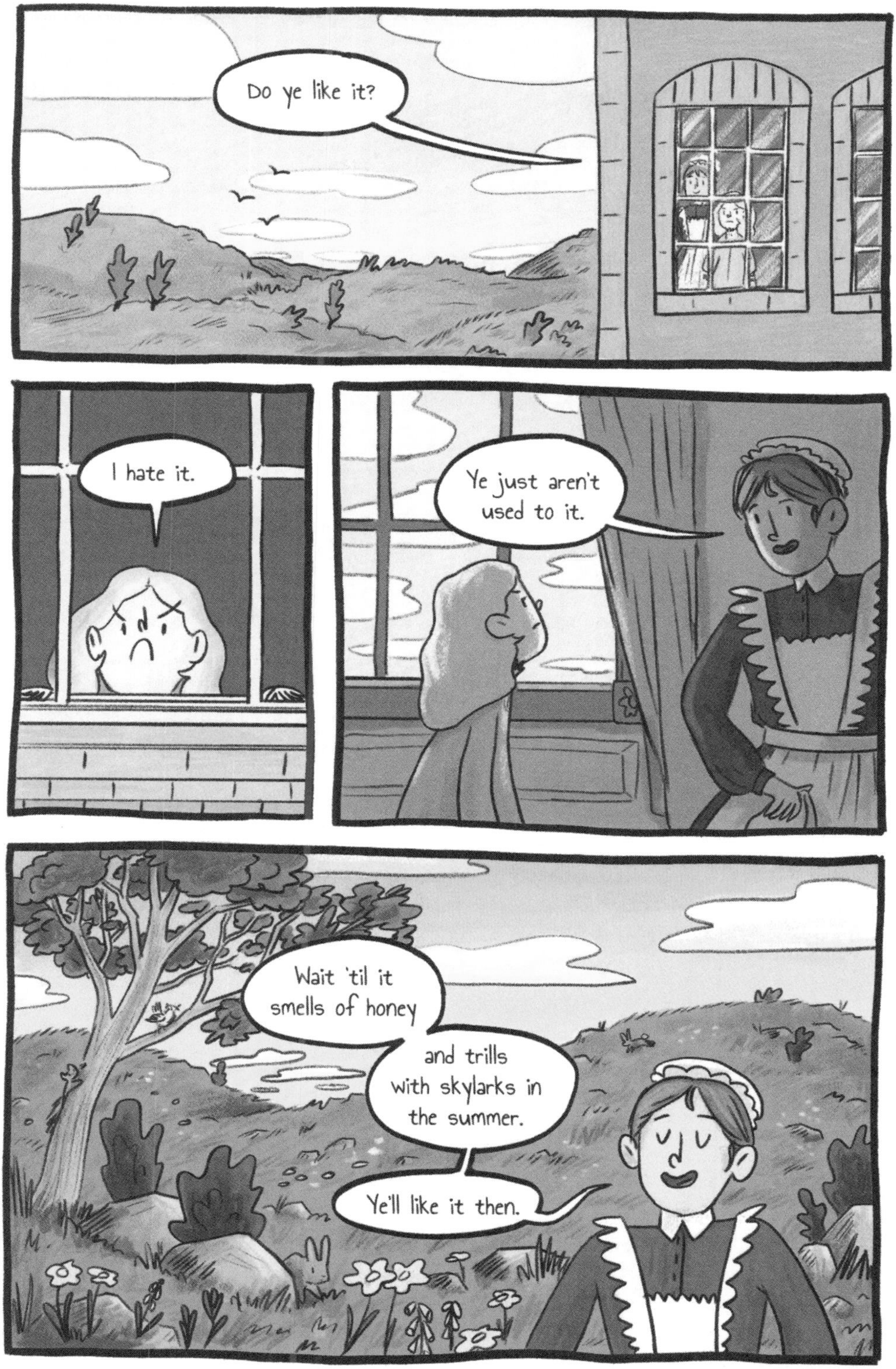
Do ye like it?
I hate it.
Ye just aren't used to it.
Wait 'til it smells of honey
and trills with skylarks in the summer.
Ye'll like it then.

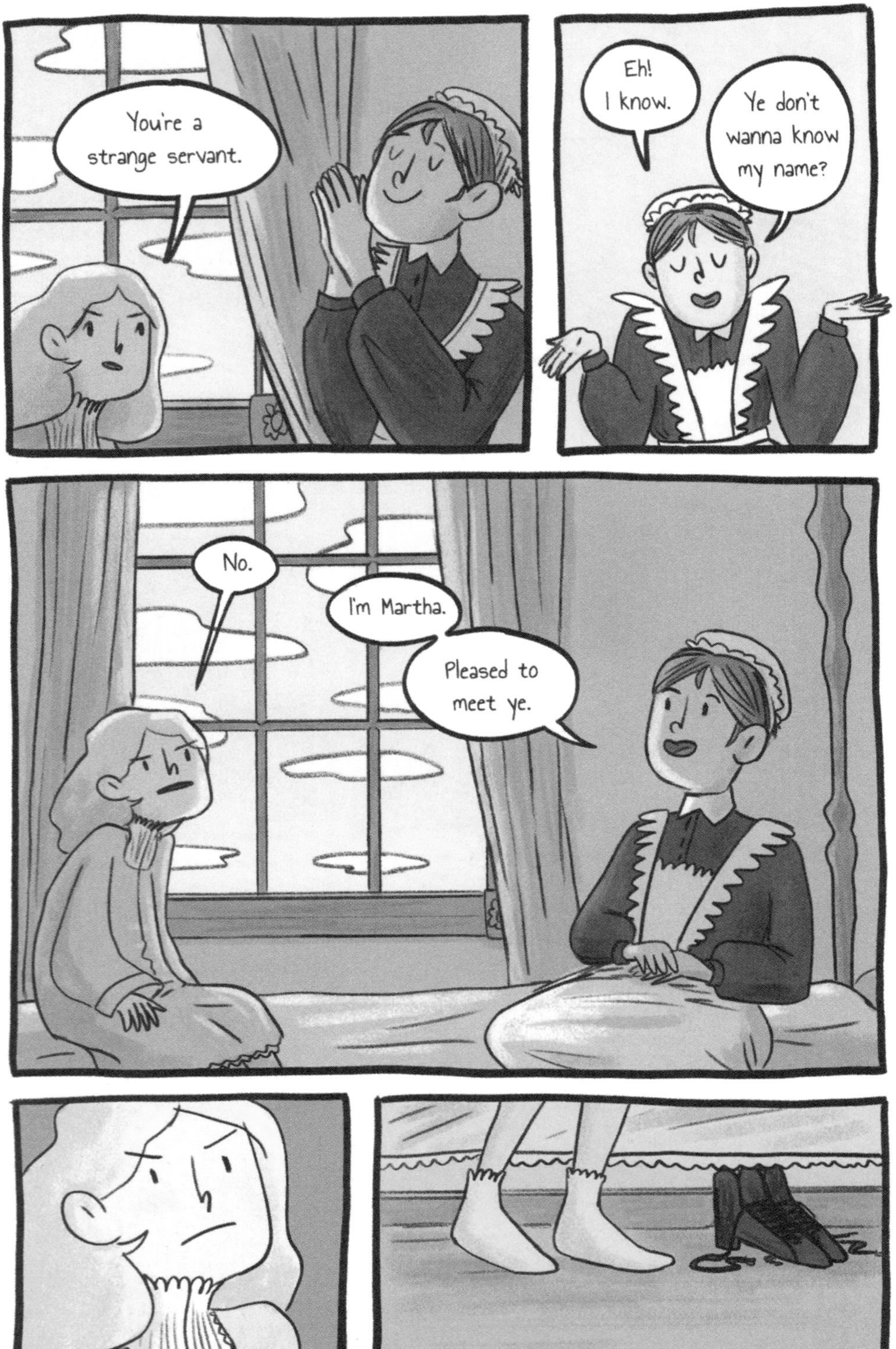
You're a strange servant.
Eh! I know.
Ye don't wanna know my name?
No.
I'm Martha.
Pleased to meet ye.

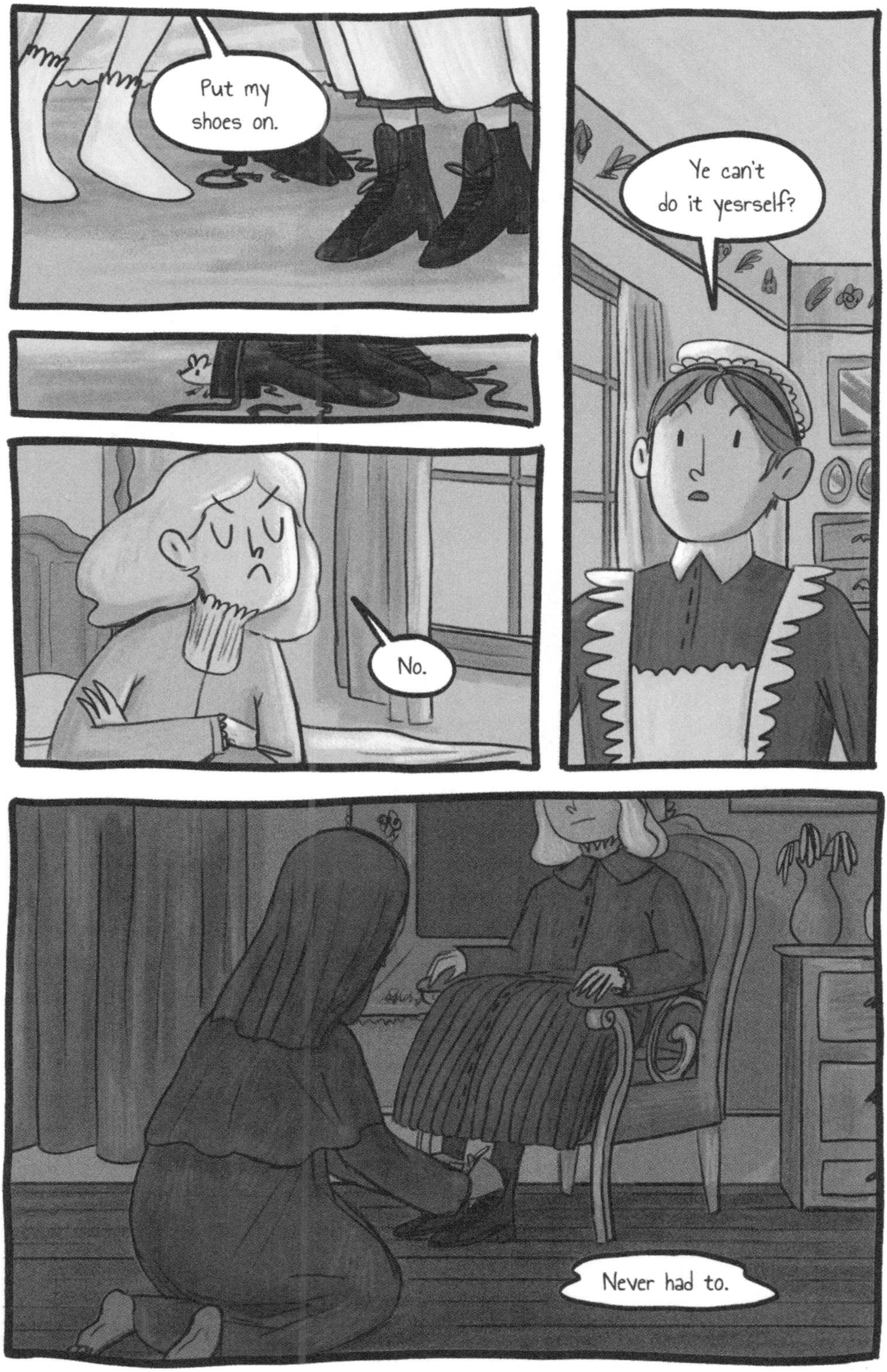
Put my shoes on.
Ye can't do it yesrself?
No.
Never had to.

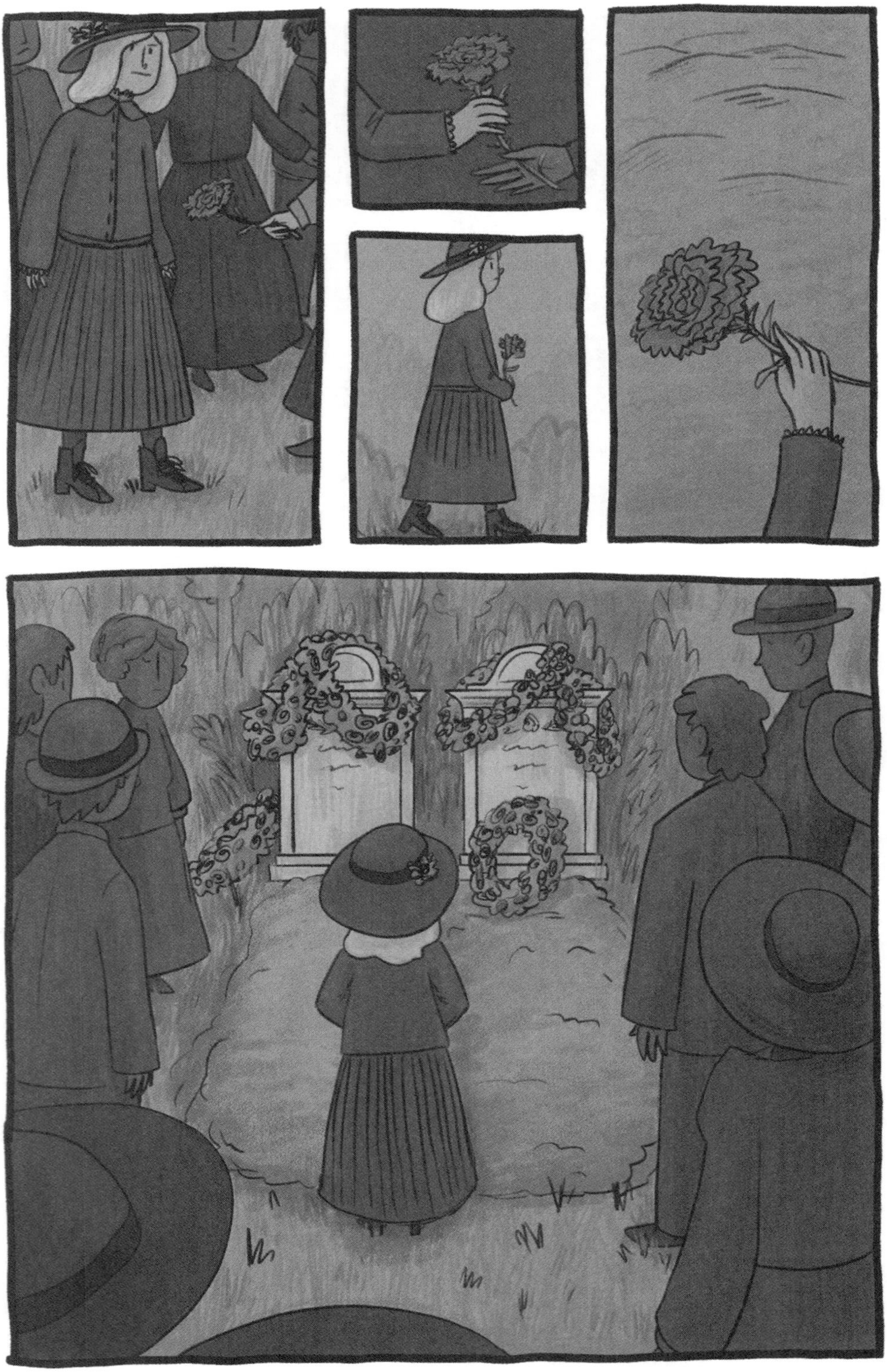

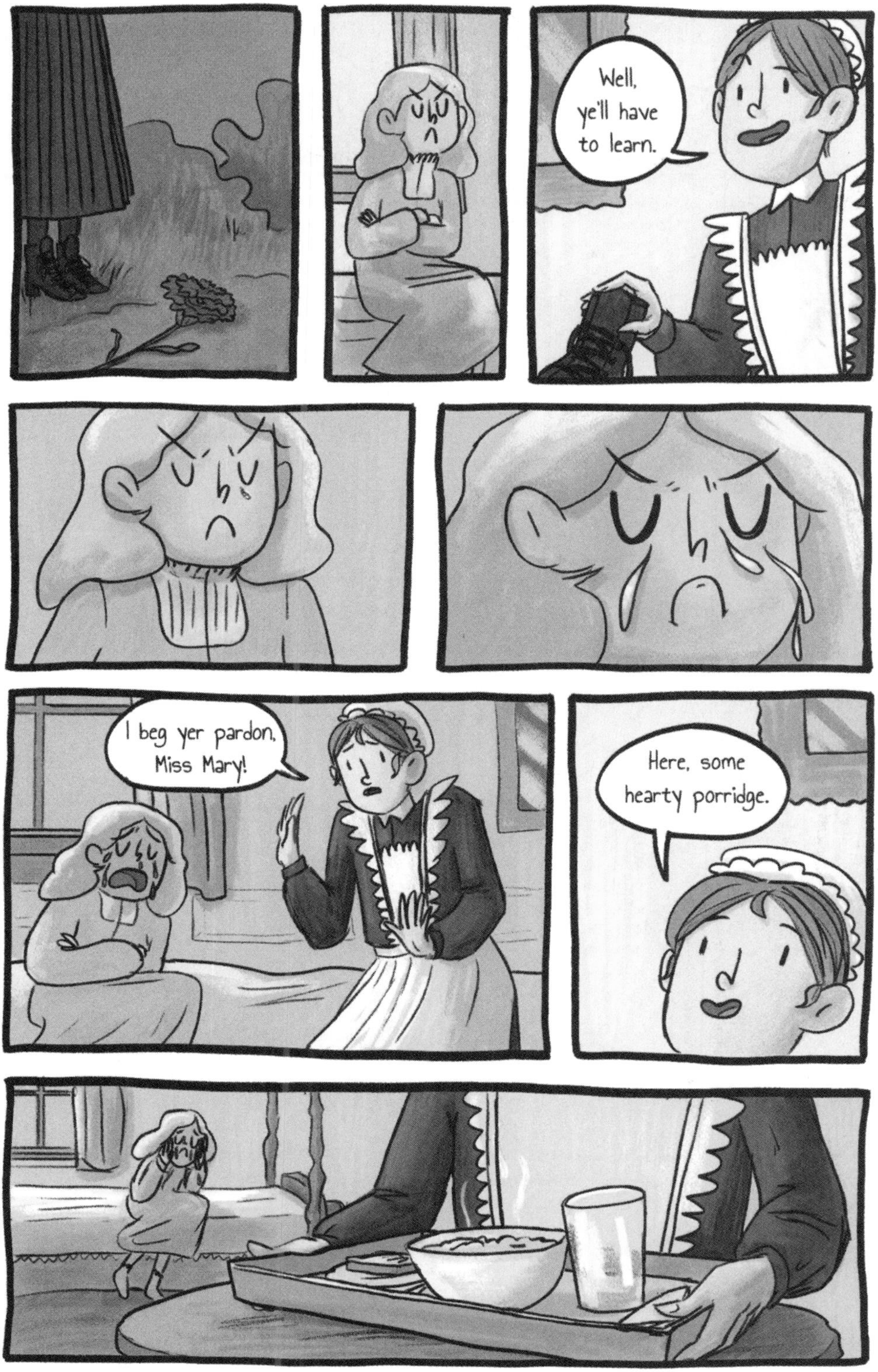
Well, ye'll have to learn.
I beg yer pardon, Miss Mary!
Here, some hearty porridge.

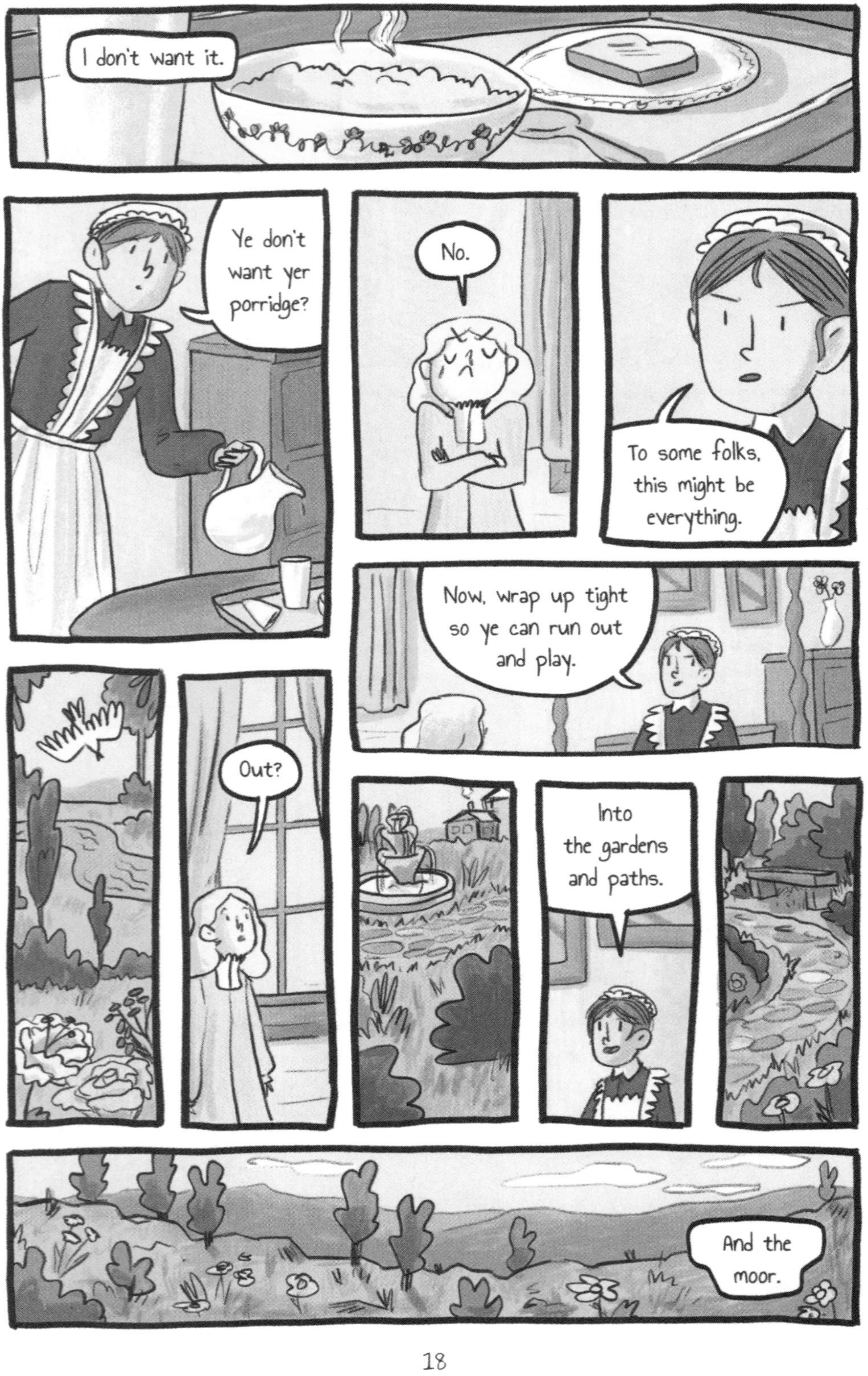
I don't want it.
Ye don't want yer porridge?
No.
To some folks, this might be everything.
Now, wrap up tight so ye can run out and play.
Out?
Into the gardens and paths.
And the moor.

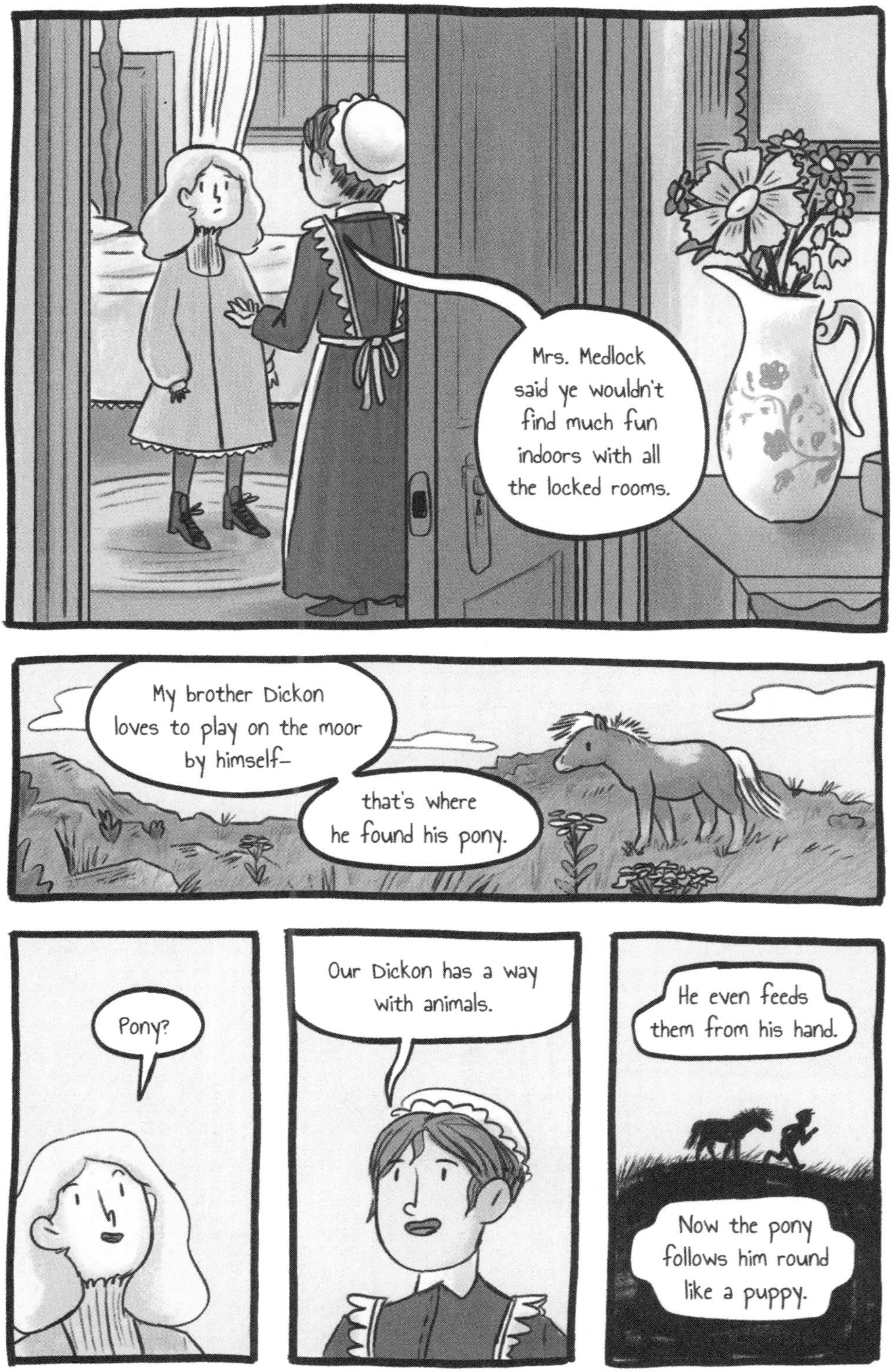
Mrs. Medlock said ye wouldn't find much fun indoors with all the locked rooms.
My brother Dickon loves to play on the moor by himself–
that's where he found his pony.
Pony?
Our Dickon has a way with animals.
He even feeds them from his hand.
Now the pony follows him round like a puppy.

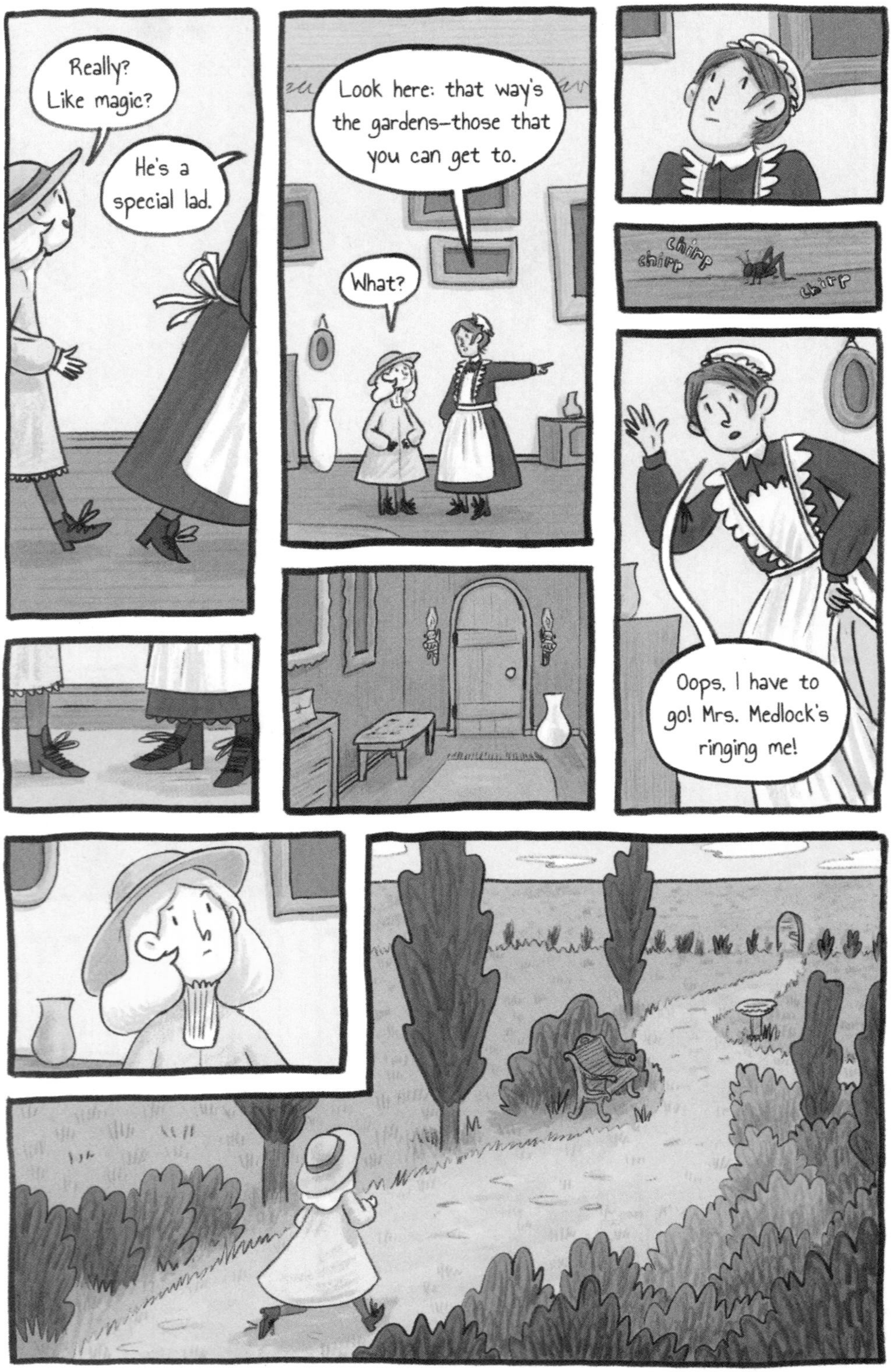
Really? Like magic?
He's a special lad.
Look here: that way's the gardens—those that you can get to.
What?
chirp
chirp
chirp
Oops, I have to go! Mrs. Medlock's ringing me!

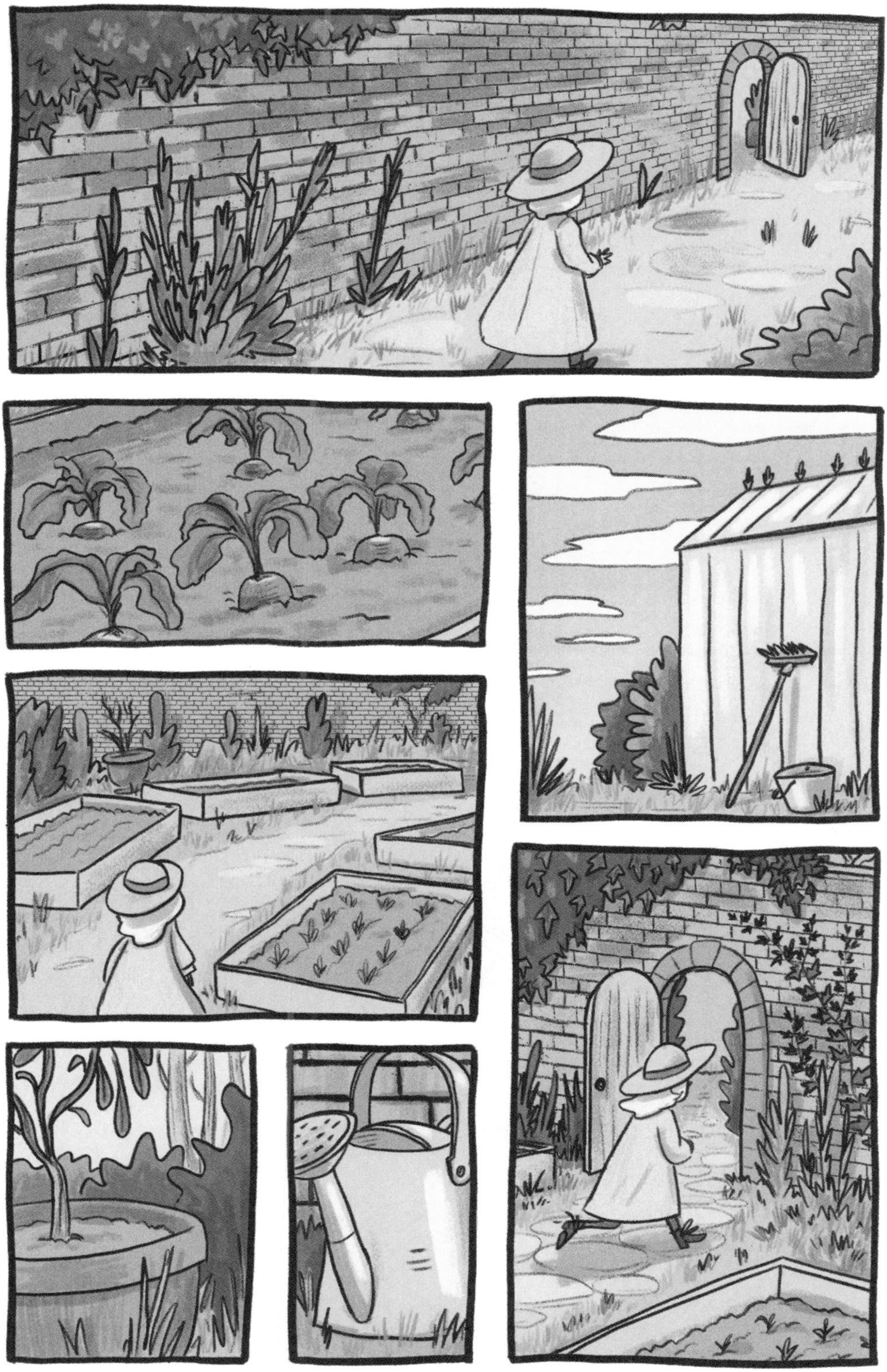

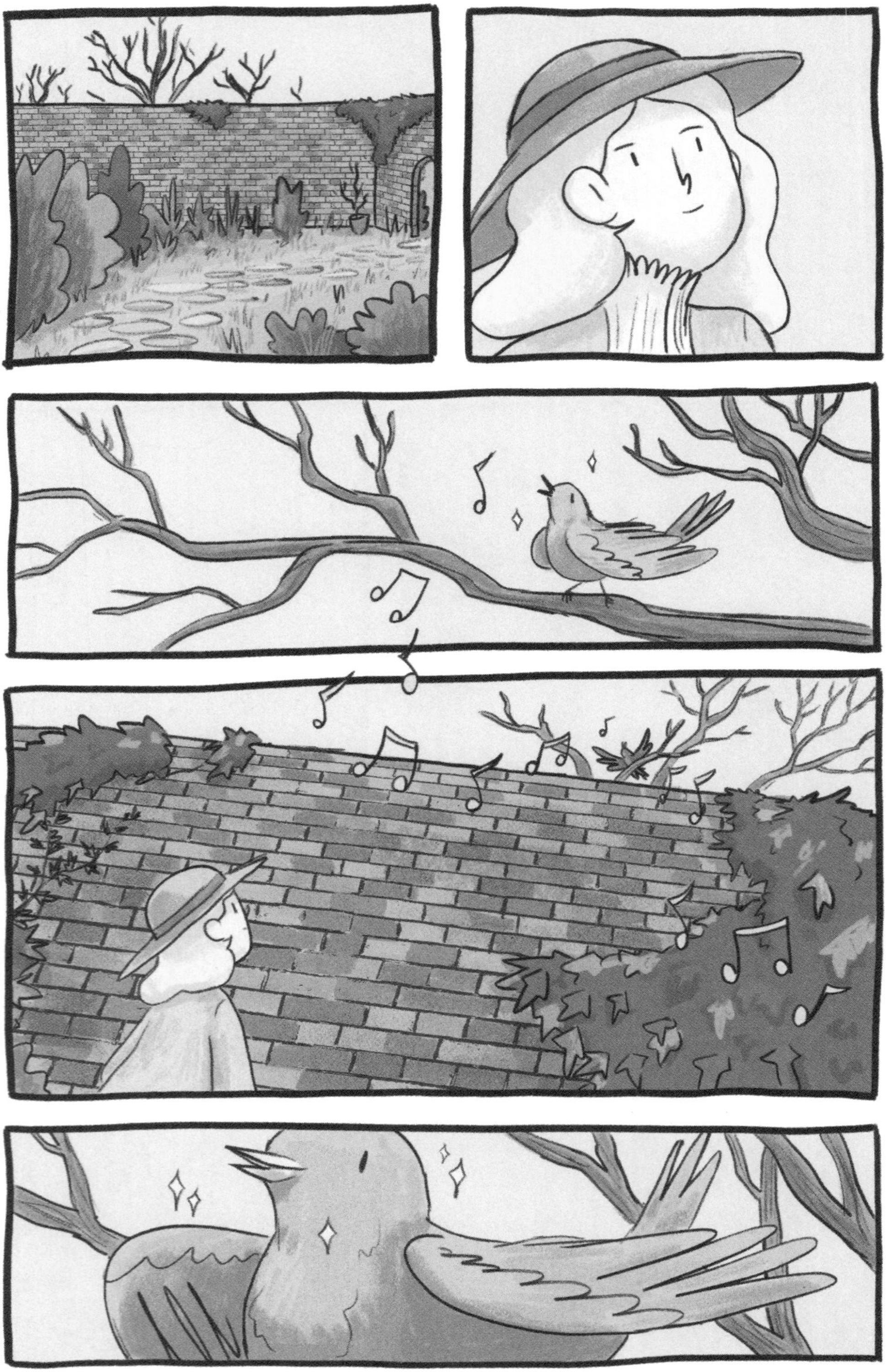

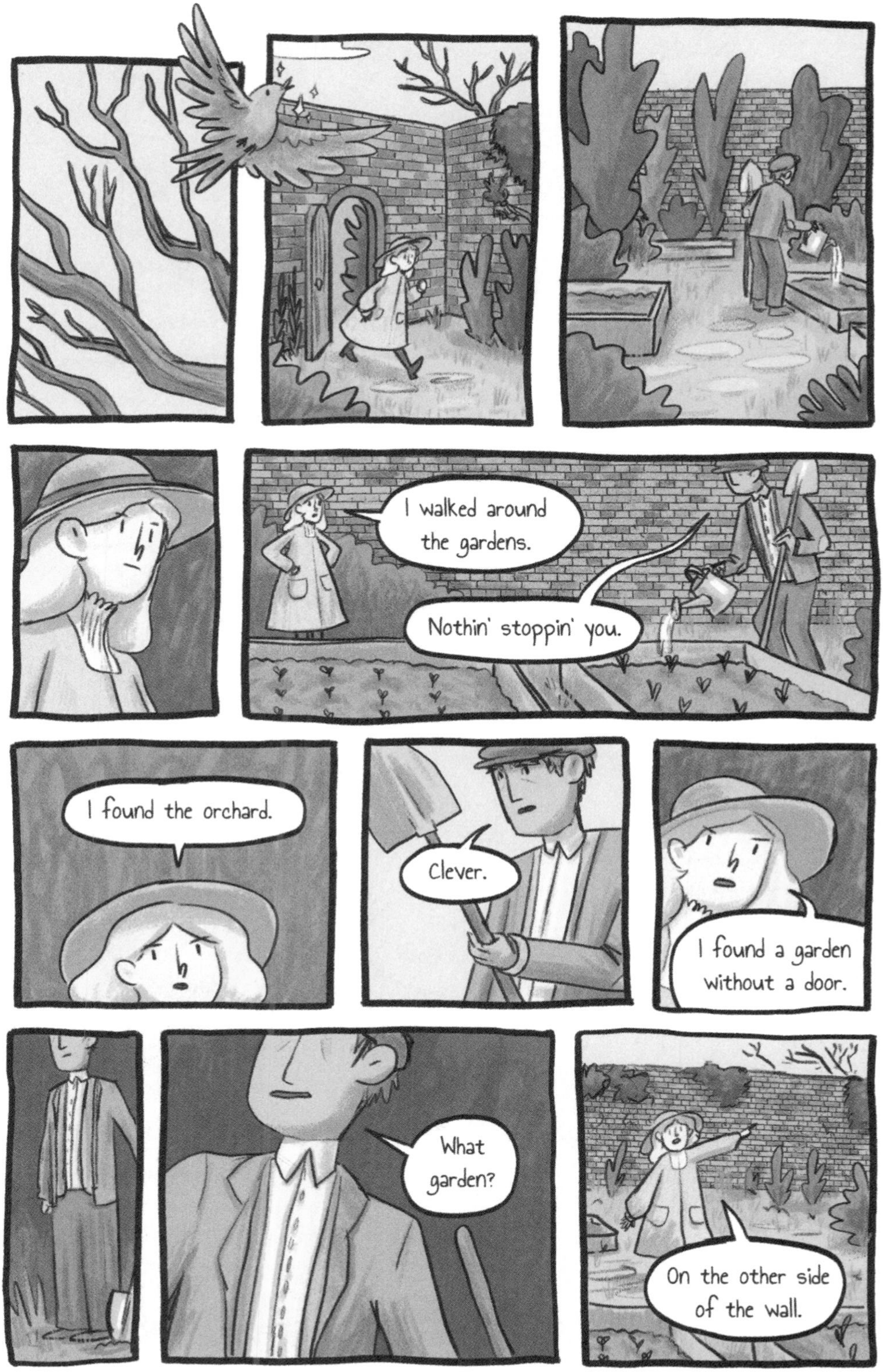
I walked around the gardens.
Nothin' stoppin' you.
I found the orchard.
Clever.
I found a garden without a door.
What garden?
On the other side of the wall.

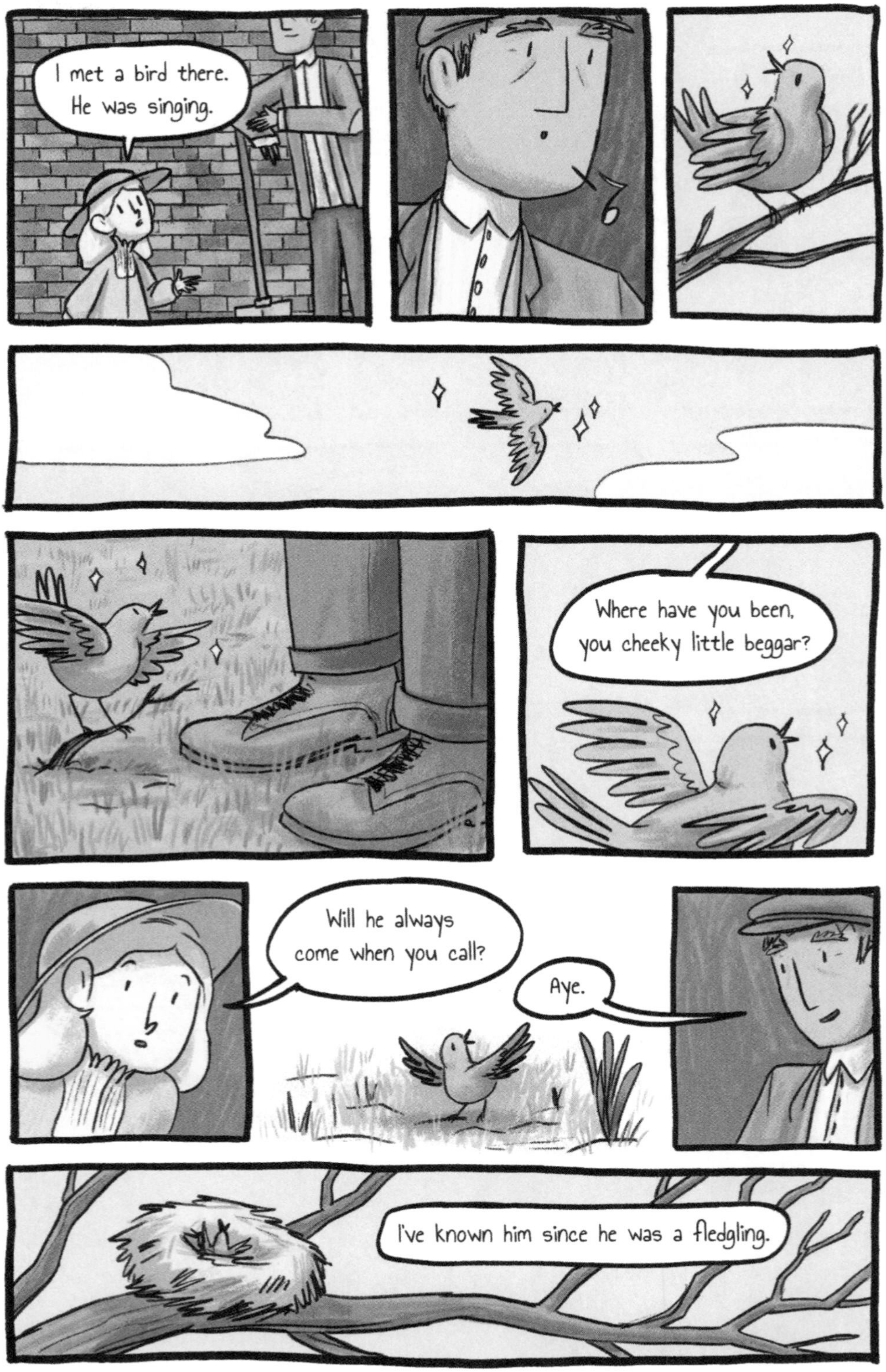
I met a bird there. He was singing.
Where have you been, you cheeky little beggar?
Will he always come when you call?
Aye.
I've known him since he was a fledgling.

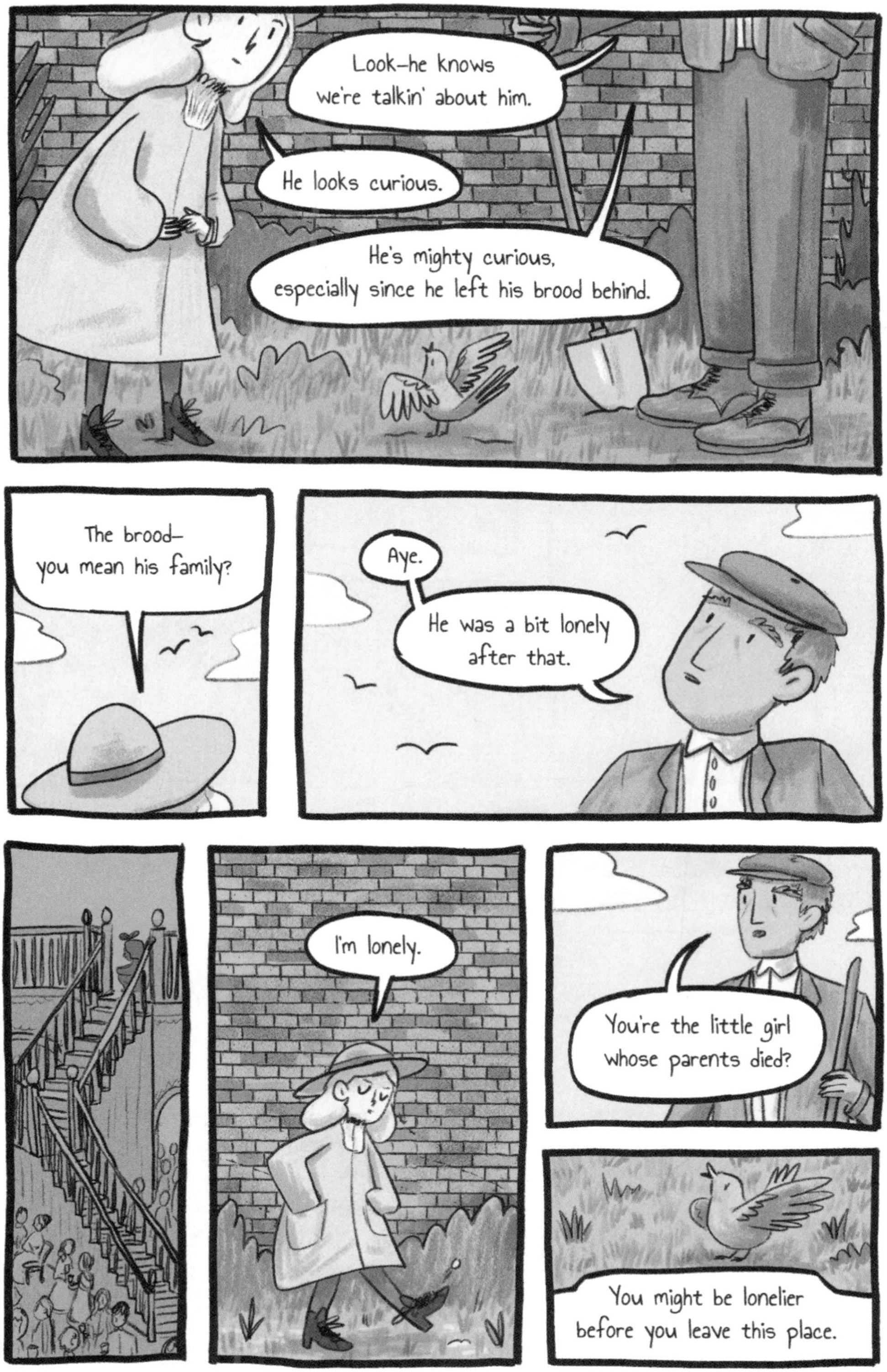
Look—he knows we're talkin' about him.
He looks curious.
He's mighty curious, especially since he left his brood behind.
The brood— you mean his family?
Aye.
He was a bit lonely after that.
I'm lonely.
You're the little girl whose parents died?
You might be lonelier before you leave this place.

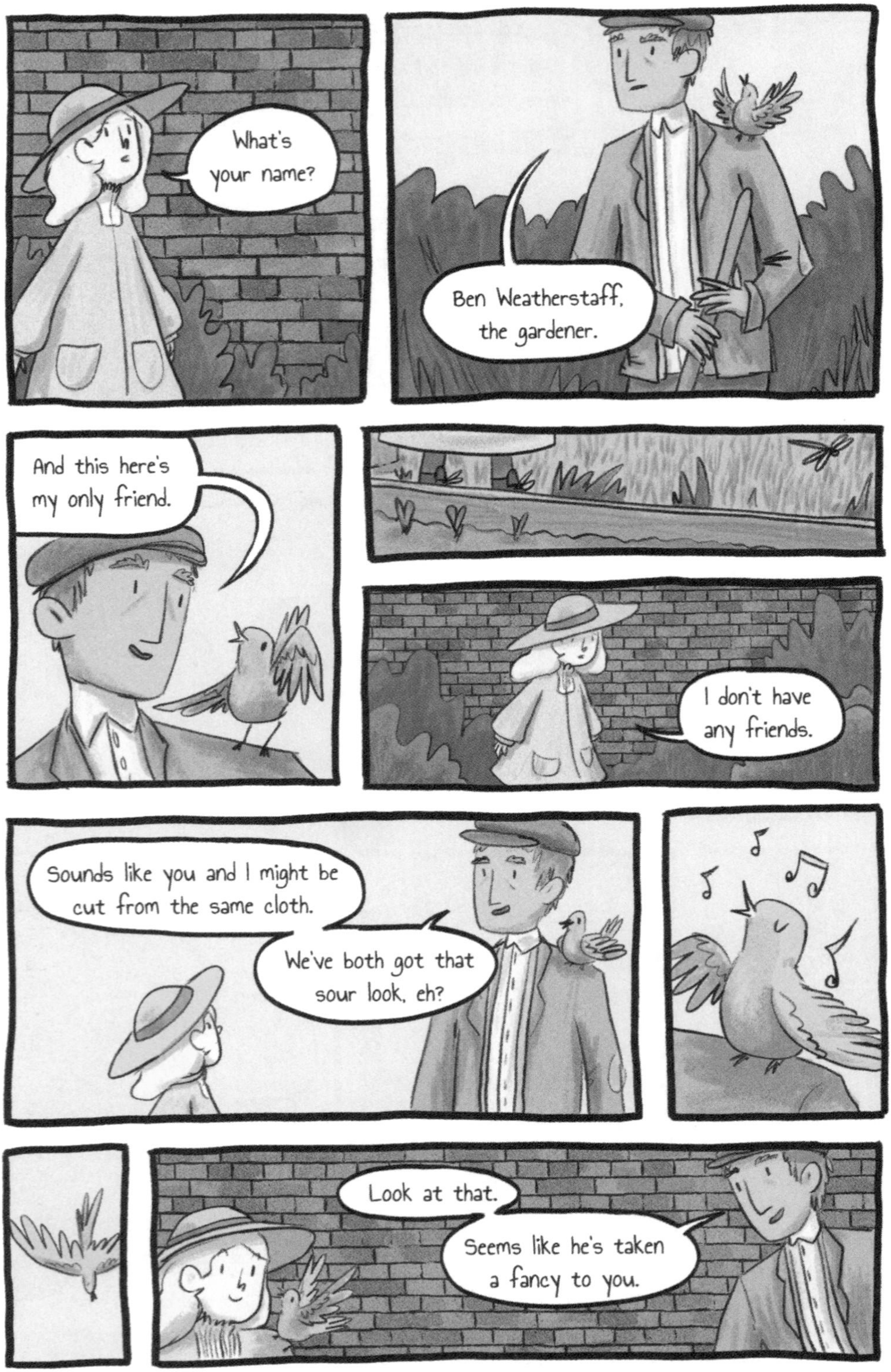
What's your name?
Ben Weatherstaff, the gardener.
And this here's my only friend.
I don't have any friends.
Sounds like you and I might be cut from the same cloth.
We've both got that sour look, eh?
Look at that.
Seems like he's taken a fancy to you.

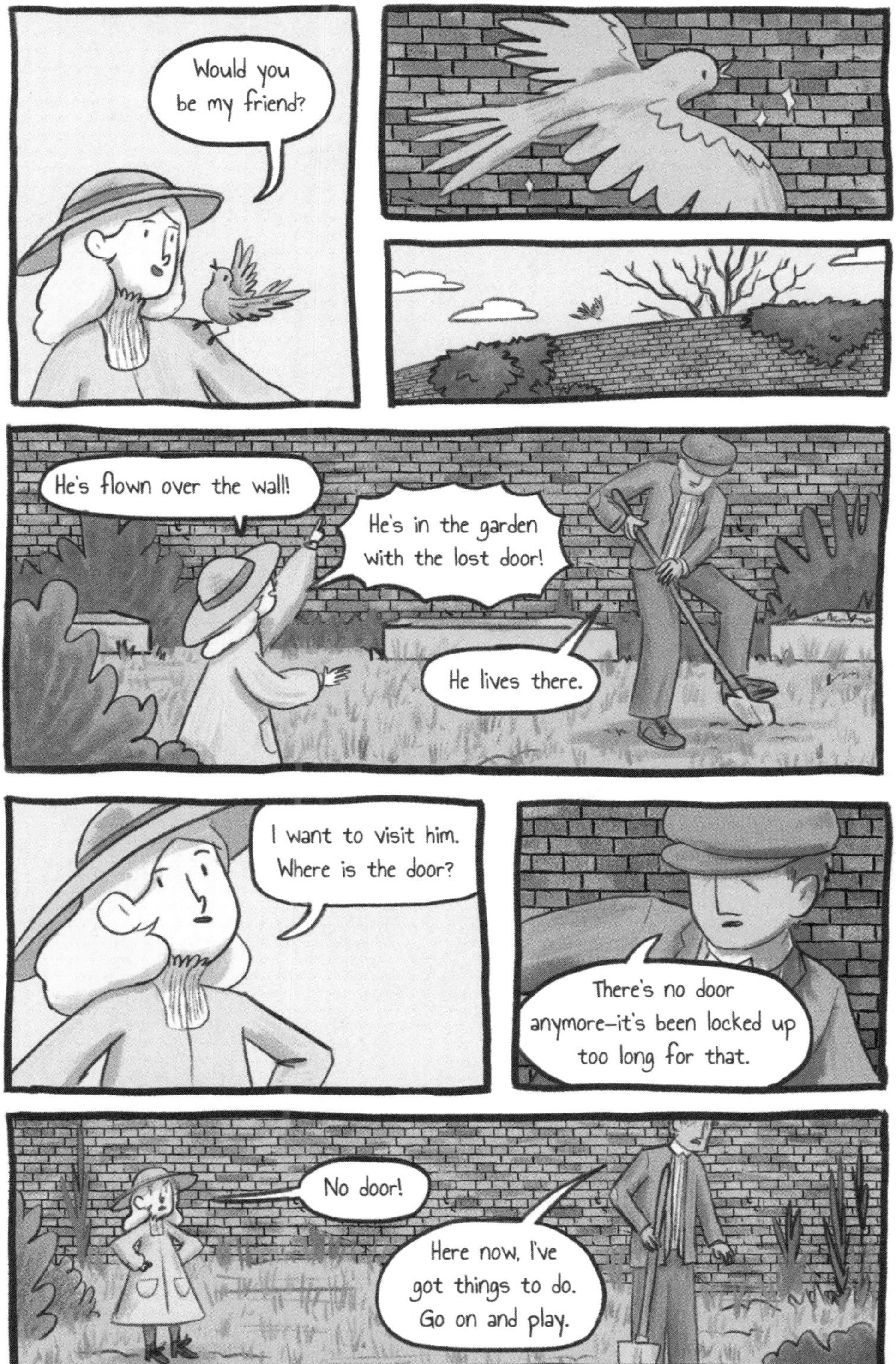
Would you be my friend?
He's flown over the wall!
He's in the garden with the lost door!
He lives there.
I want to visit him. Where is the door?
There's no door anymore—it's been locked up too long for that.
No door!
Here now, I've got things to do. Go on and play.

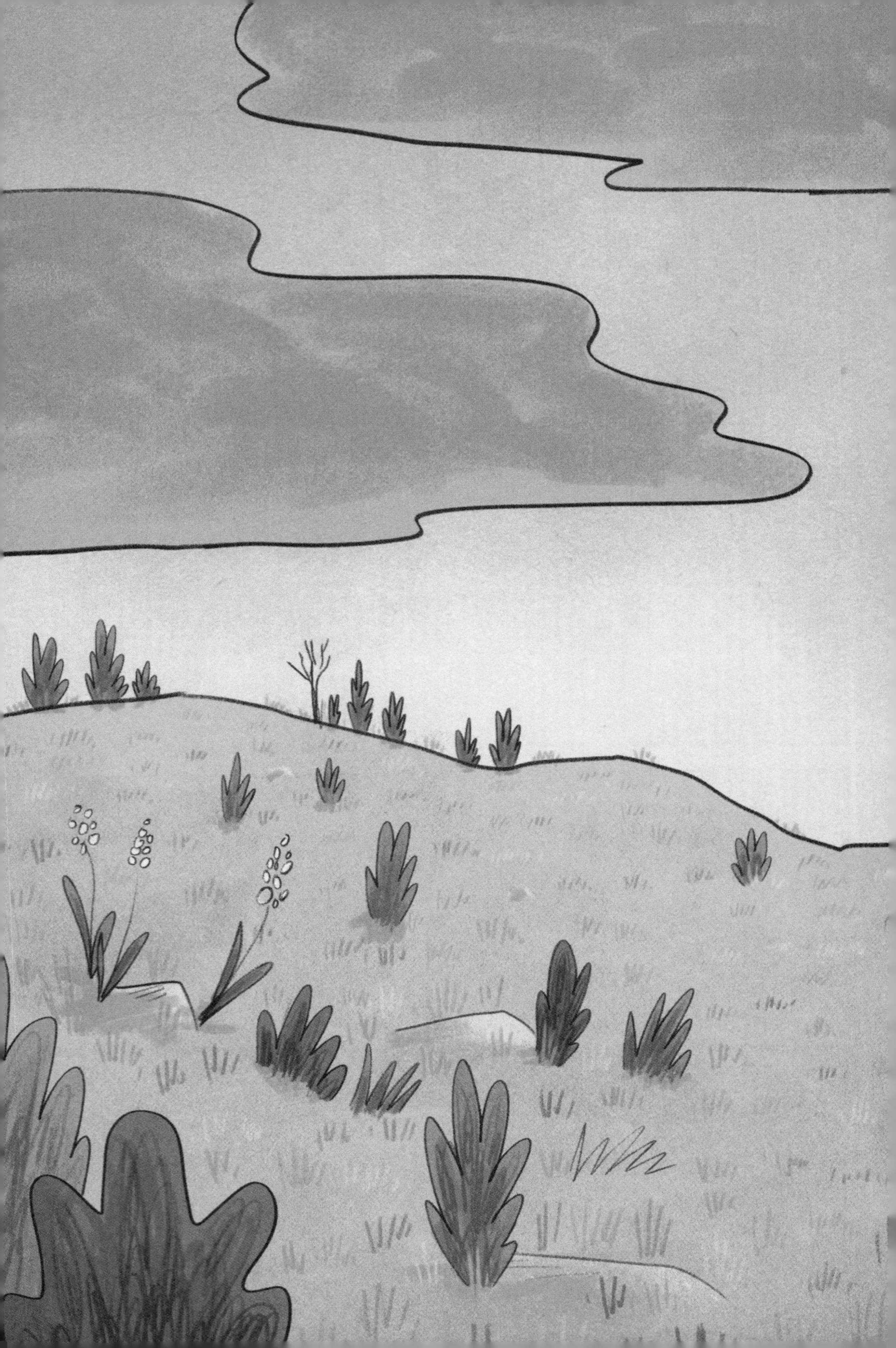

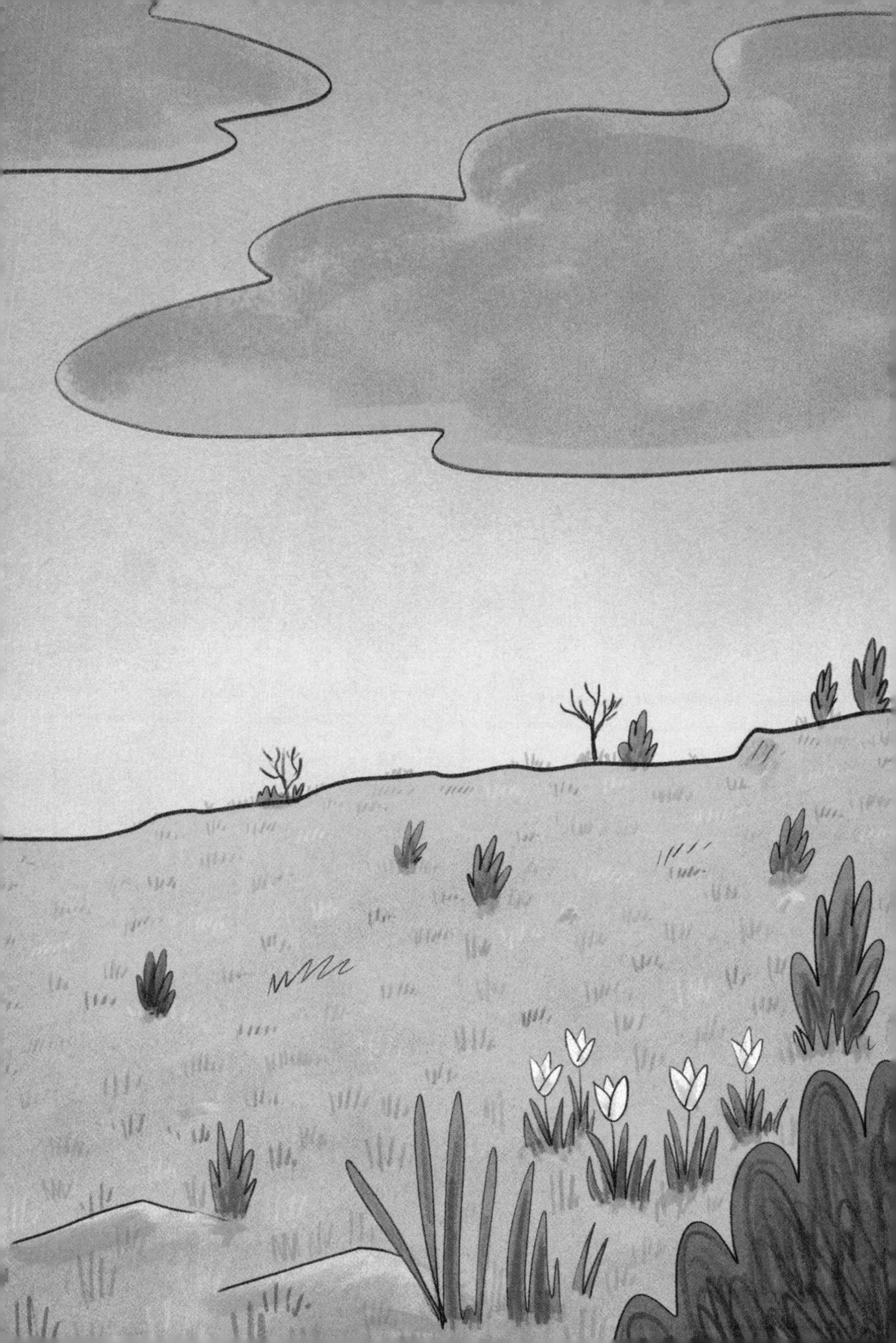

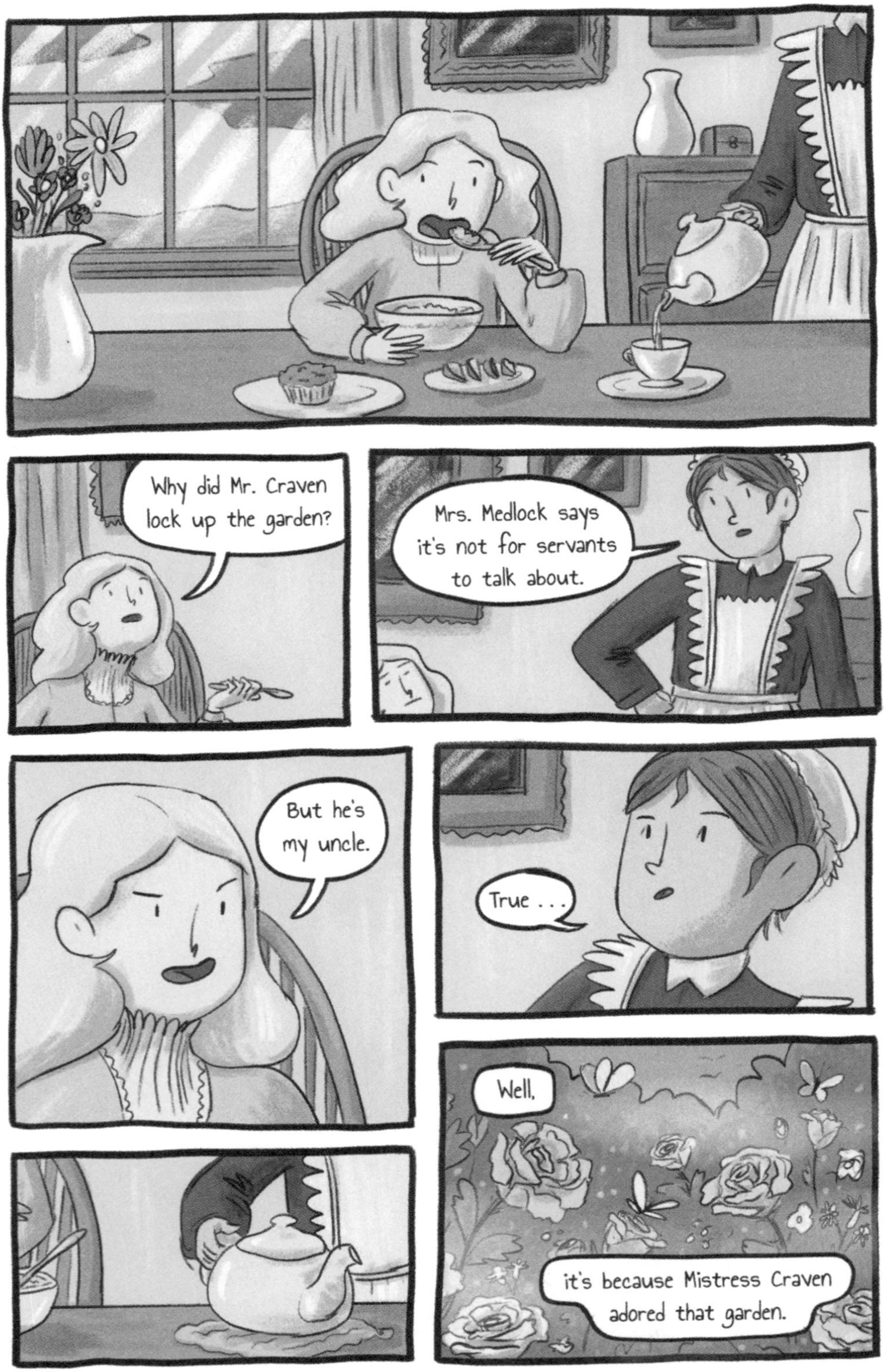
Why did Mr. Craven lock up the garden?
Mrs. Medlock says it's not for servants to talk about.
But he's my uncle.
True . . .
Well,
it's because Mistress Craven adored that garden.

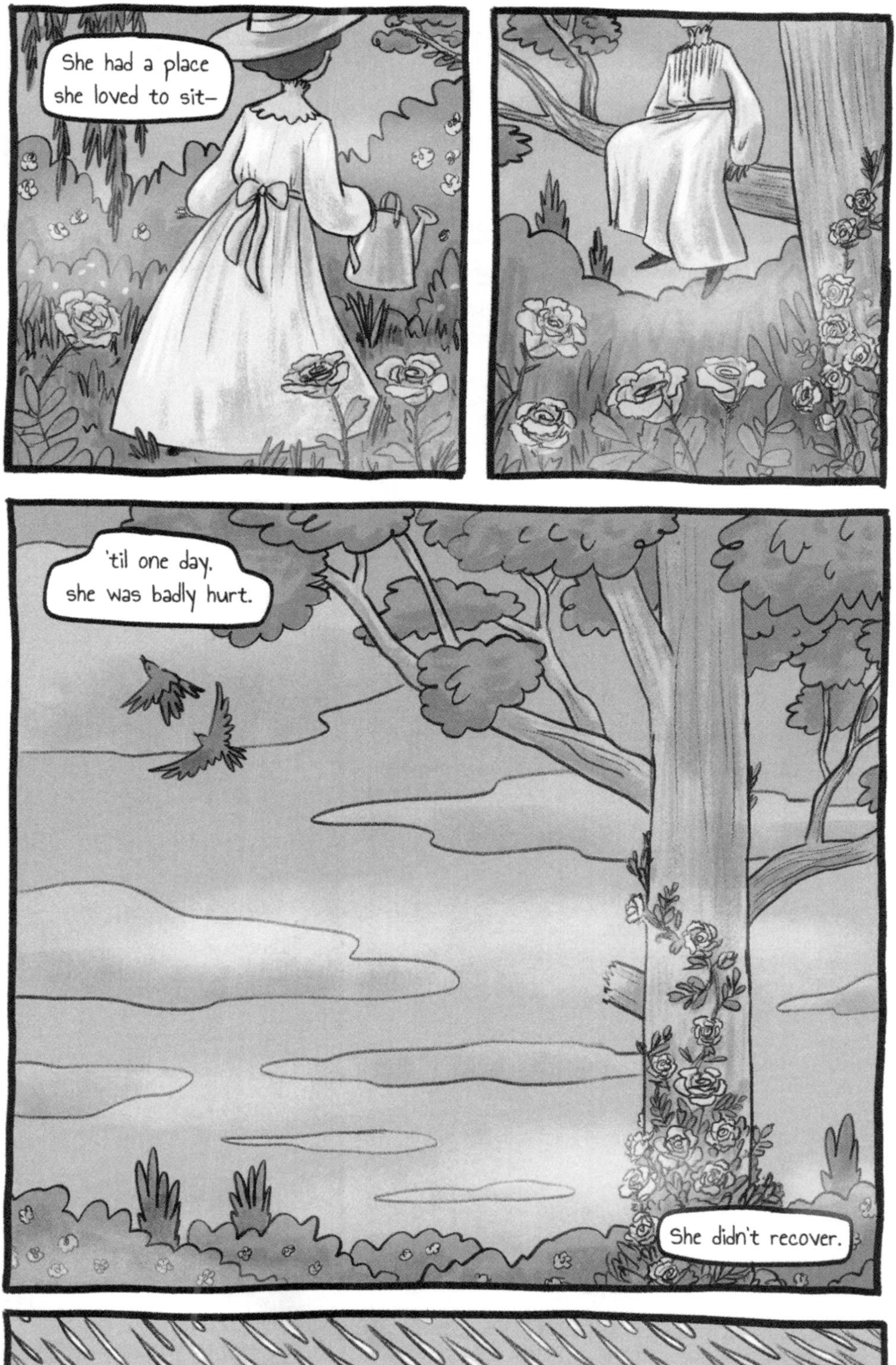
She had a place
she loved to sit–
'til one day,
she was badly hurt.
She didn't recover.

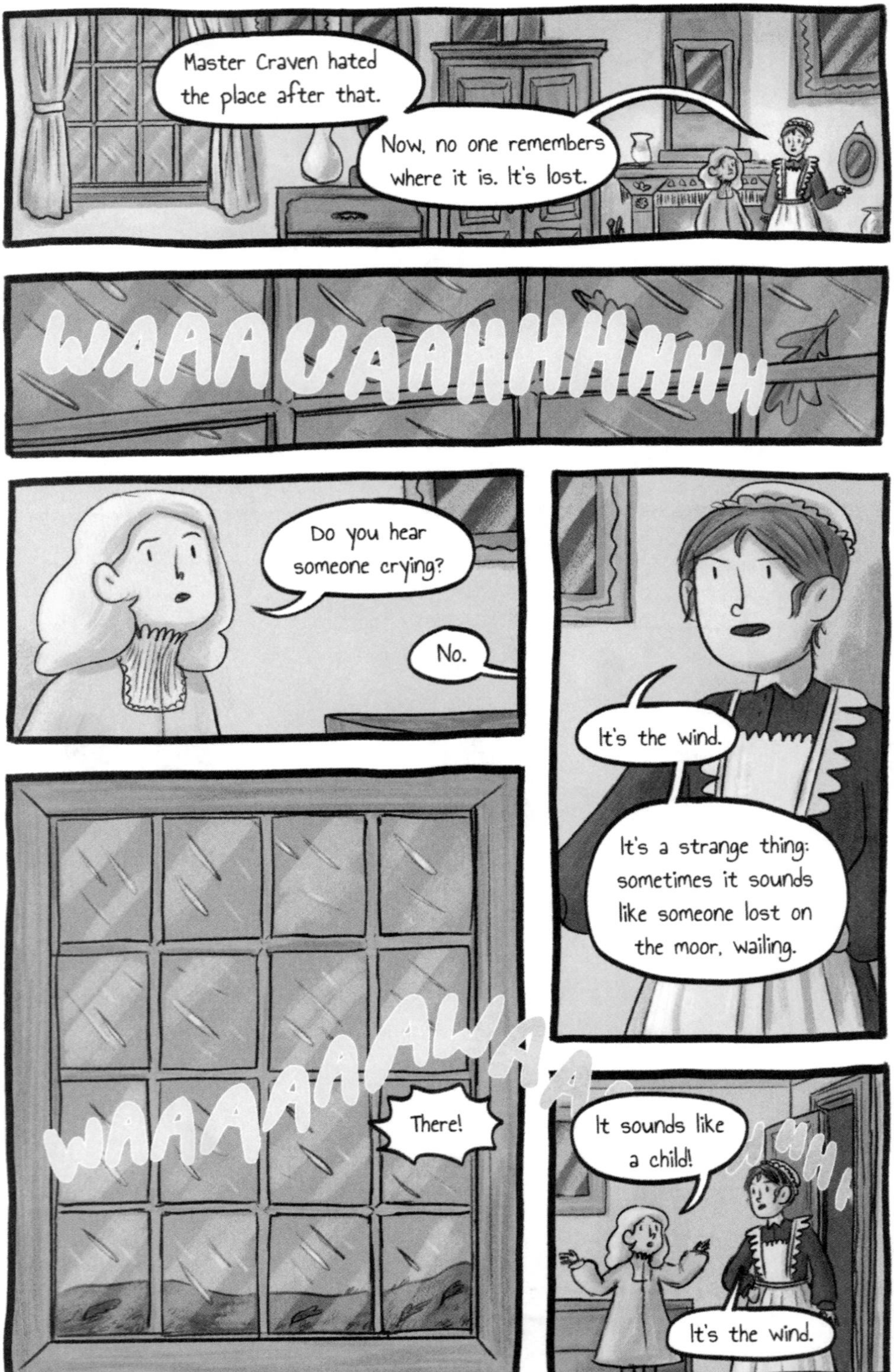
Master Craven hated the place after that.
Now, no one remembers where it is. It's lost.
WAAAUAAHHHHHH
Do you hear someone crying?
No.
It's the wind.
It's a strange thing: sometimes it sounds like someone lost on the moor, wailing.
WAAAAAAWAA
There!
It sounds like a child!
It's the wind.

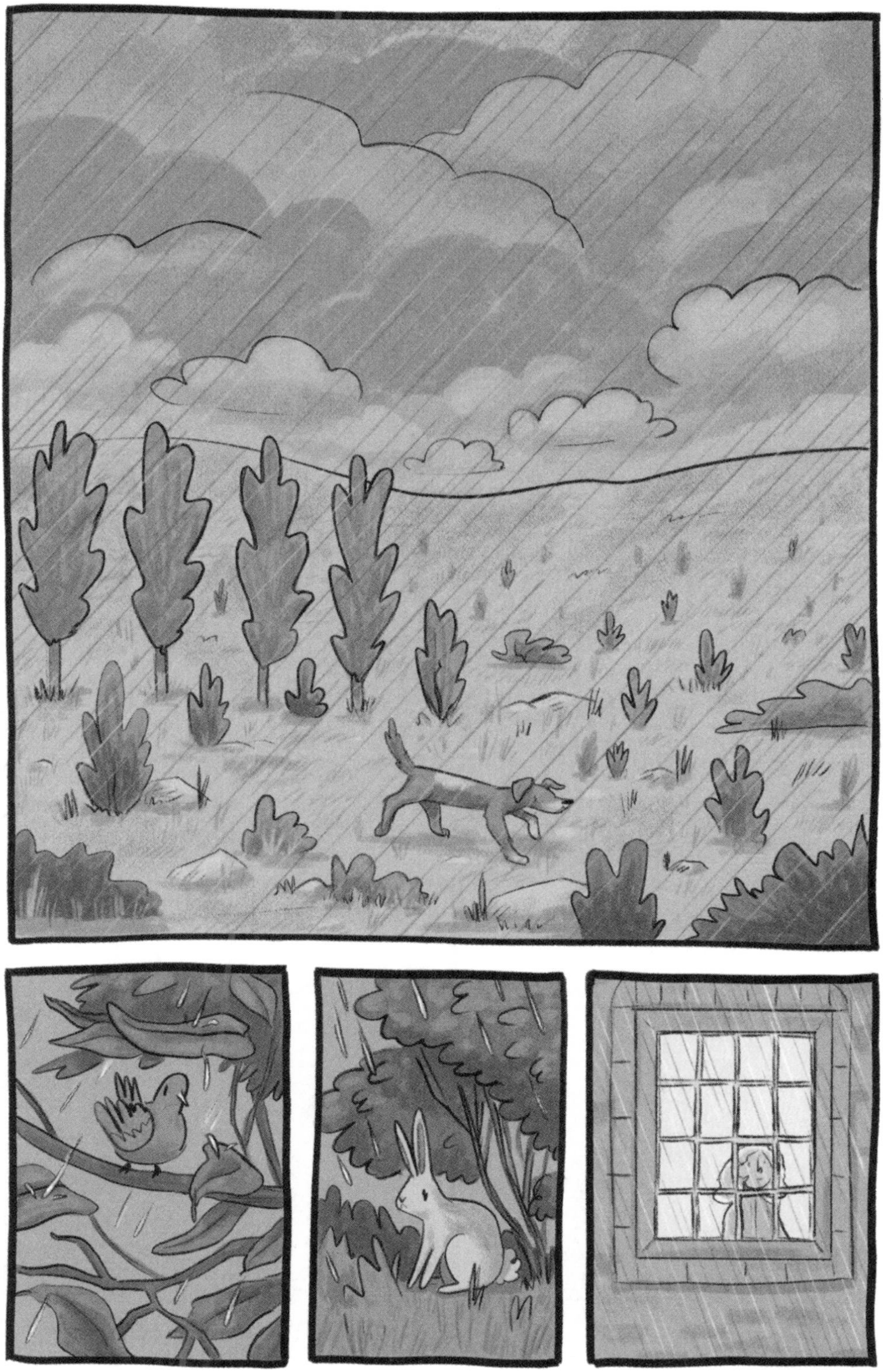

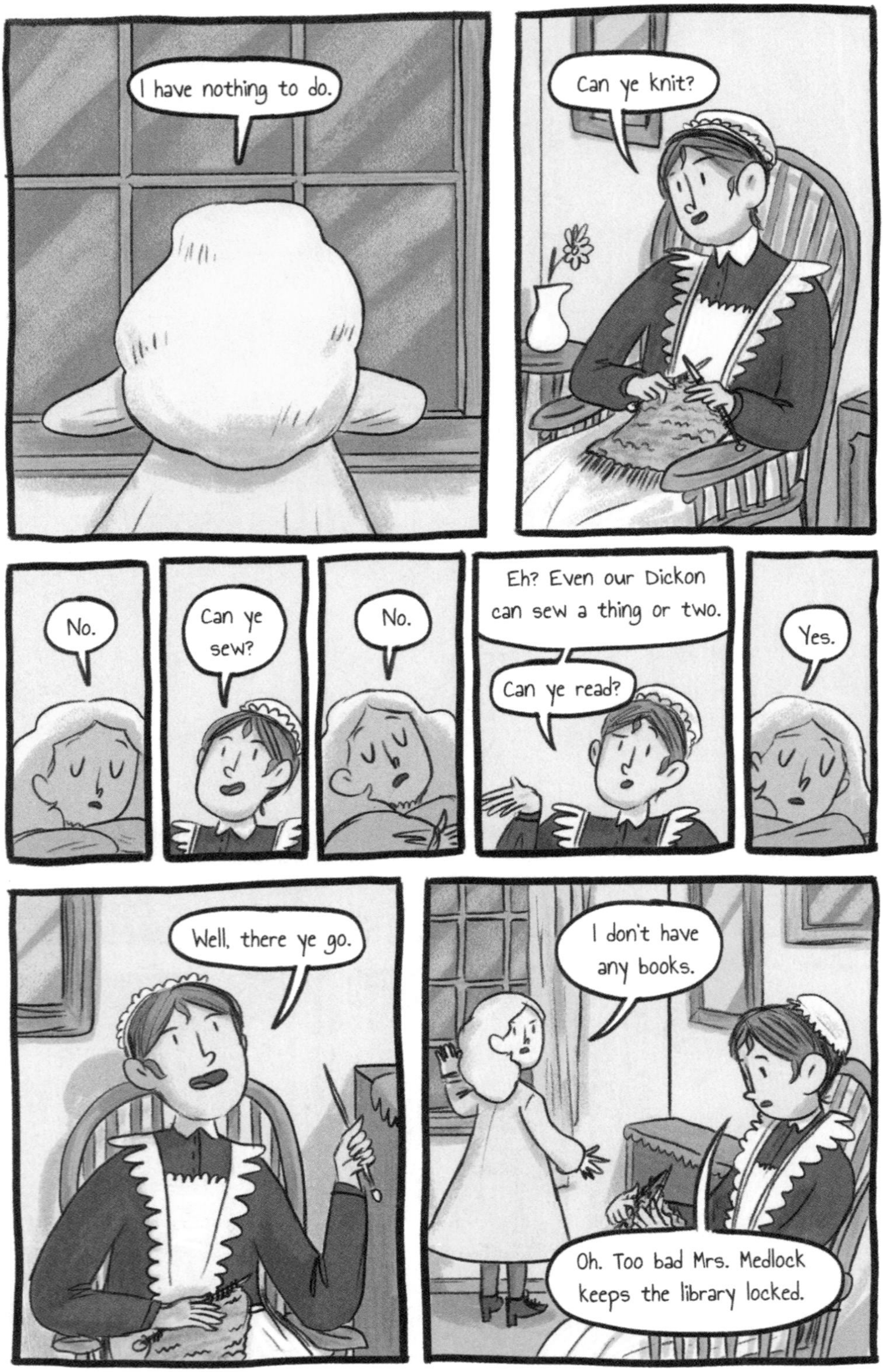
I have nothing to do.
Can ye knit?
No.
Can ye sew?
No.
Eh? Even our Dickon can sew a thing or two.
Can ye read?
Yes.
Well, there ye go.
I don't have any books.
Oh. Too bad Mrs. Medlock keeps the library locked.

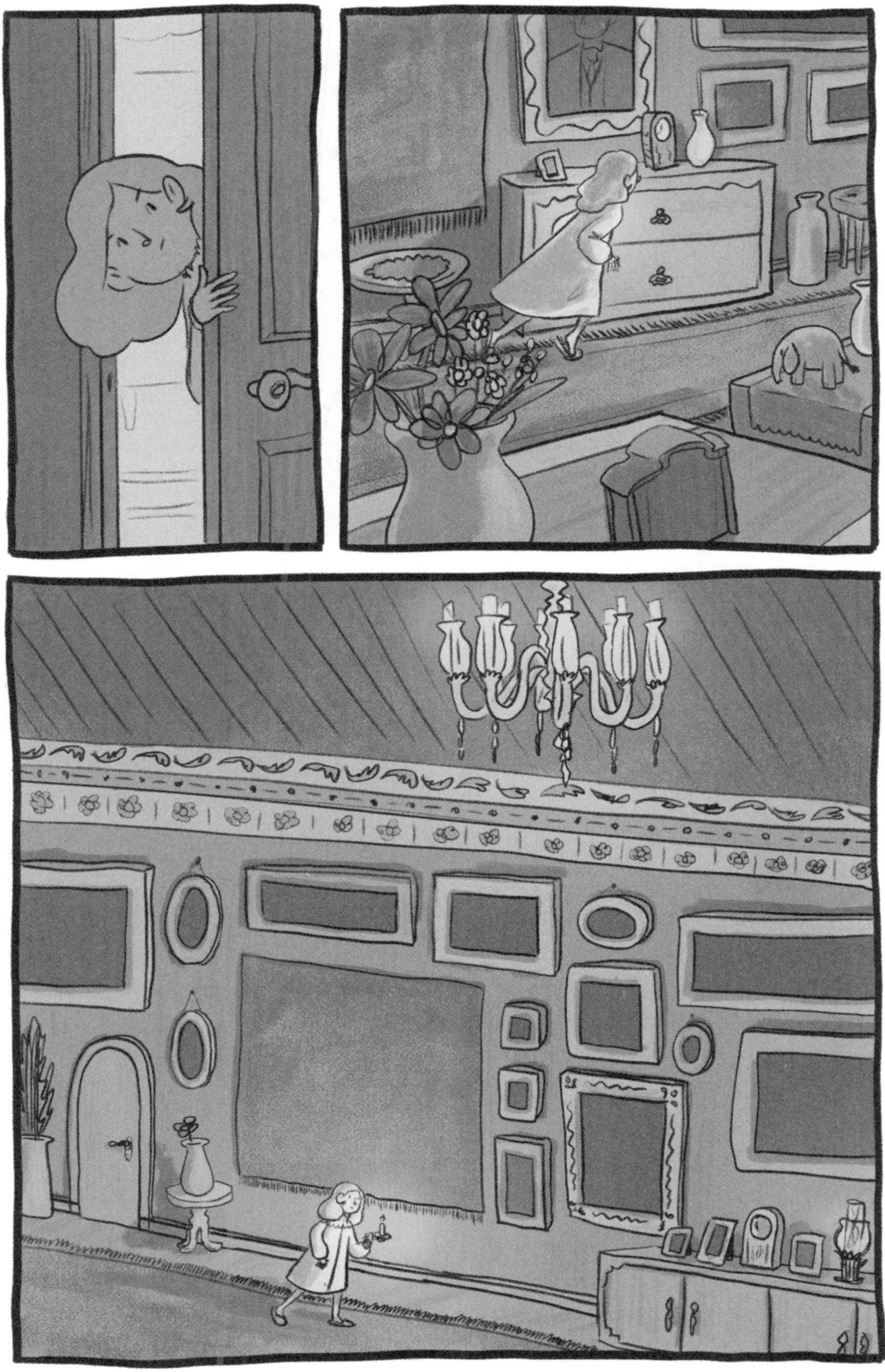

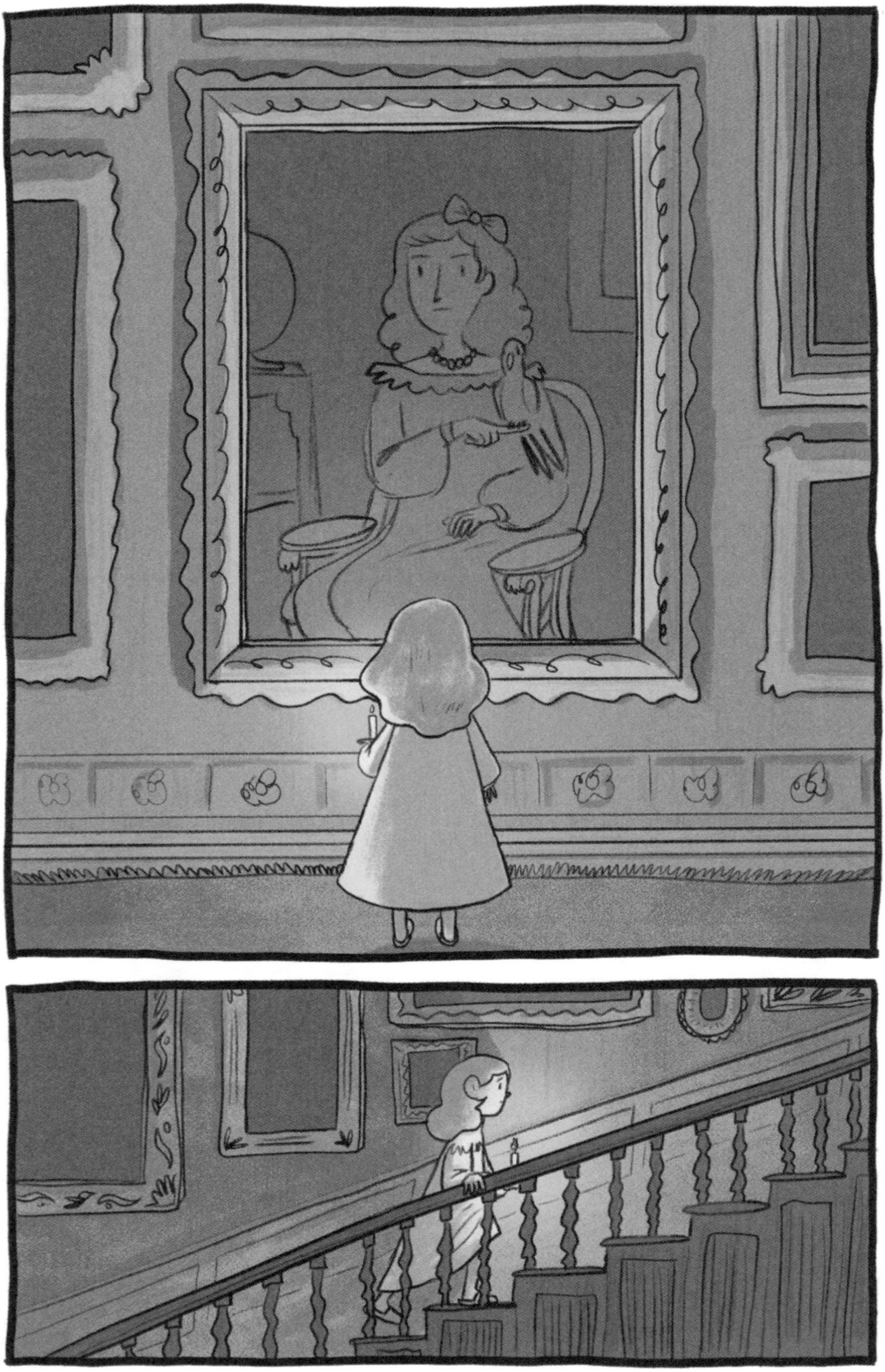

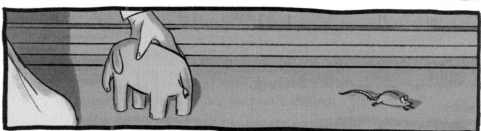

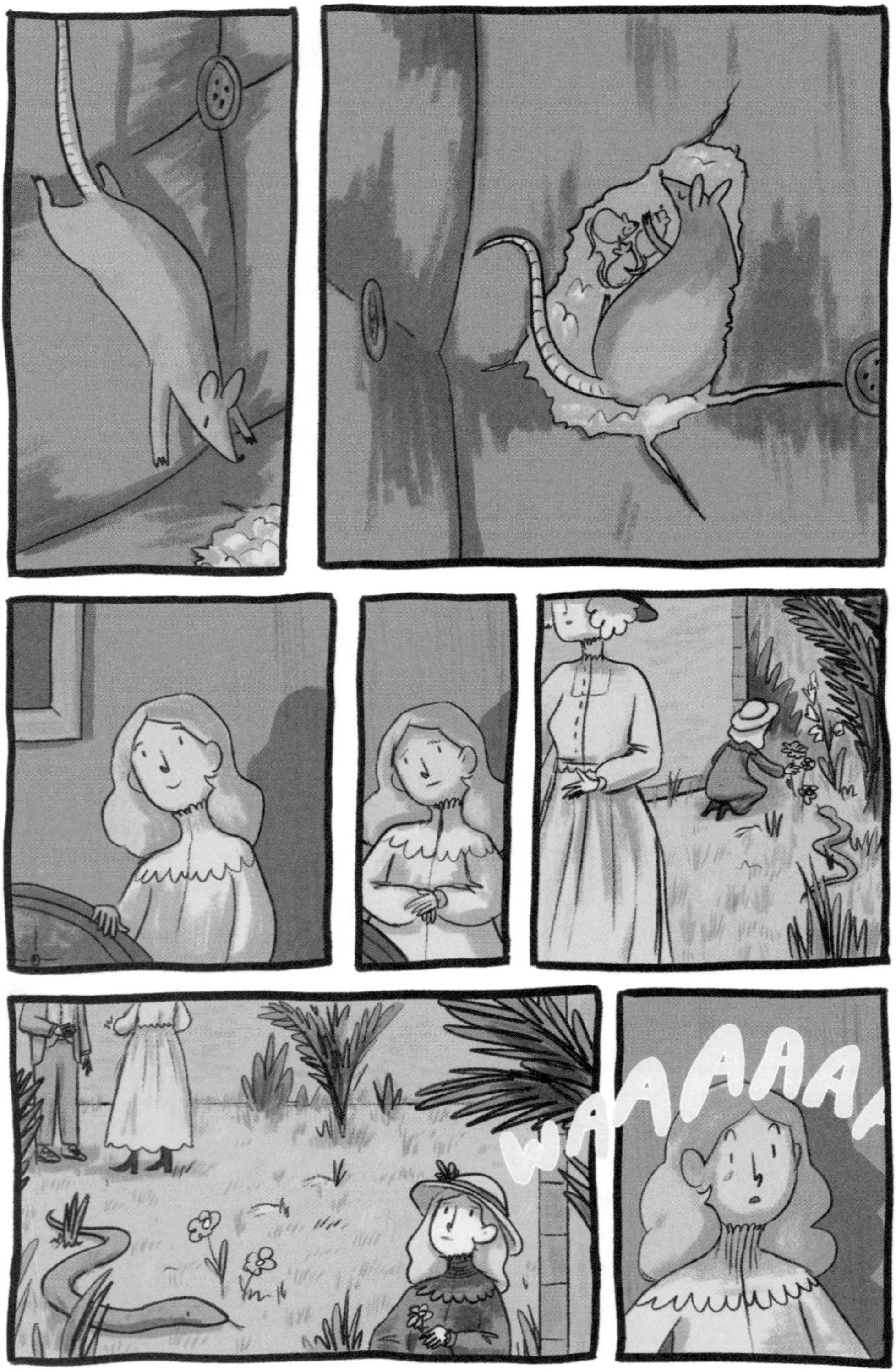
WAAAAAA

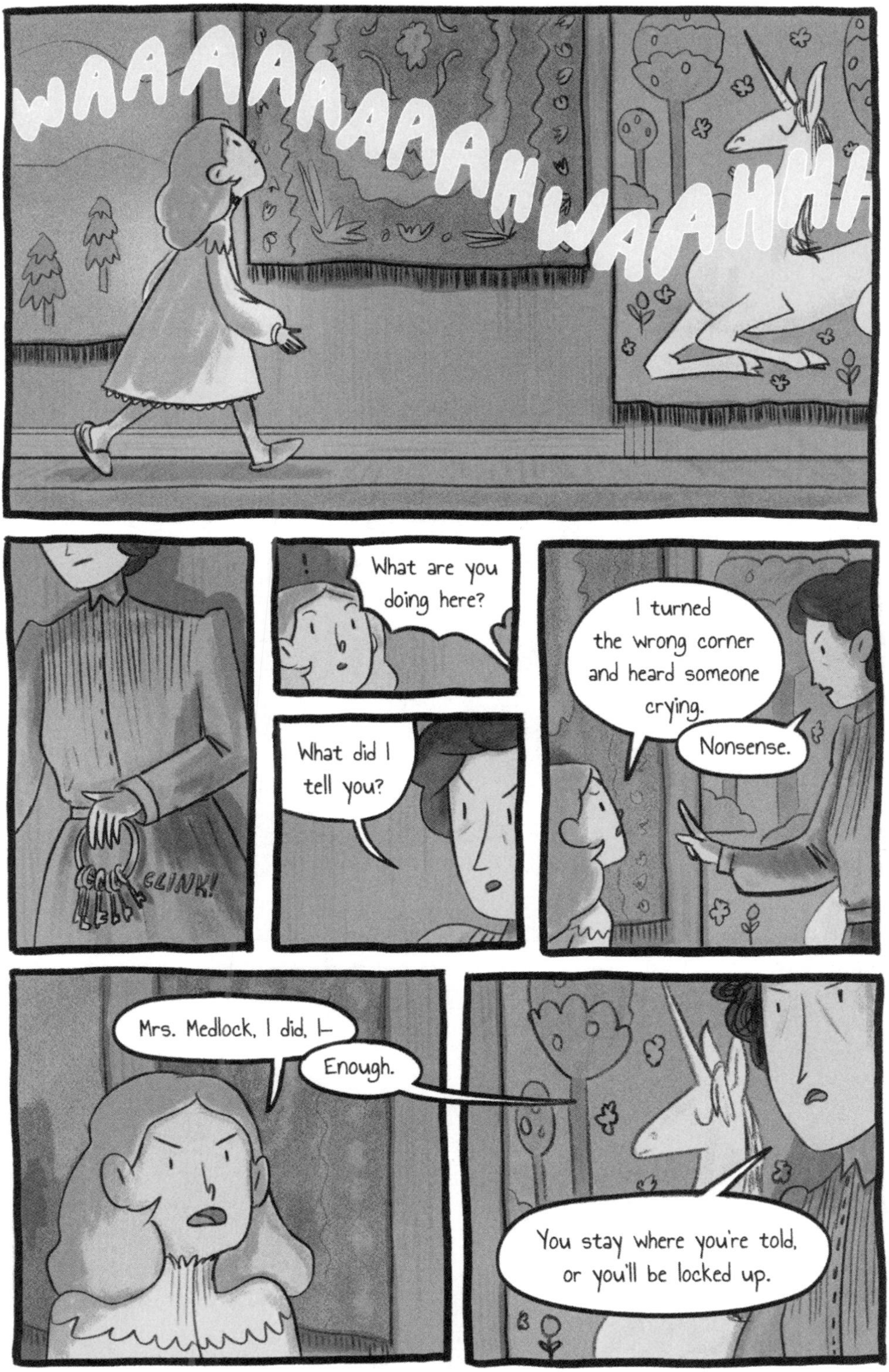
WAAAAAAAAAHWAAHHH
CLINK!
What are you doing here?
What did I tell you?
I turned the wrong corner and heard someone crying.
Nonsense.
Mrs. Medlock, I did, I–
Enough.
You stay where you're told, or you'll be locked up.

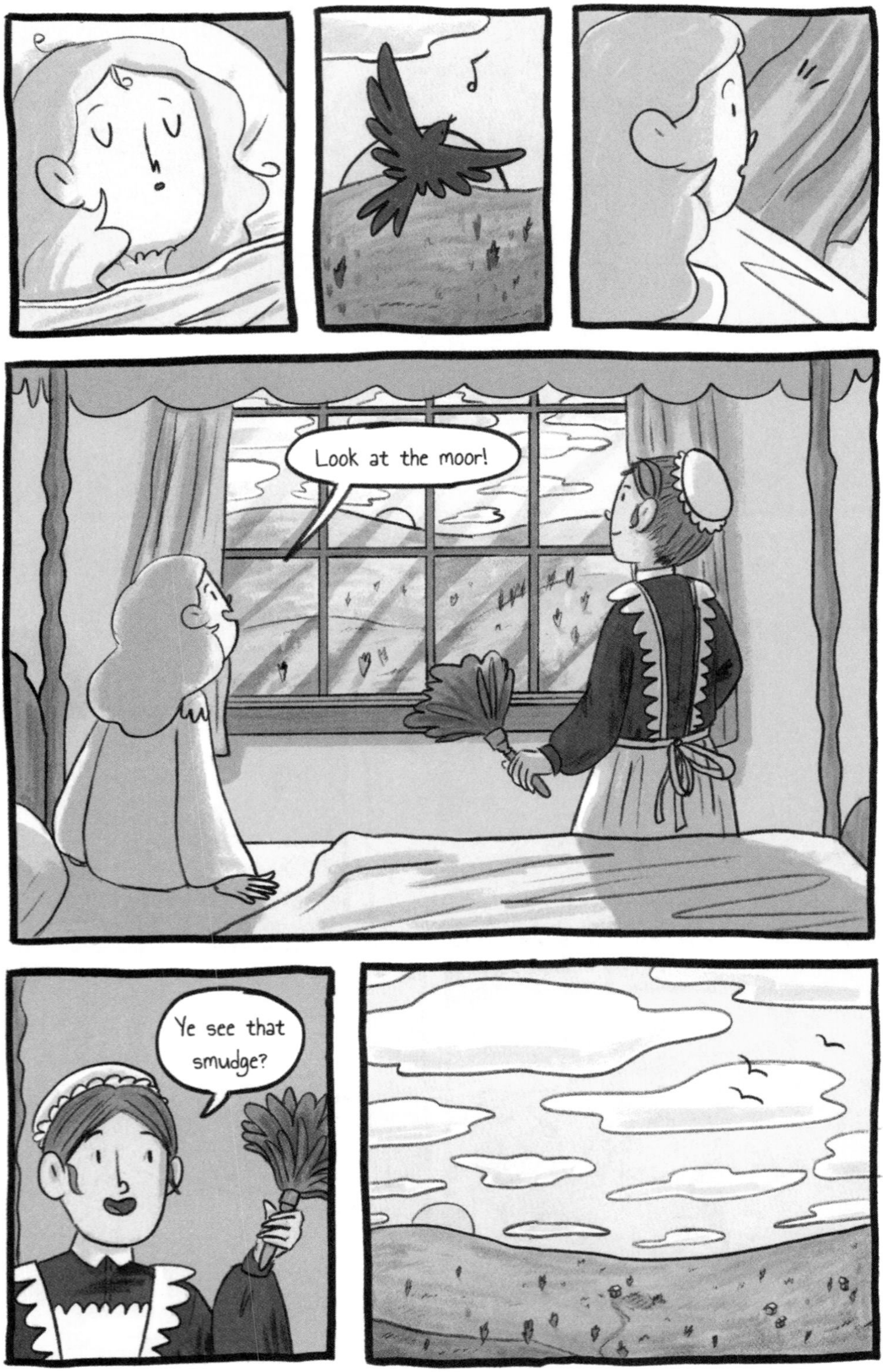
Look at the moor!
Ye see that smudge?

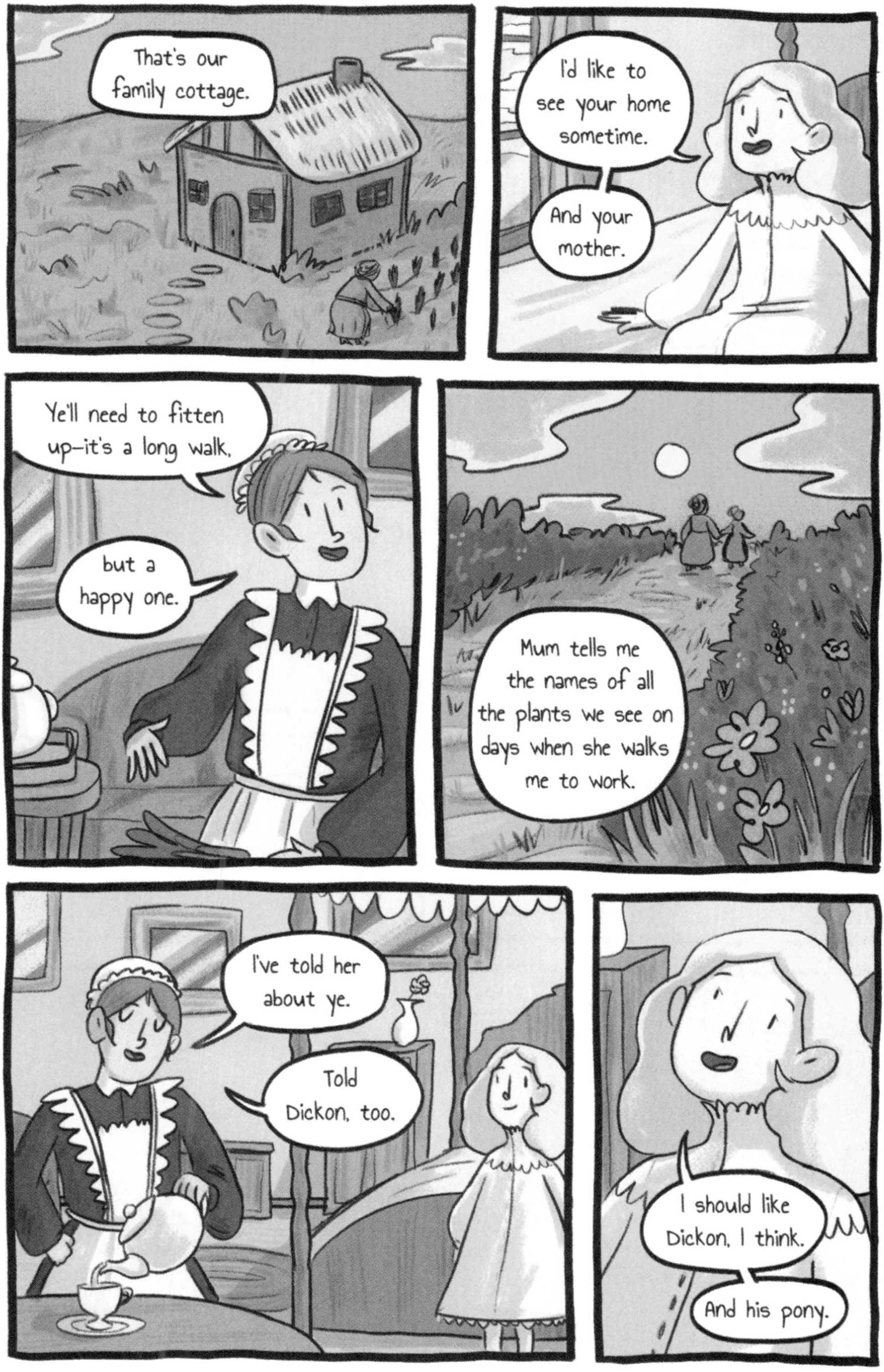
That's our family cottage.
I'd like to see your home sometime.
And your mother.
Ye'll need to fitten up–it's a long walk,
but a happy one.
Mum tells me the names of all the plants we see on days when she walks me to work.
I've told her about ye.
Told Dickon, too.
I should like Dickon, I think.
And his pony.

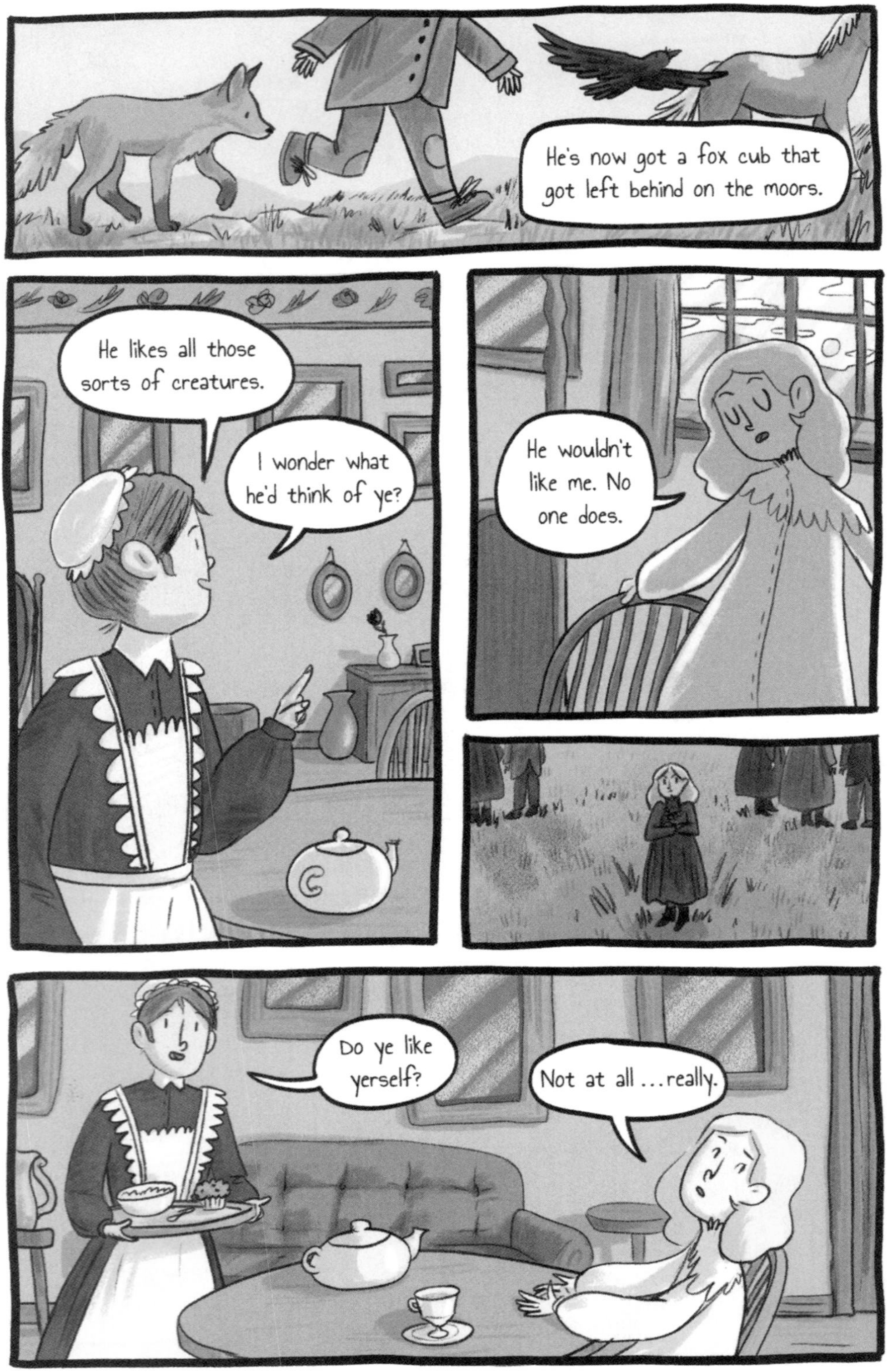
He's now got a fox cub that got left behind on the moors.
He likes all those sorts of creatures.
I wonder what he'd think of ye?
He wouldn't like me. No one does.
Do ye like yerself?
Not at all ...really.

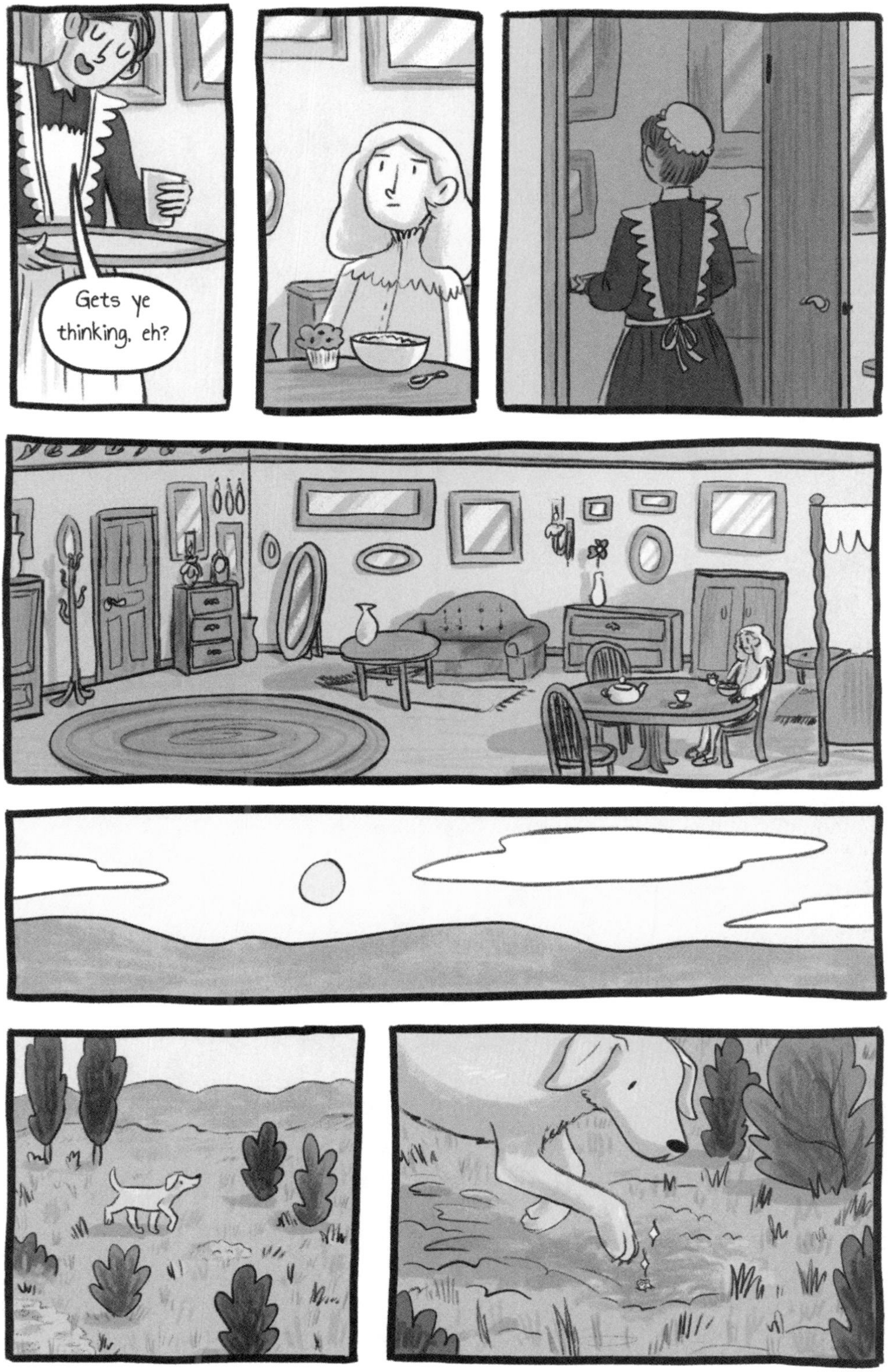
Gets ye thinking, eh?

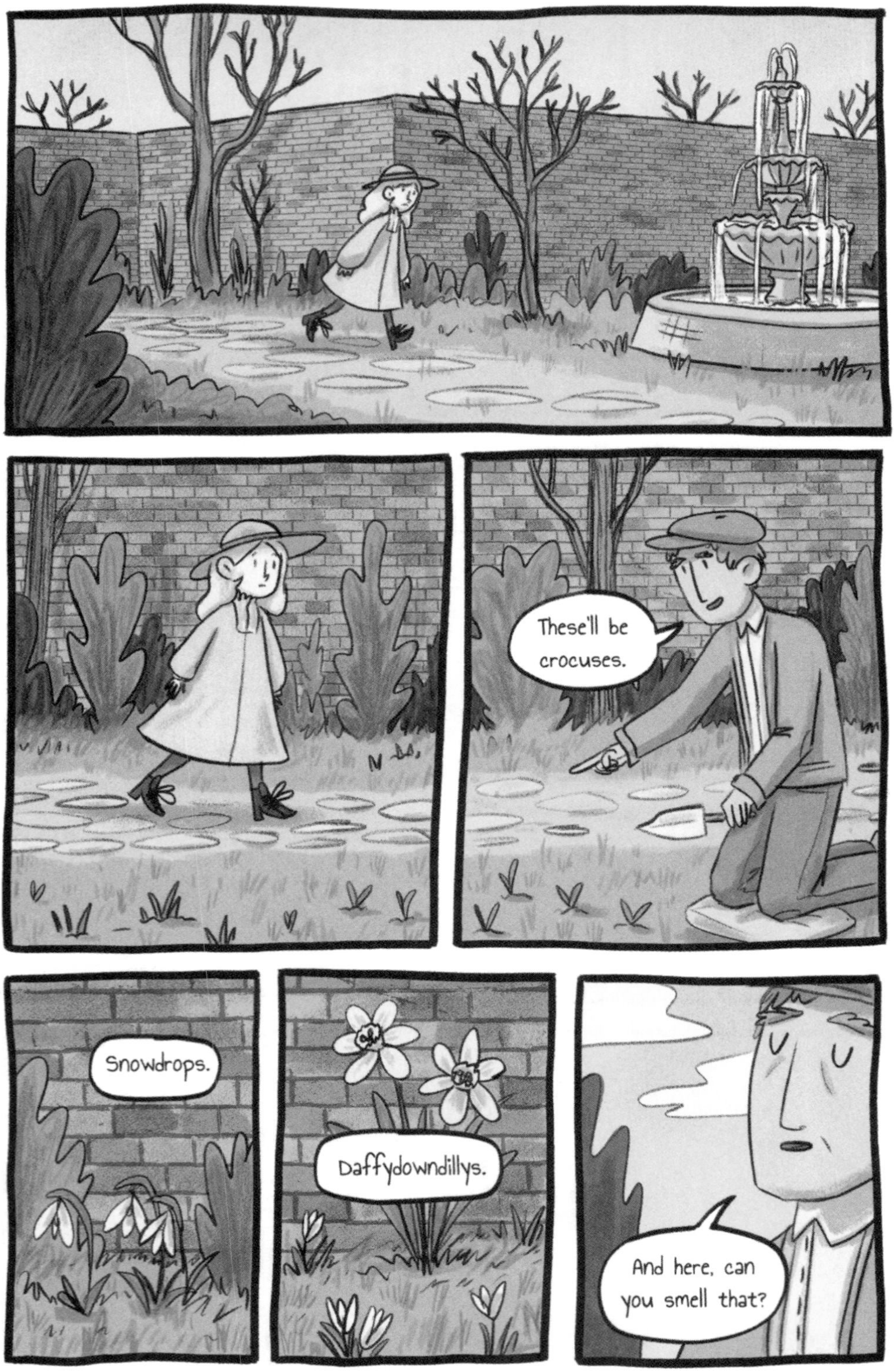
These'll be crocuses.
Snowdrops.
Daffydowndillys.
And here, can you smell that?

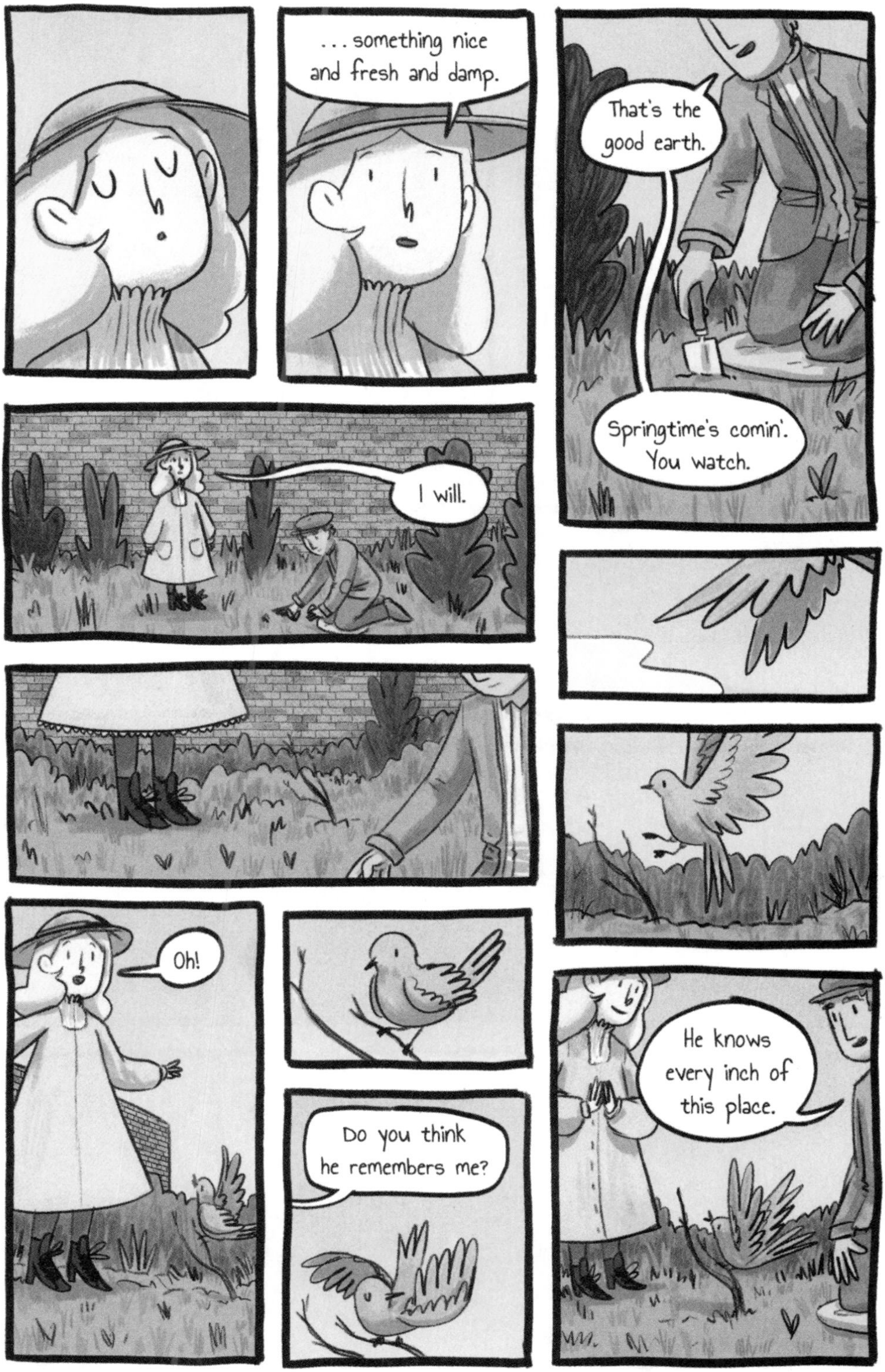

. . . something nice and fresh and damp.
That's the good earth.
Springtime's comin'. You watch.
I will.
Oh!
Do you think he remembers me?
He knows every inch of this place.

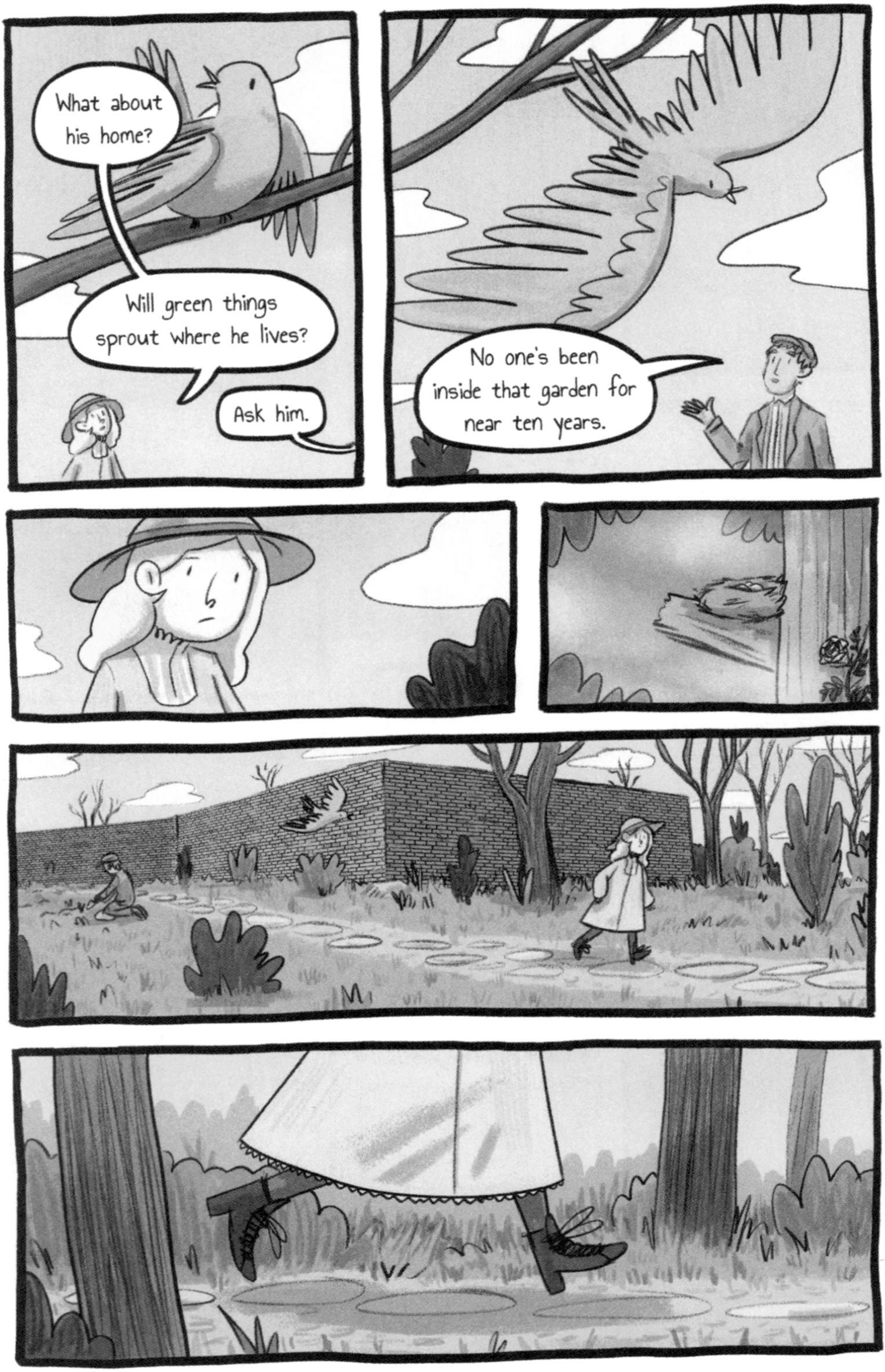
What about his home?
Will green things sprout where he lives?
Ask him.
No one's been inside that garden for near ten years.

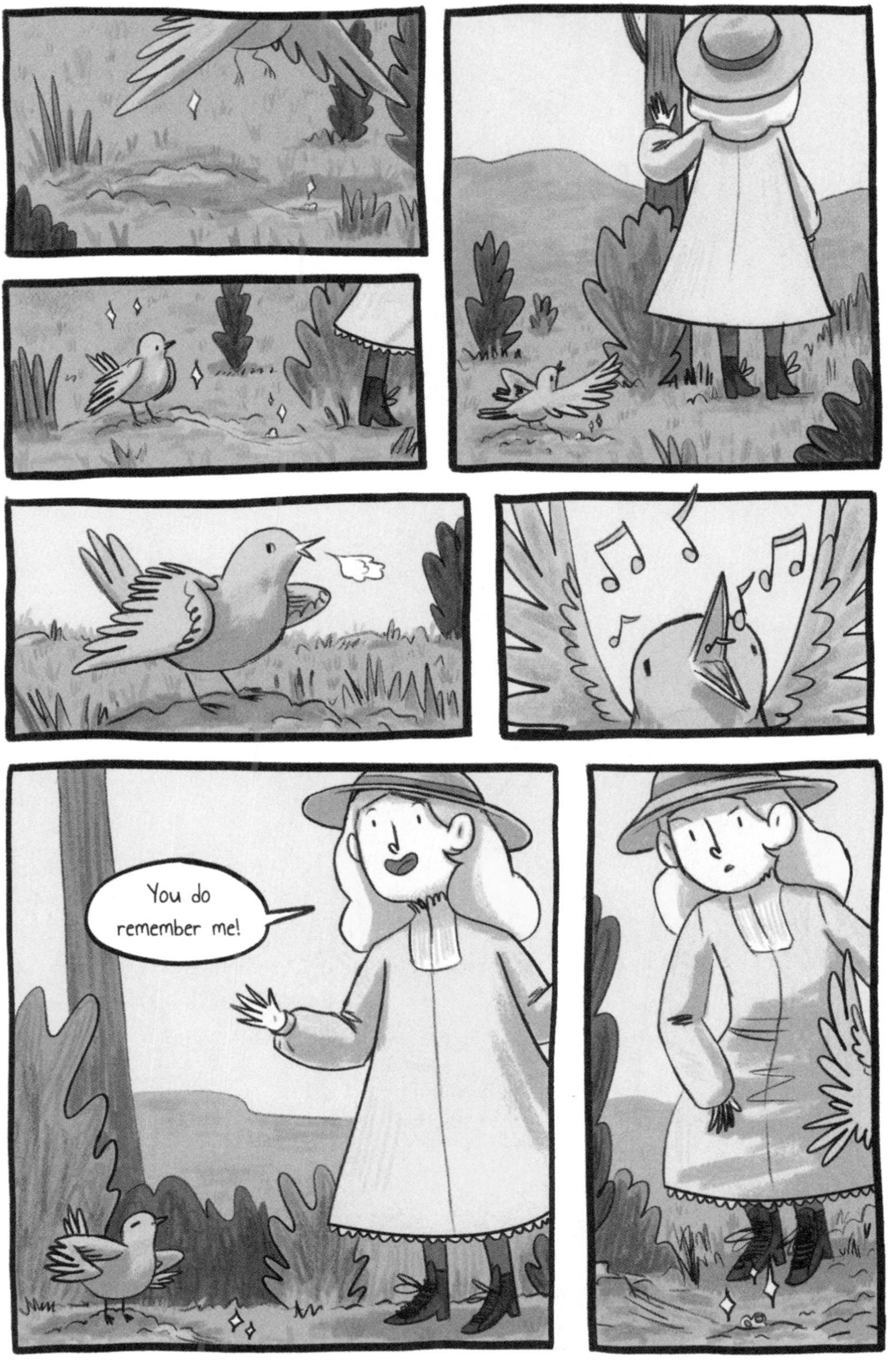
You do remember me!

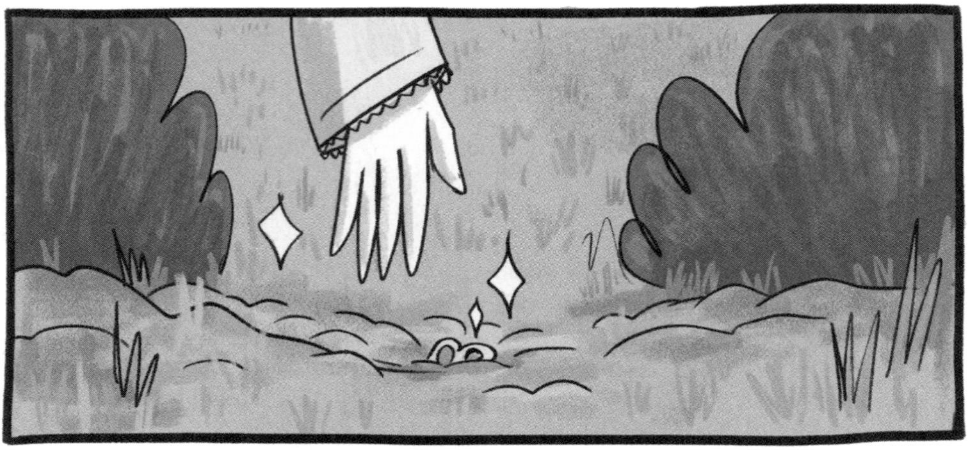
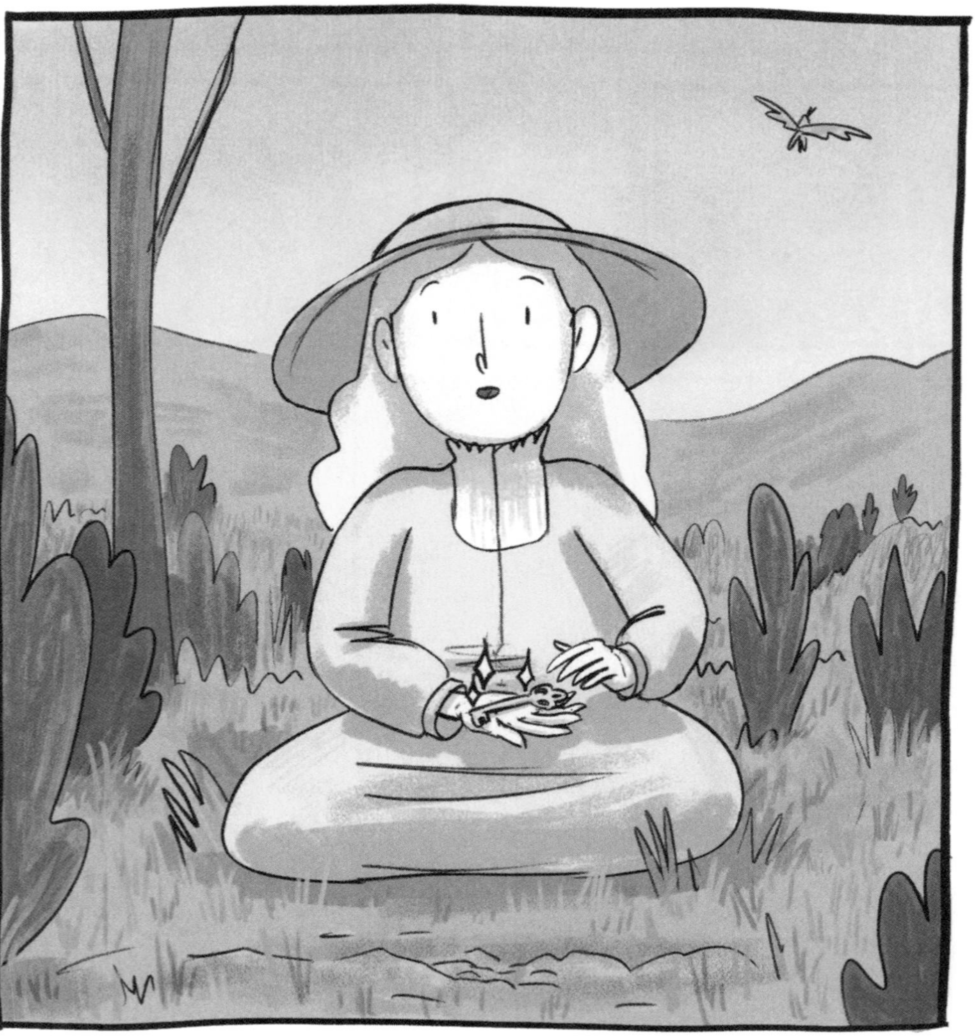

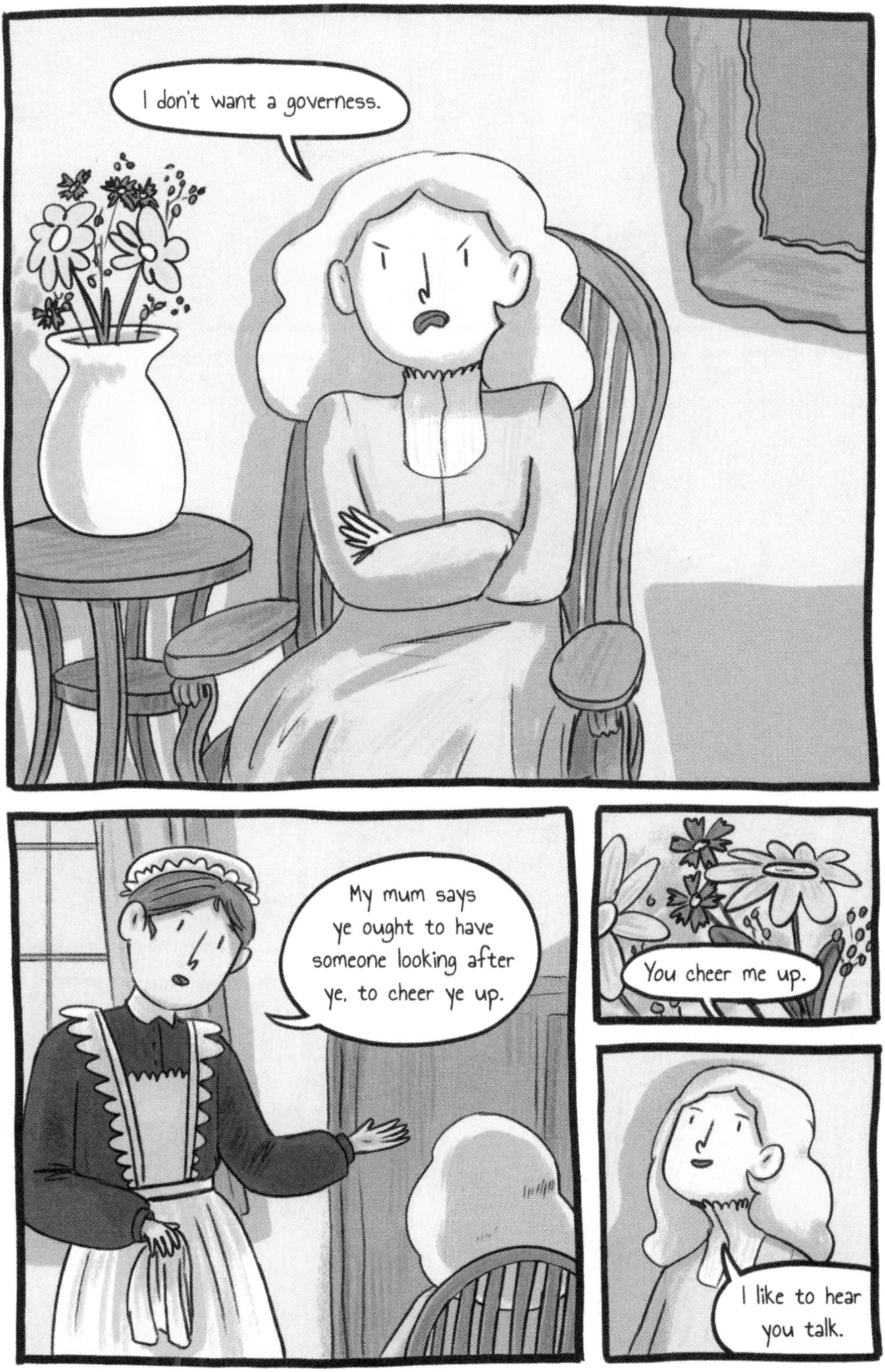
I don't want a governess.
My mum says ye ought to have someone looking after ye, to cheer ye up.
You cheer me up.
I like to hear you talk.

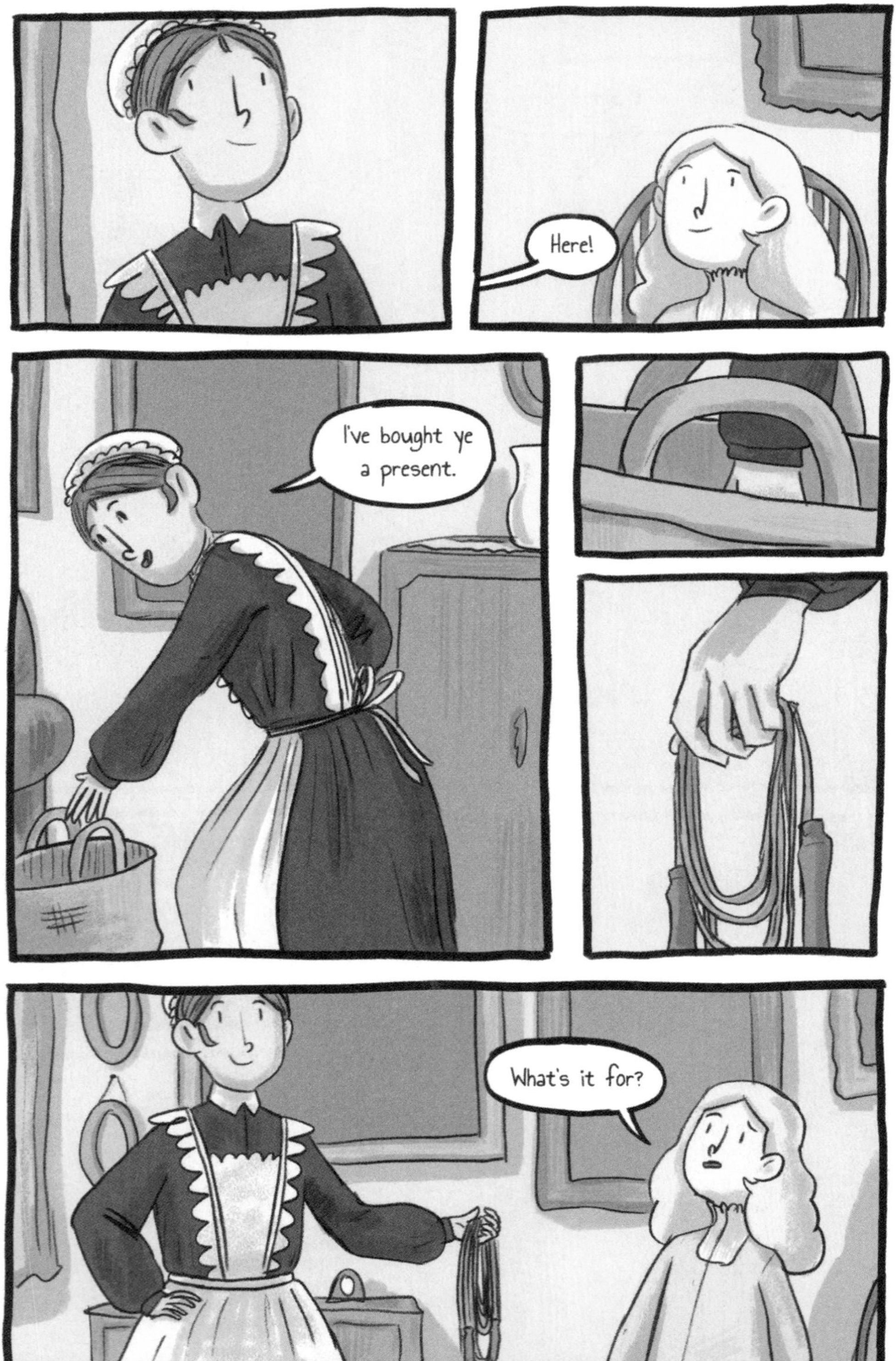
Here!
I've bought ye a present.
What's it for?

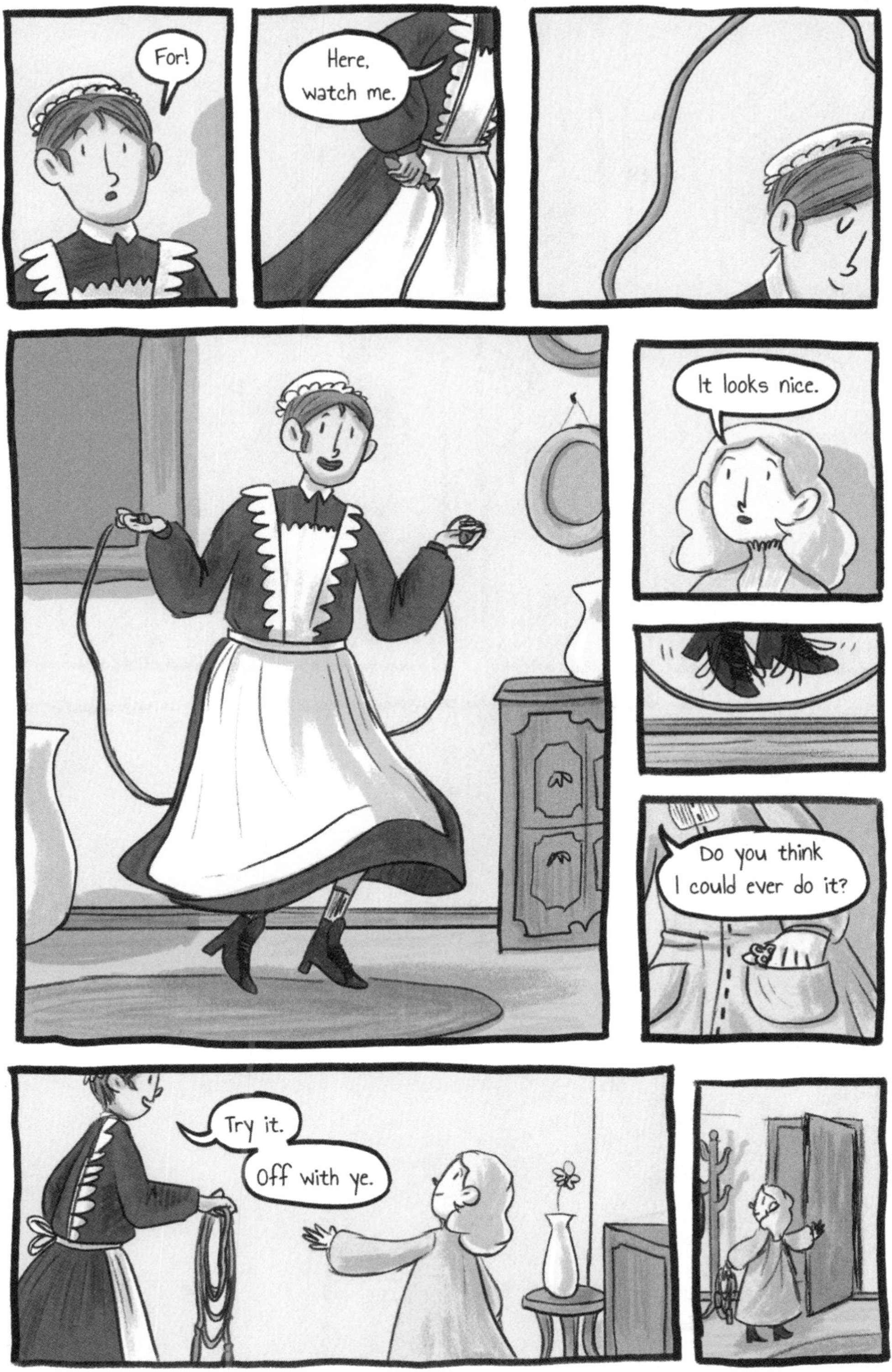
For!
Here, watch me.
It looks nice.
Do you think I could ever do it?
Try it.
Off with ye.

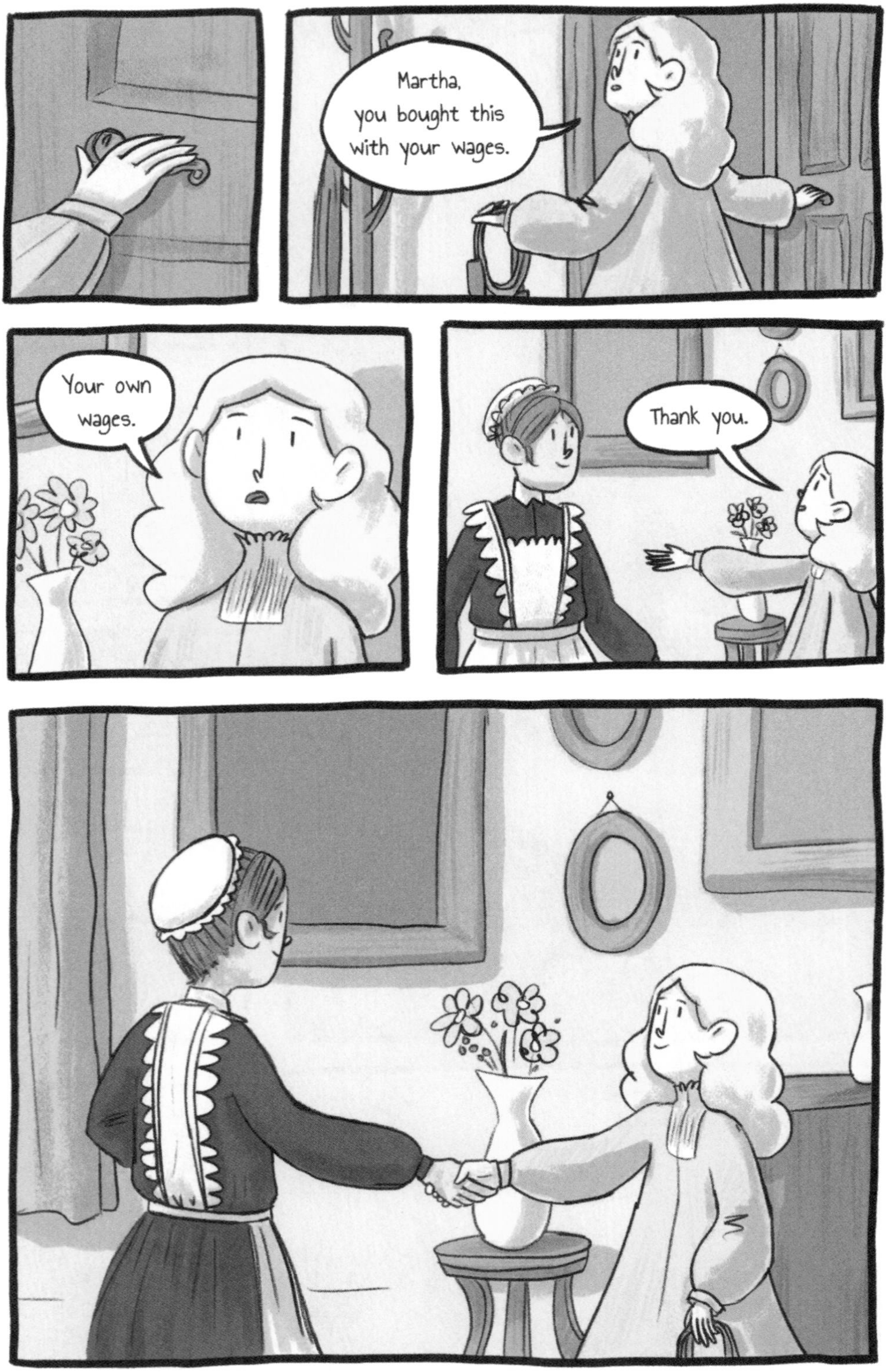
Martha, you bought this with your wages.
Your own wages.
Thank you.

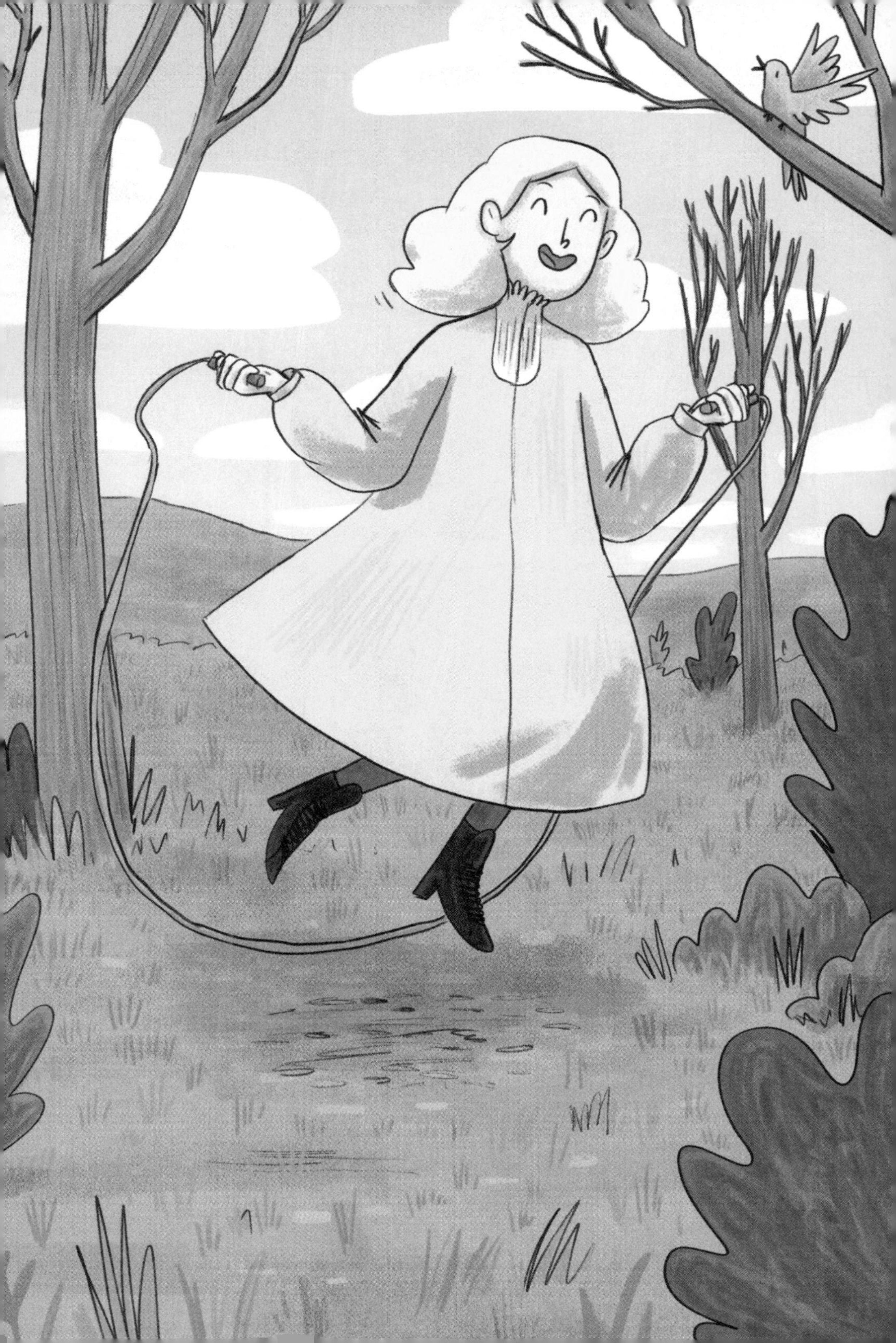

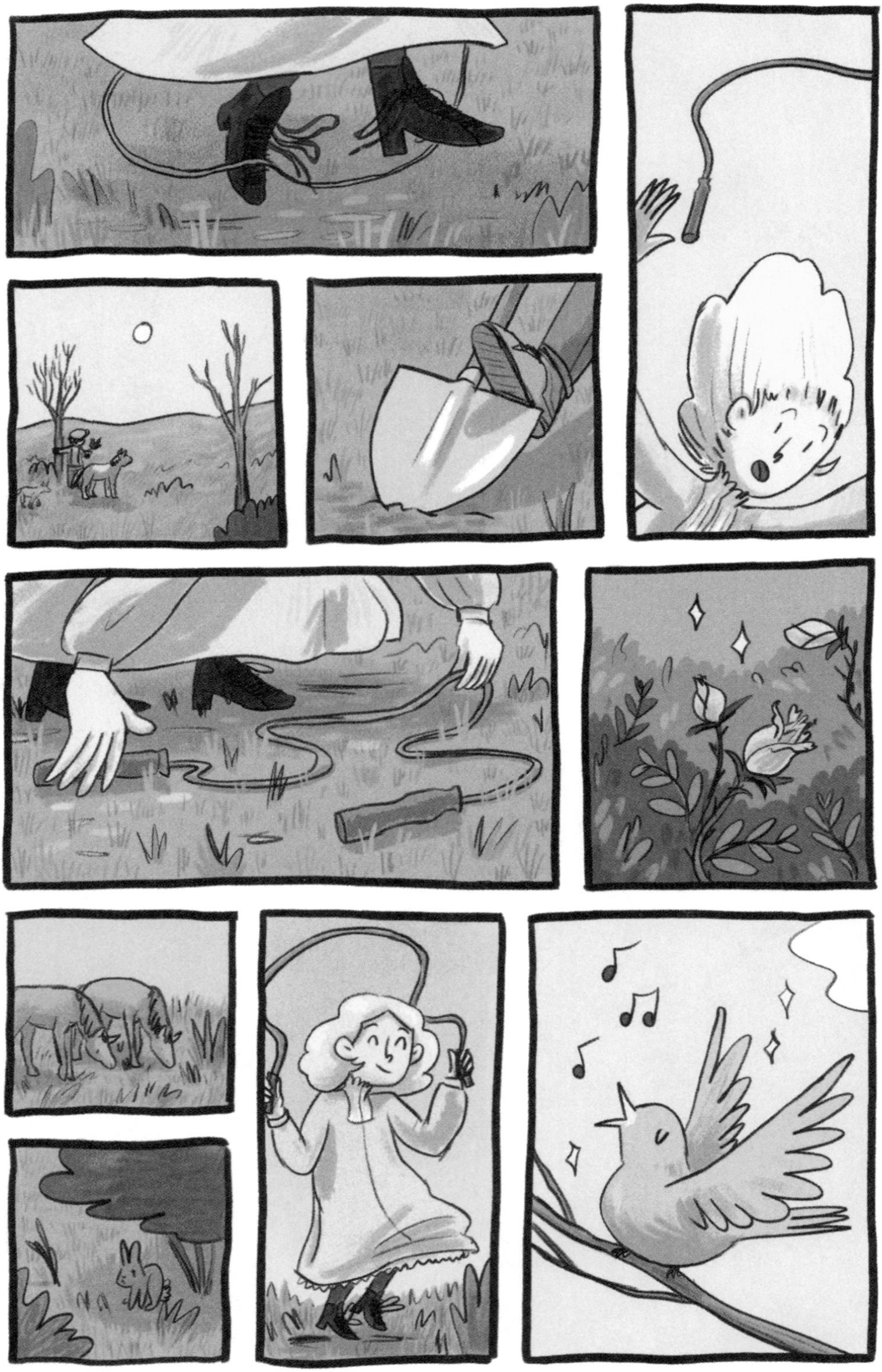

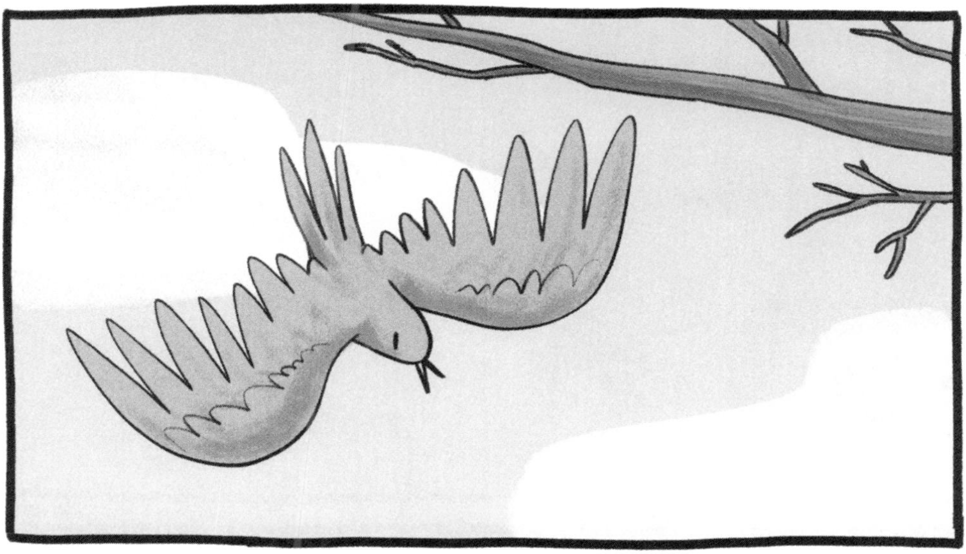

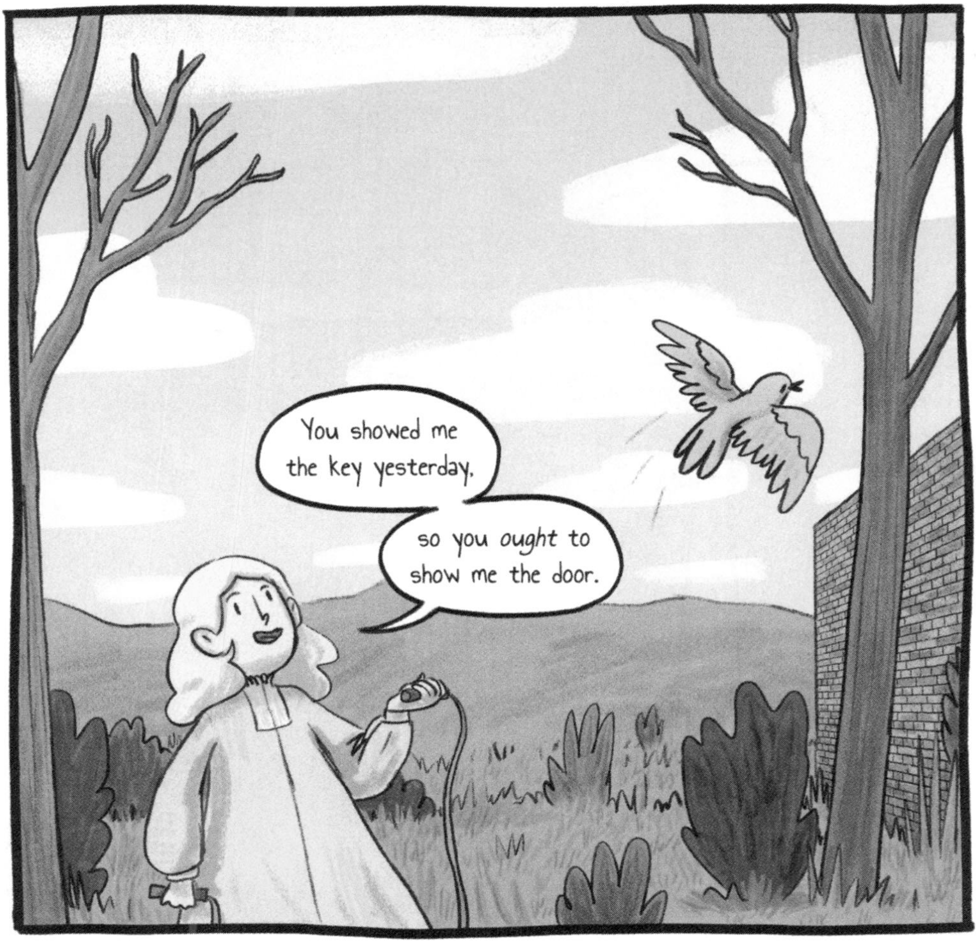

You showed me the key yesterday,
so you *ought* to show me the door.

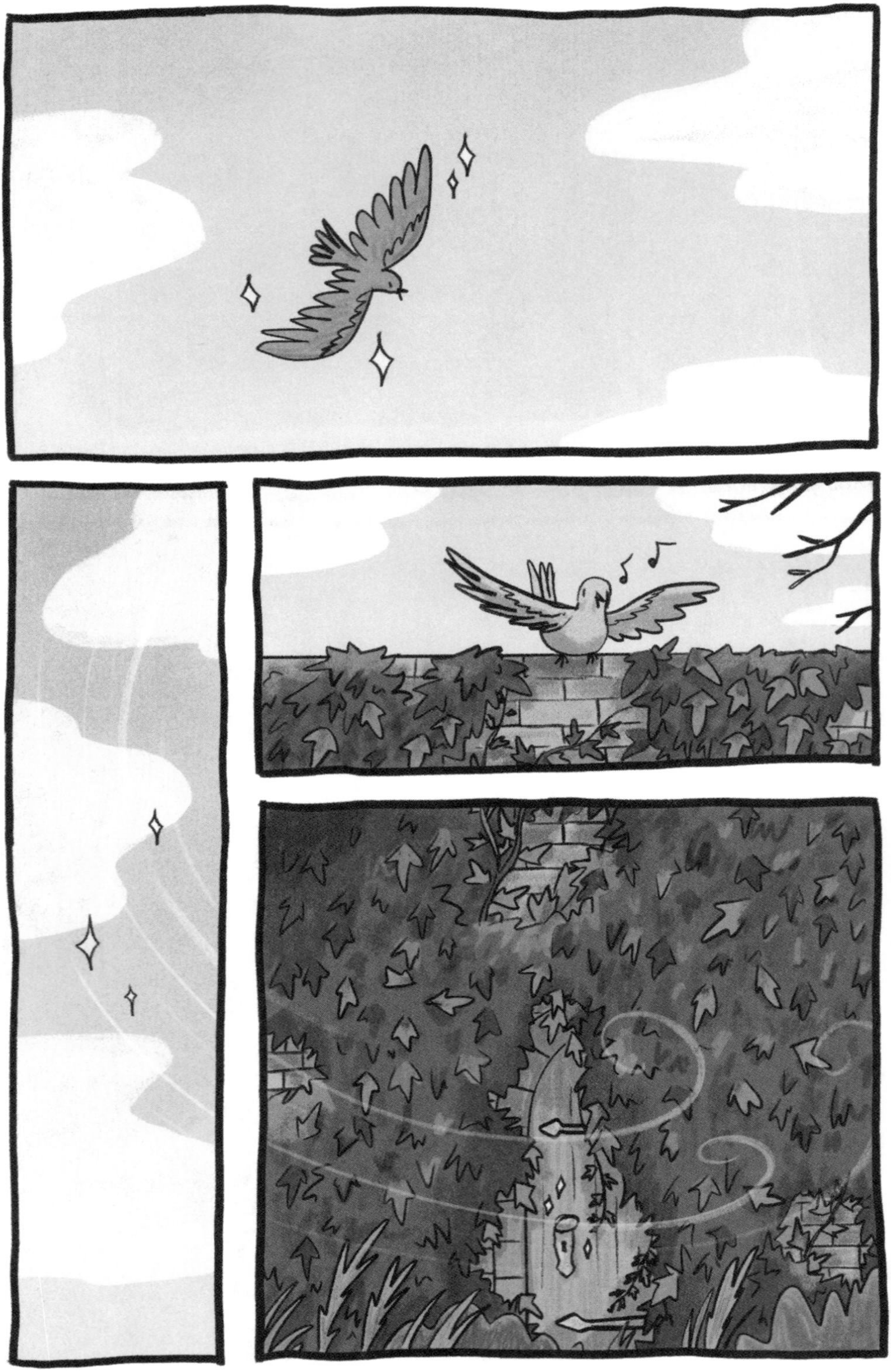

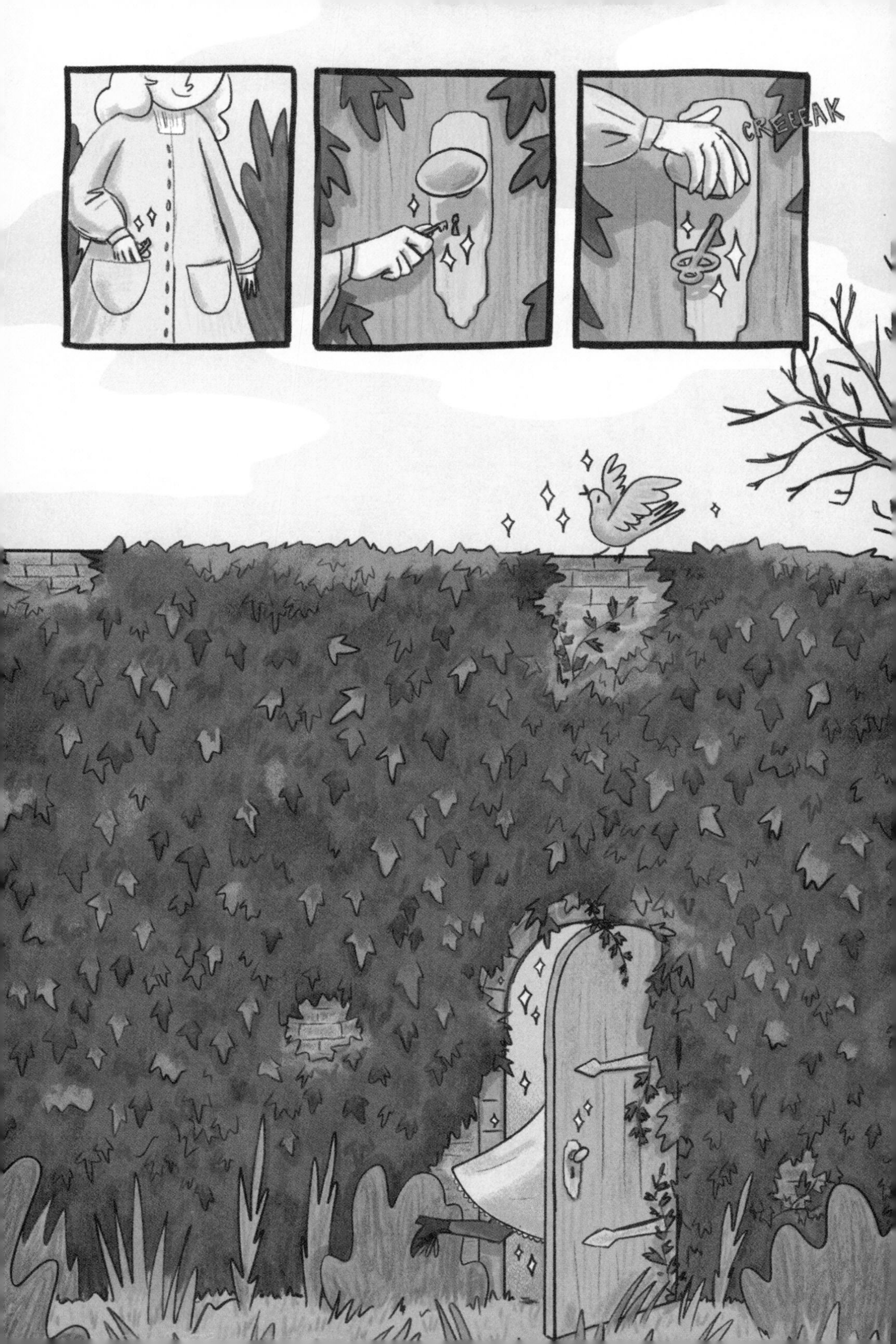
CREEEAK

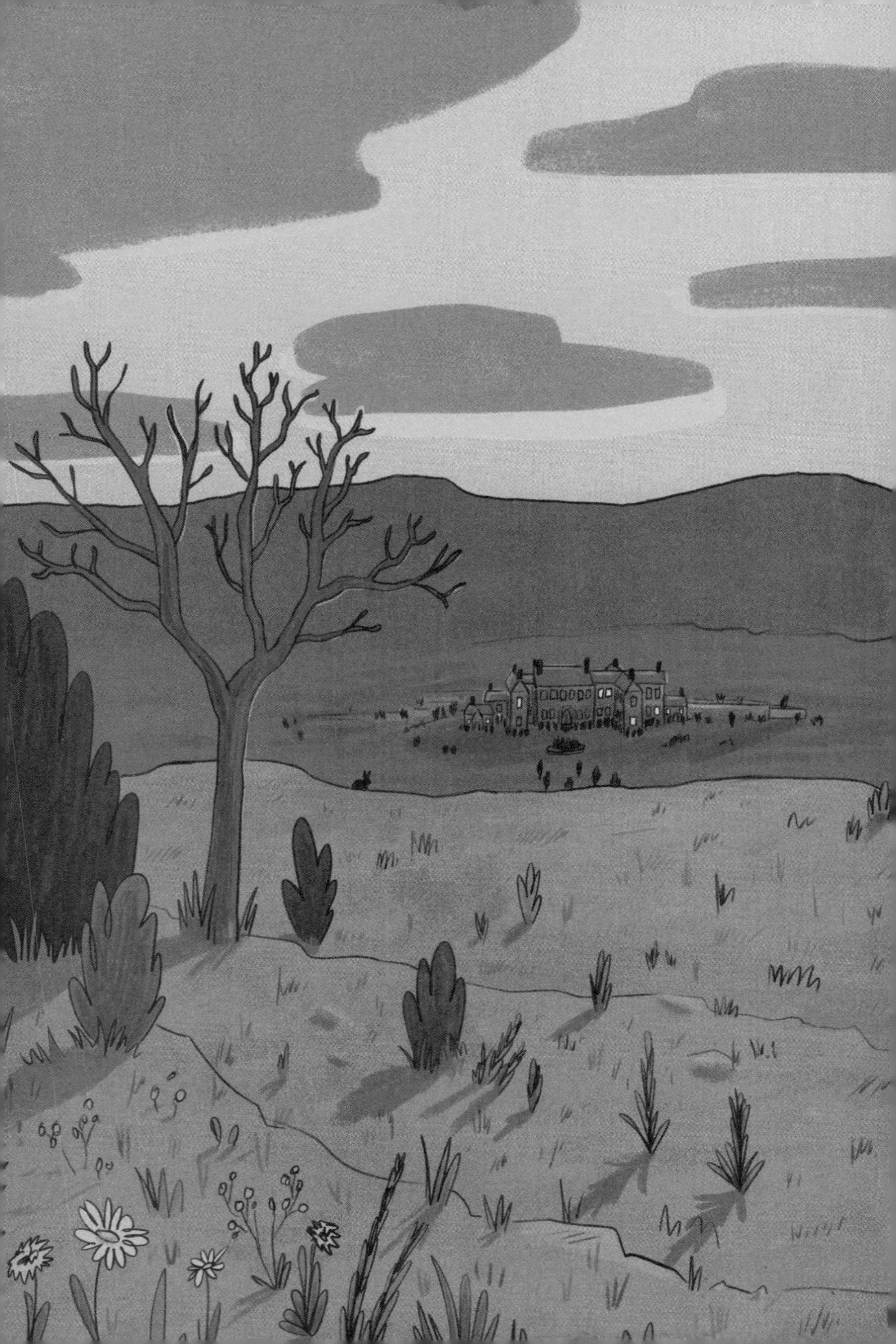

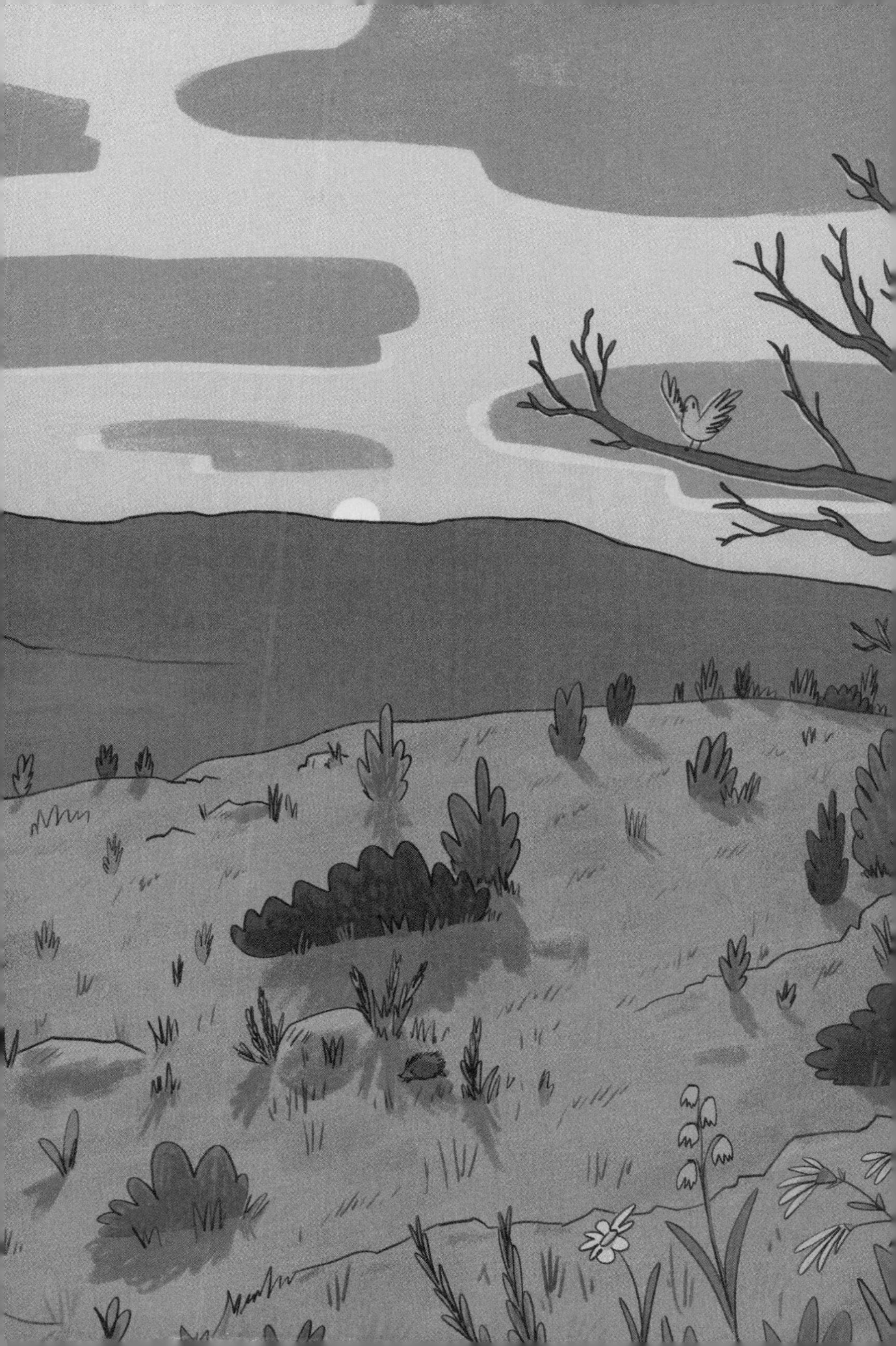

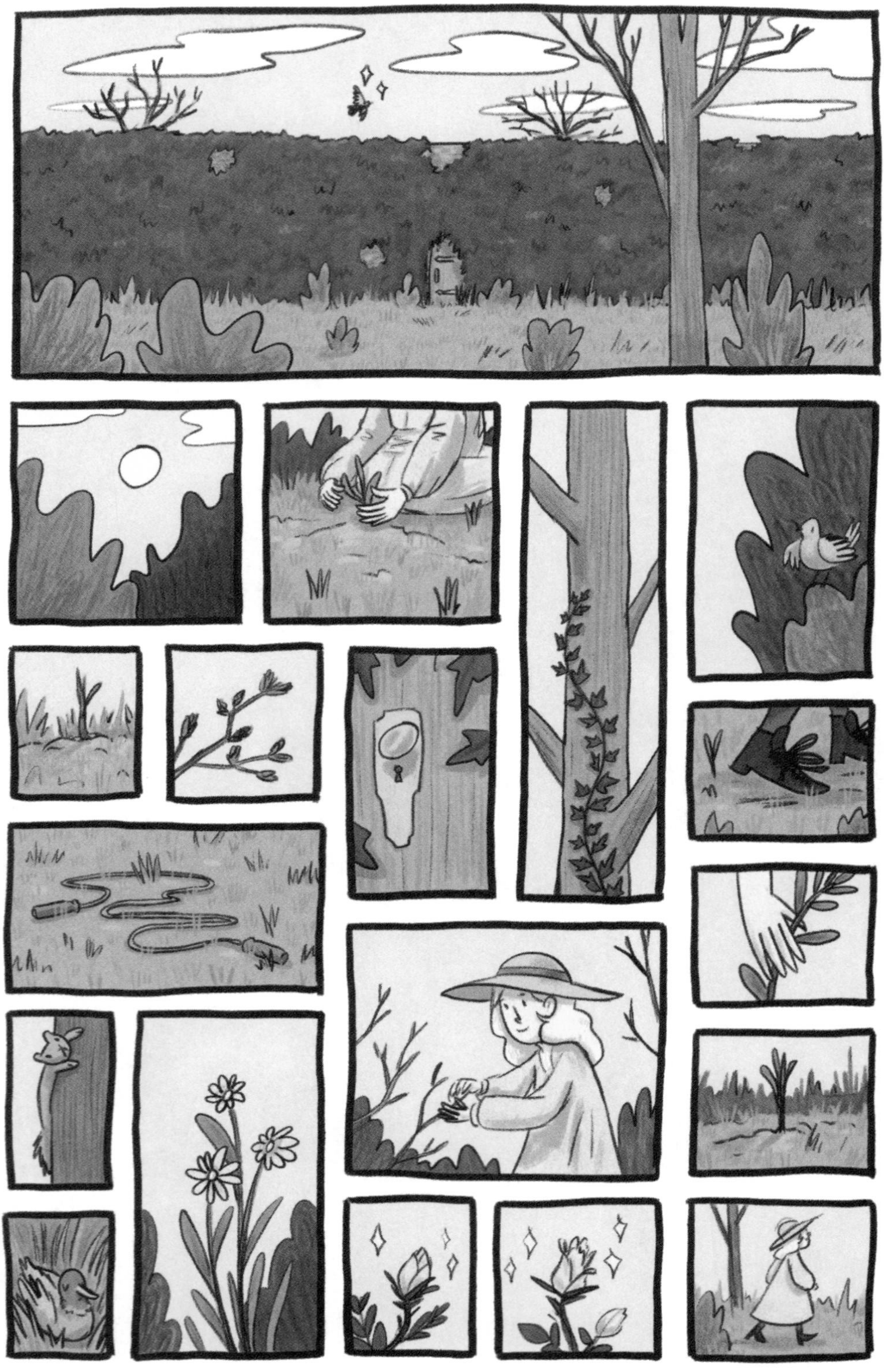

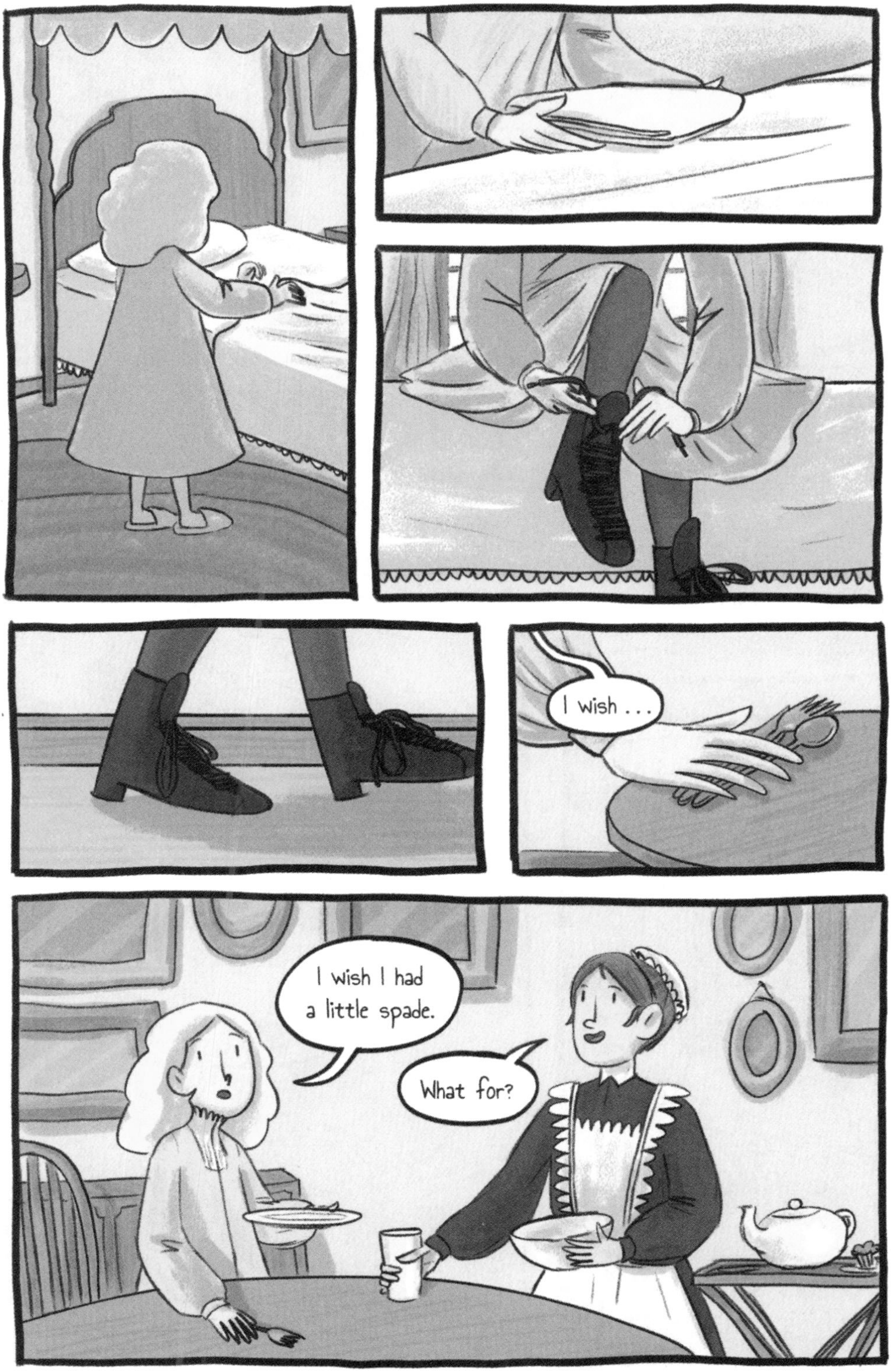
I wish . . .
I wish I had a little spade.
What for?

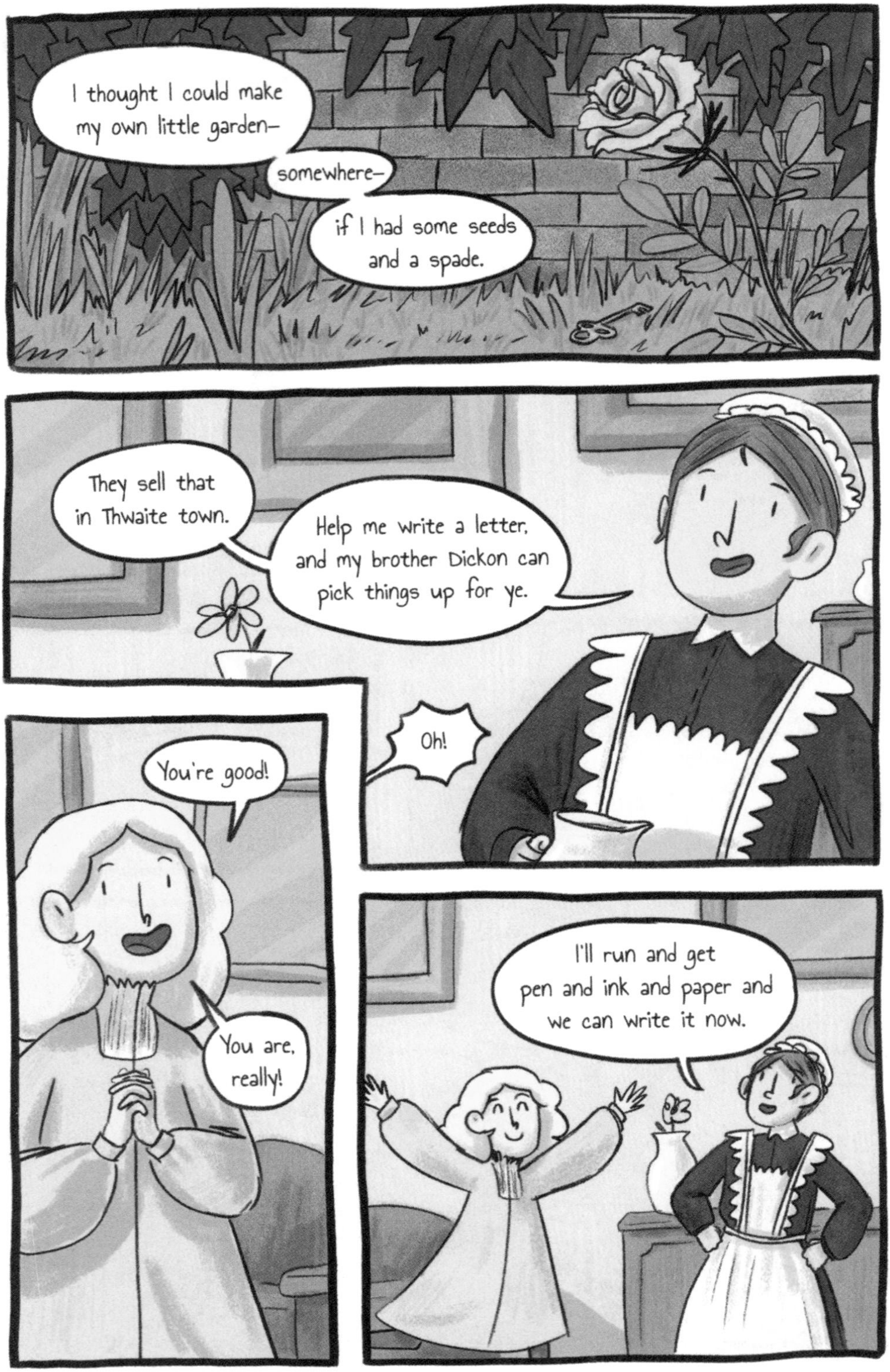
I thought I could make my own little garden—
somewhere—
if I had some seeds and a spade.
They sell that in Thwaite town.
Help me write a letter, and my brother Dickon can pick things up for ye.
Oh!
You're good!
You are, really!
I'll run and get pen and ink and paper and we can write it now.

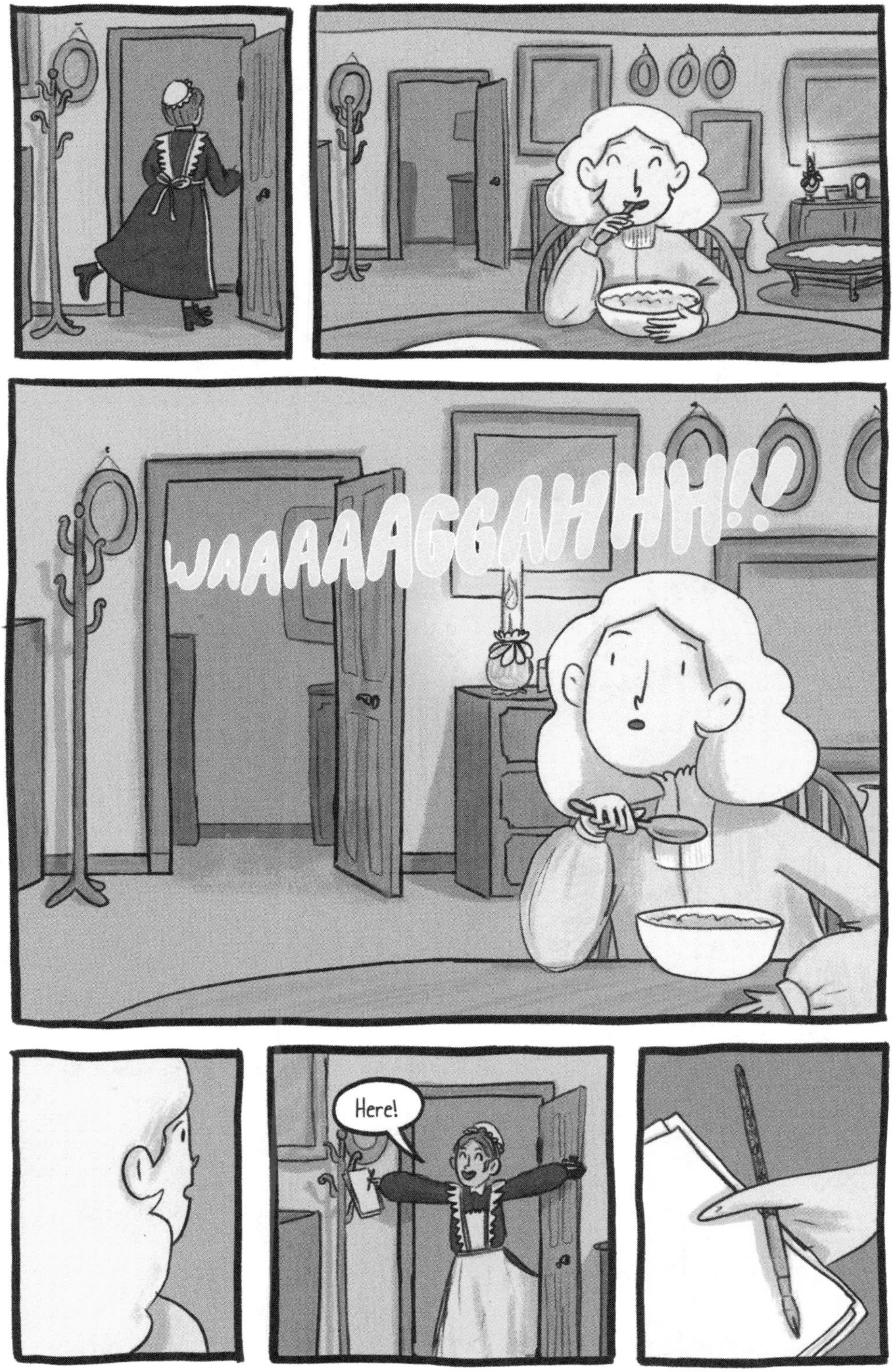
WAAAAAGGAHHH!!
Here!

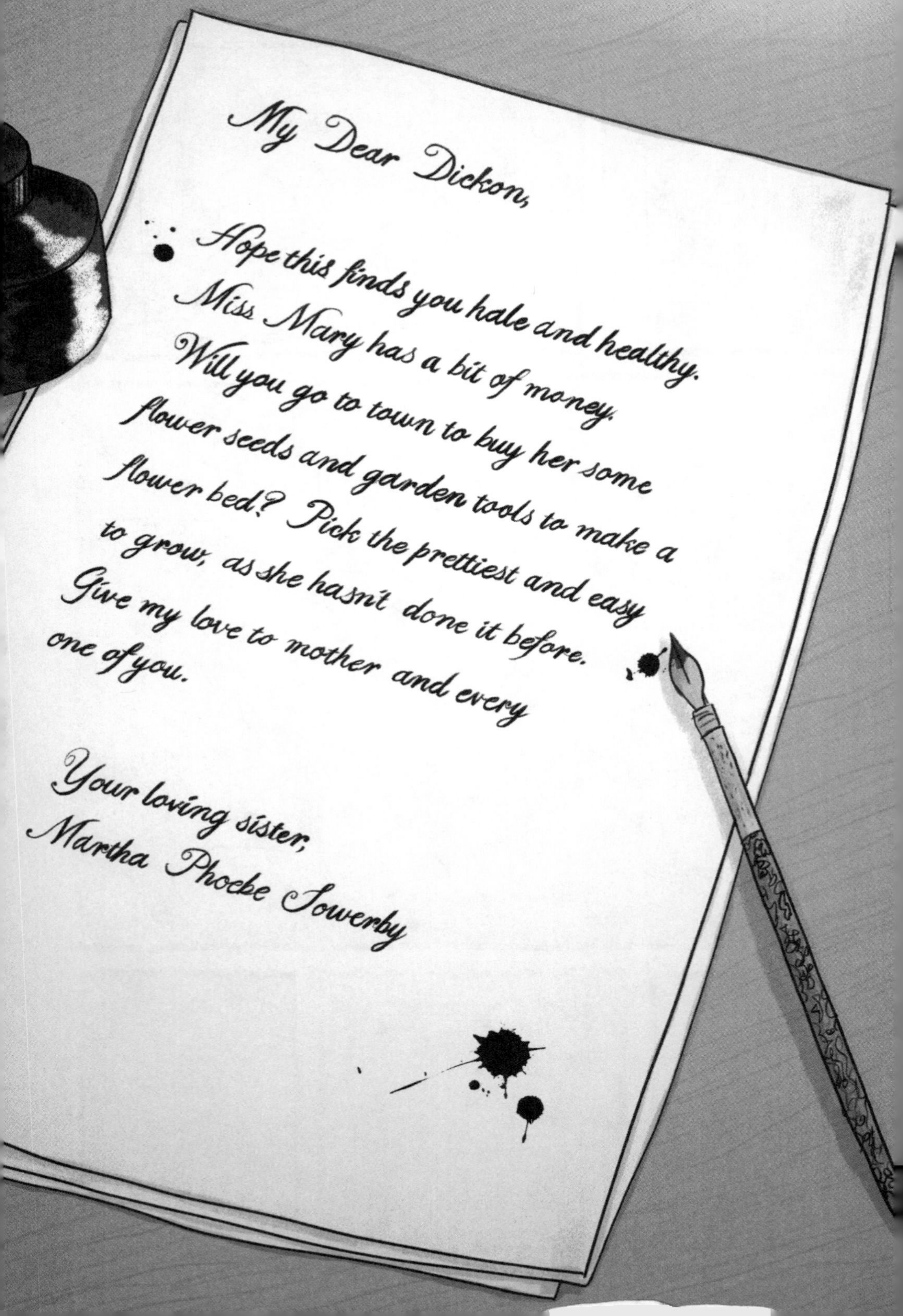

My Dear Dickon,

Hope this finds you hale and healthy.
Miss Mary has a bit of money.
Will you go to town to buy her some
flower seeds and garden tools to make a
flower bed? Pick the prettiest and easy
to grow, as she hasn't done it before.
Give my love to mother and every
one of you.

Your loving sister,
Martha Phoebe Sowerby

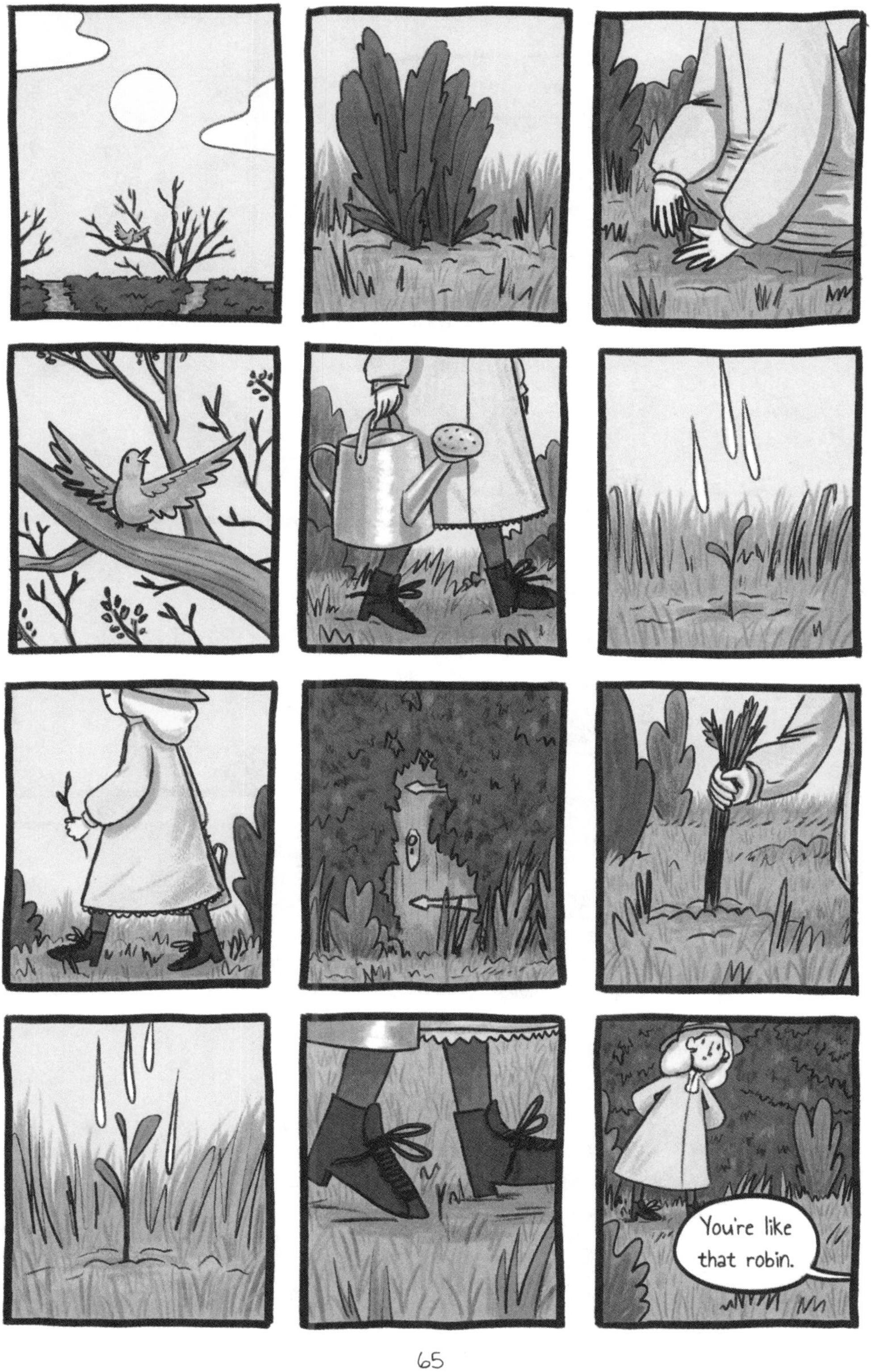
You're like
that robin.

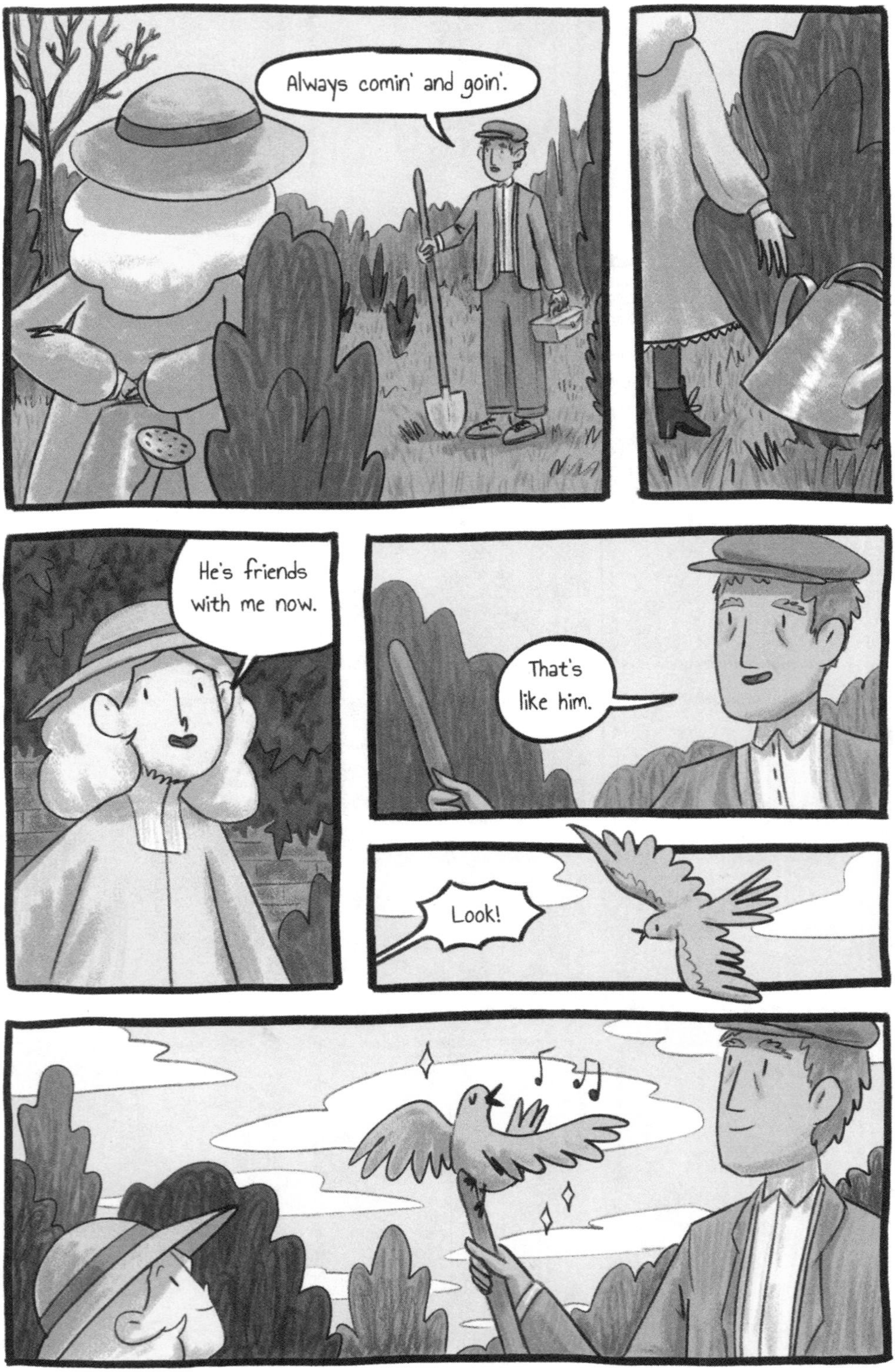

Always comin' and goin'.
He's friends with me now.
That's like him.
Look!

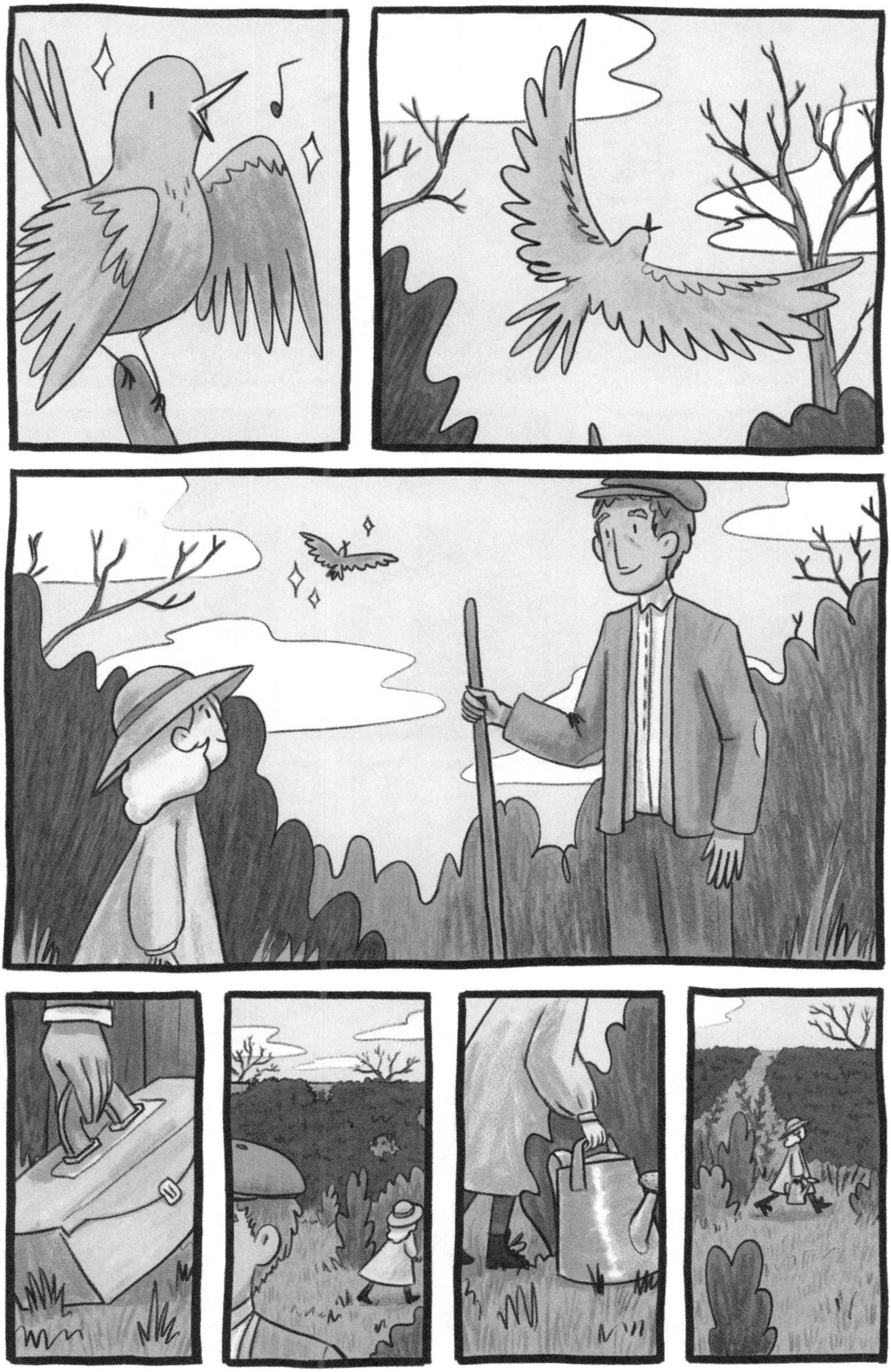

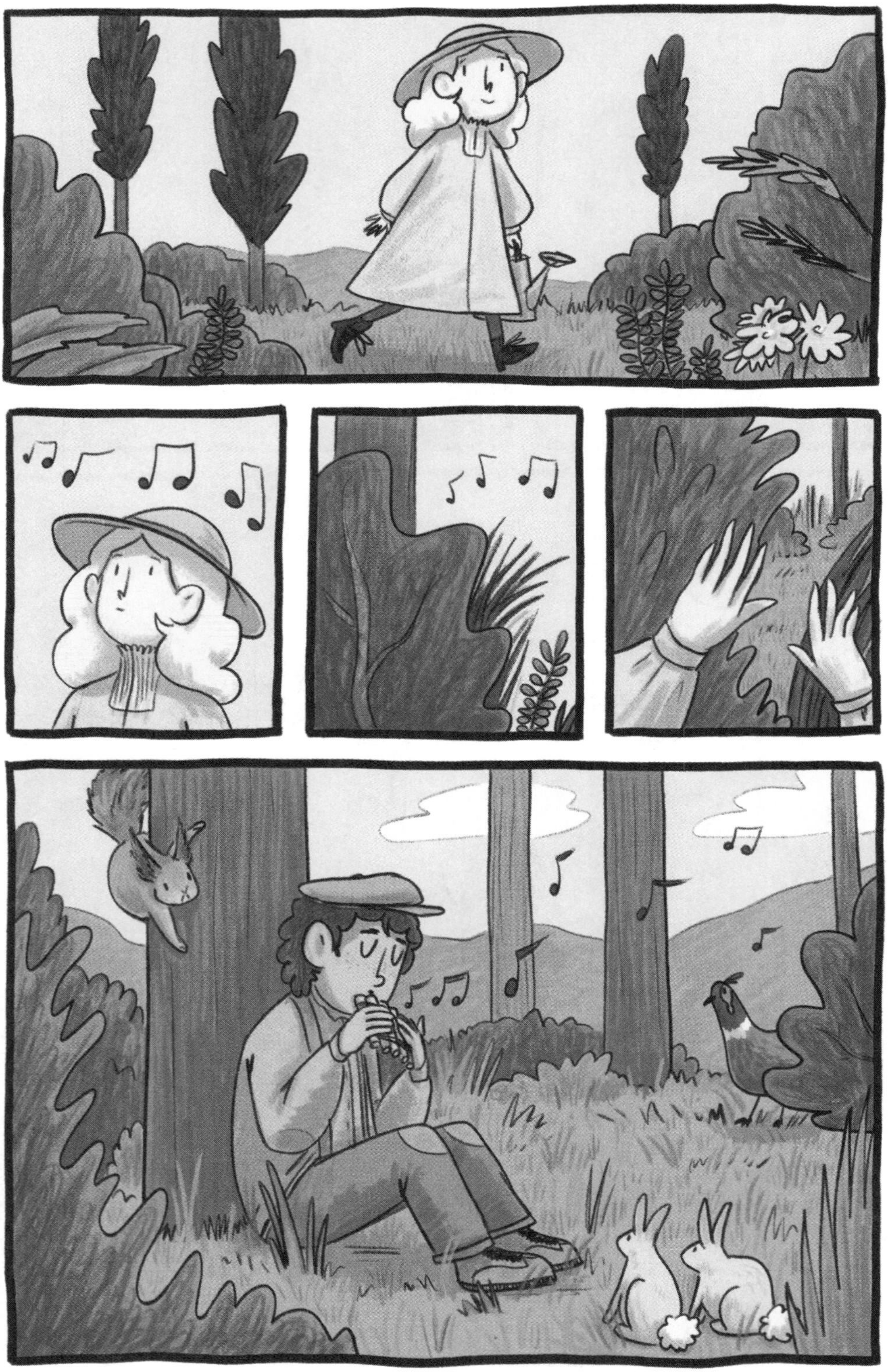

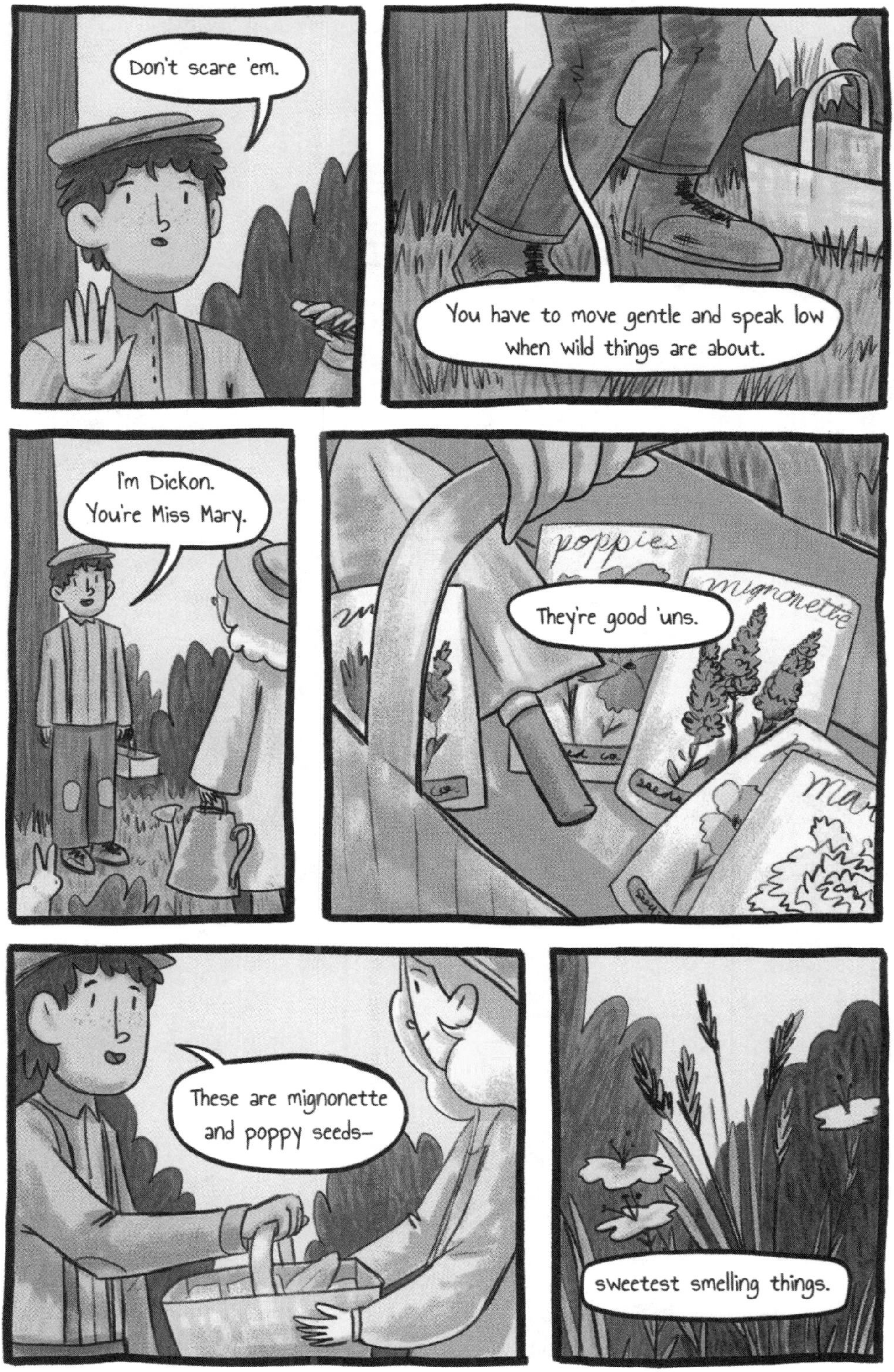
Don't scare 'em.
You have to move gentle and speak low when wild things are about.
I'm Dickon. You're Miss Mary.
They're good 'uns.
poppies
mignonette
These are mignonette and poppy seeds–
sweetest smelling things.

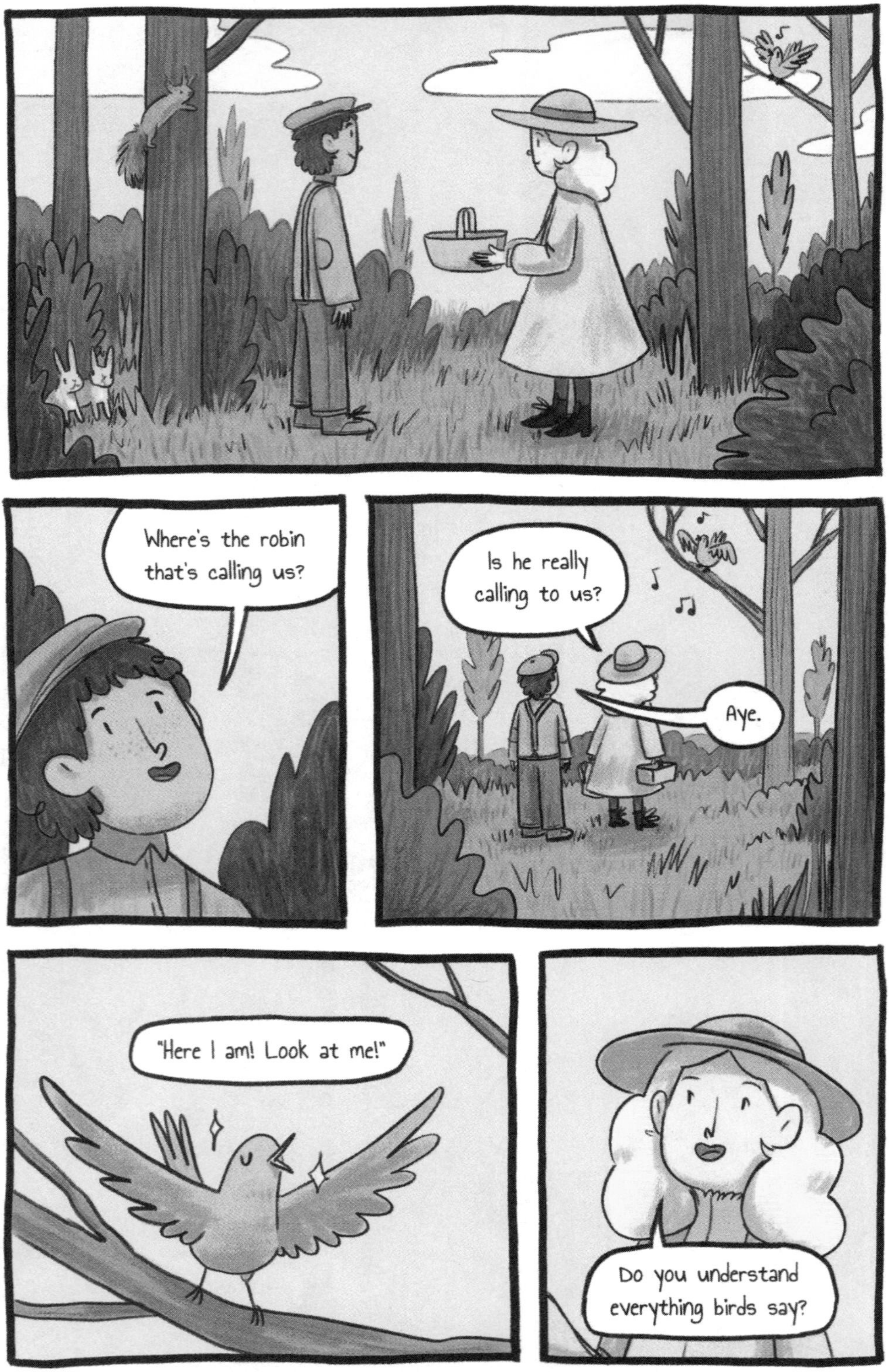
Where's the robin that's calling us?
Is he really calling to us?
Aye.
"Here I am! Look at me!"
Do you understand everything birds say?

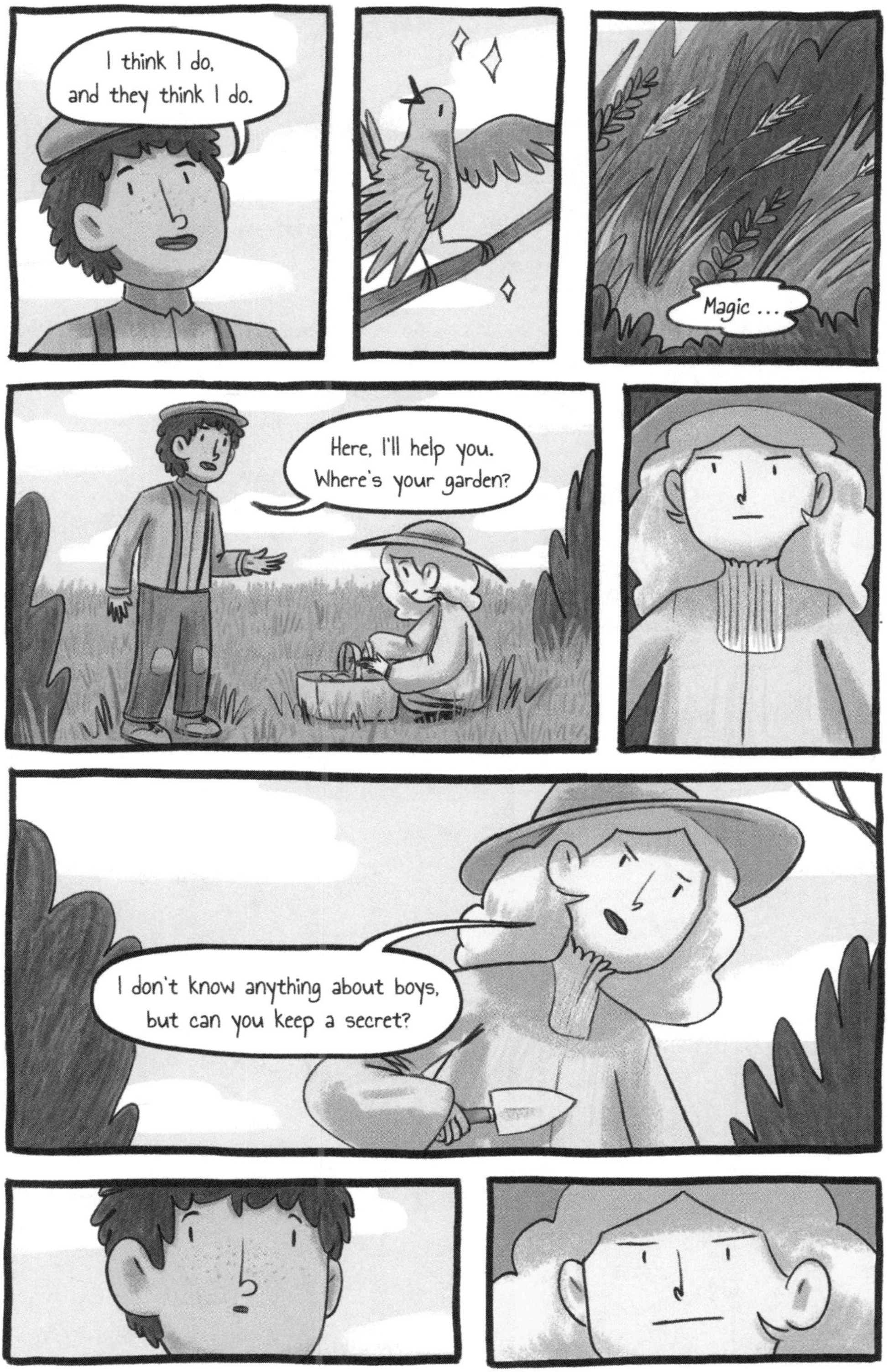
I think I do, and they think I do.
Magic ...
Here, I'll help you. Where's your garden?
I don't know anything about boys, but can you keep a secret?

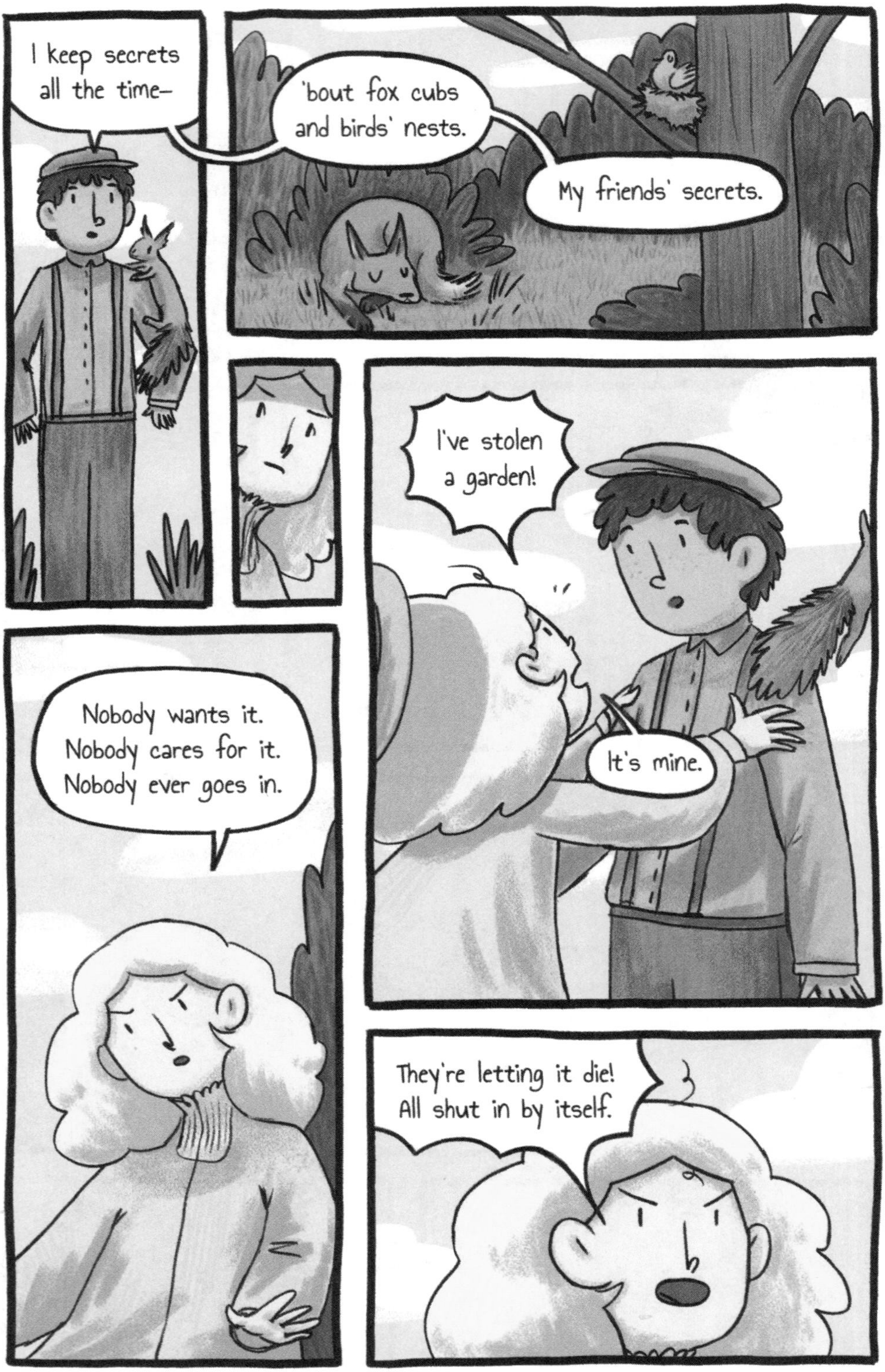
I keep secrets all the time—
'bout fox cubs and birds' nests.
My friends' secrets.
I've stolen a garden!
It's mine.
Nobody wants it. Nobody cares for it. Nobody ever goes in.
They're letting it die! All shut in by itself.

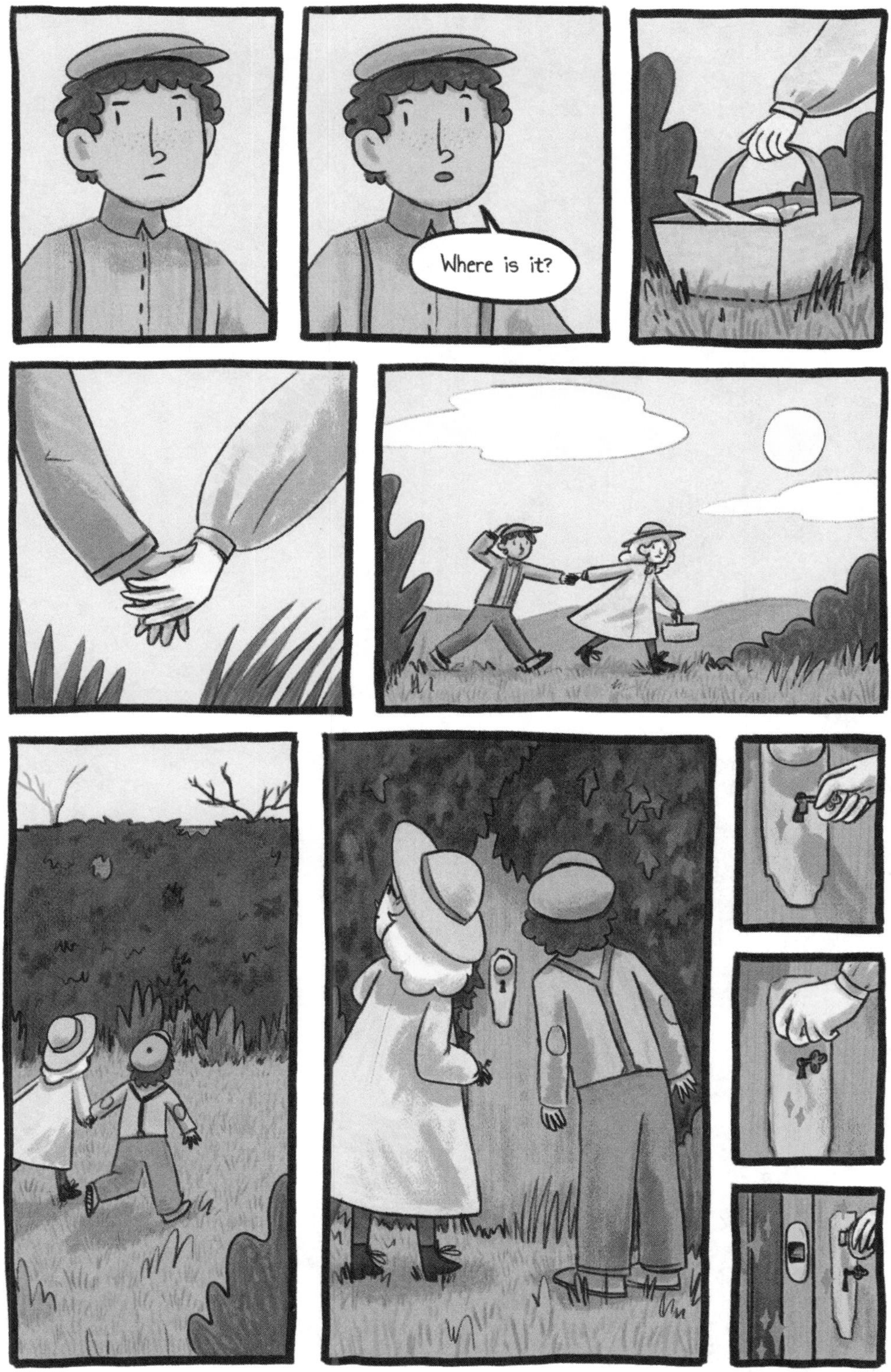
Where is it?

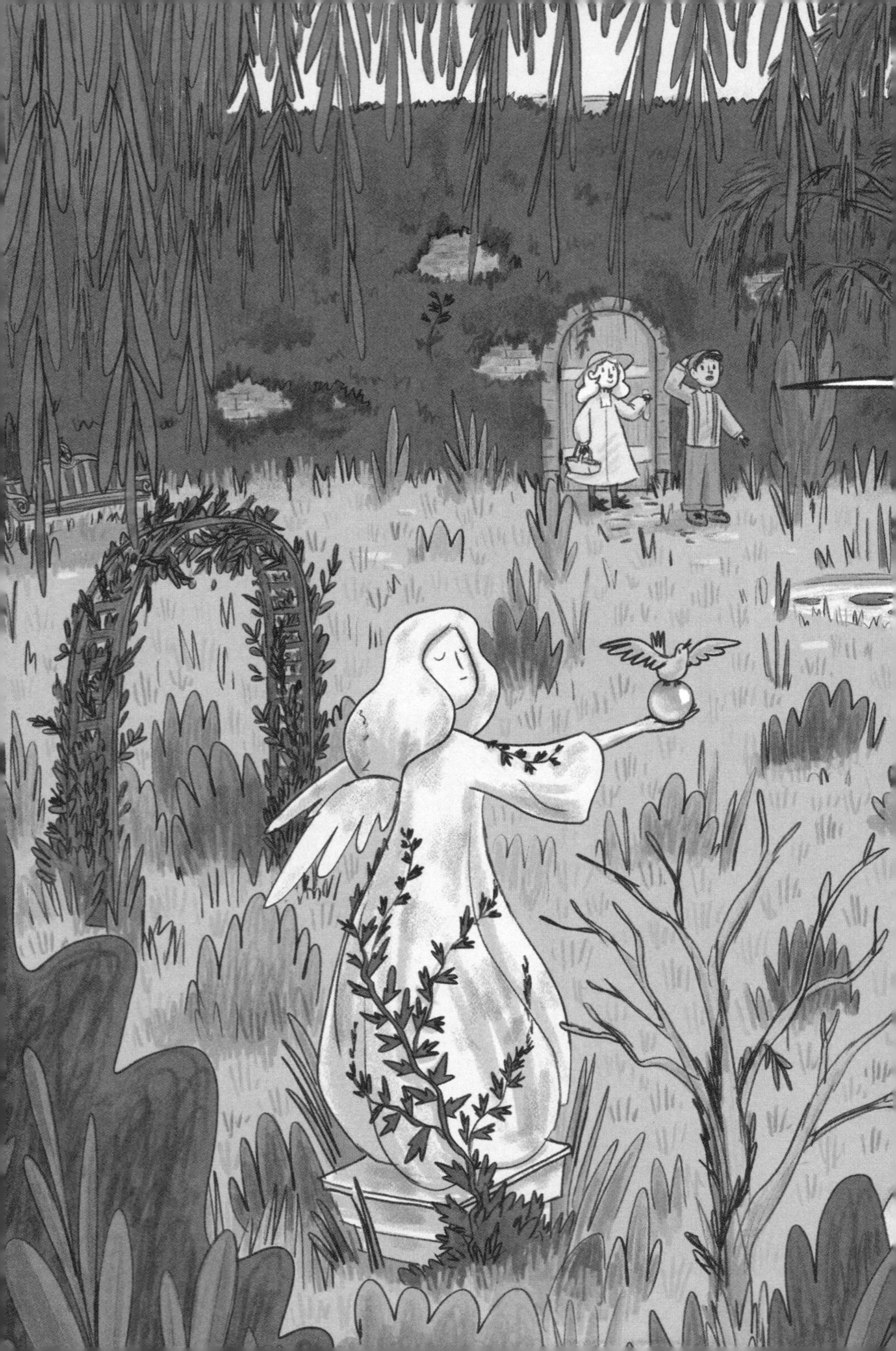

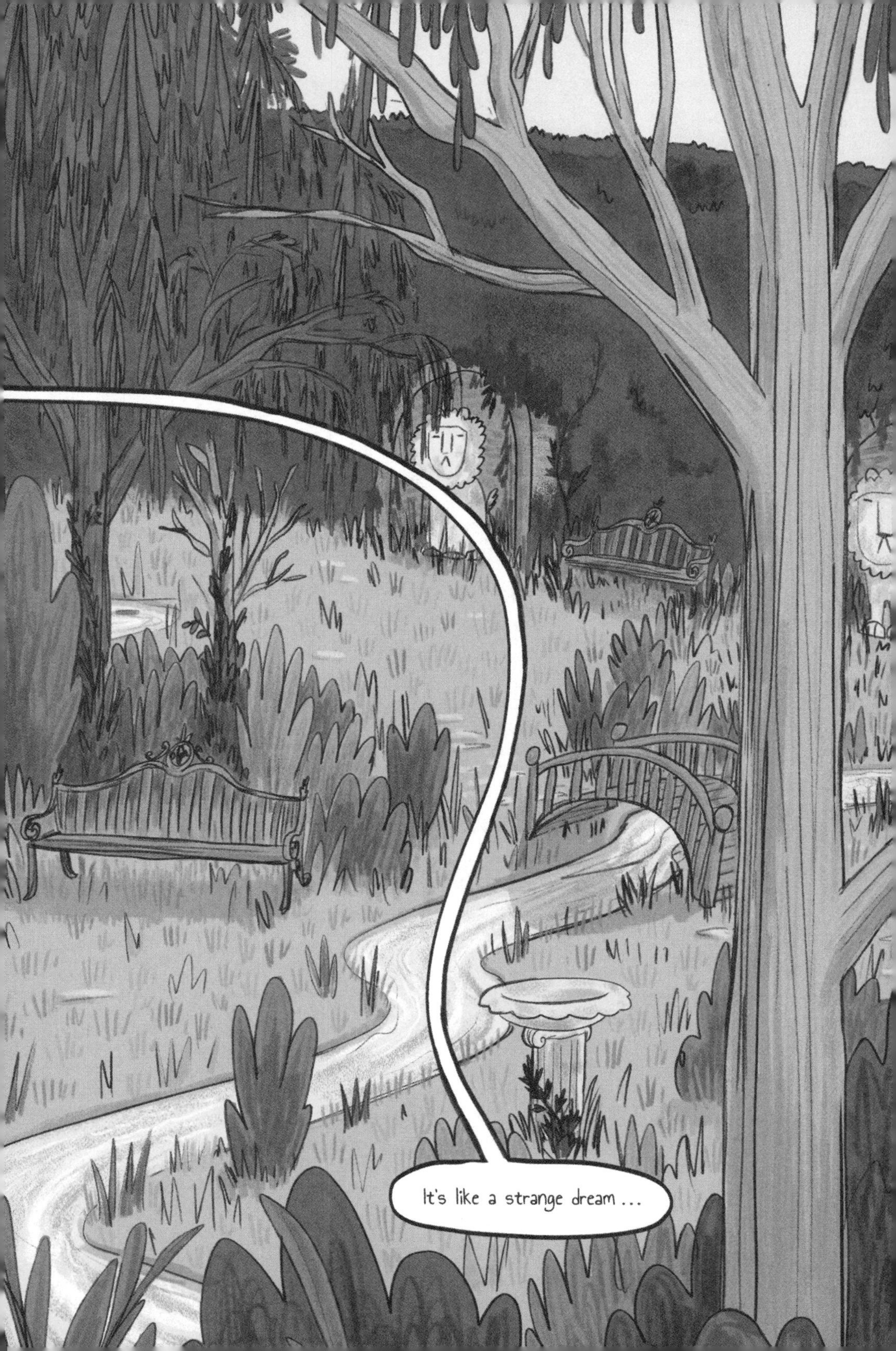
It's like a strange dream ...

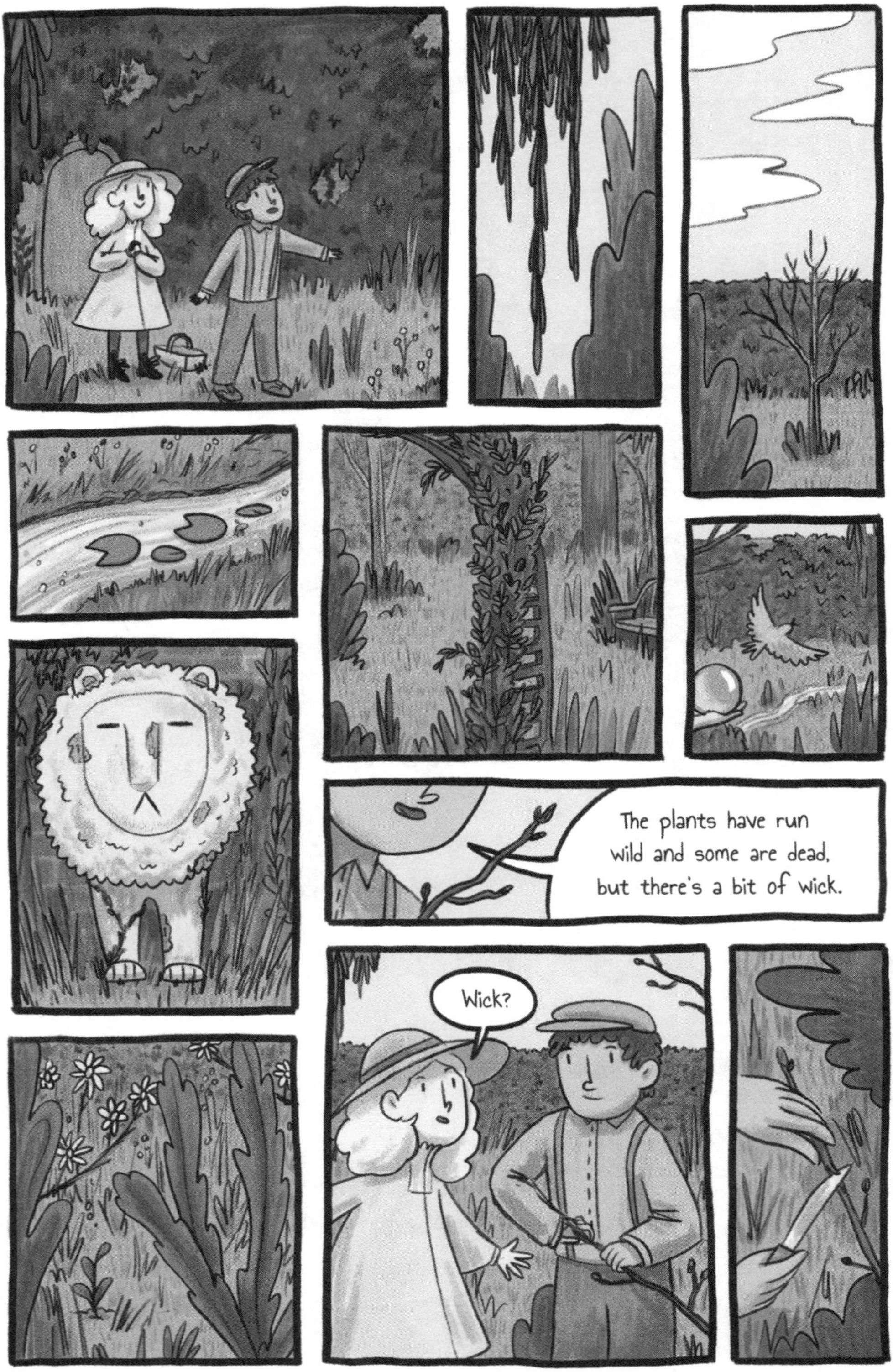
The plants have run wild and some are dead, but there's a bit of wick.
Wick?

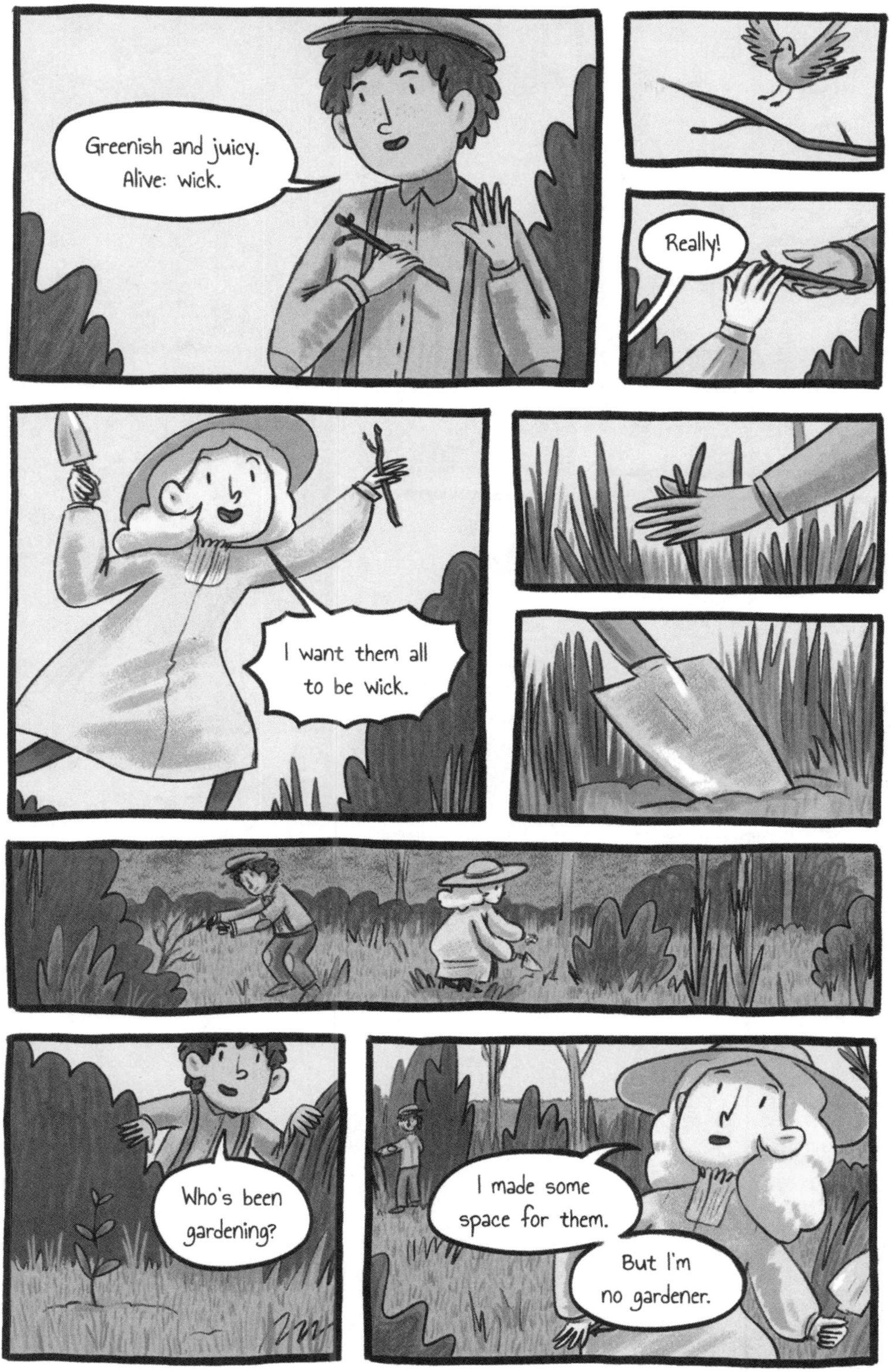
Greenish and juicy. Alive: wick.
Really!
I want them all to be wick.
Who's been gardening?
I made some space for them.
But I'm no gardener.

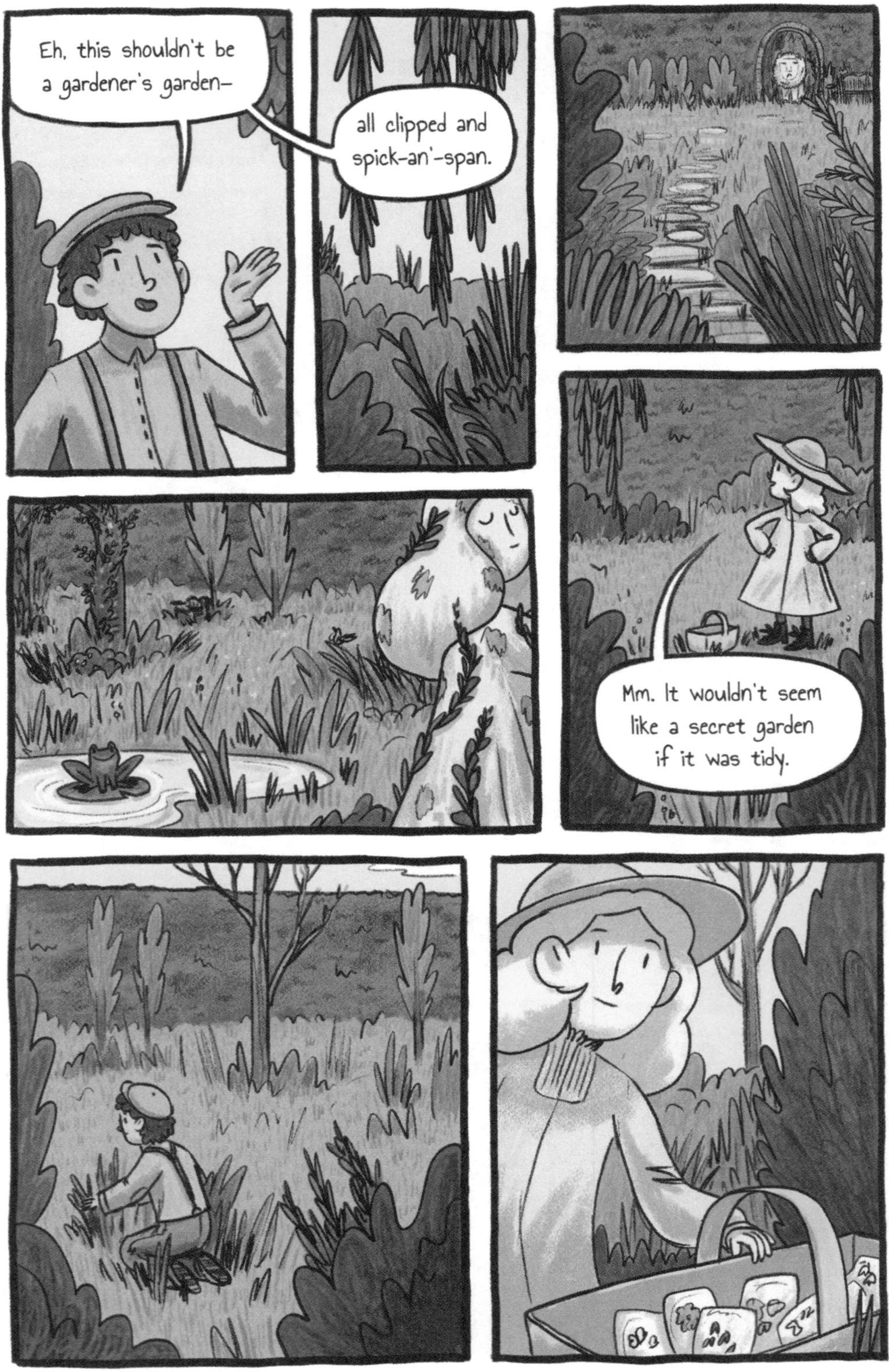
Eh, this shouldn't be a gardener's garden–
all clipped and spick-an'-span.
Mm. It wouldn't seem like a secret garden if it was tidy.

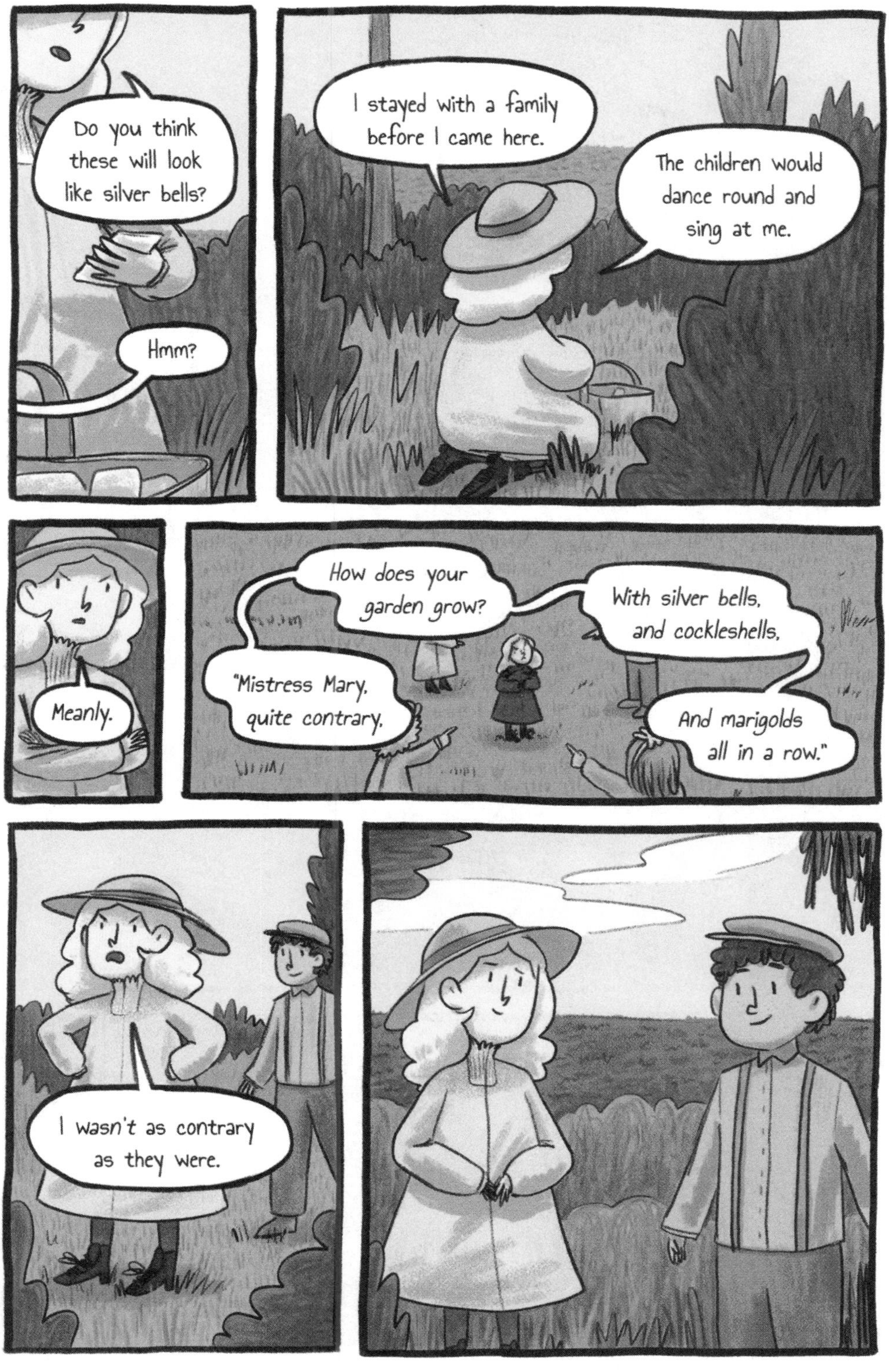
Do you think these will look like silver bells?
Hmm?
I stayed with a family before I came here.
The children would dance round and sing at me.
Meanly.
"Mistress Mary, quite contrary,
How does your garden grow?
With silver bells, and cockleshells,
And marigolds all in a row."
I wasn't as contrary as they were.

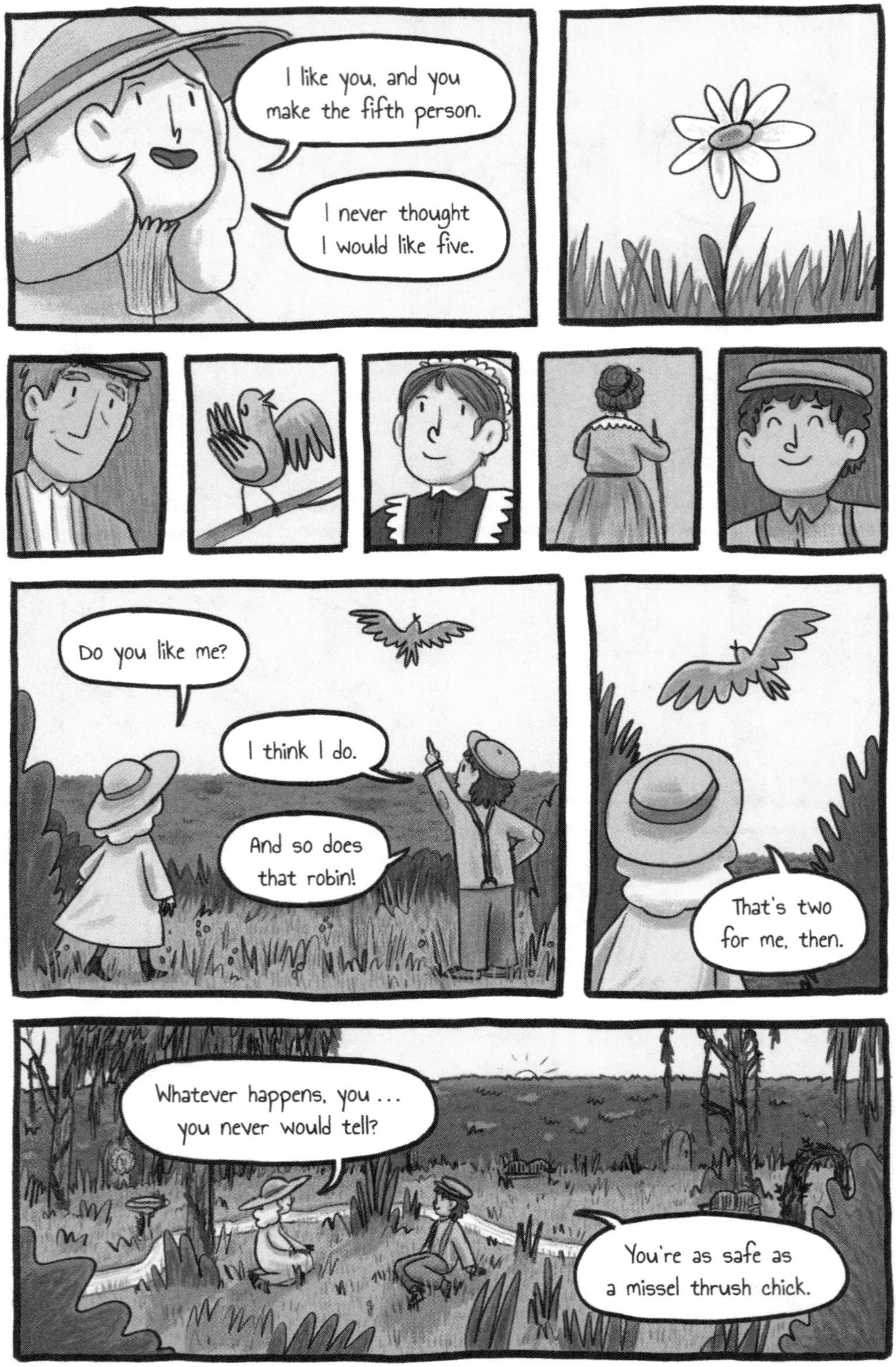
I like you, and you make the fifth person.
I never thought I would like five.
Do you like me?
I think I do.
And so does that robin!
That's two for me, then.
Whatever happens, you . . . you never would tell?
You're as safe as a missel thrush chick.

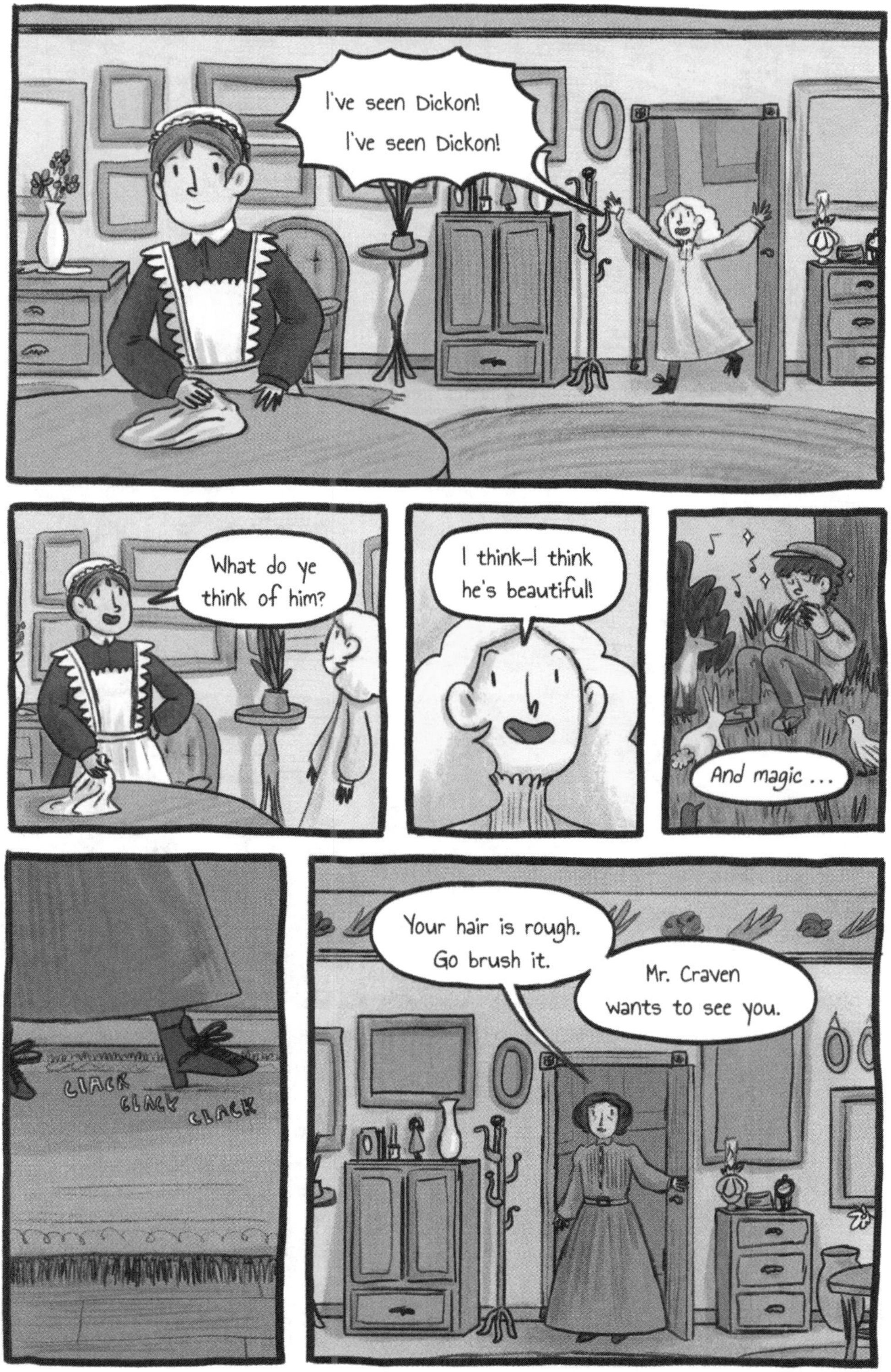

I've seen Dickon!
I've seen Dickon!
What do ye think of him?
I think—I think he's beautiful!
And magic . . .
CLACK
CLACK
CLACK
Your hair is rough. Go brush it.
Mr. Craven wants to see you.

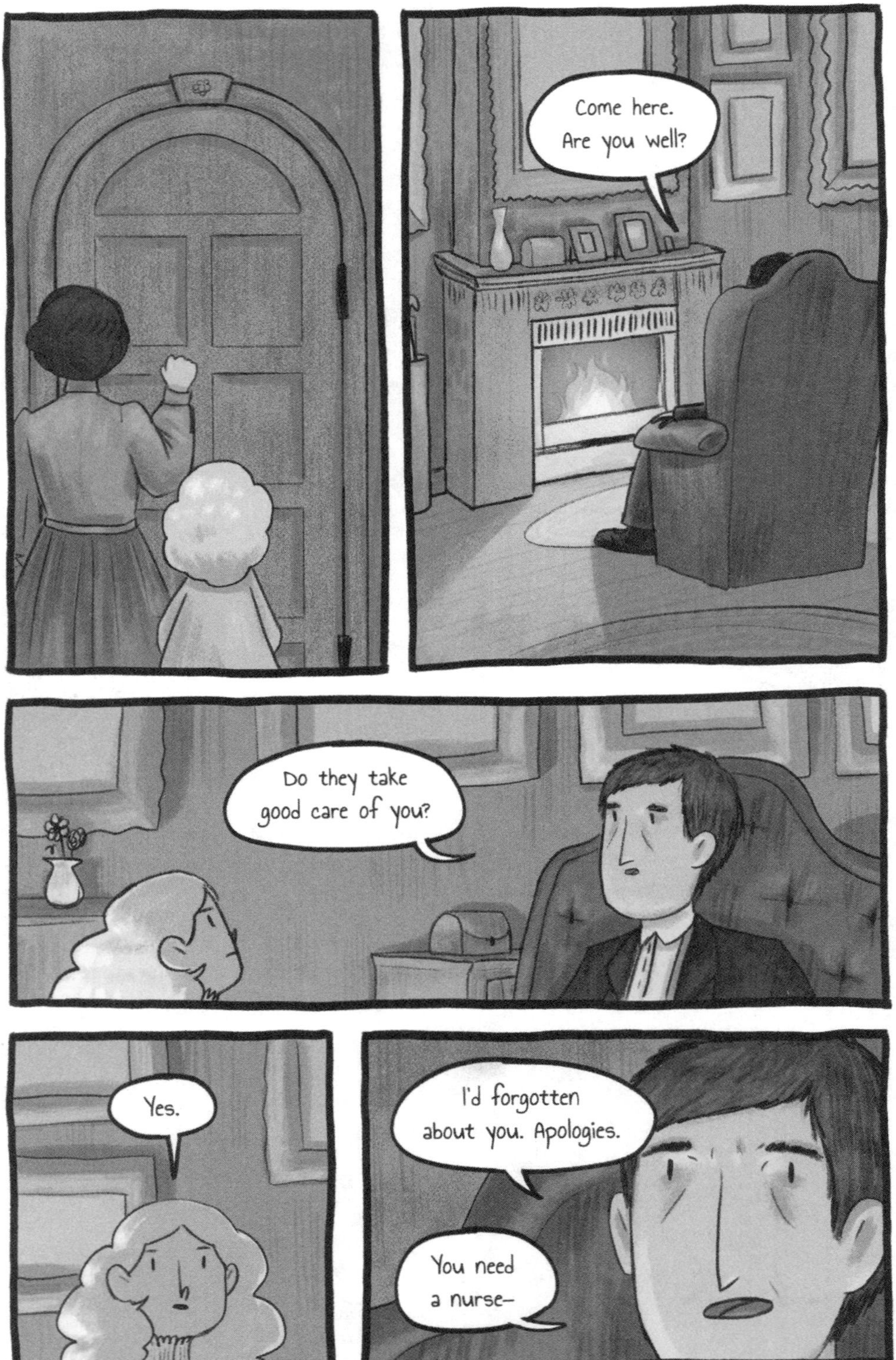
Come here.
Are you well?
Do they take
good care of you?
Yes.
I'd forgotten
about you. Apologies.
You need
a nurse–

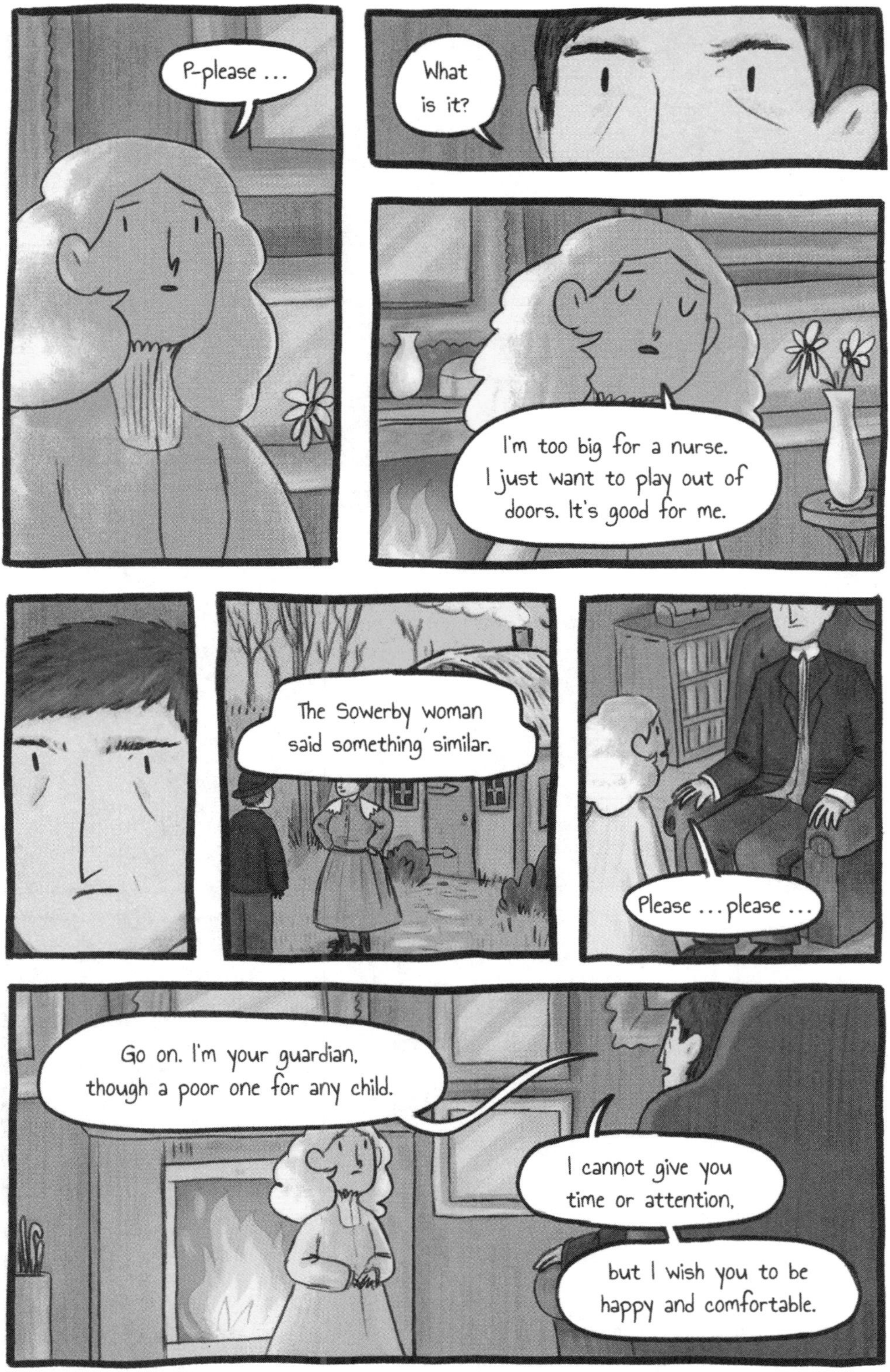
P-please ...
What is it?
I'm too big for a nurse. I just want to play out of doors. It's good for me.
The Sowerby woman said something similar.
Please ... please ...
Go on. I'm your guardian, though a poor one for any child.
I cannot give you time or attention,
but I wish you to be happy and comfortable.

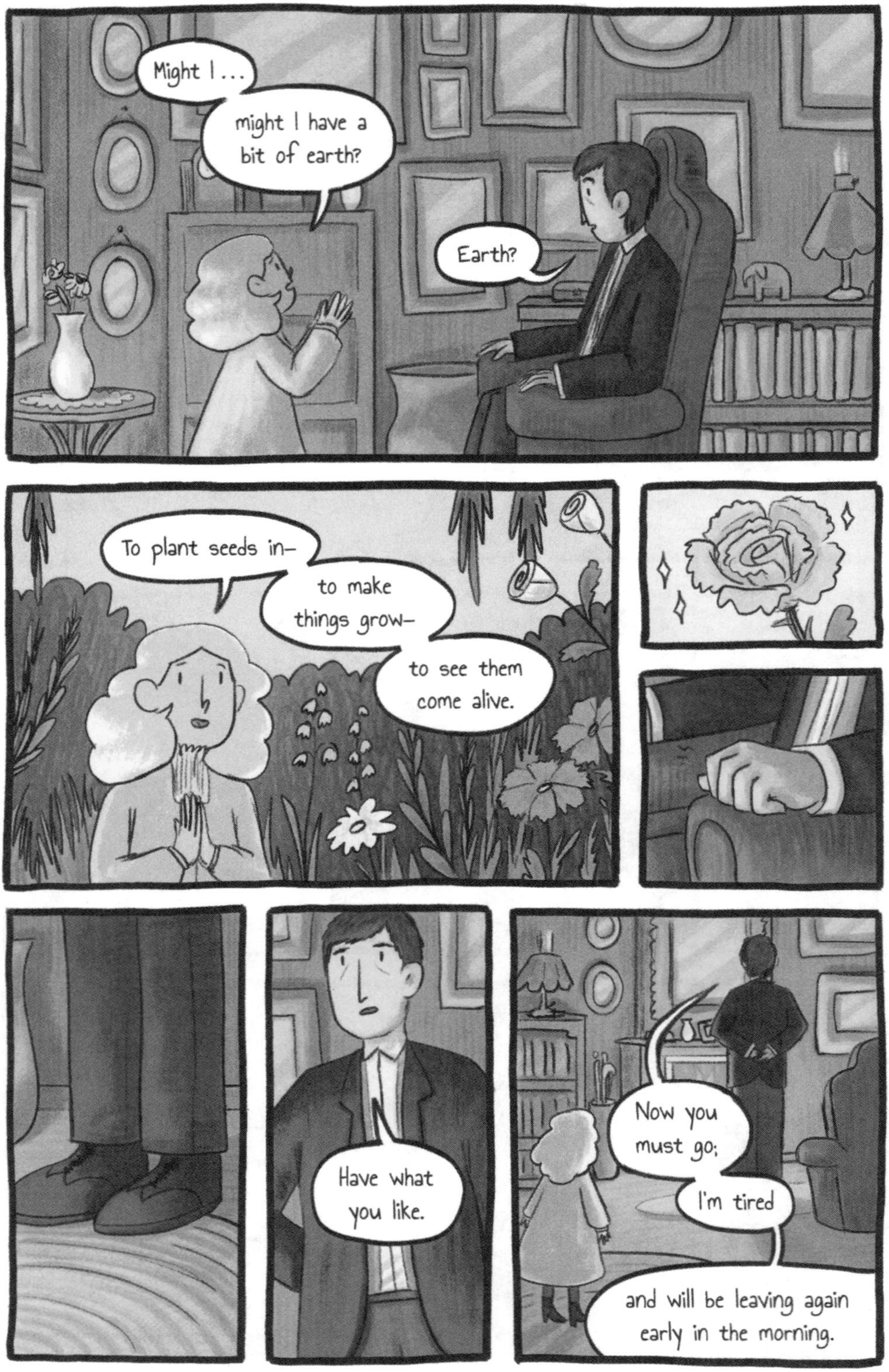
Might I...
might I have a bit of earth?
Earth?
To plant seeds in–
to make things grow–
to see them come alive.
Have what you like.
Now you must go;
I'm tired
and will be leaving again early in the morning.

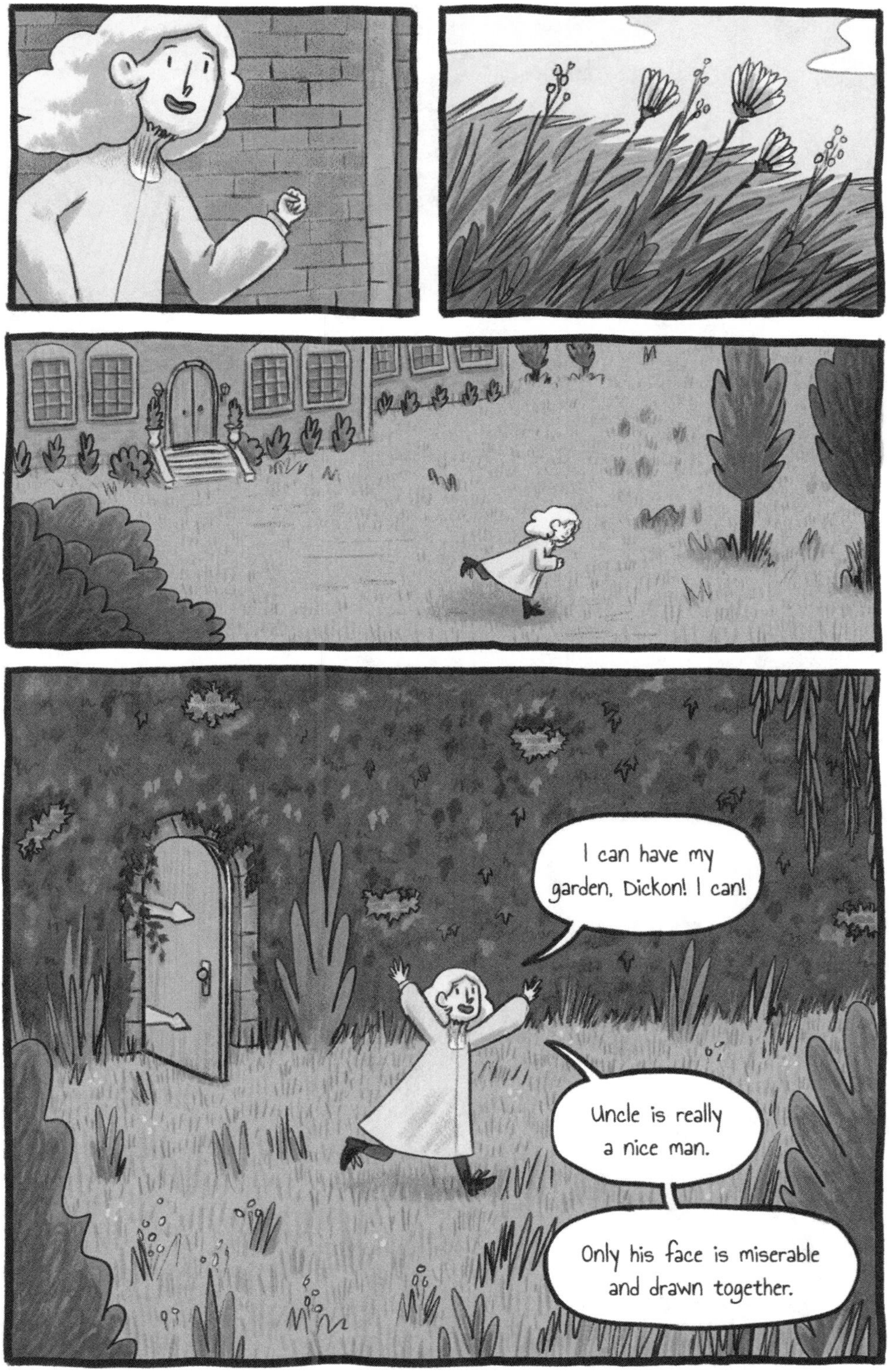
I can have my garden, Dickon! I can!
Uncle is really a nice man.
Only his face is miserable and drawn together.

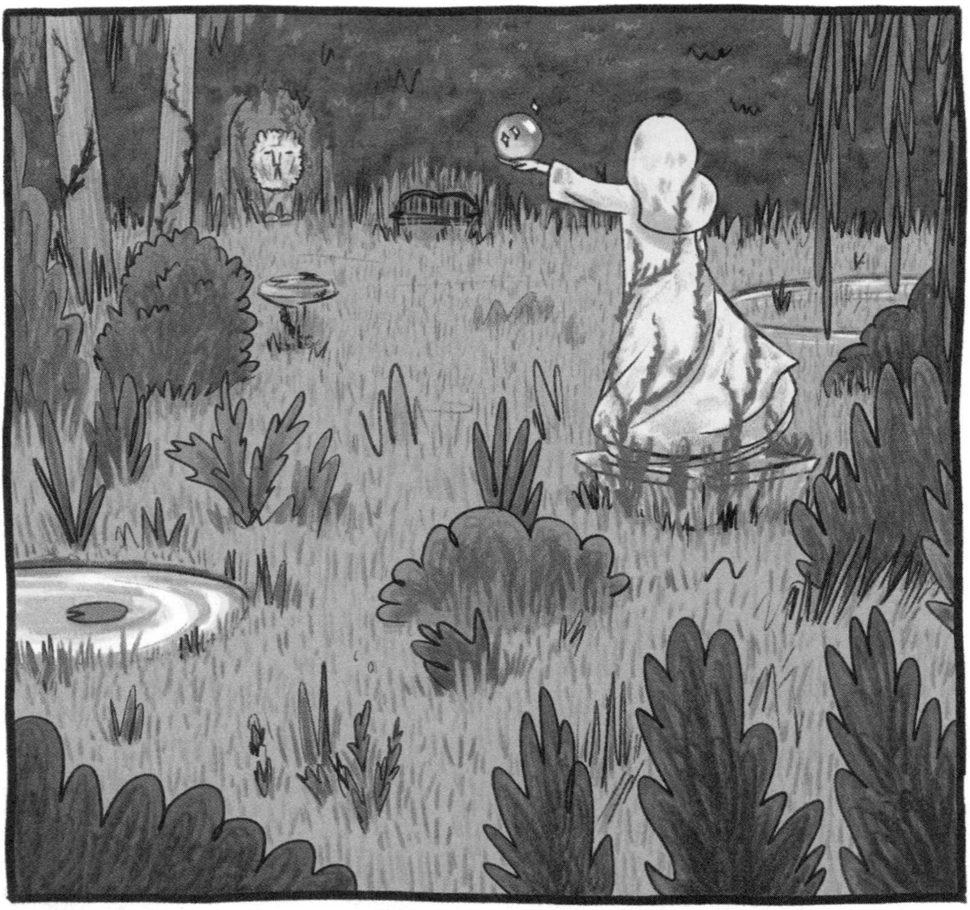

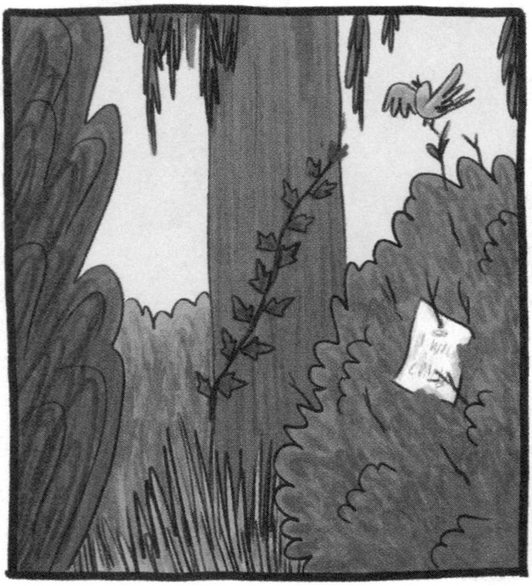

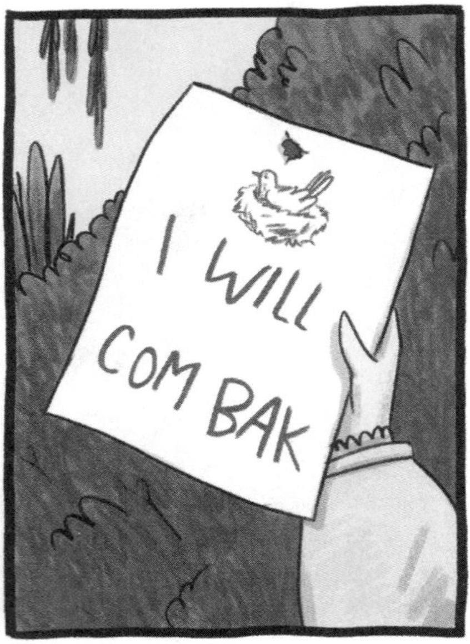
I WILL
COM BAK

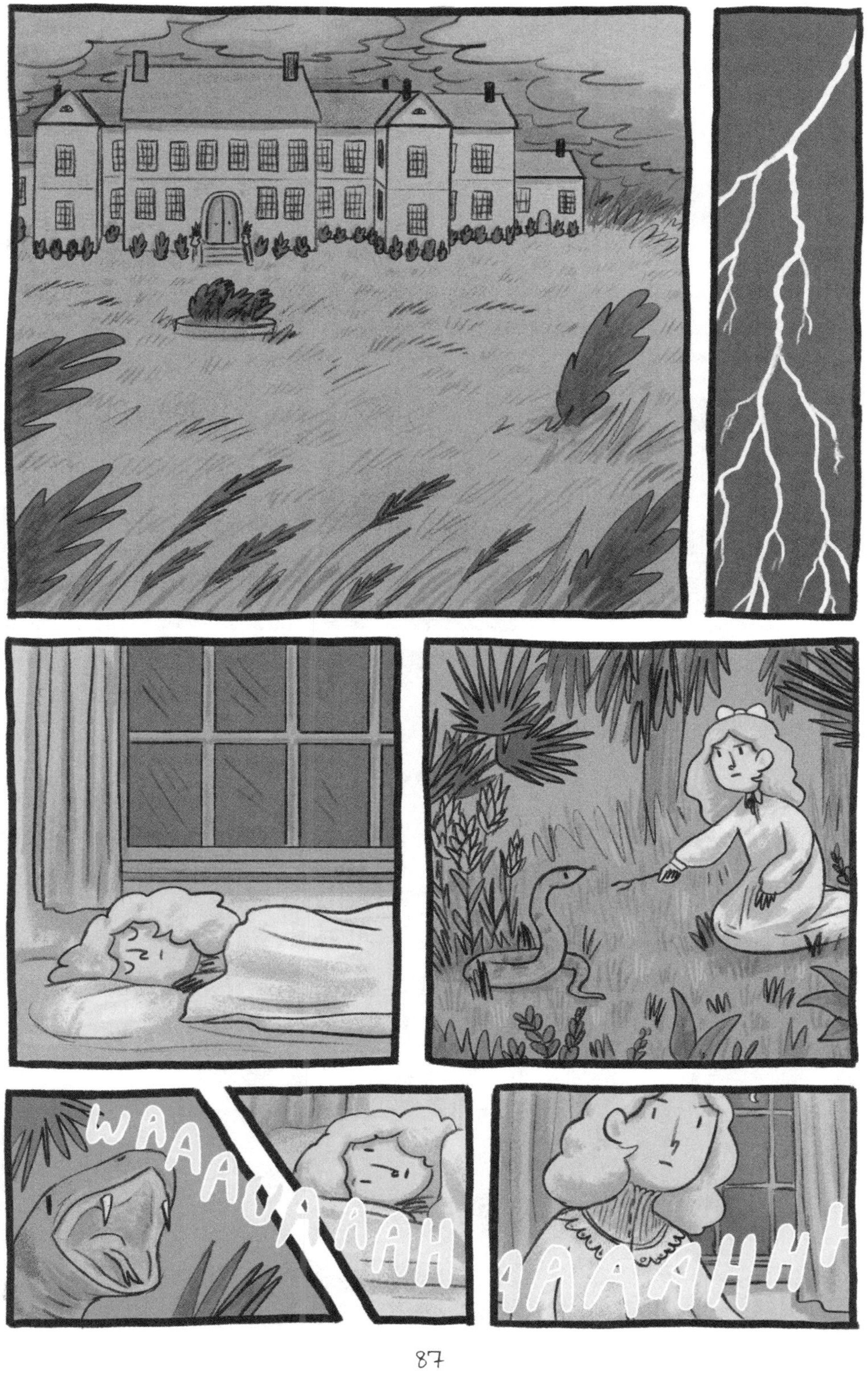
WAAAUAAAAH
AAAAHHH

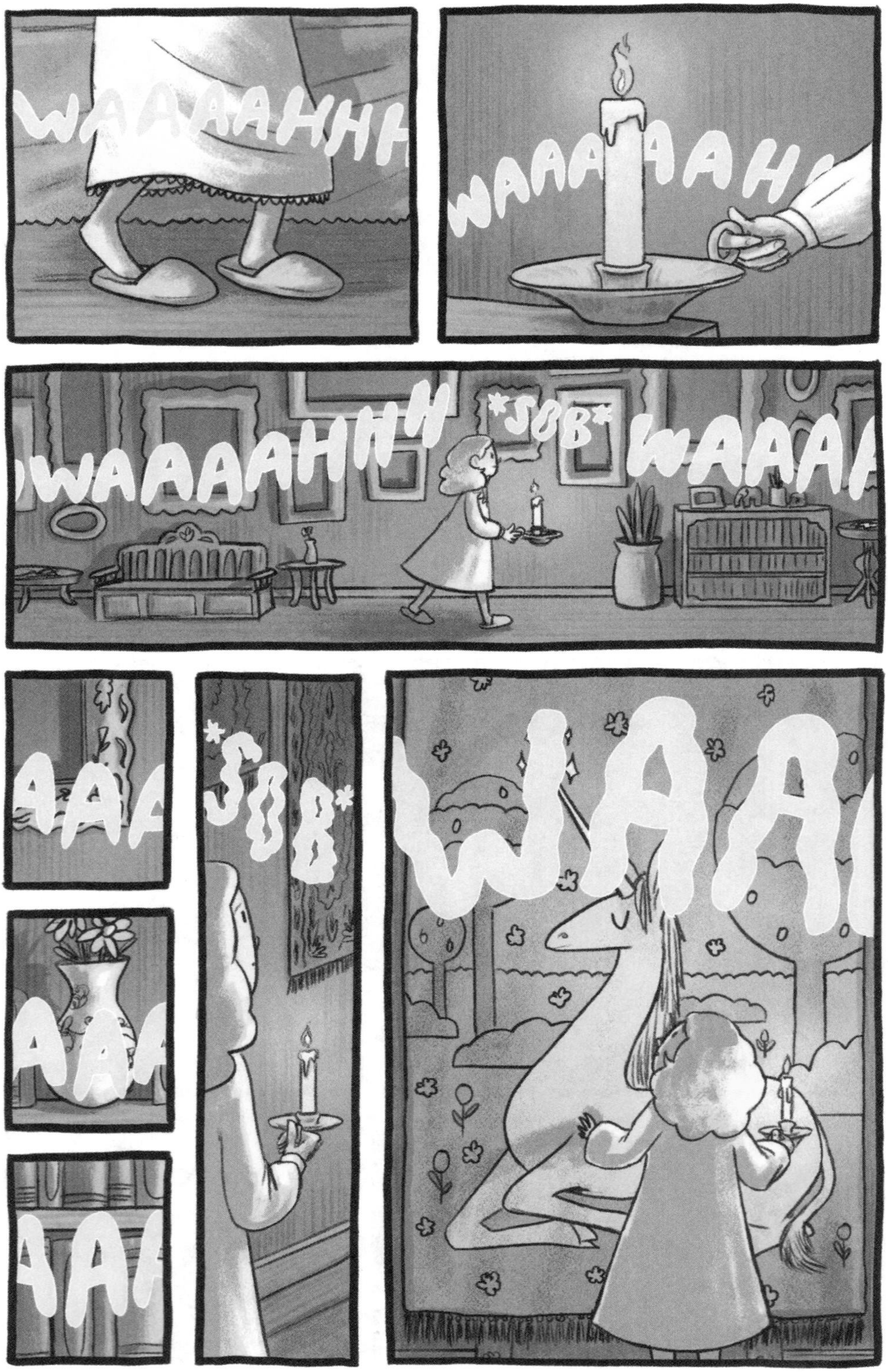
WAAAAHHH
WAAAAAH
WAAAAAHHH *SOB* WAAAA
AAA
SOB
WAA
AAA
AAA

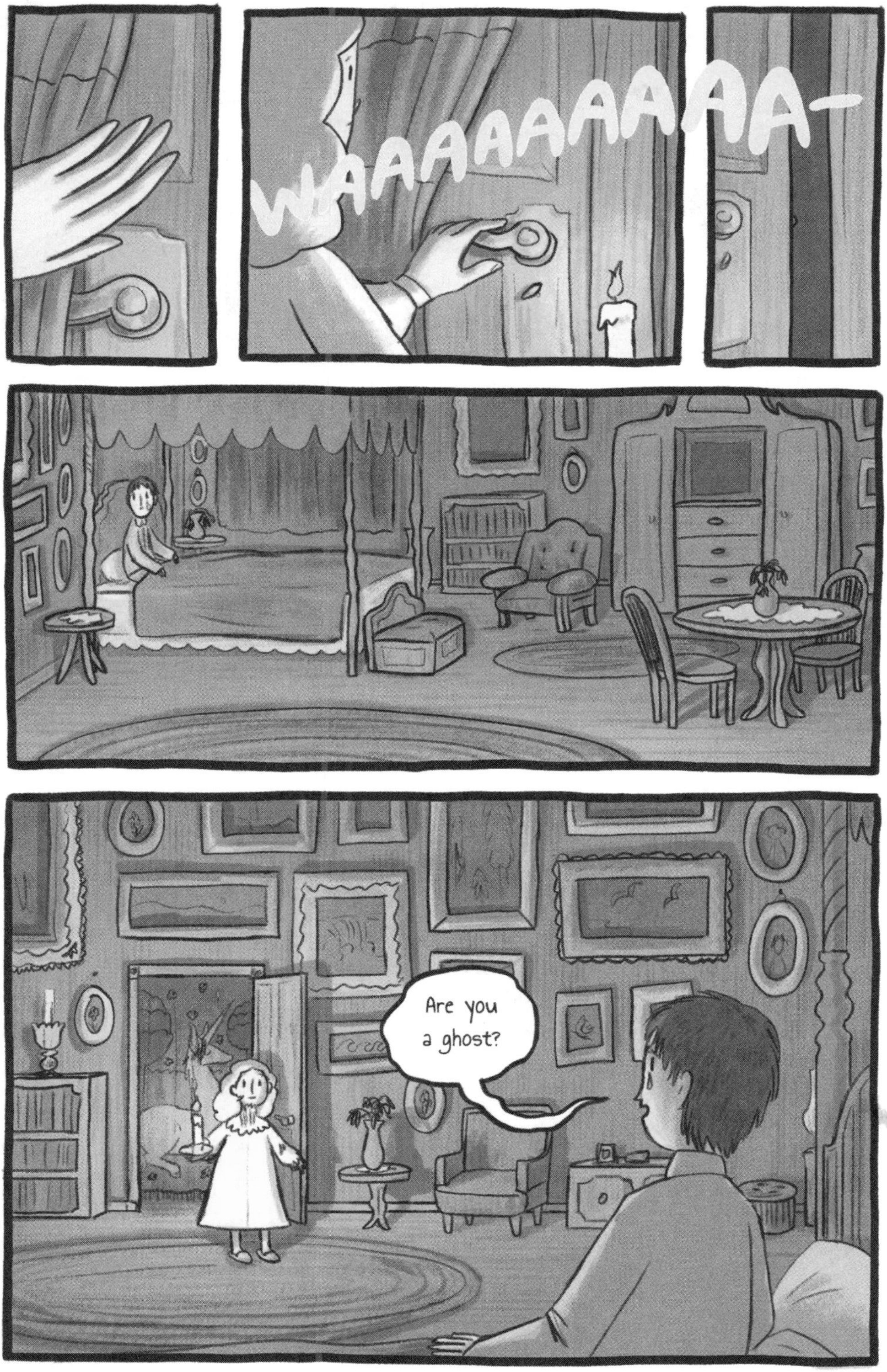
WAAAAAAAAAA-
Are you a ghost?

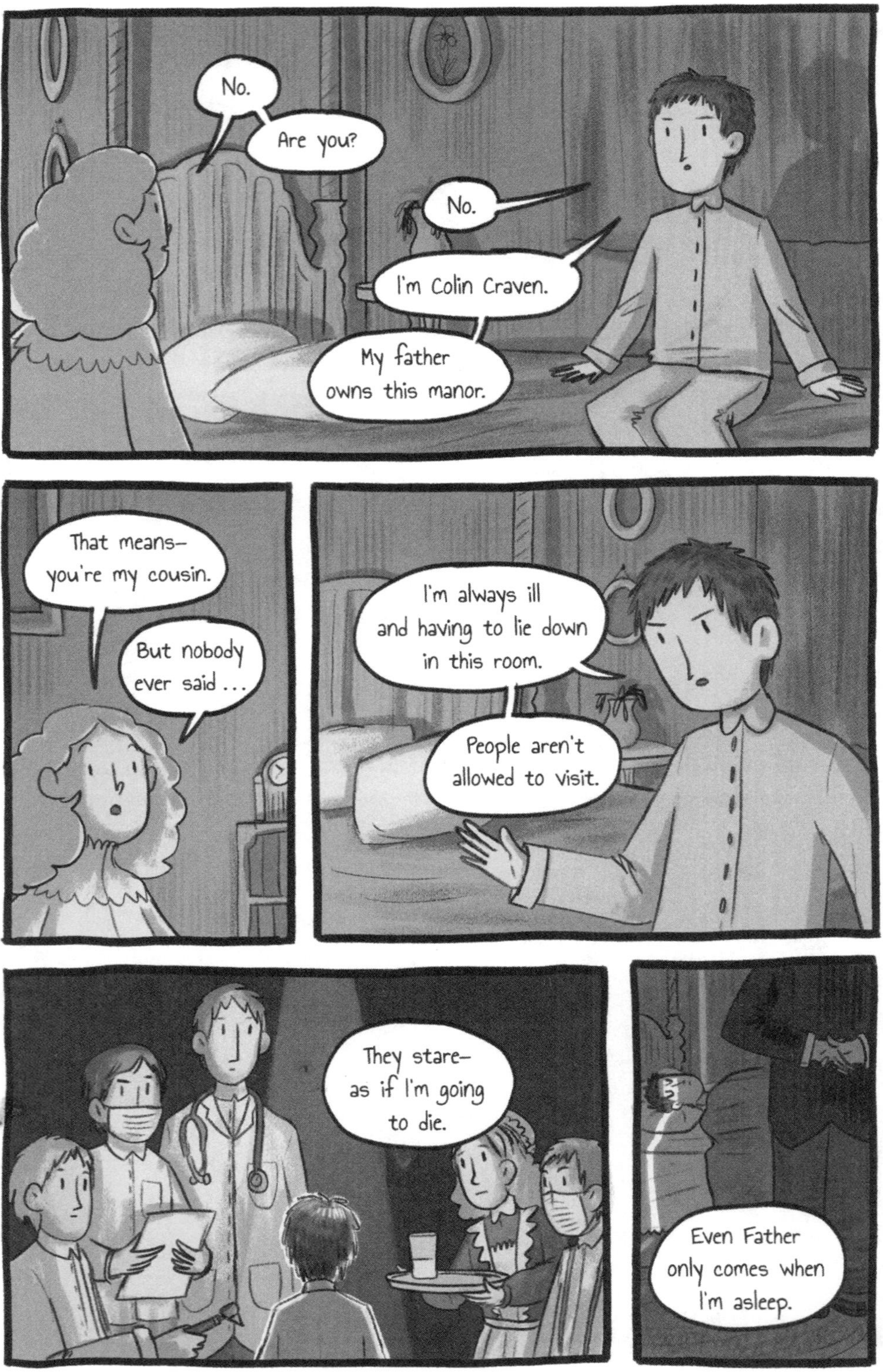
No.
Are you?
No.
I'm Colin Craven.
My father owns this manor.
That means— you're my cousin.
But nobody ever said . . .
I'm always ill and having to lie down in this room.
People aren't allowed to visit.
They stare— as if I'm going to die.
Even Father only comes when I'm asleep.

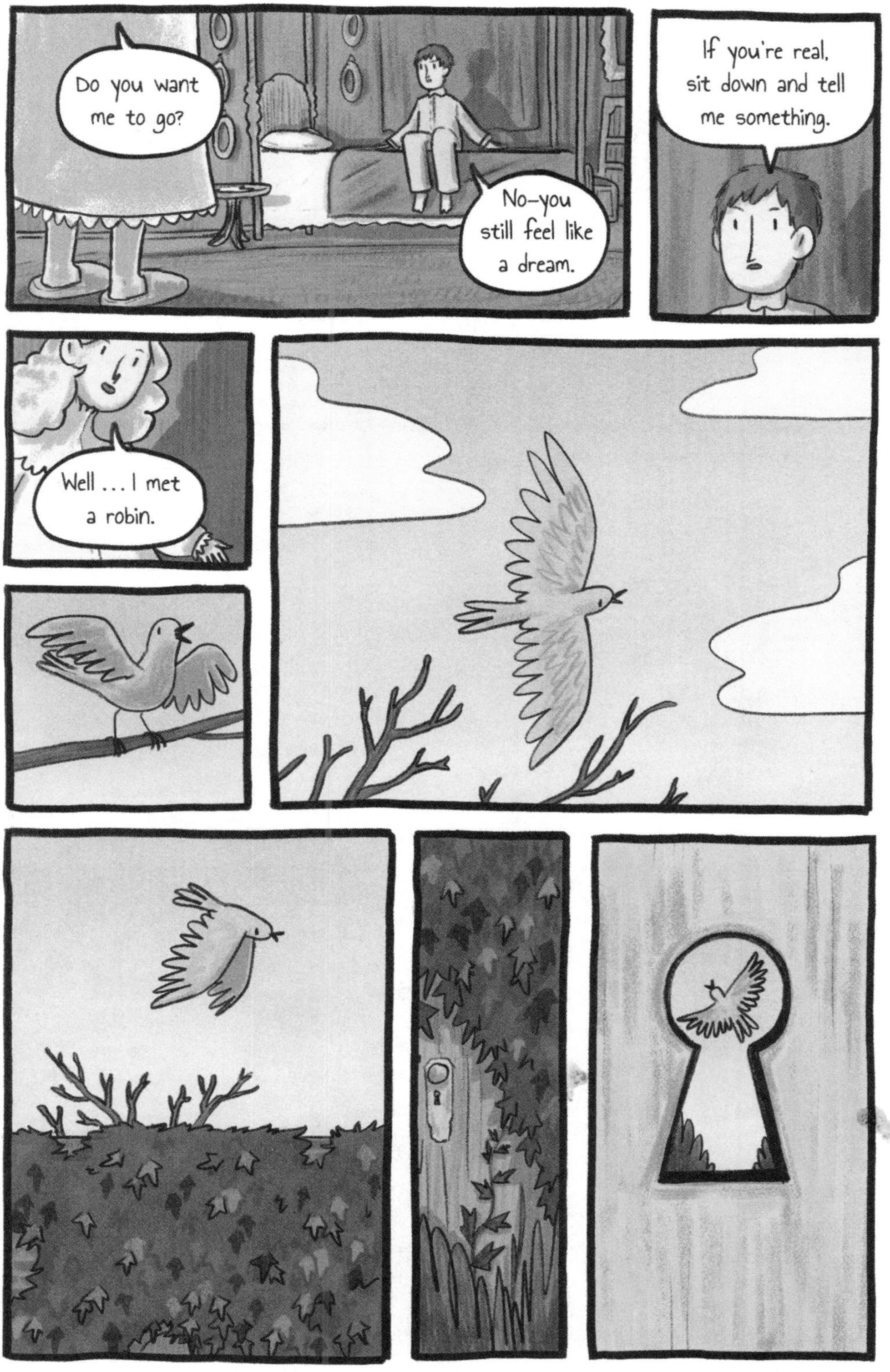

Do you want me to go?
No–you still feel like a dream.
If you're real, sit down and tell me something.
Well . . . I met a robin.

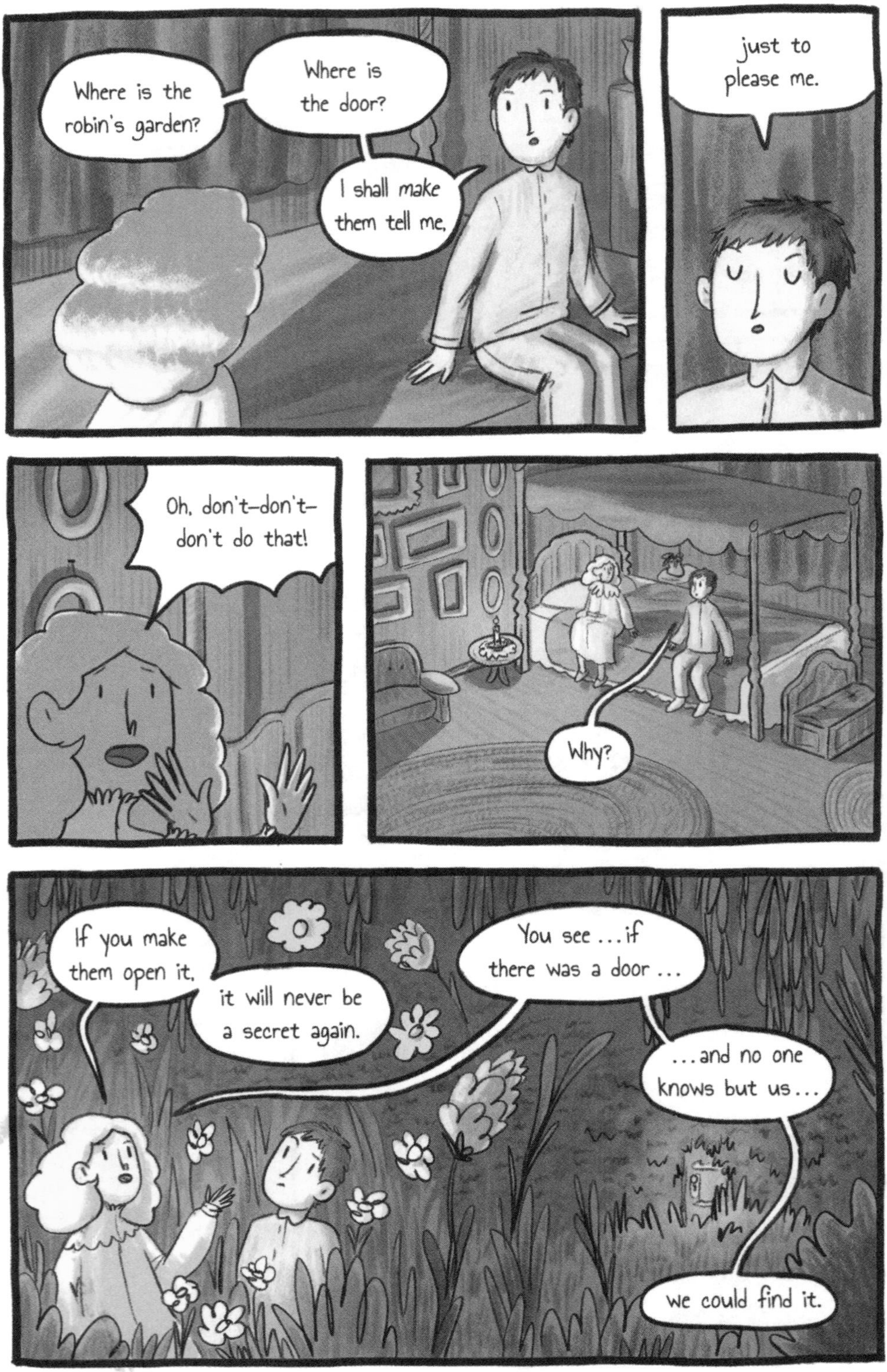
Where is the robin's garden?
Where is the door?
I shall make them tell me,
just to please me.
Oh, don't—don't—don't do that!
Why?
If you make them open it,
it will never be a secret again.
You see ... if there was a door ...
...and no one knows but us...
we could find it.

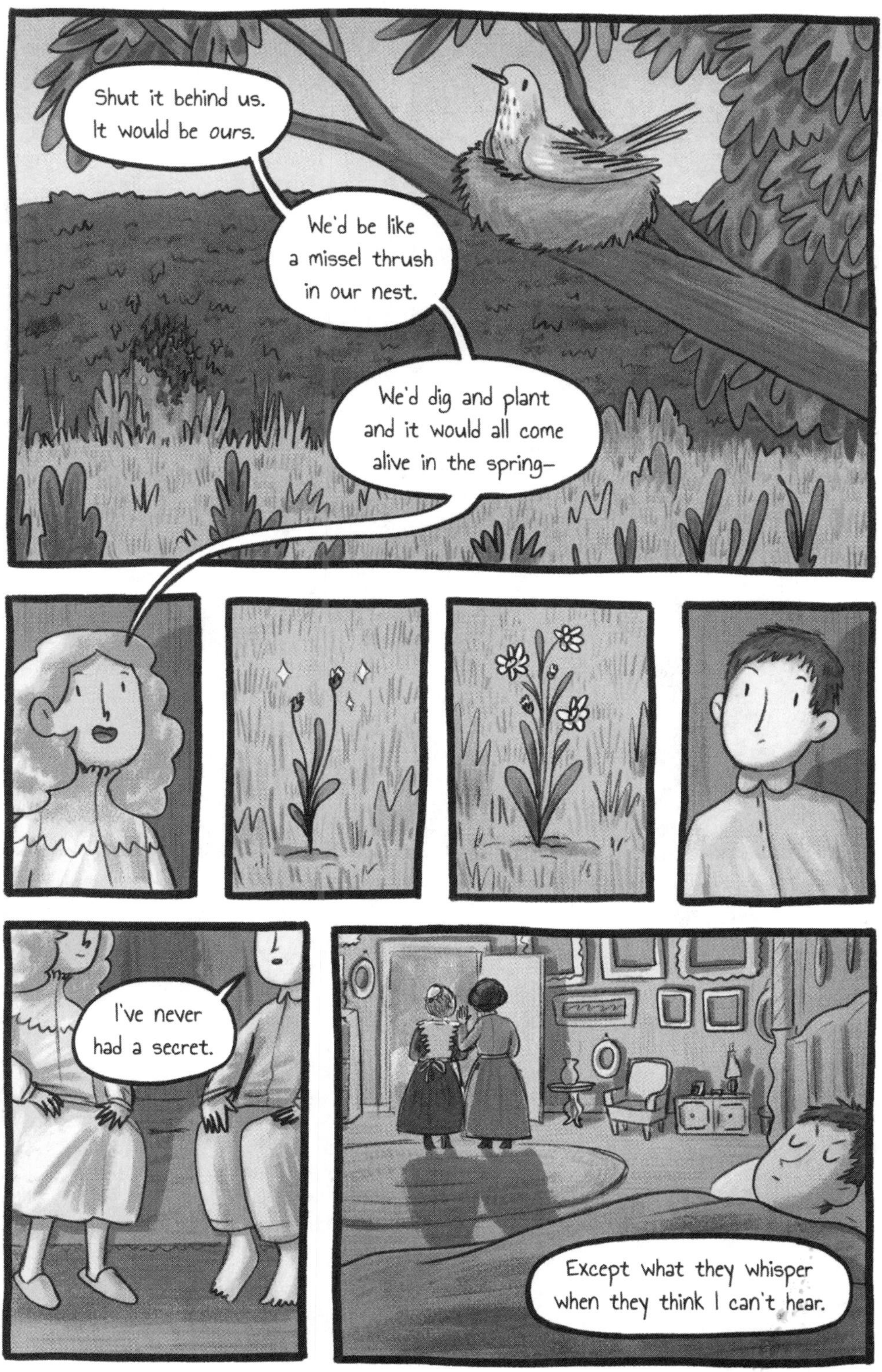
Shut it behind us. It would be ours.
We'd be like a missel thrush in our nest.
We'd dig and plant and it would all come alive in the spring—
I've never had a secret.
Except what they whisper when they think I can't hear.

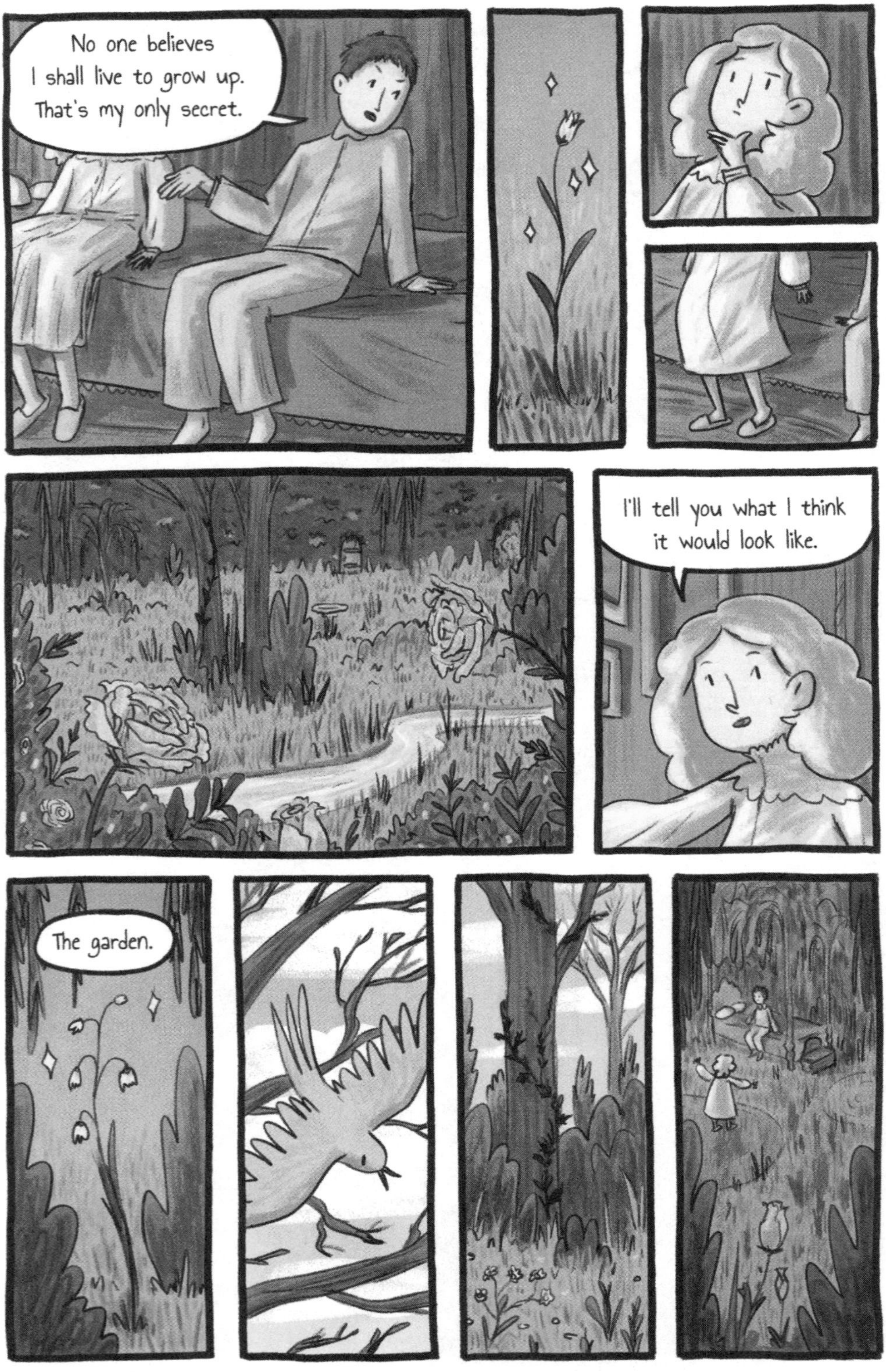
No one believes I shall live to grow up. That's my only secret.
I'll tell you what I think it would look like.
The garden.

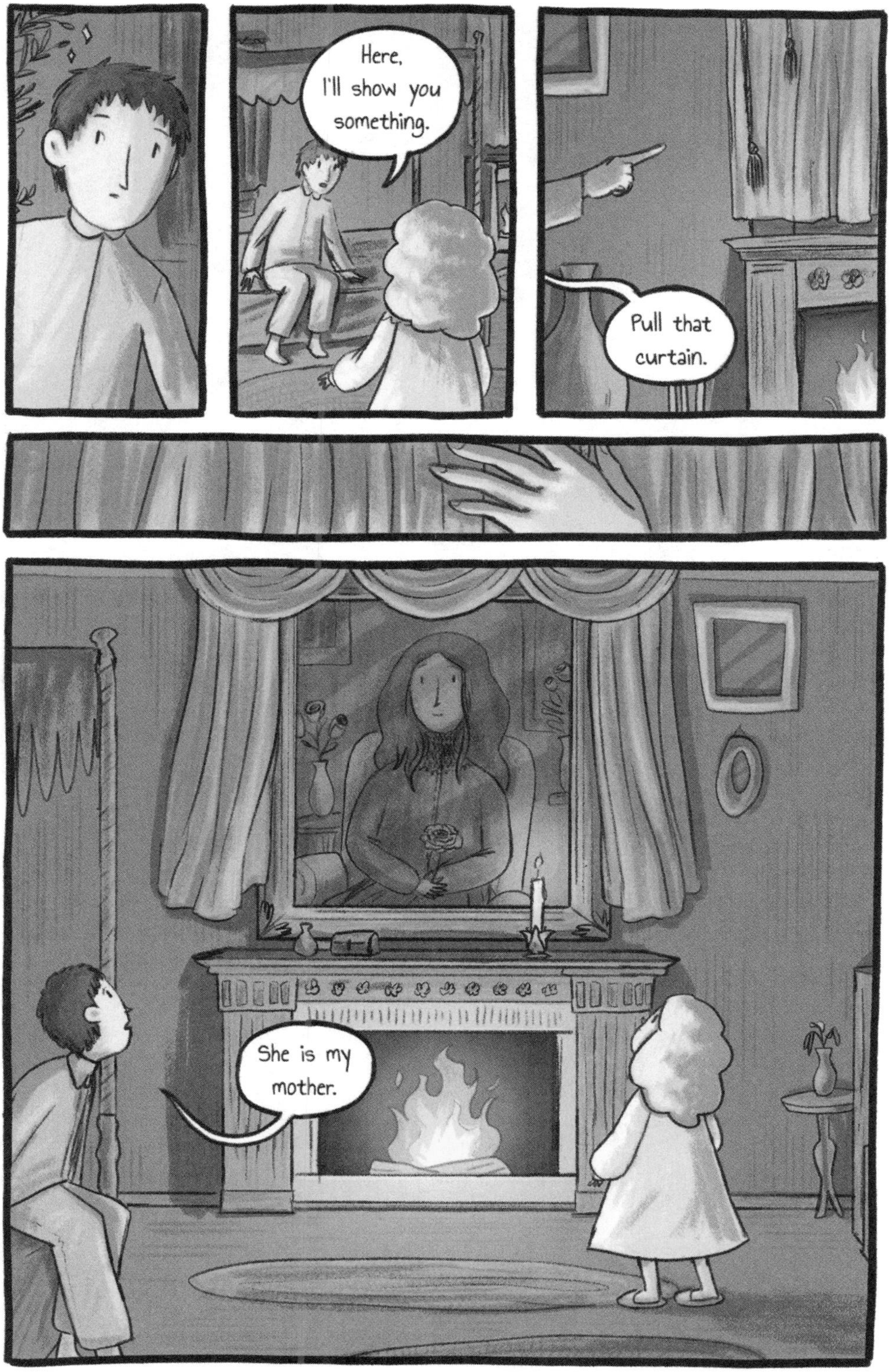
Here, I'll show you something.
Pull that curtain.
She is my mother.

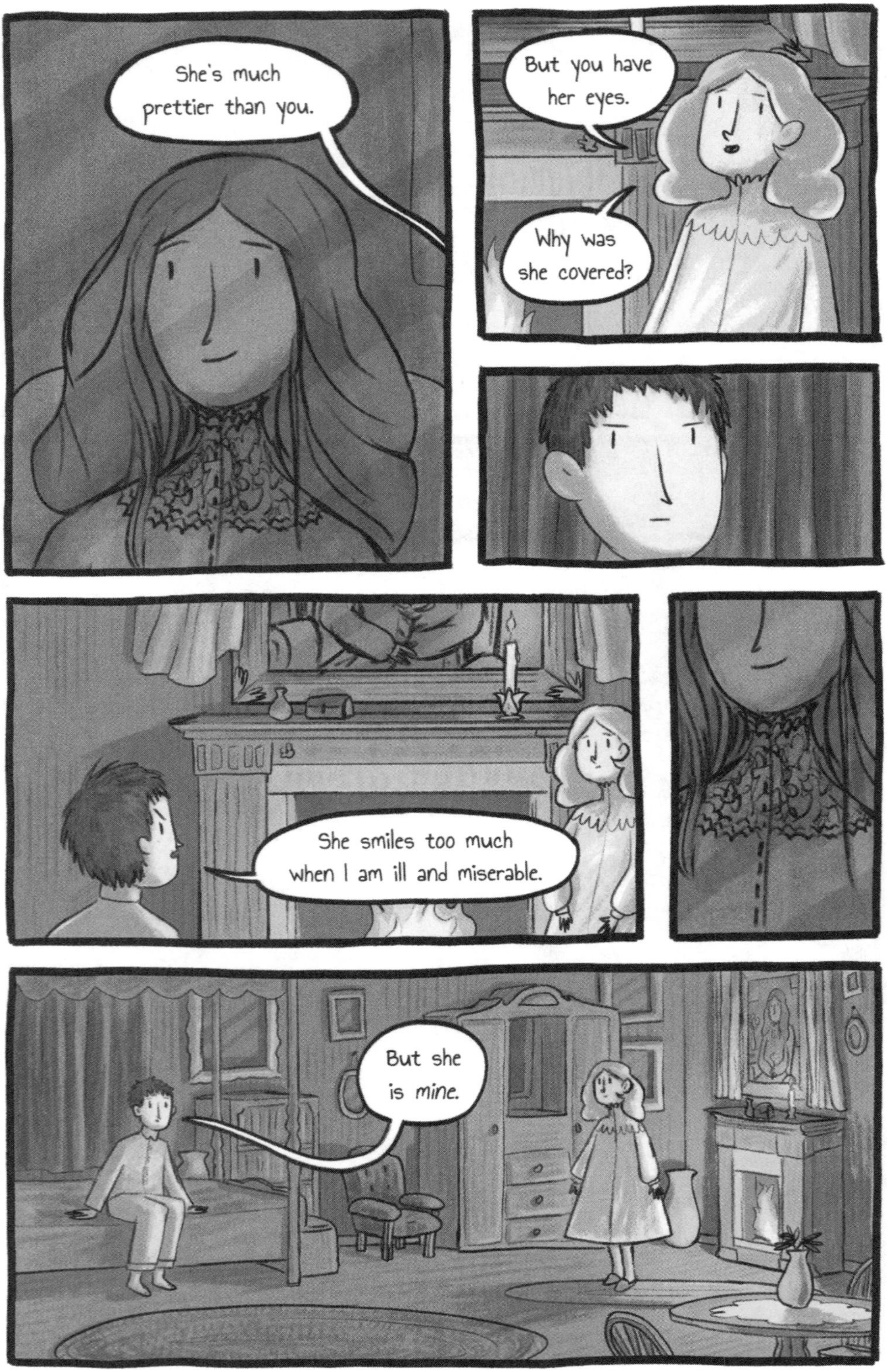
She's much prettier than you.
But you have her eyes.
Why was she covered?
She smiles too much when I am ill and miserable.
But she is mine.

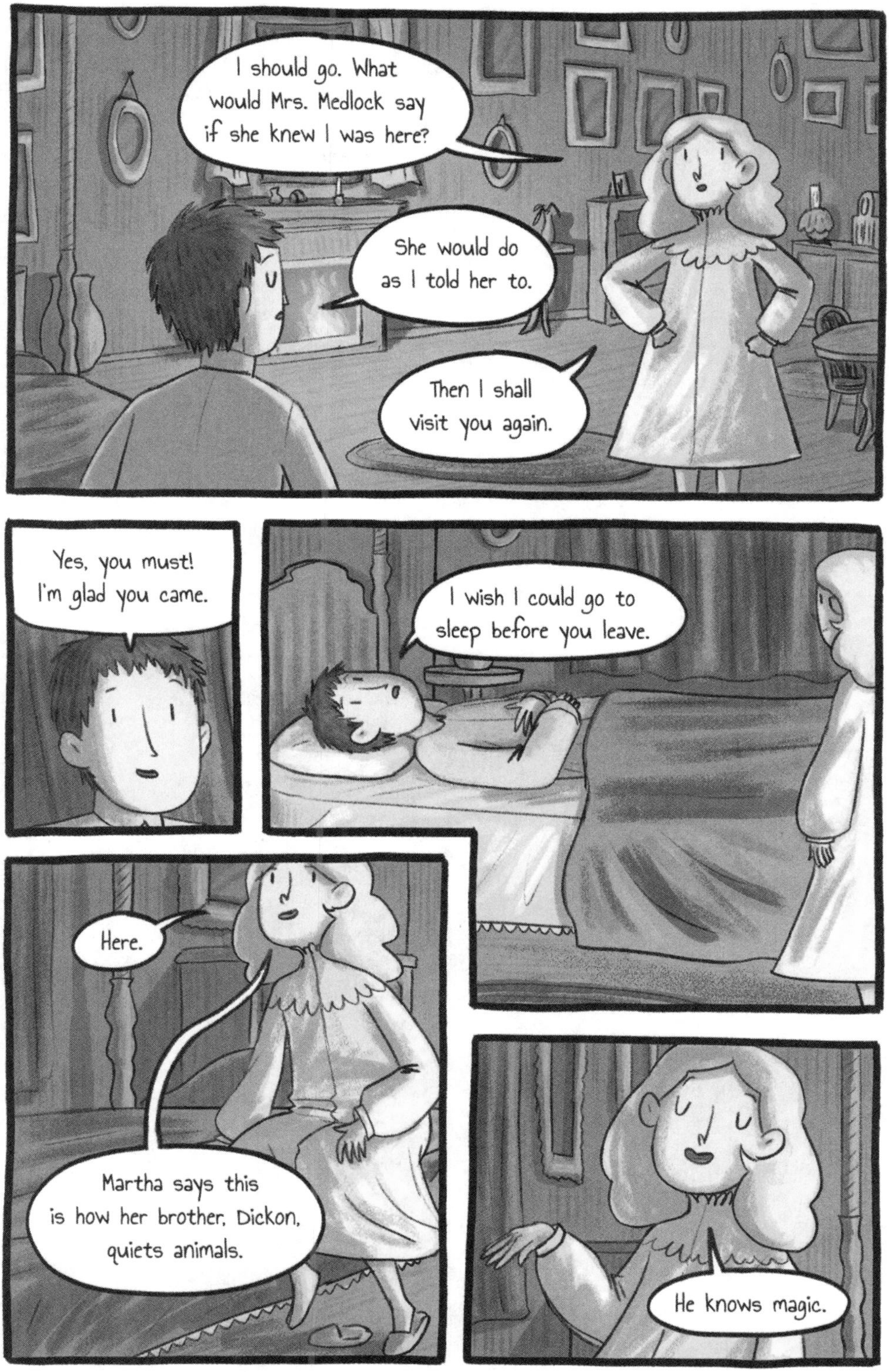
I should go. What would Mrs. Medlock say if she knew I was here?
She would do as I told her to.
Then I shall visit you again.
Yes, you must! I'm glad you came.
I wish I could go to sleep before you leave.
Here.
Martha says this is how her brother, Dickon, quiets animals.
He knows magic.

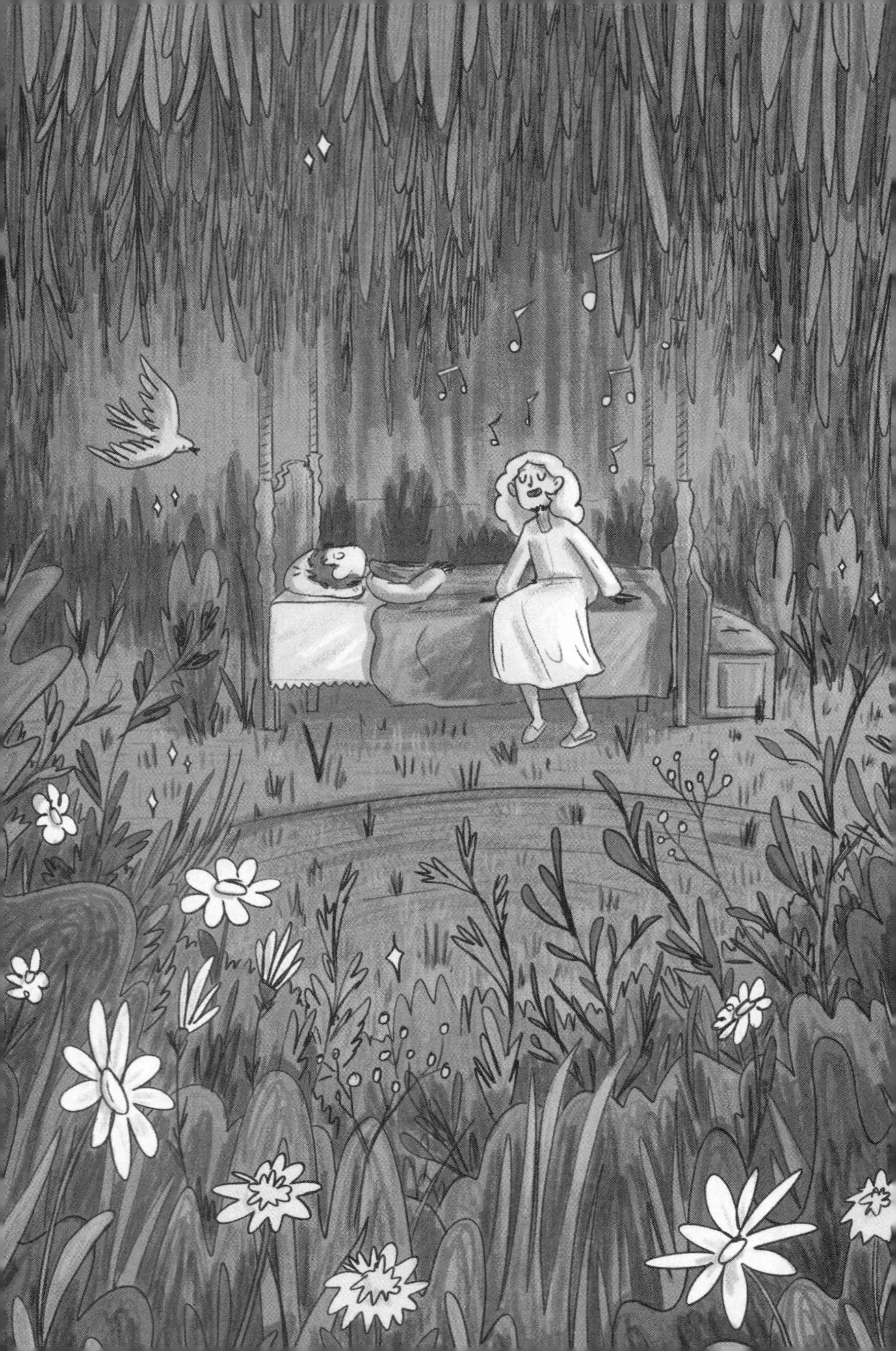

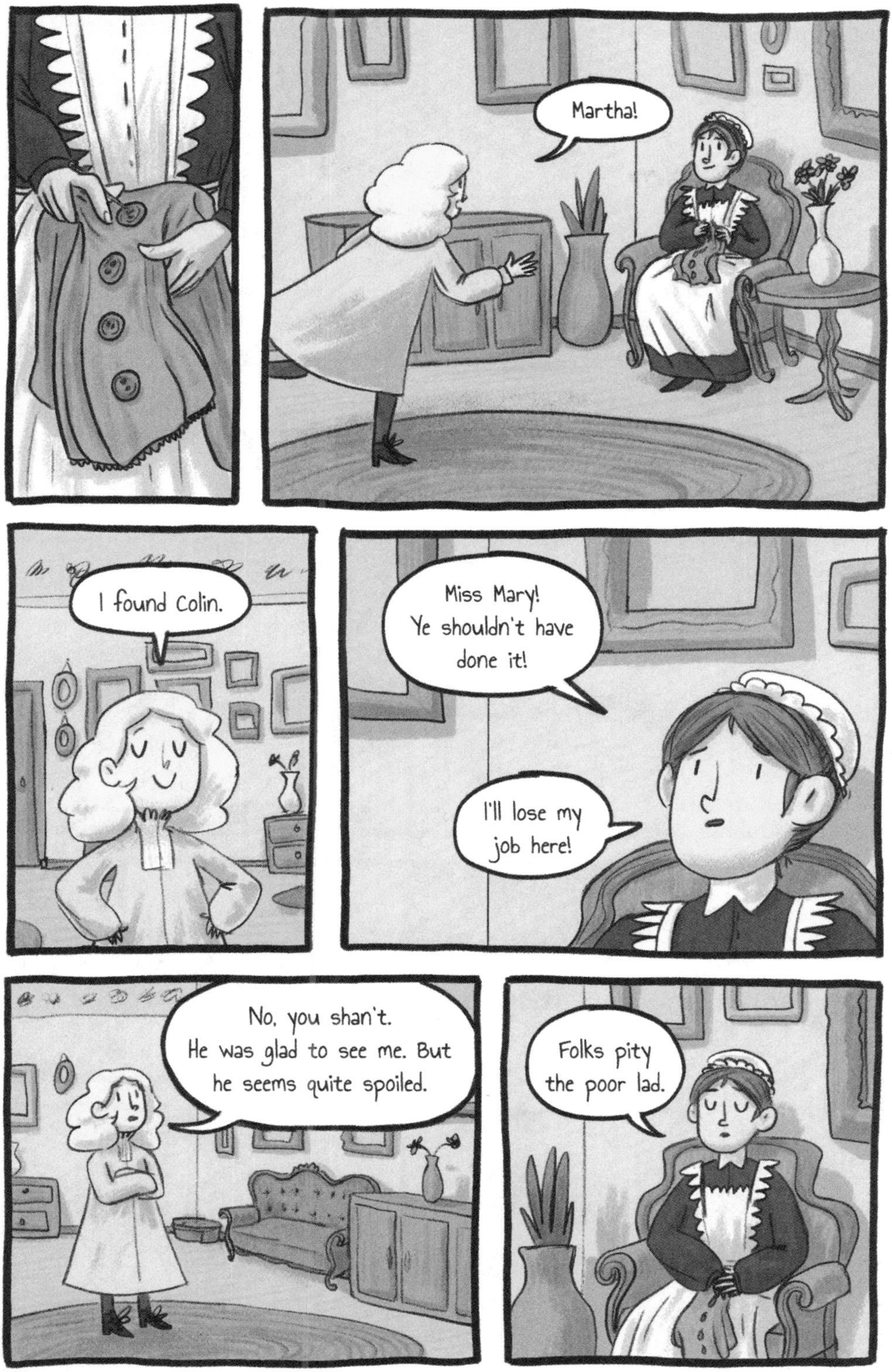
Martha!
I found Colin.
Miss Mary! Ye shouldn't have done it!
I'll lose my job here!
No, you shan't. He was glad to see me. But he seems quite spoiled.
Folks pity the poor lad.

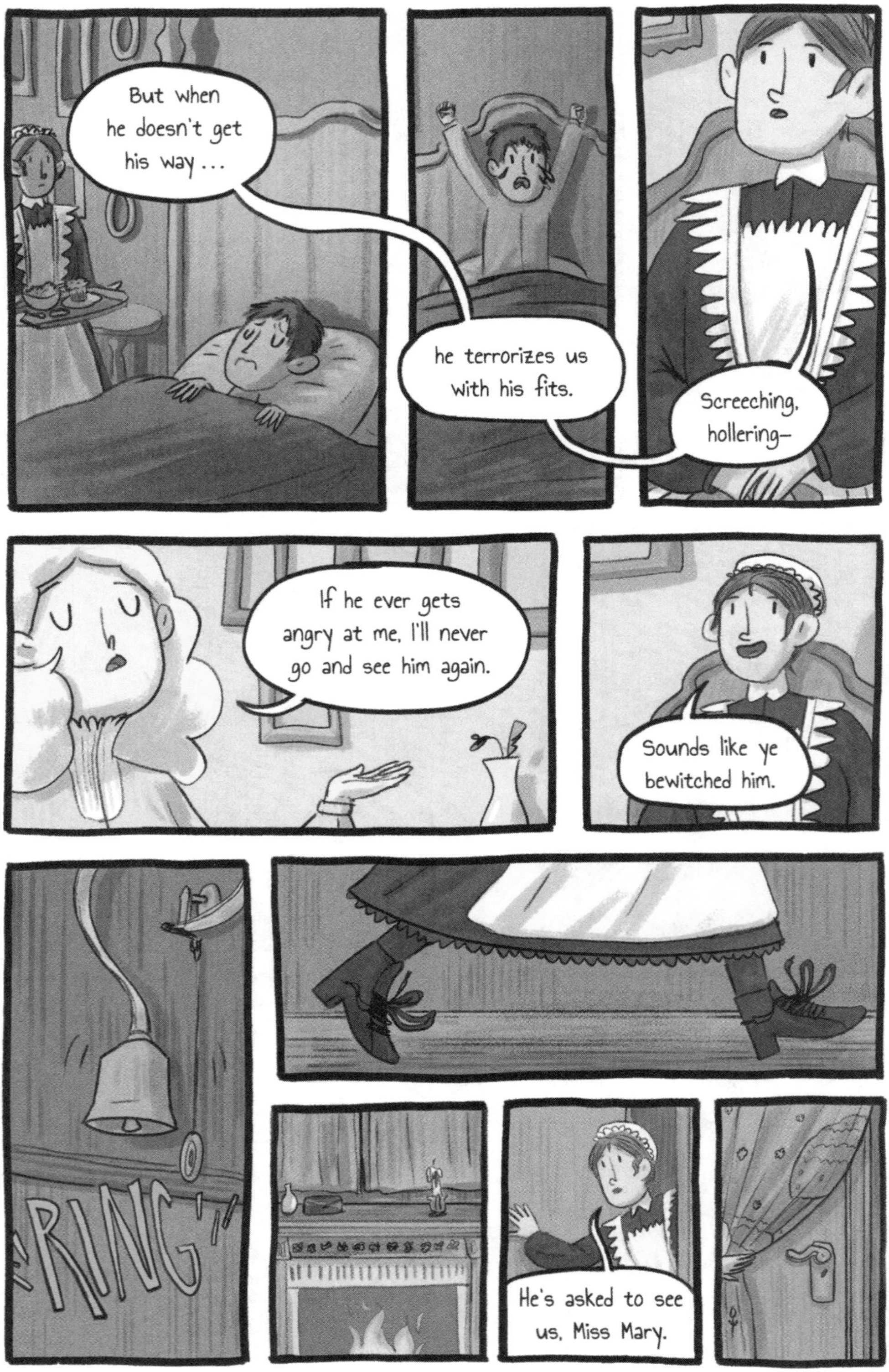
But when he doesn't get his way…
he terrorizes us with his fits.
Screeching, hollering–
If he ever gets angry at me, I'll never go and see him again.
Sounds like ye bewitched him.
RING
He's asked to see us, Miss Mary.

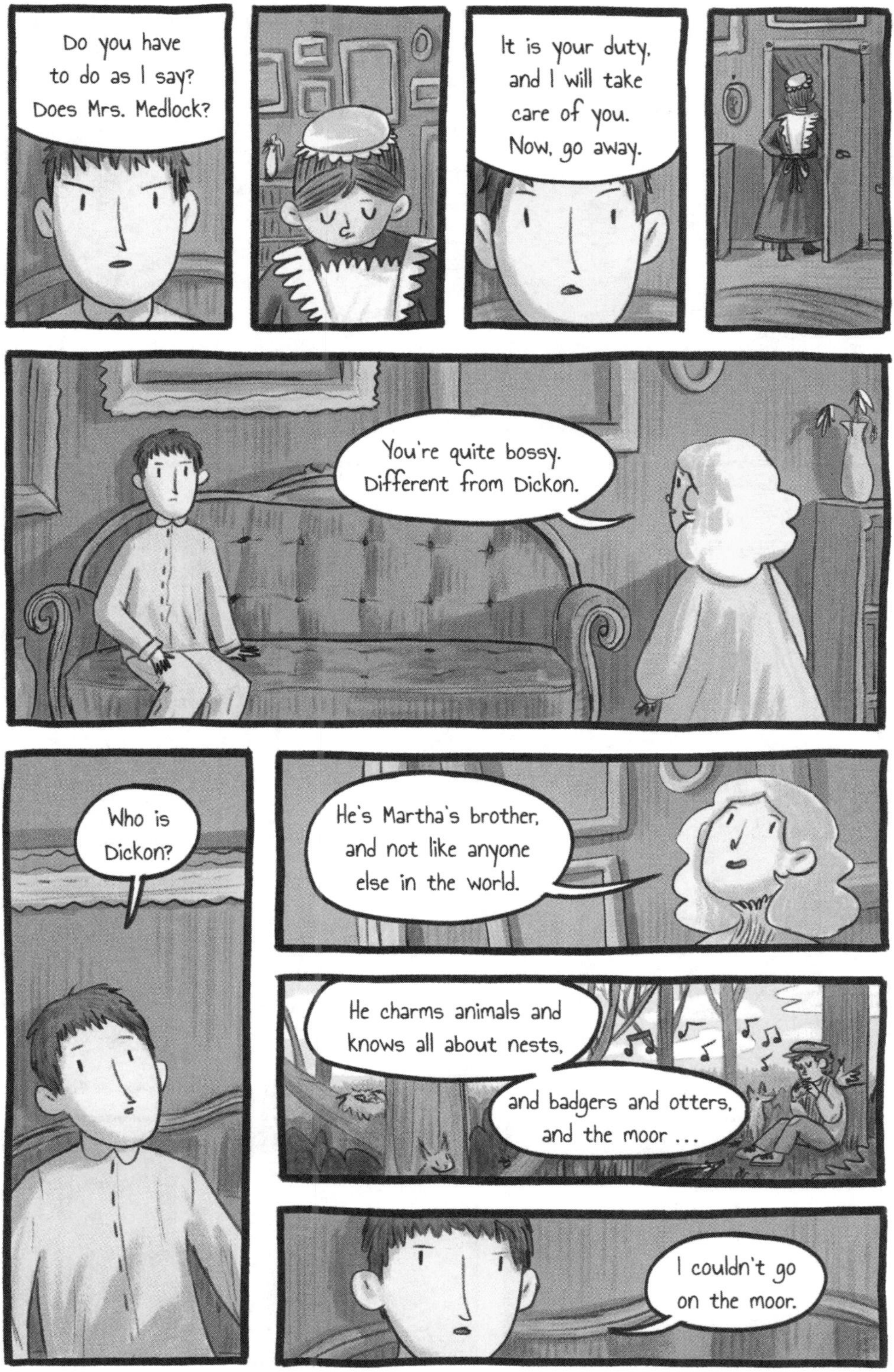

Do you have to do as I say? Does Mrs. Medlock?
It is your duty, and I will take care of you. Now, go away.
You're quite bossy. Different from Dickon.
Who is Dickon?
He's Martha's brother, and not like anyone else in the world.
He charms animals and knows all about nests,
and badgers and otters, and the moor ...
I couldn't go on the moor.

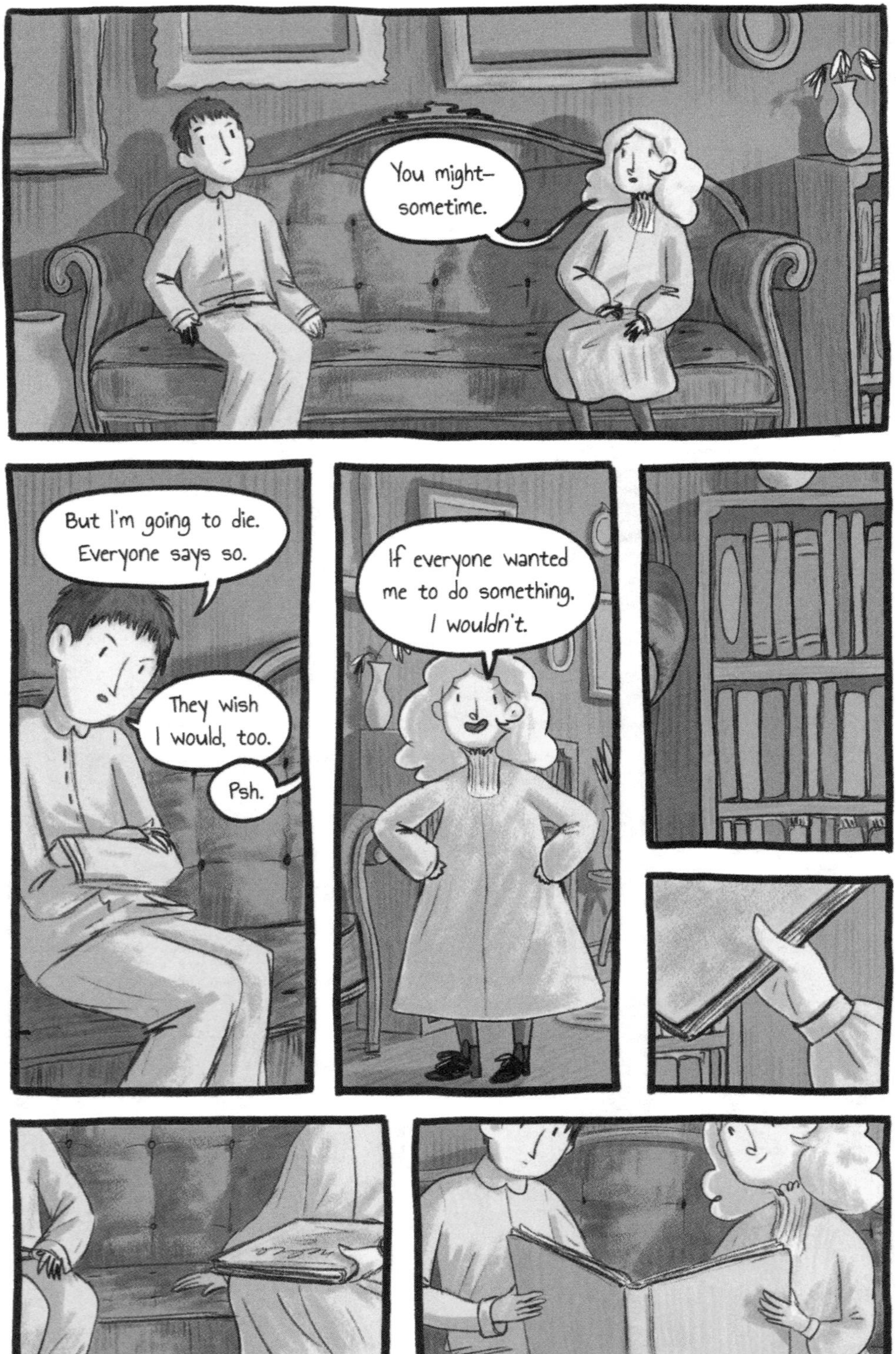
You might—
sometime.
But I'm going to die.
Everyone says so.
They wish
I would, too.
Psh.
If everyone wanted
me to do something,
I wouldn't.

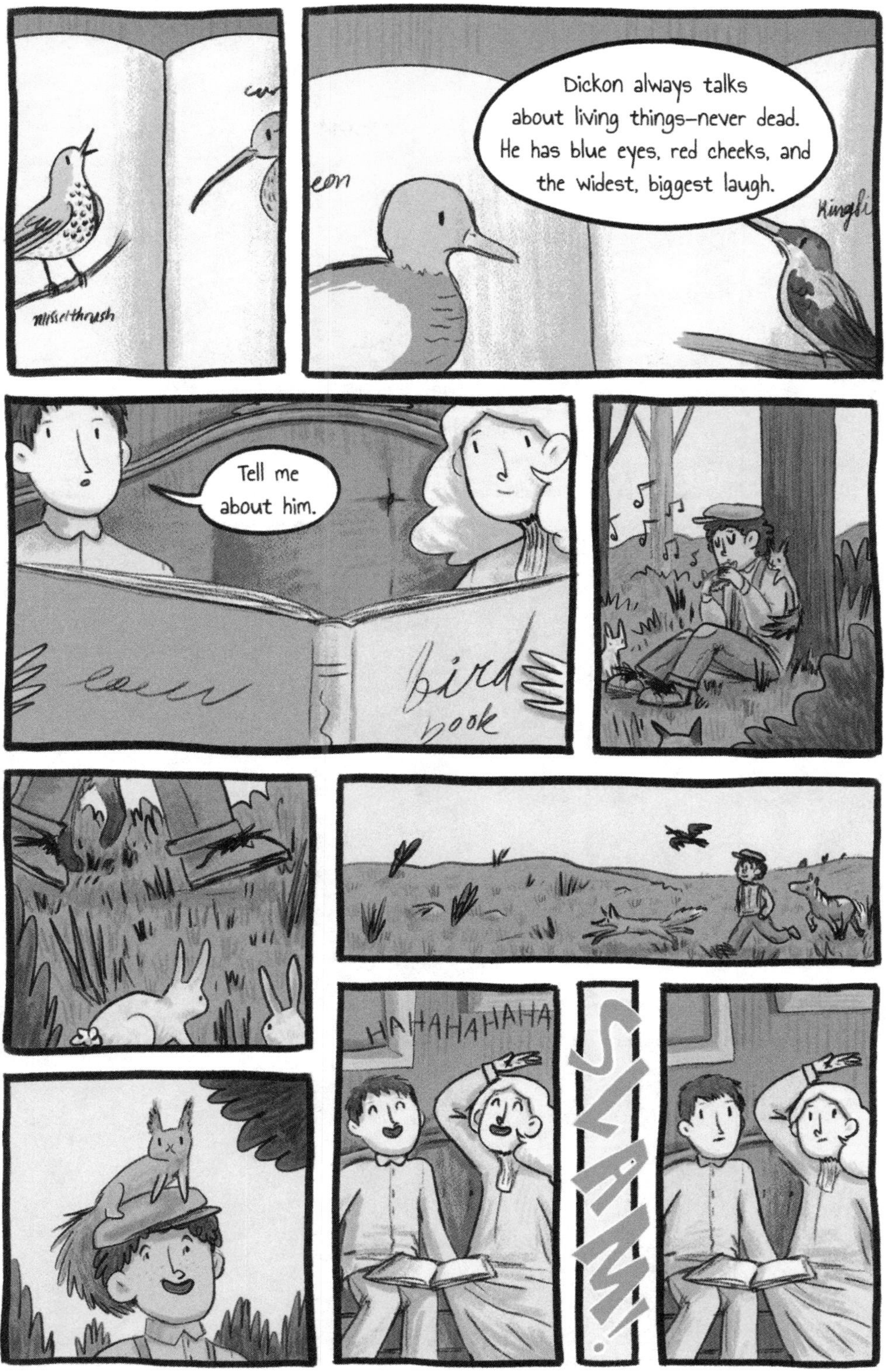
misselthrush
Dickon always talks about living things—never dead. He has blue eyes, red cheeks, and the widest, biggest laugh.
Tell me about him.
bird book
HAHAHAHAHA
SLAM!

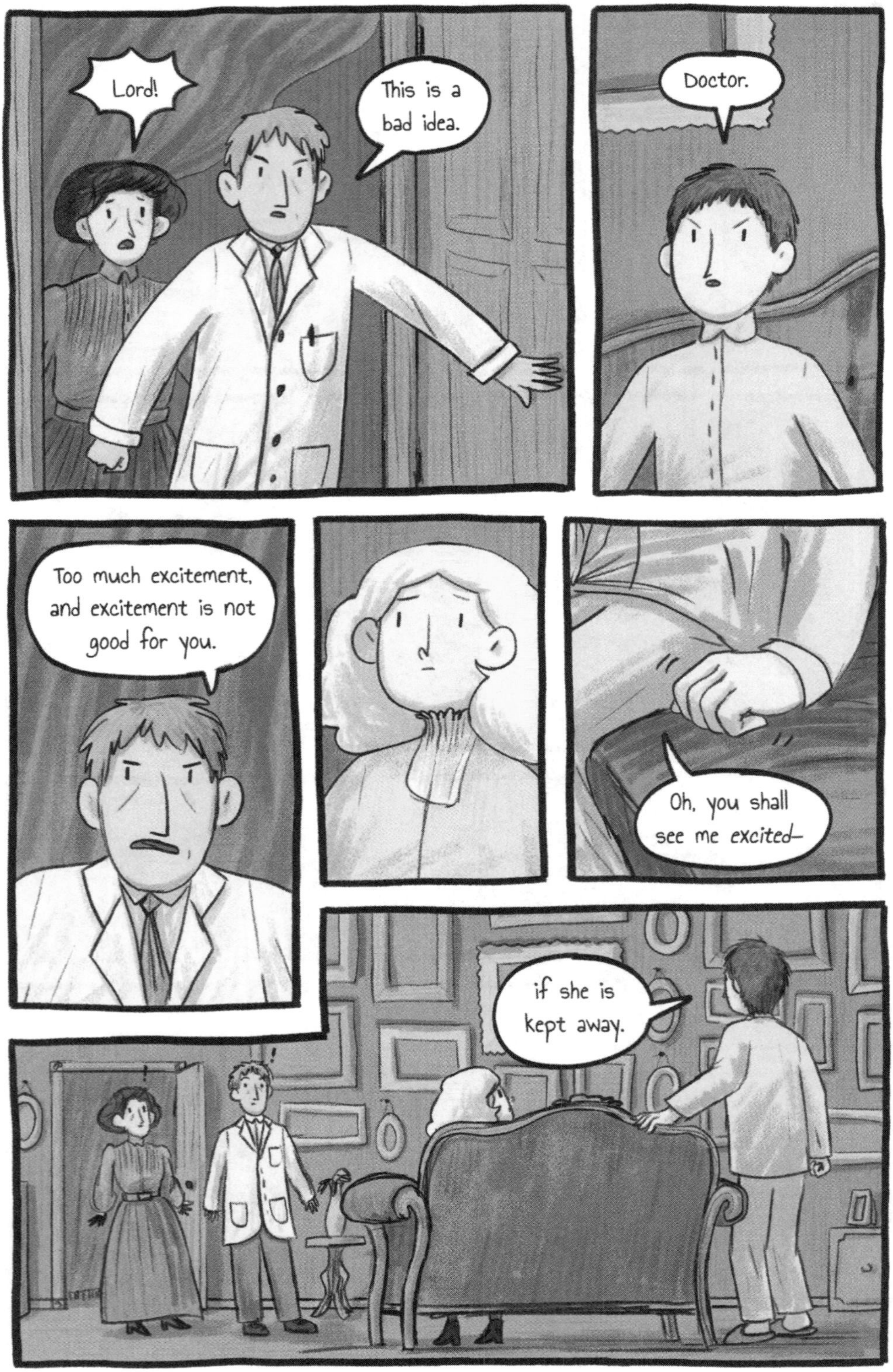
Lord!
This is a bad idea.
Doctor.
Too much excitement, and excitement is not good for you.
Oh, you shall see me *excited*—
if she is kept away.

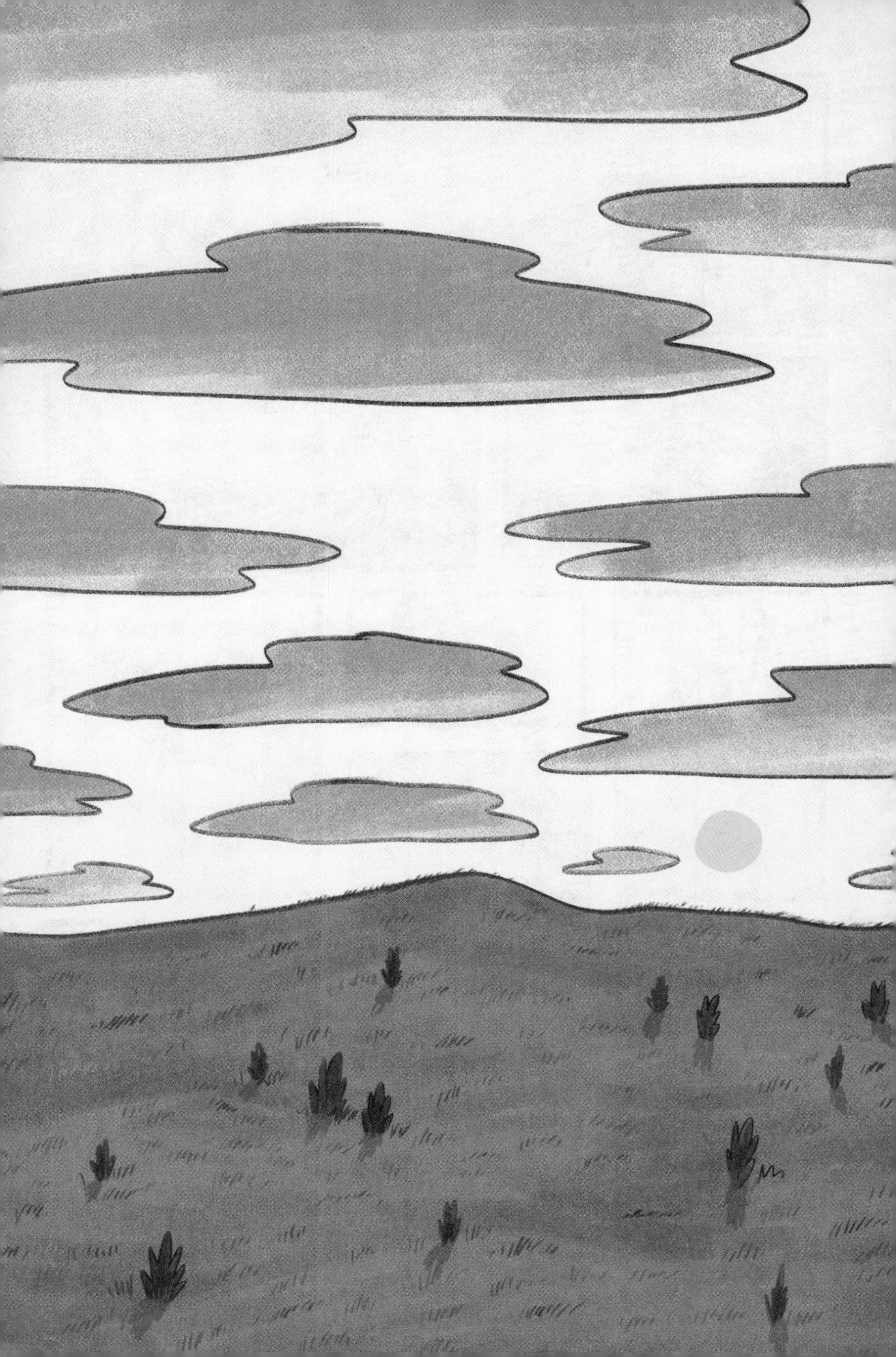

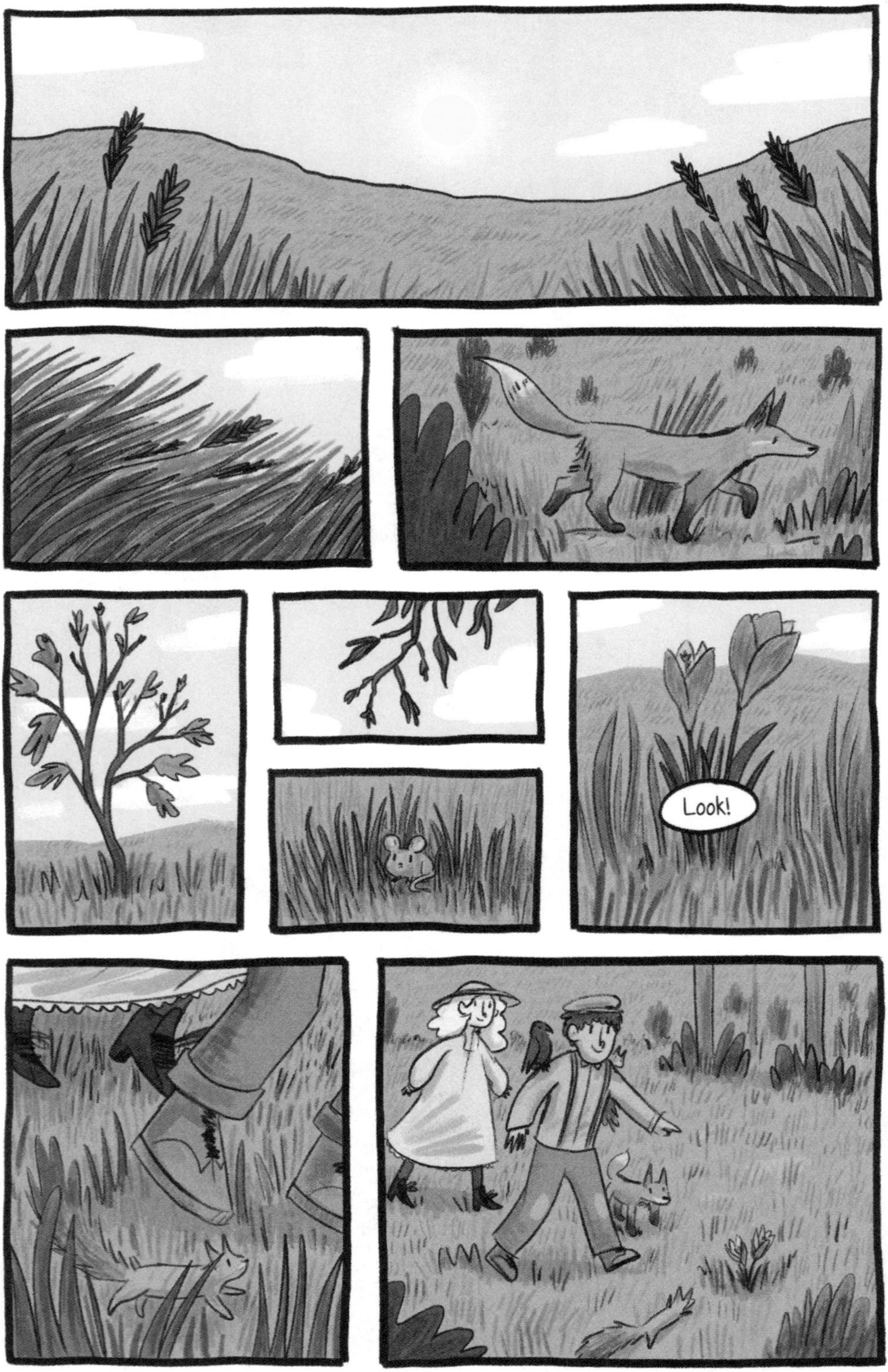
Look!

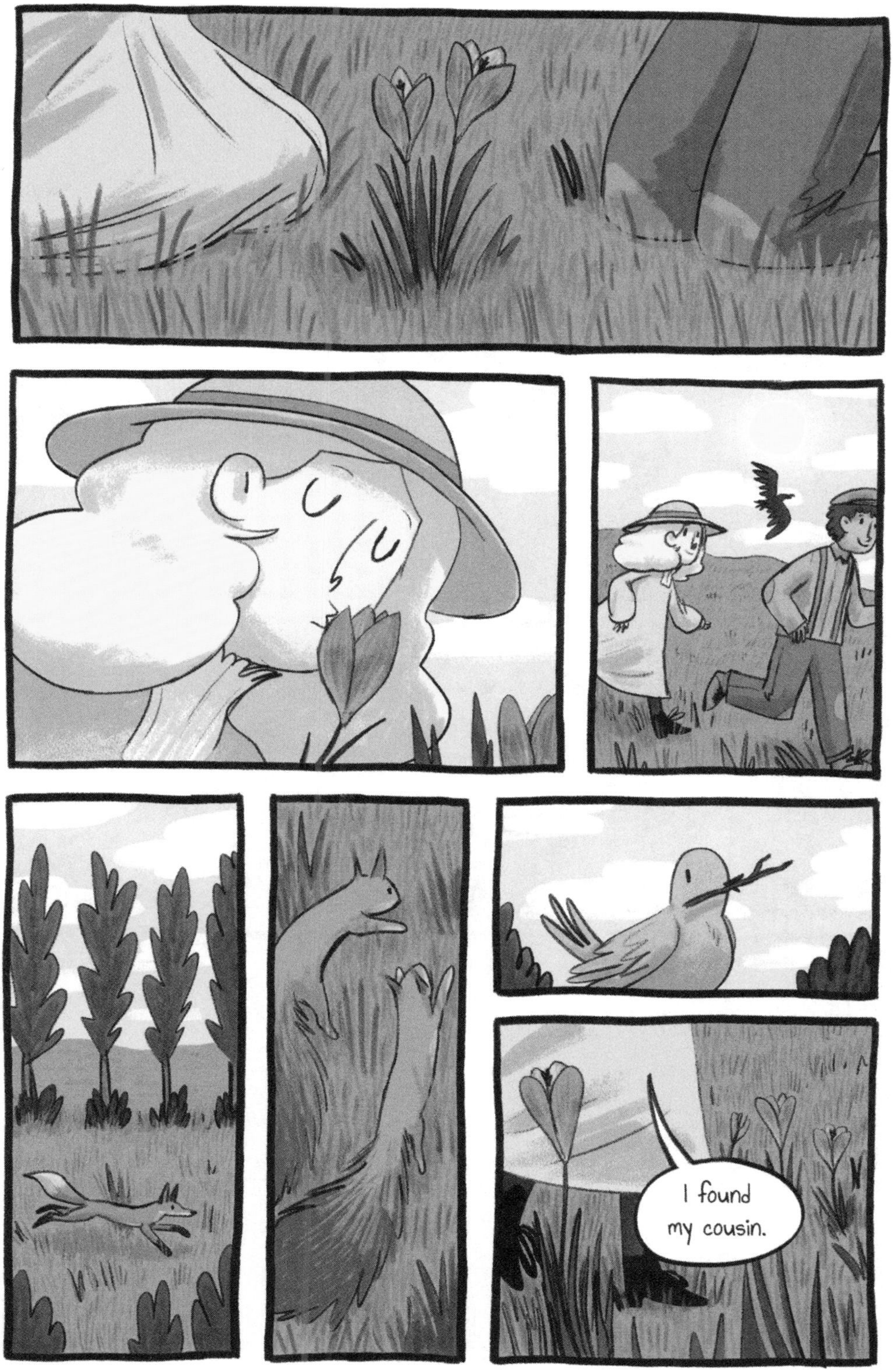
I found
my cousin.

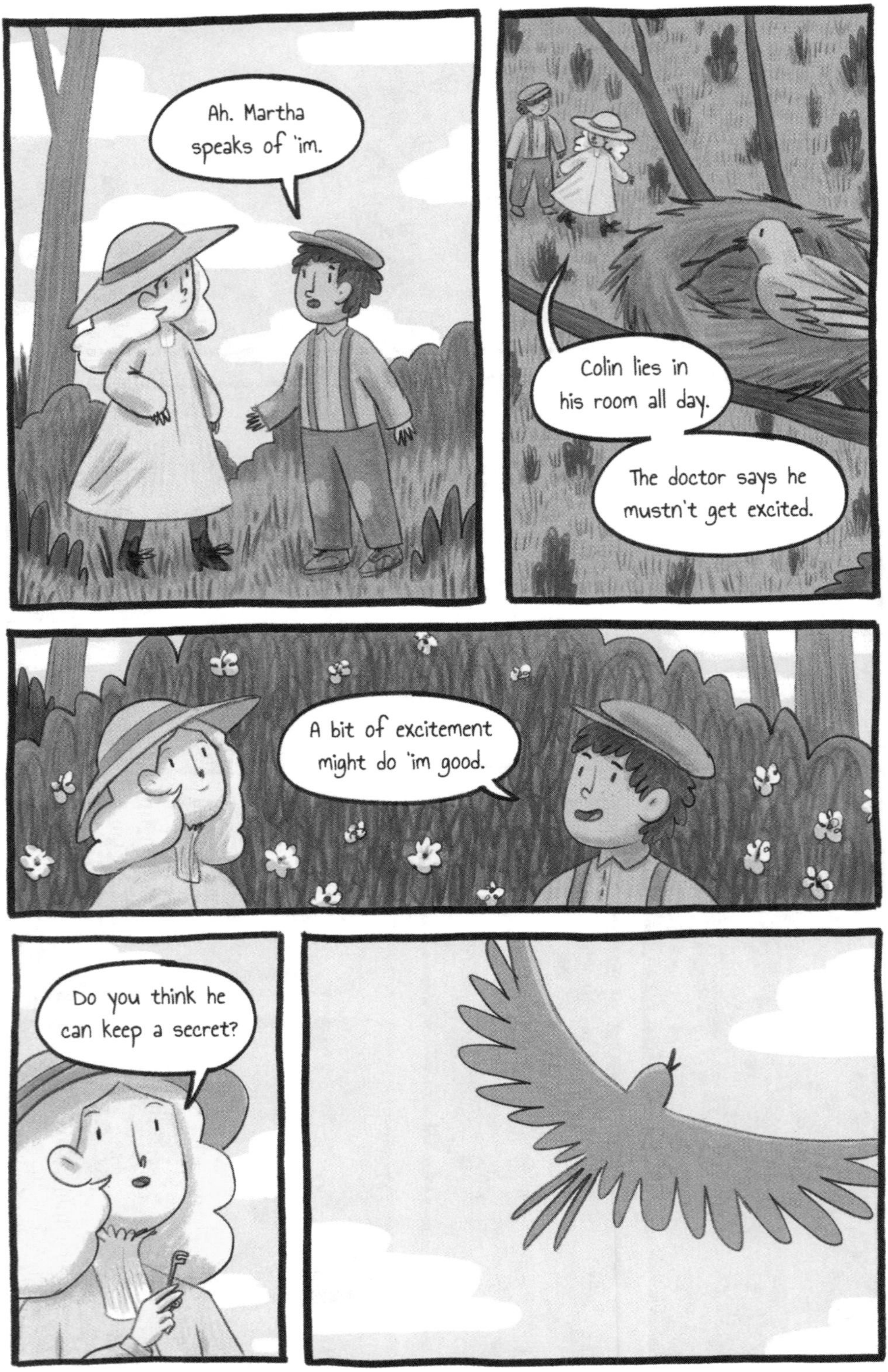
Ah. Martha speaks of 'im.
Colin lies in his room all day.
The doctor says he mustn't get excited.
A bit of excitement might do 'im good.
Do you think he can keep a secret?

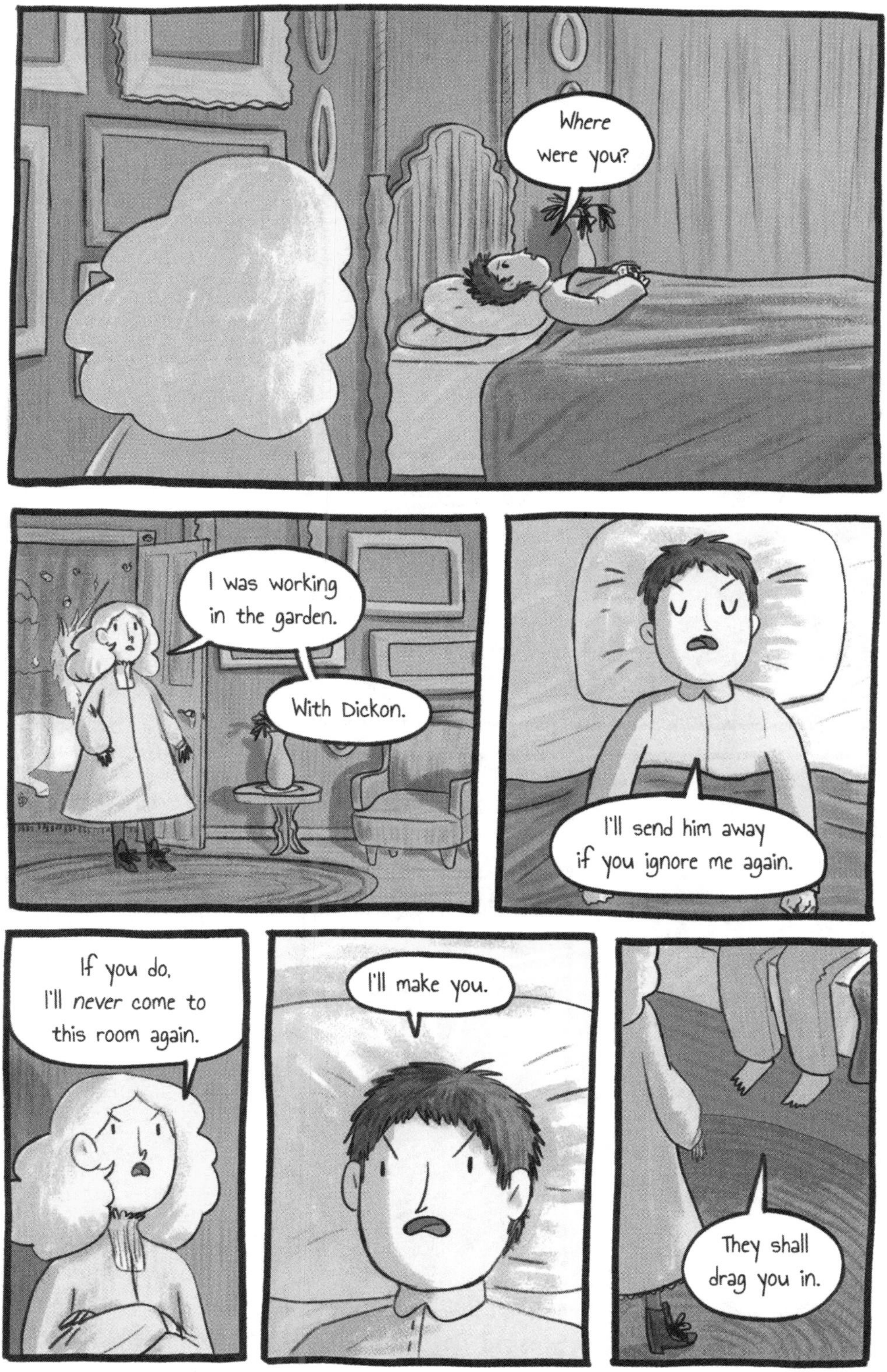
Where were you?
I was working in the garden.
With Dickon.
I'll send him away if you ignore me again.
If you do, I'll *never* come to this room again.
I'll make you.
They shall drag you in.

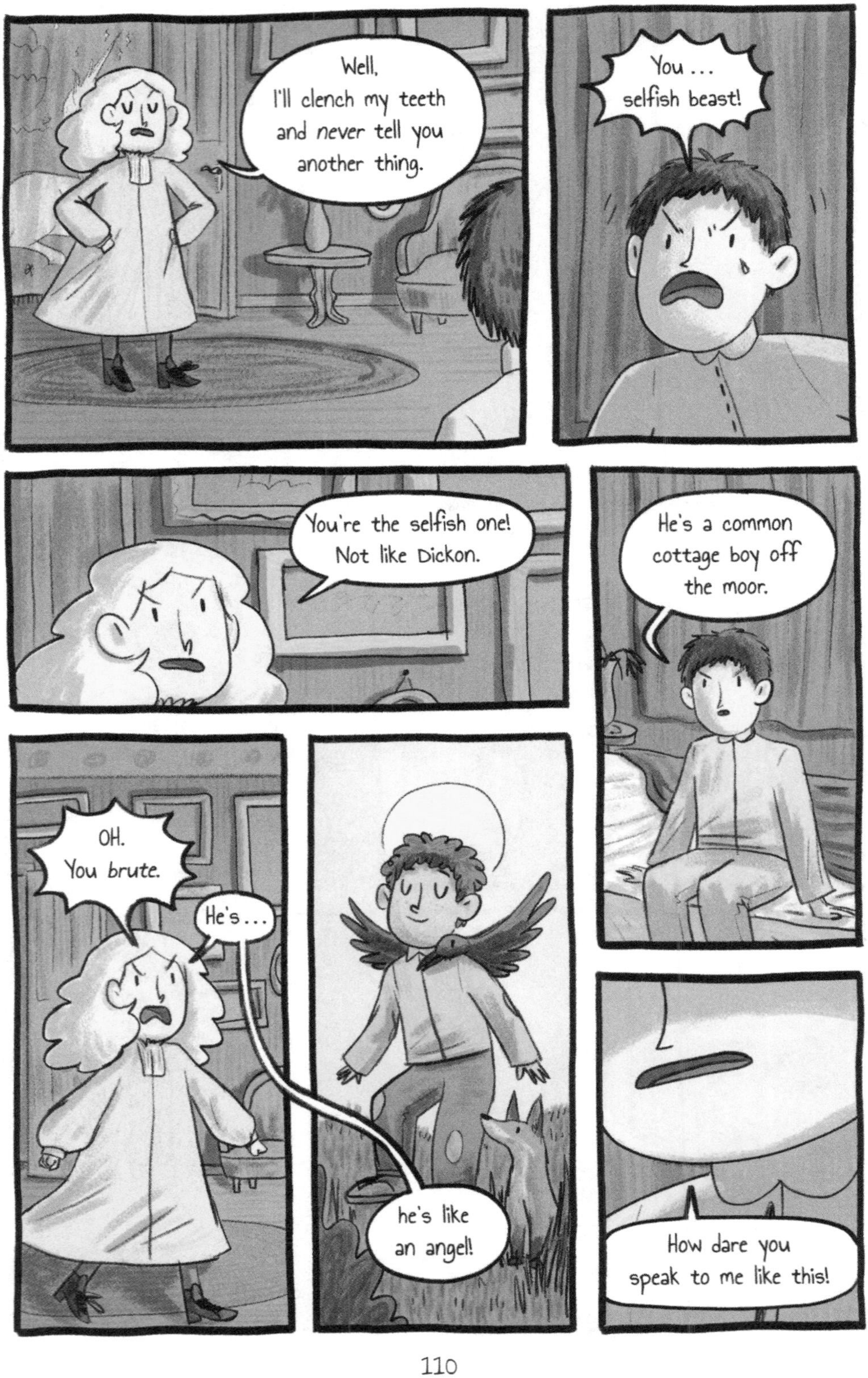
Well, I'll clench my teeth and *never* tell you another thing.
You ... selfish beast!
You're the selfish one! Not like Dickon.
He's a common cottage boy off the moor.
OH. You *brute.*
He's ...
he's like an angel!
How dare you speak to me like this!

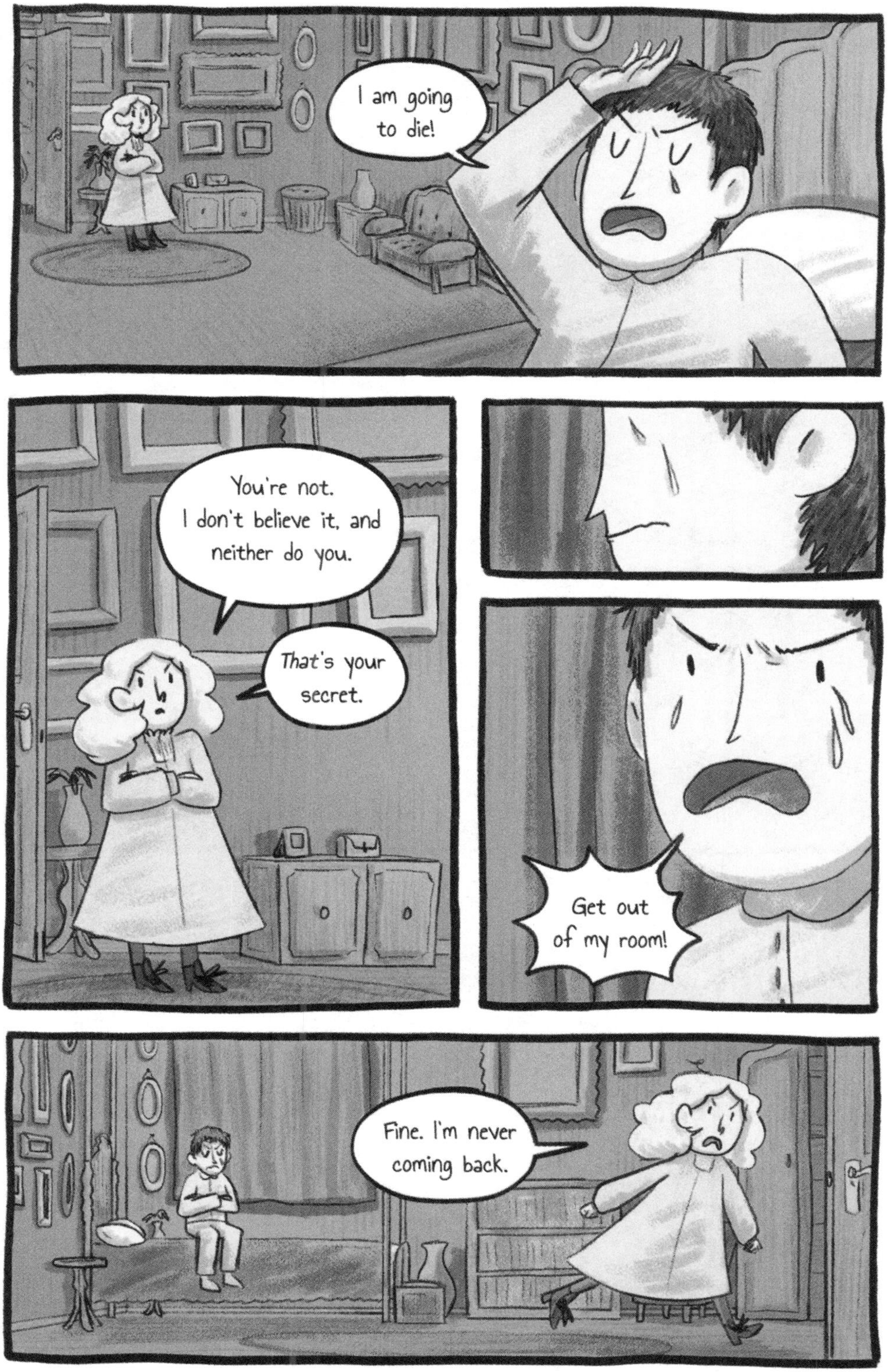
I am going to die!
You're not. I don't believe it, and neither do you.
That's your secret.
Get out of my room!
Fine. I'm never coming back.

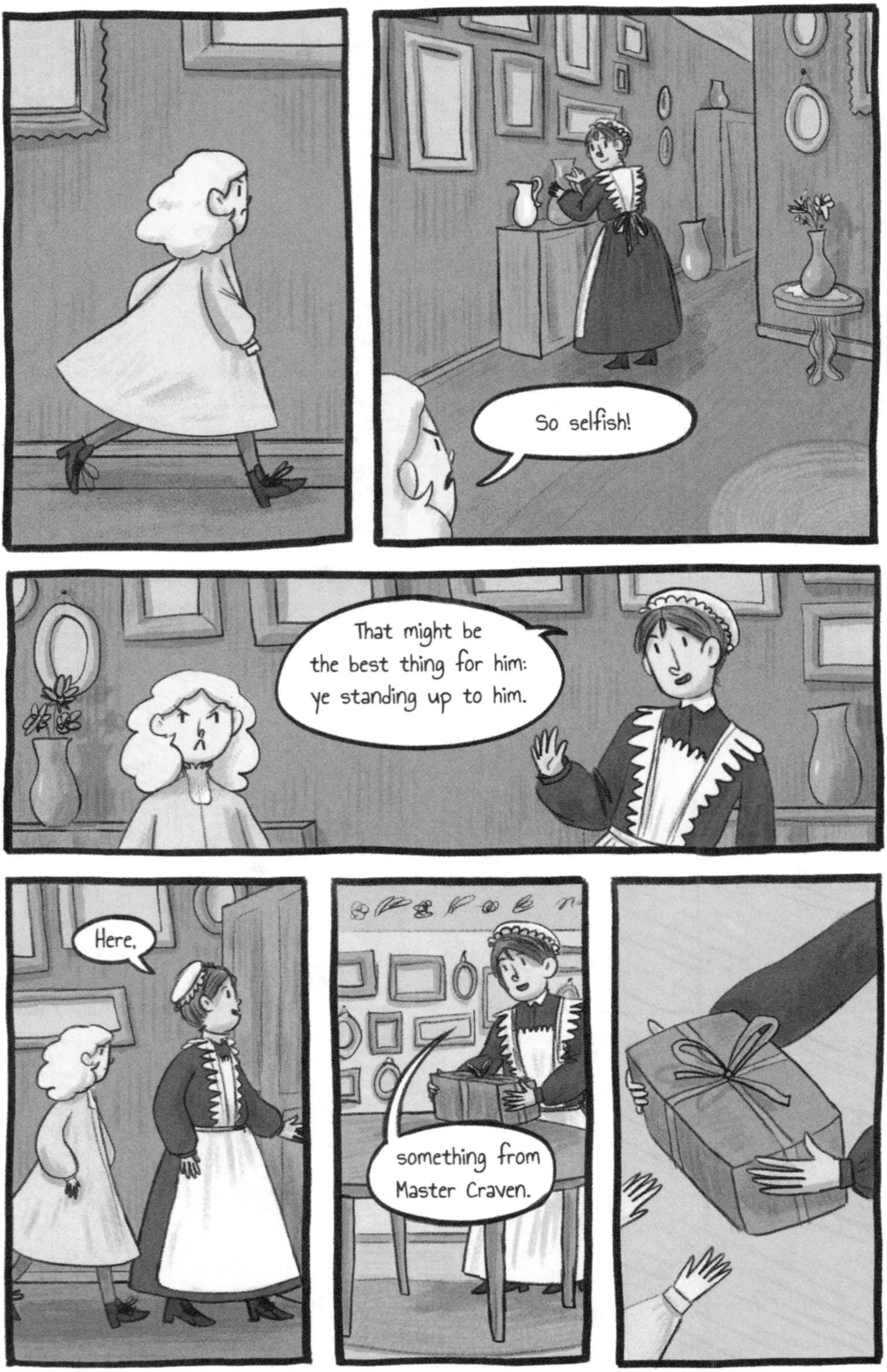
So selfish!
That might be the best thing for him: ye standing up to him.
Here,
something from Master Craven.

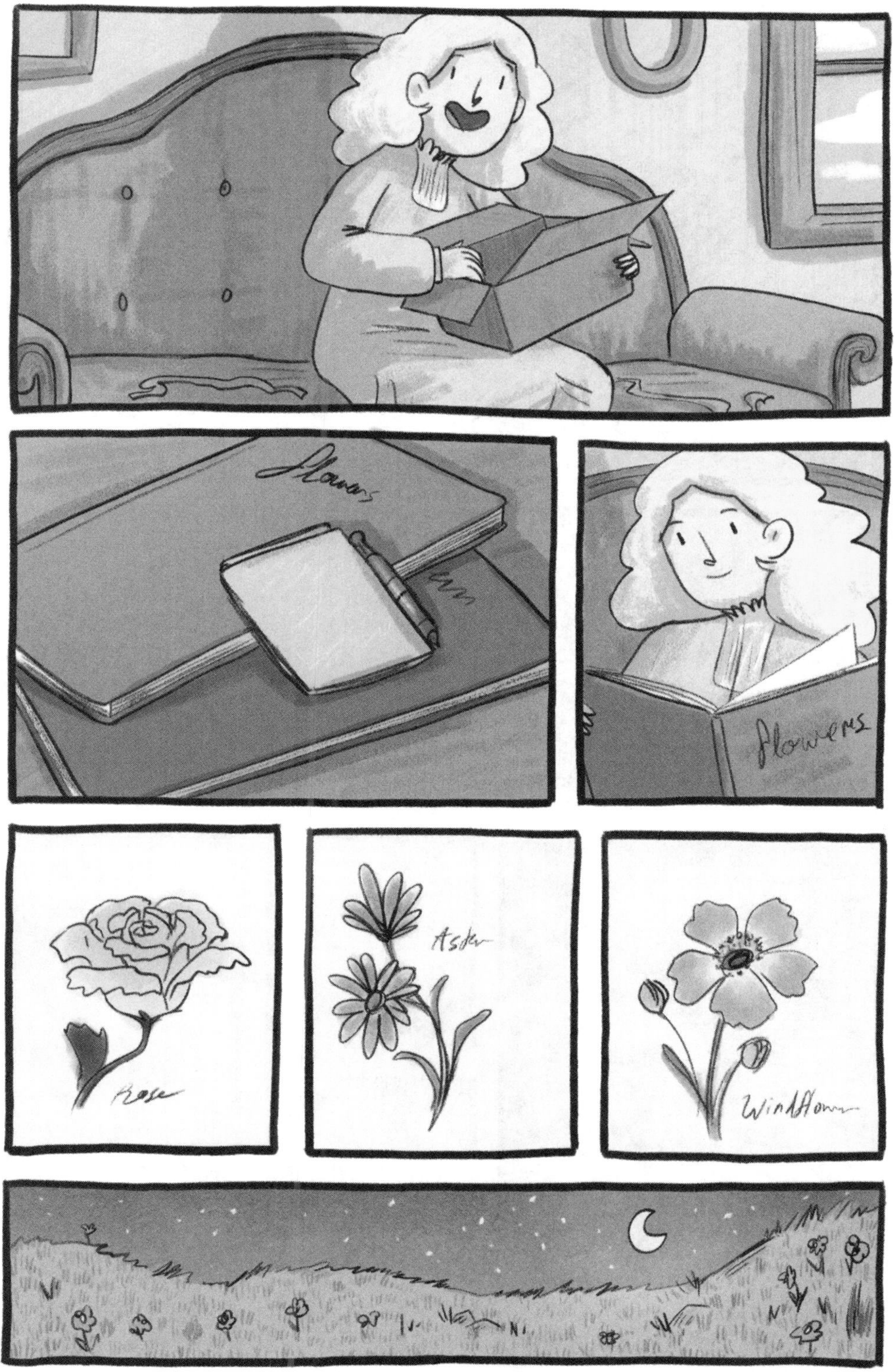
Flowers
Flowers
Rose
Aster
Windflower

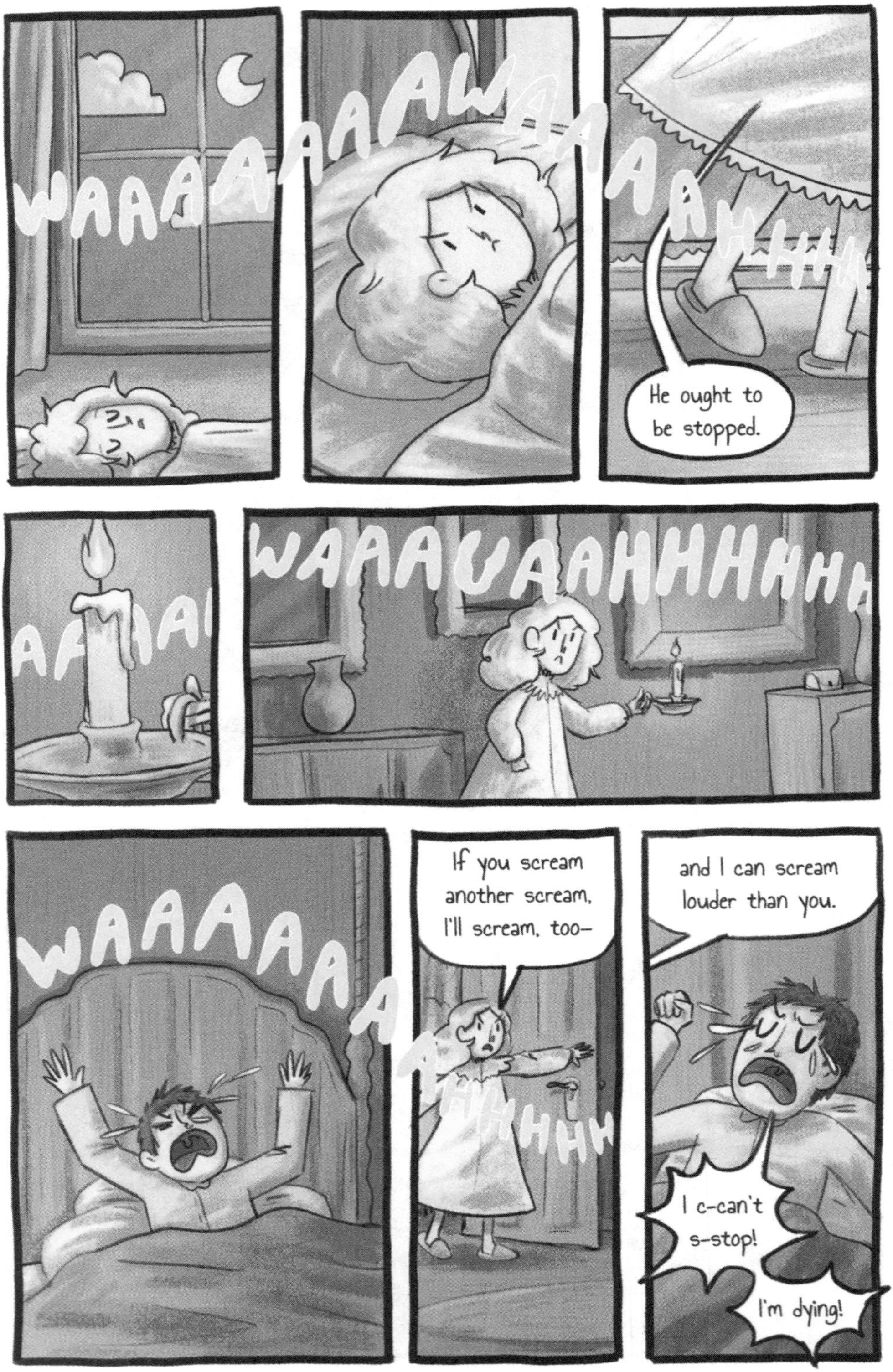
WAAAAAAAAAWAAAAAHHHH
He ought to be stopped.
AAAA
WAAAWAAHHHHHH
WAAAAAAAAAHHHHH
If you scream another scream, I'll scream, too–
and I can scream louder than you.
I c-can't s-stop!
I'm dying!

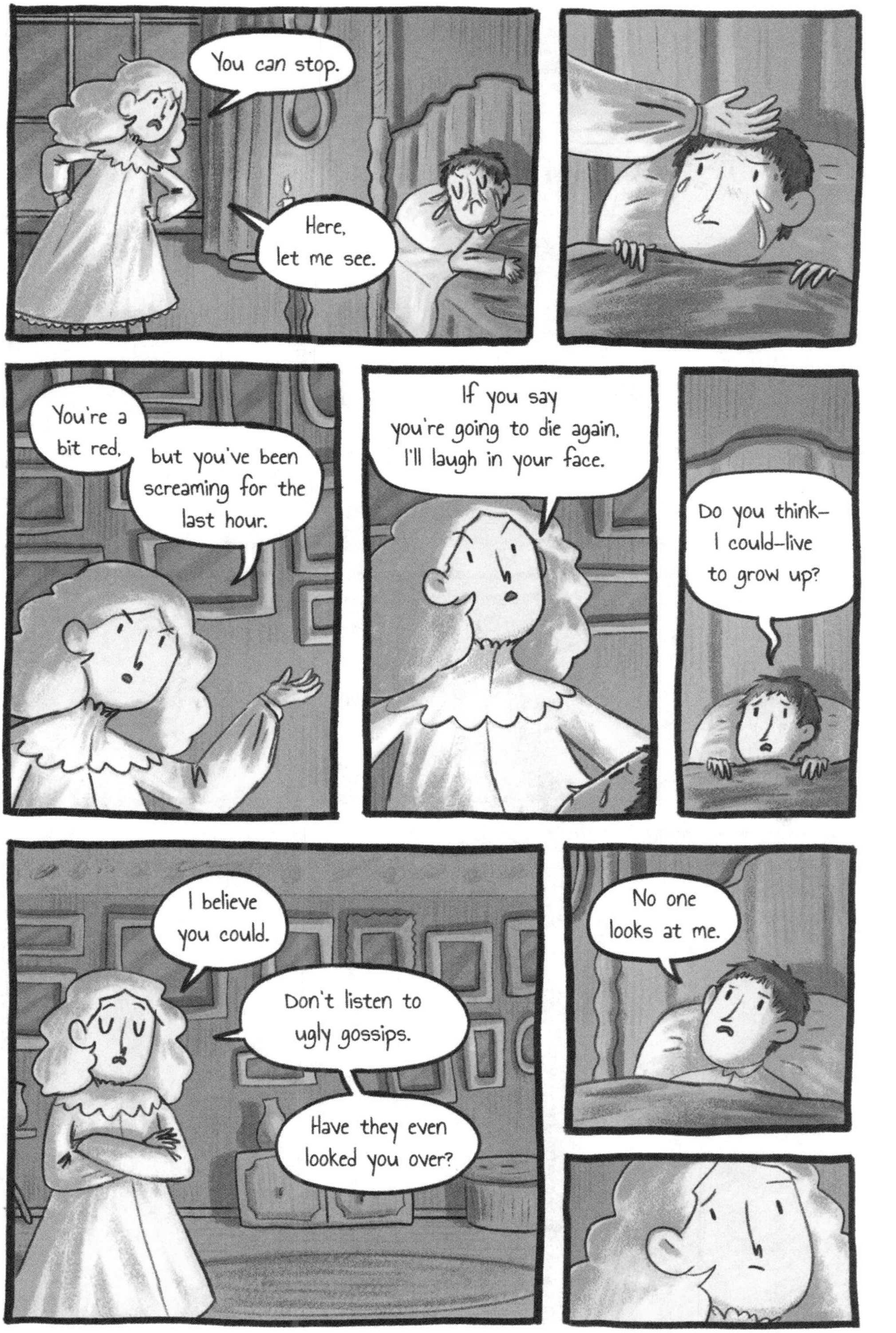
You can stop.
Here, let me see.
You're a bit red,
but you've been screaming for the last hour.
If you say you're going to die again, I'll laugh in your face.
Do you think– I could–live to grow up?
I believe you could.
Don't listen to ugly gossips.
Have they even looked you over?
No one looks at me.

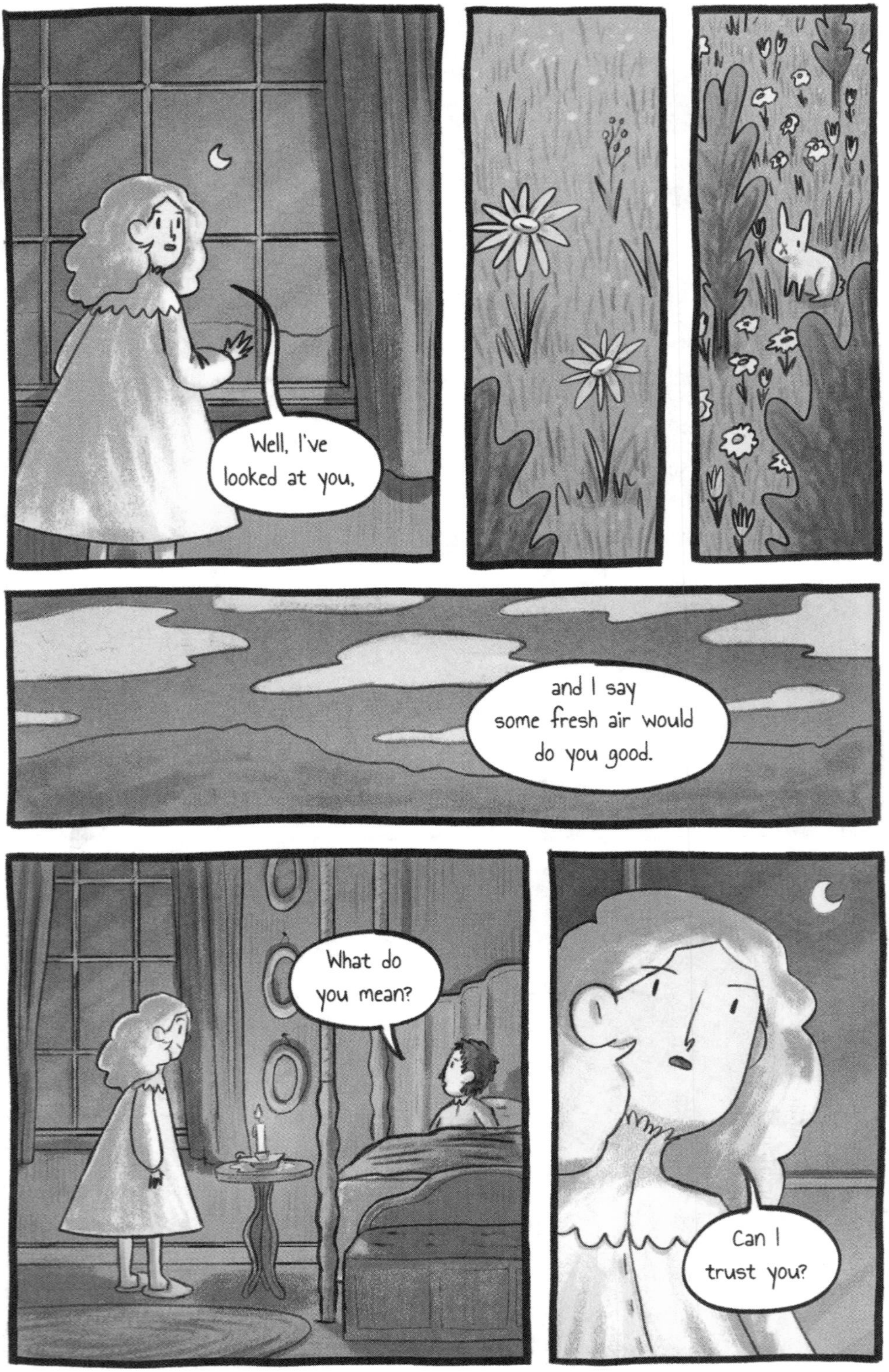
Well, I've looked at you,
and I say some fresh air would do you good.
What do you mean?
Can I trust you?

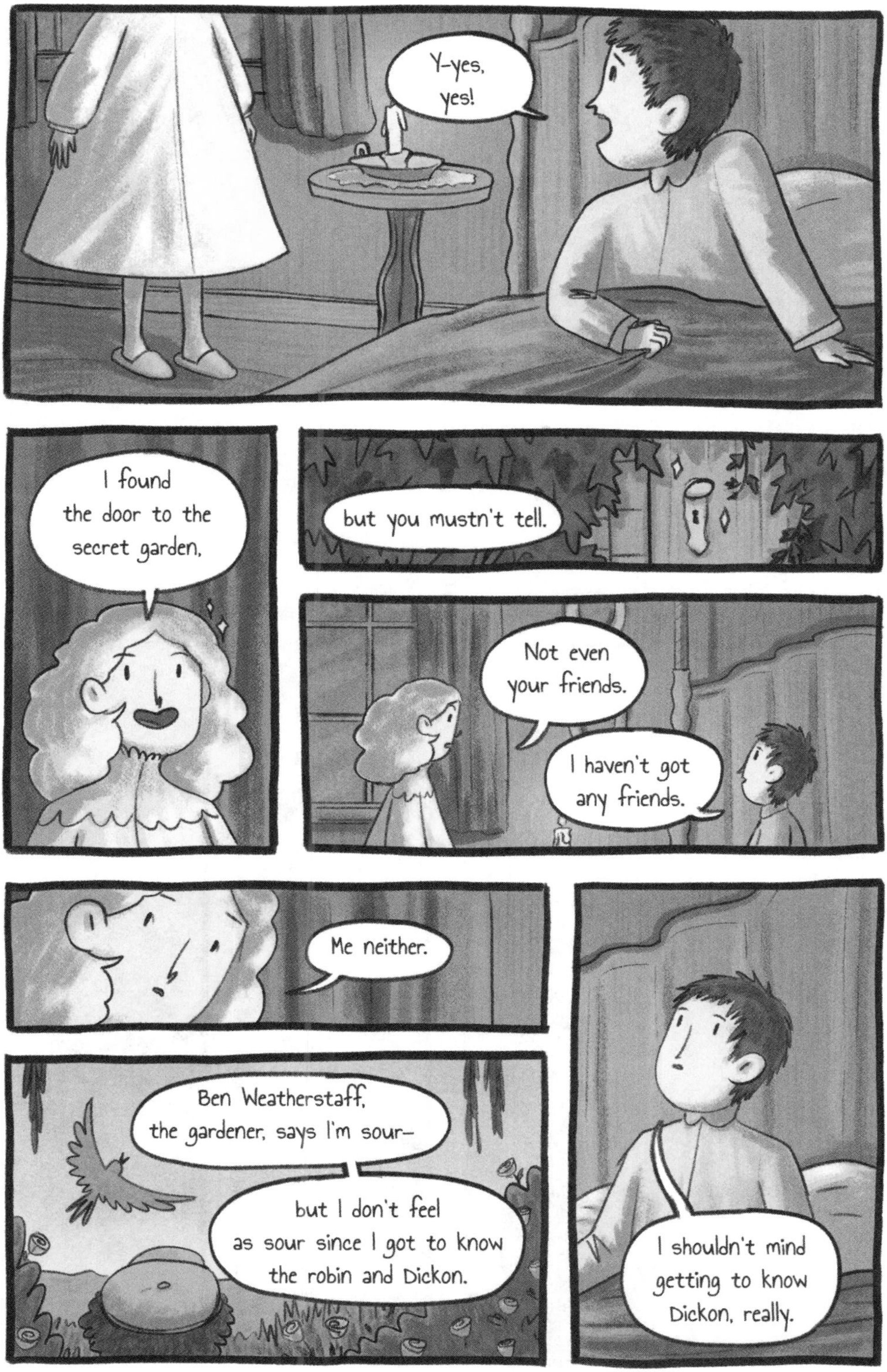
Y-yes, yes!
I found the door to the secret garden,
but you mustn't tell.
Not even your friends.
I haven't got any friends.
Me neither.
Ben Weatherstaff, the gardener, says I'm sour—
but I don't feel as sour since I got to know the robin and Dickon.
I shouldn't mind getting to know Dickon, really.

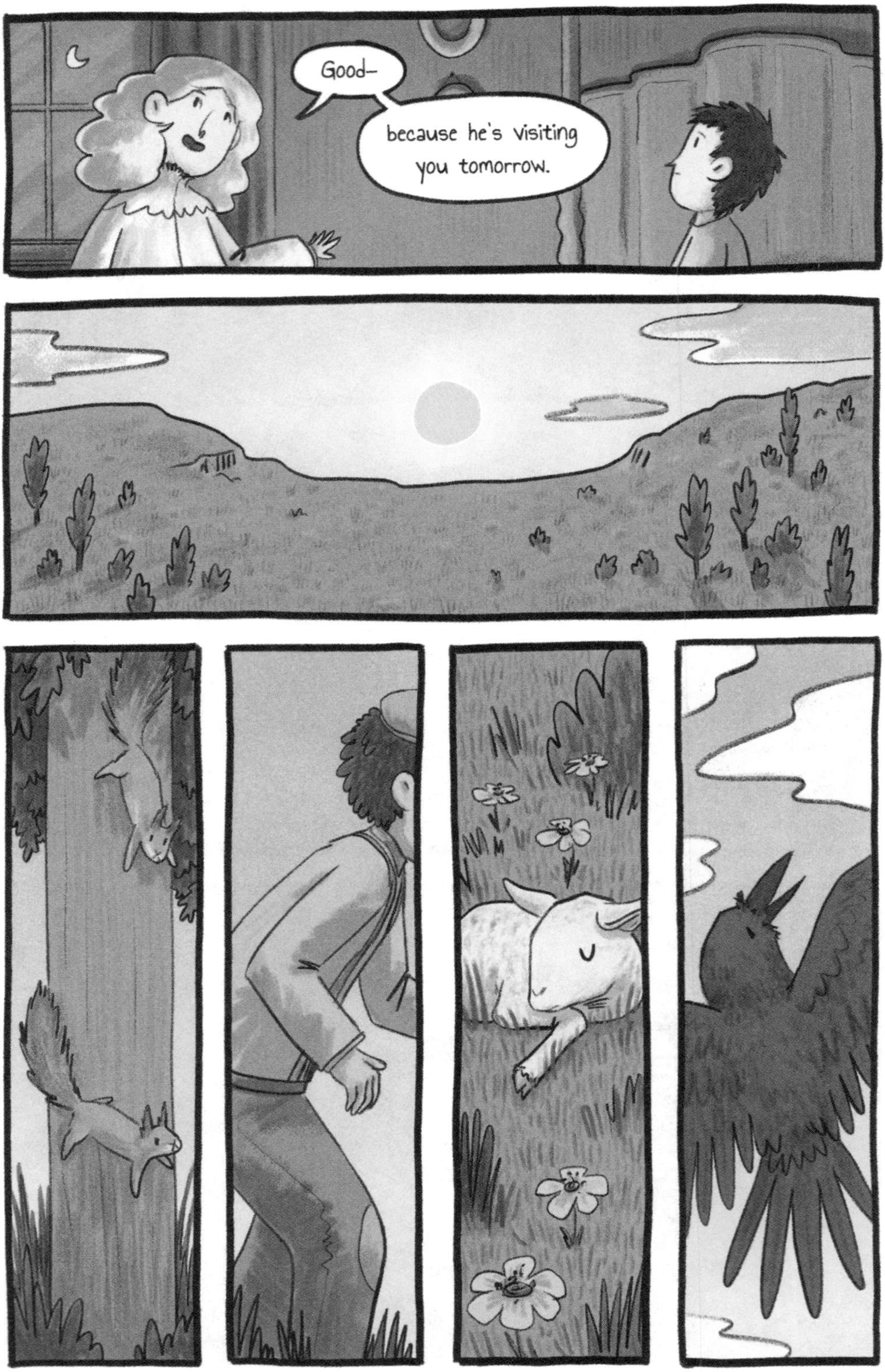
Good–
because he's visiting you tomorrow.

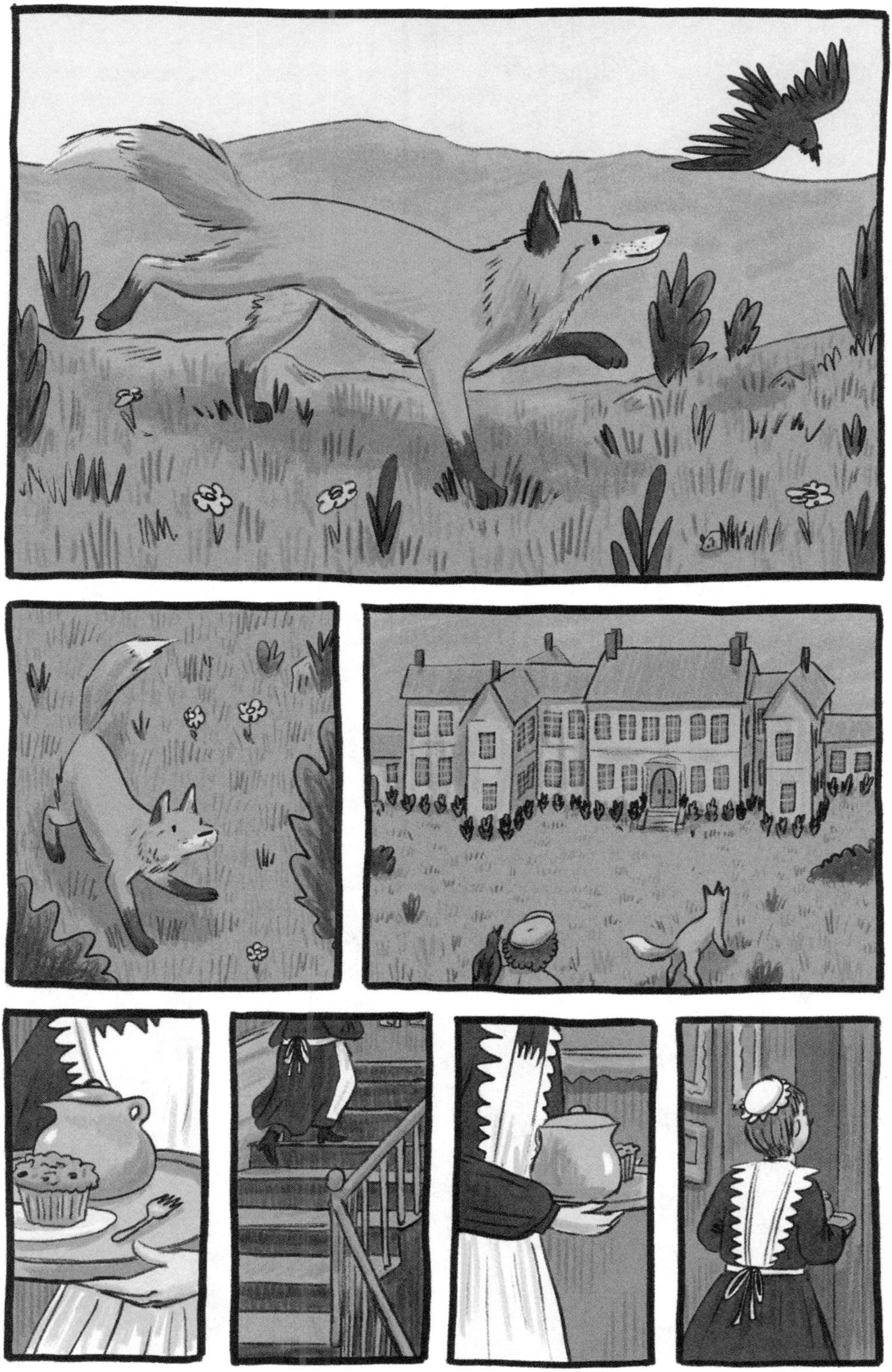

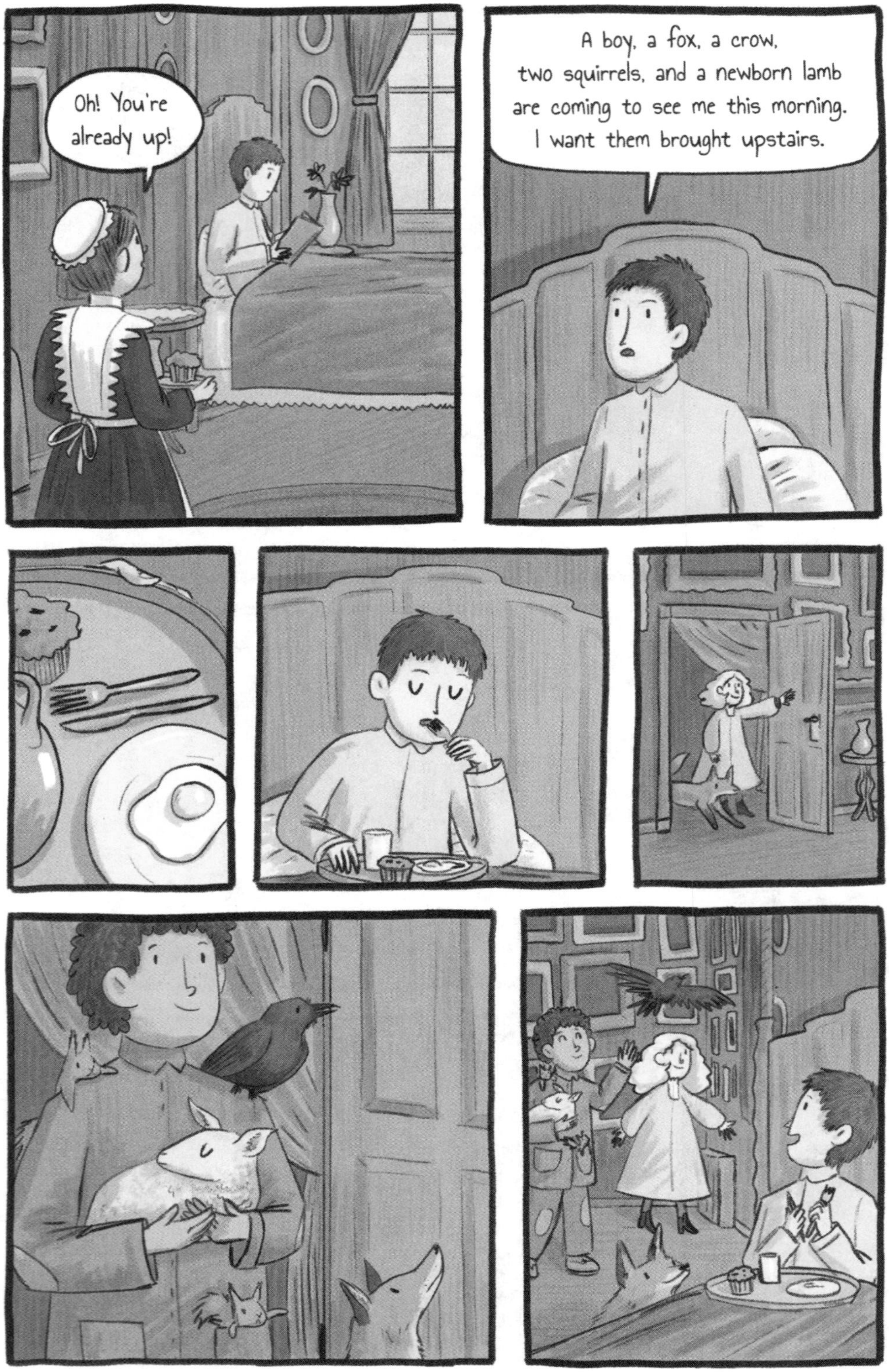
Oh! You're already up!
A boy, a fox, a crow, two squirrels, and a newborn lamb are coming to see me this morning. I want them brought upstairs.

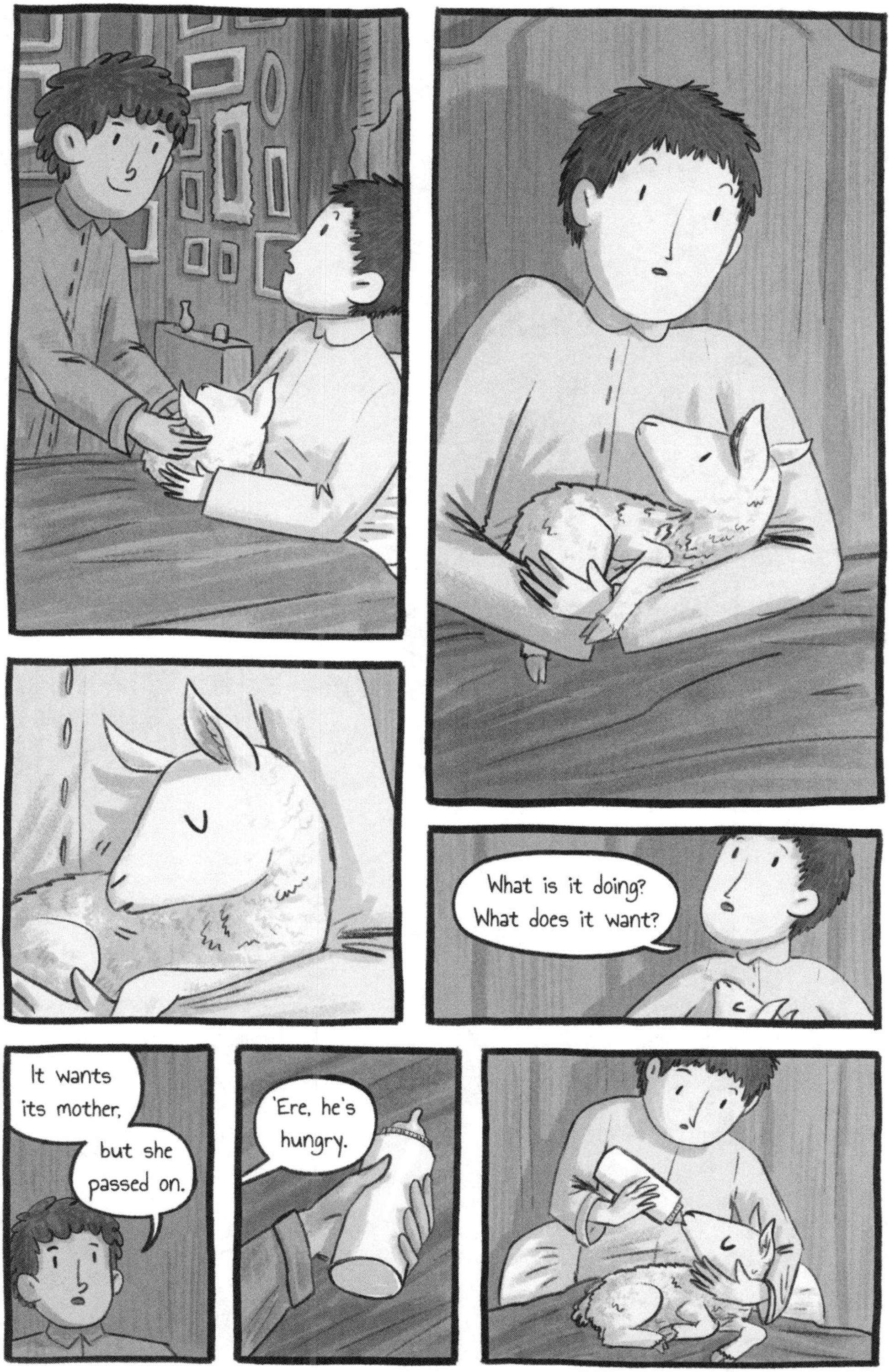
What is it doing? What does it want?
It wants its mother,
but she passed on.
'Ere, he's hungry.

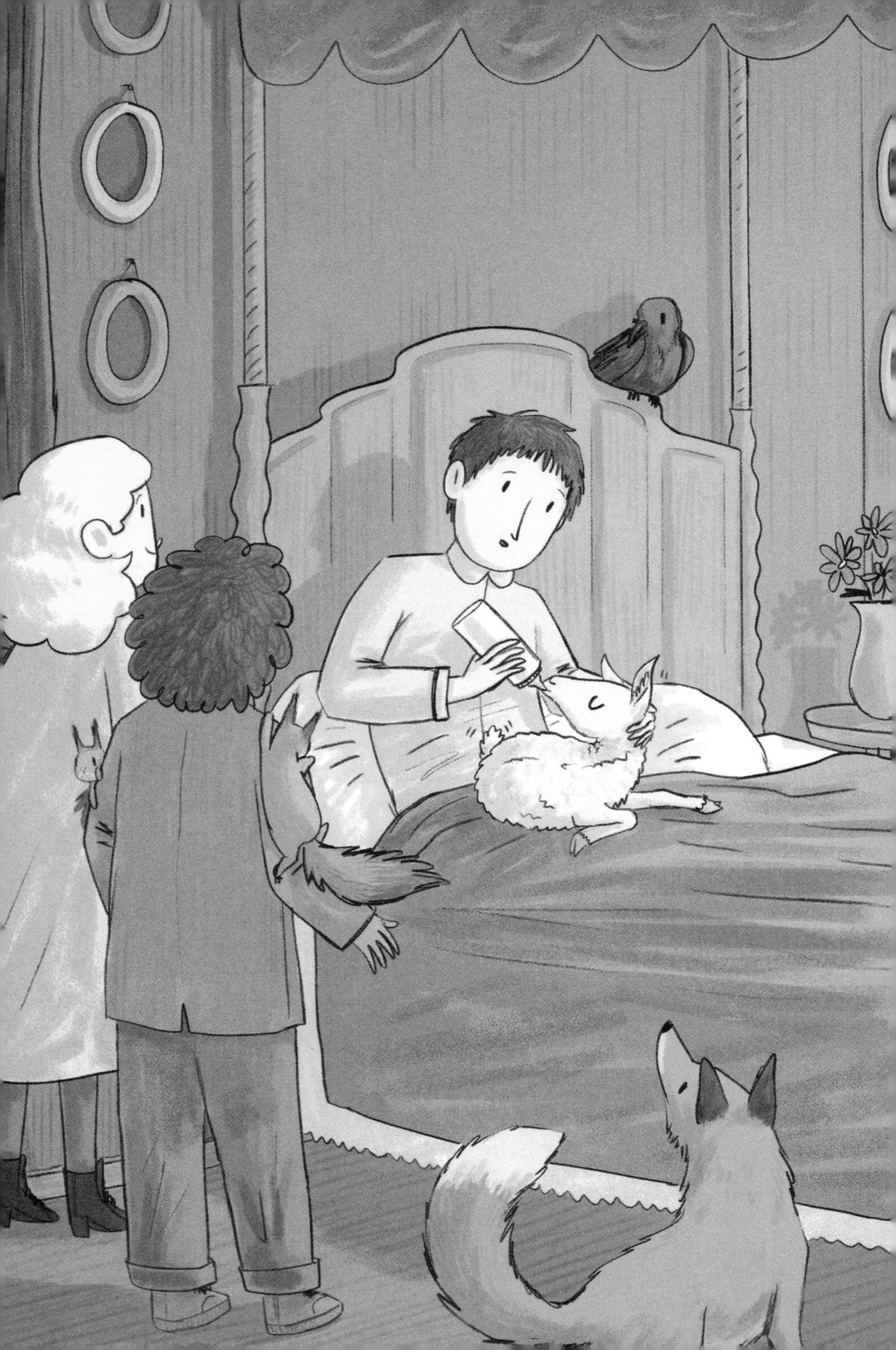

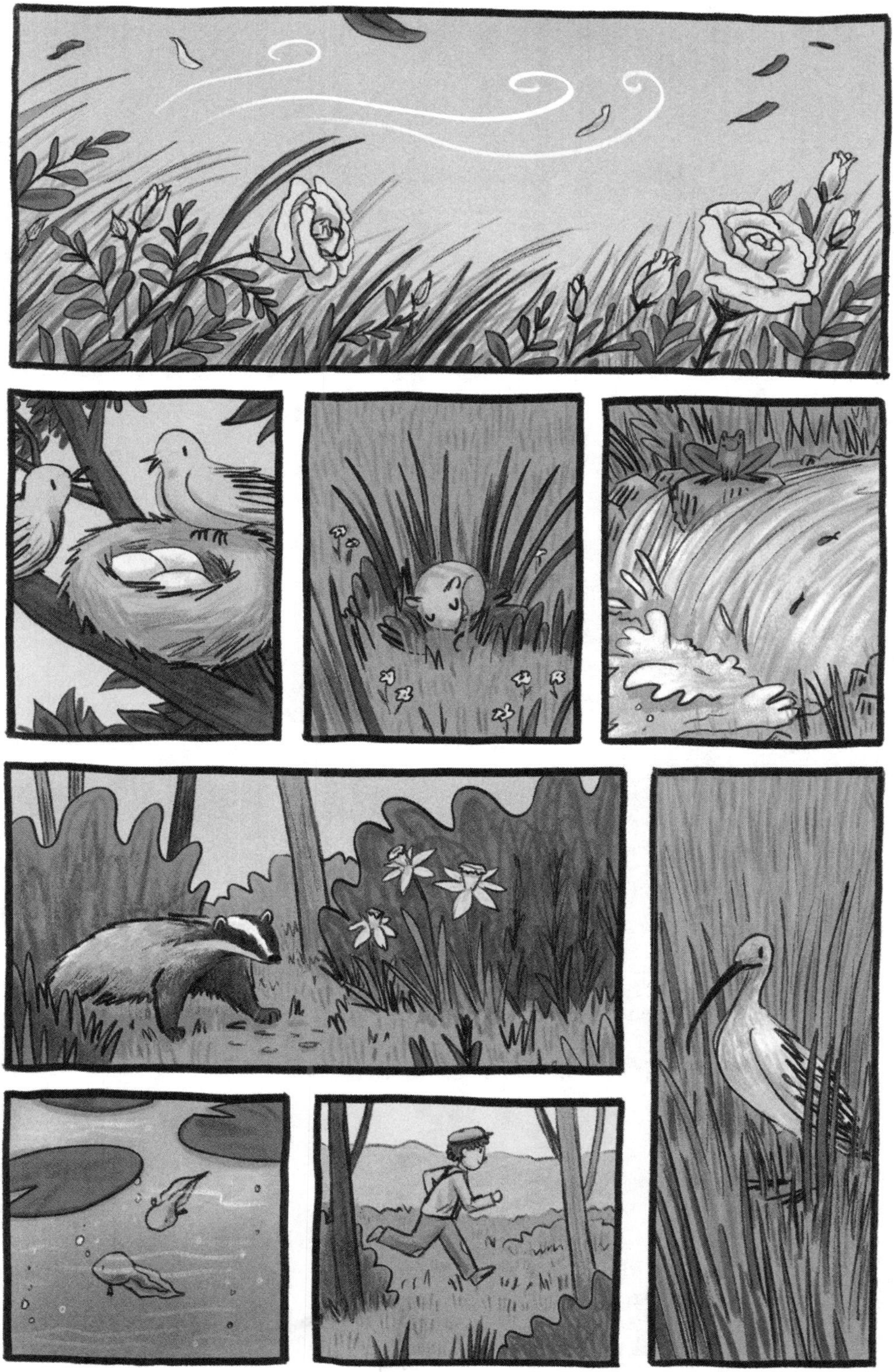

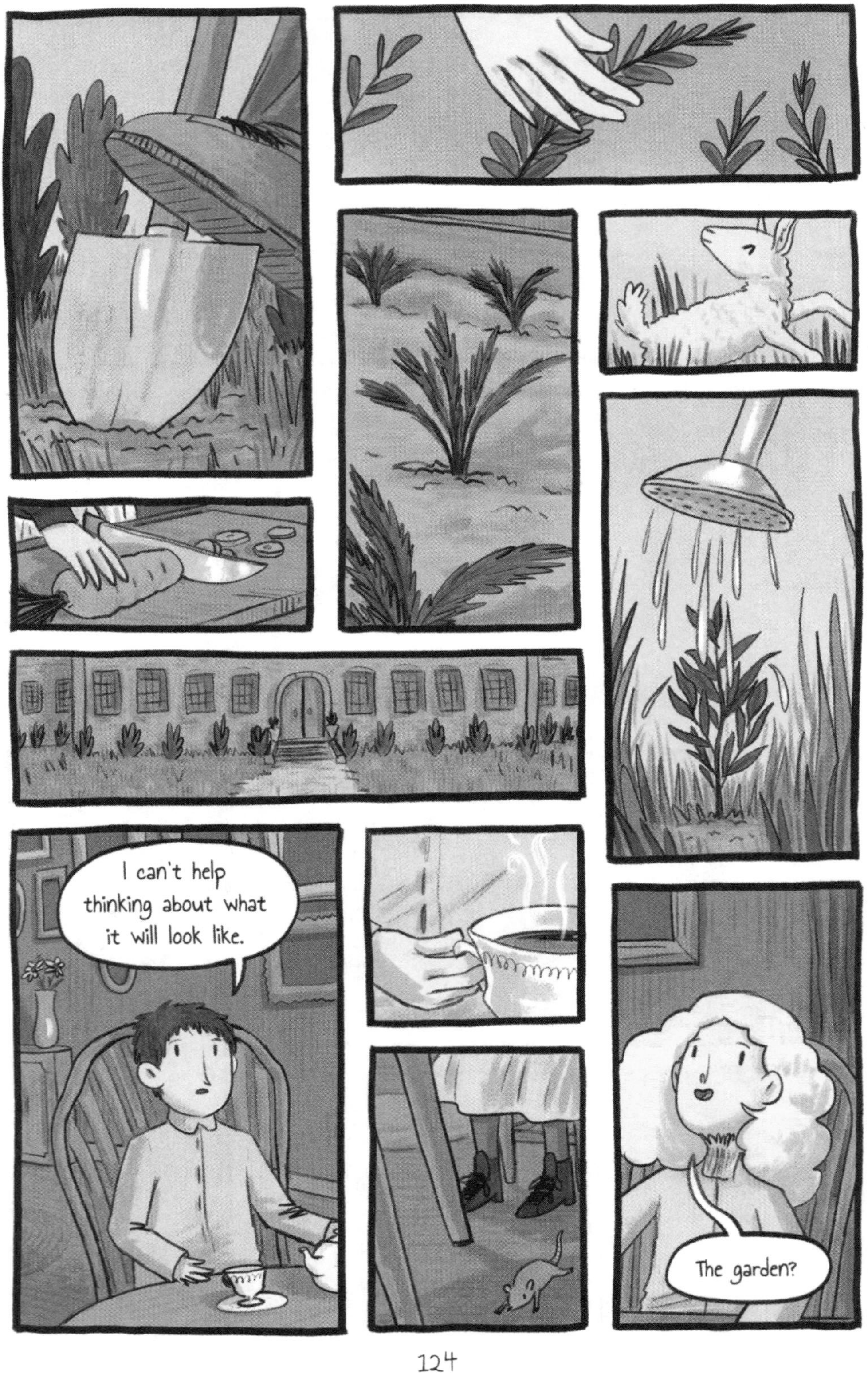
I can't help thinking about what it will look like.
The garden?

Springtime.

It must remain
our secret—

but here's how
we will do it.

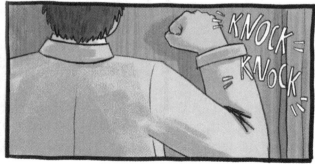
KNOCK
KNOCK

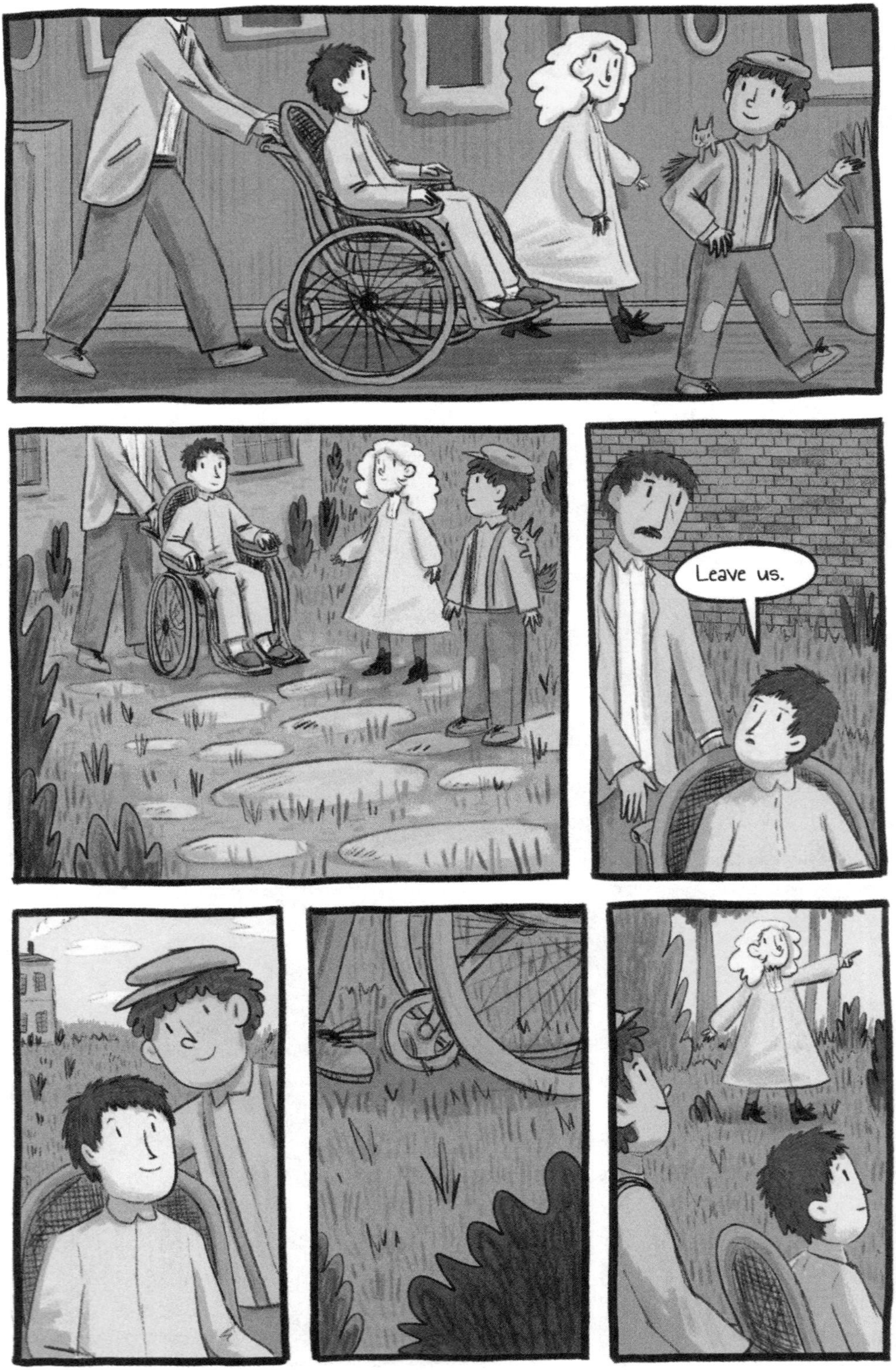
Leave us.

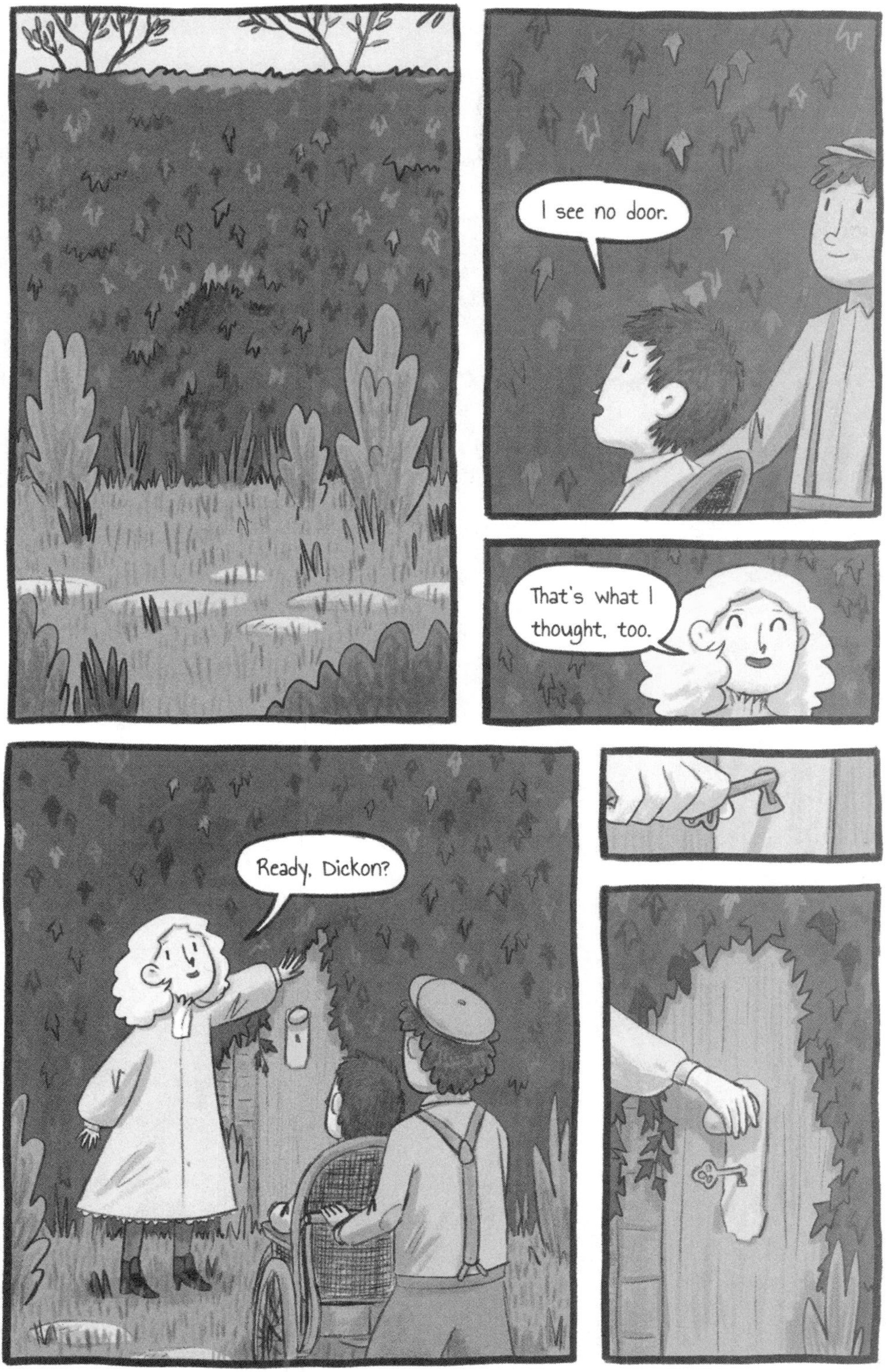
I see no door.
That's what I thought, too.
Ready, Dickon?

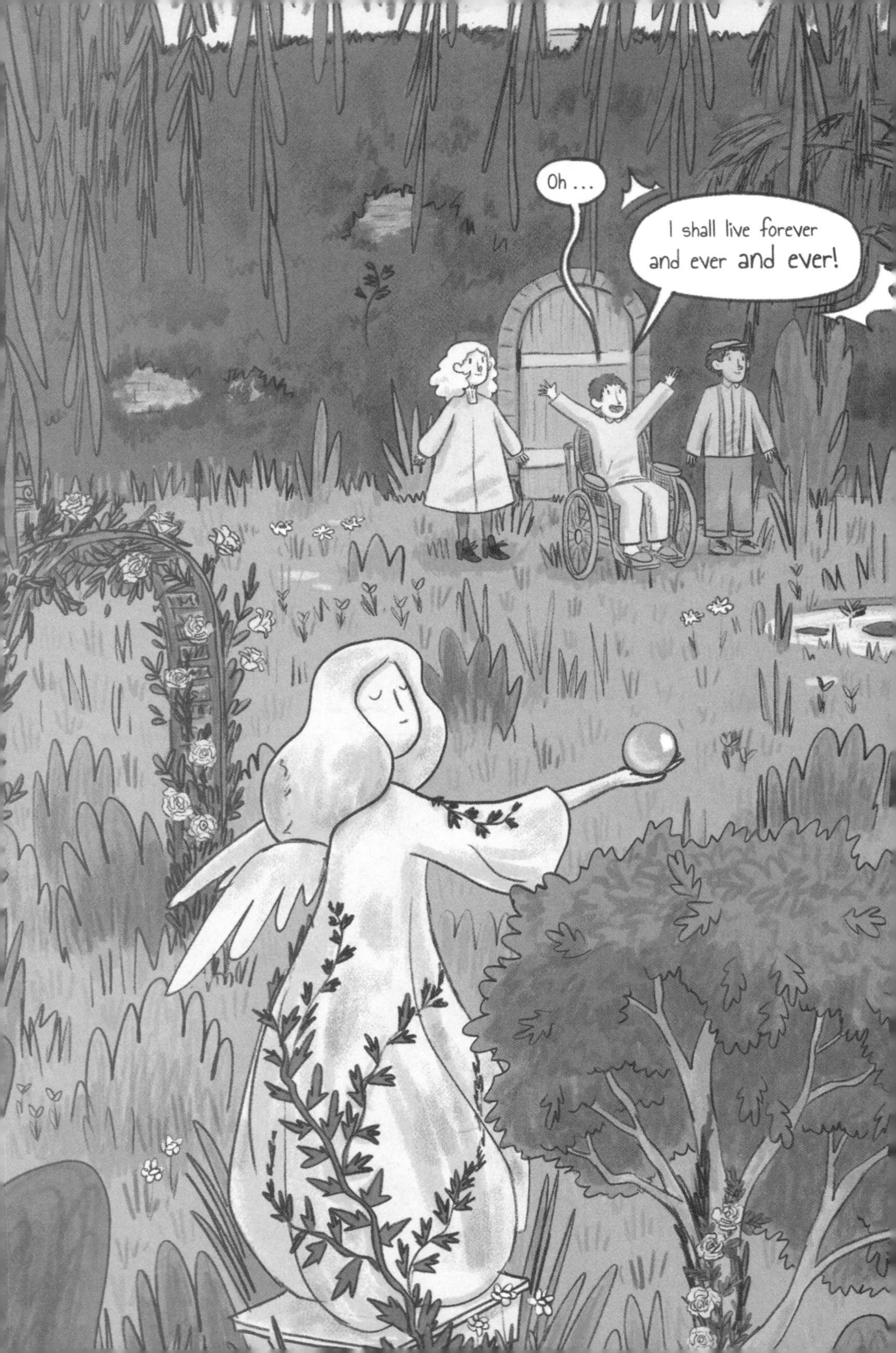
Oh . . .
I shall live forever and ever and ever!

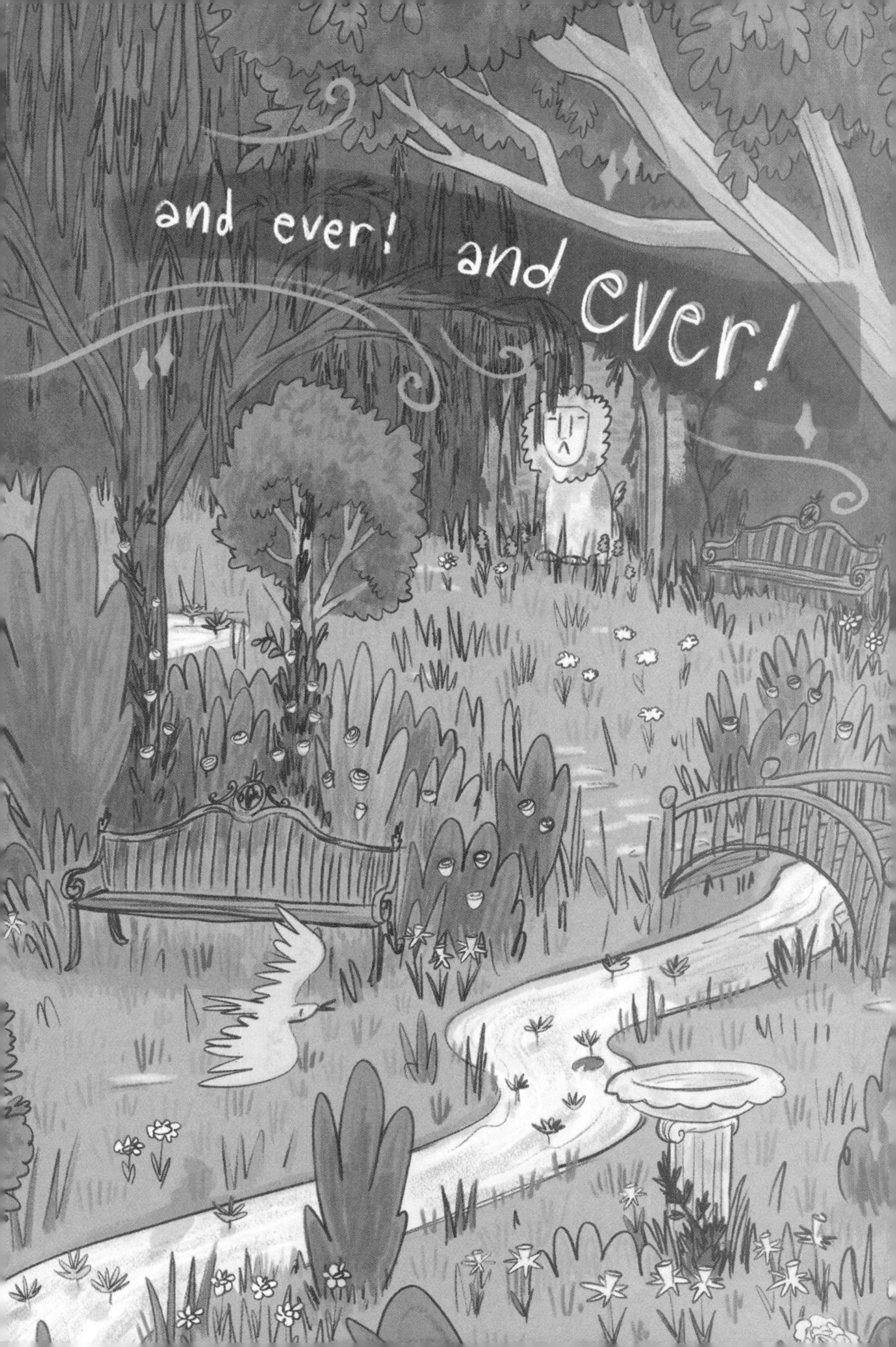
and ever!
and ever!

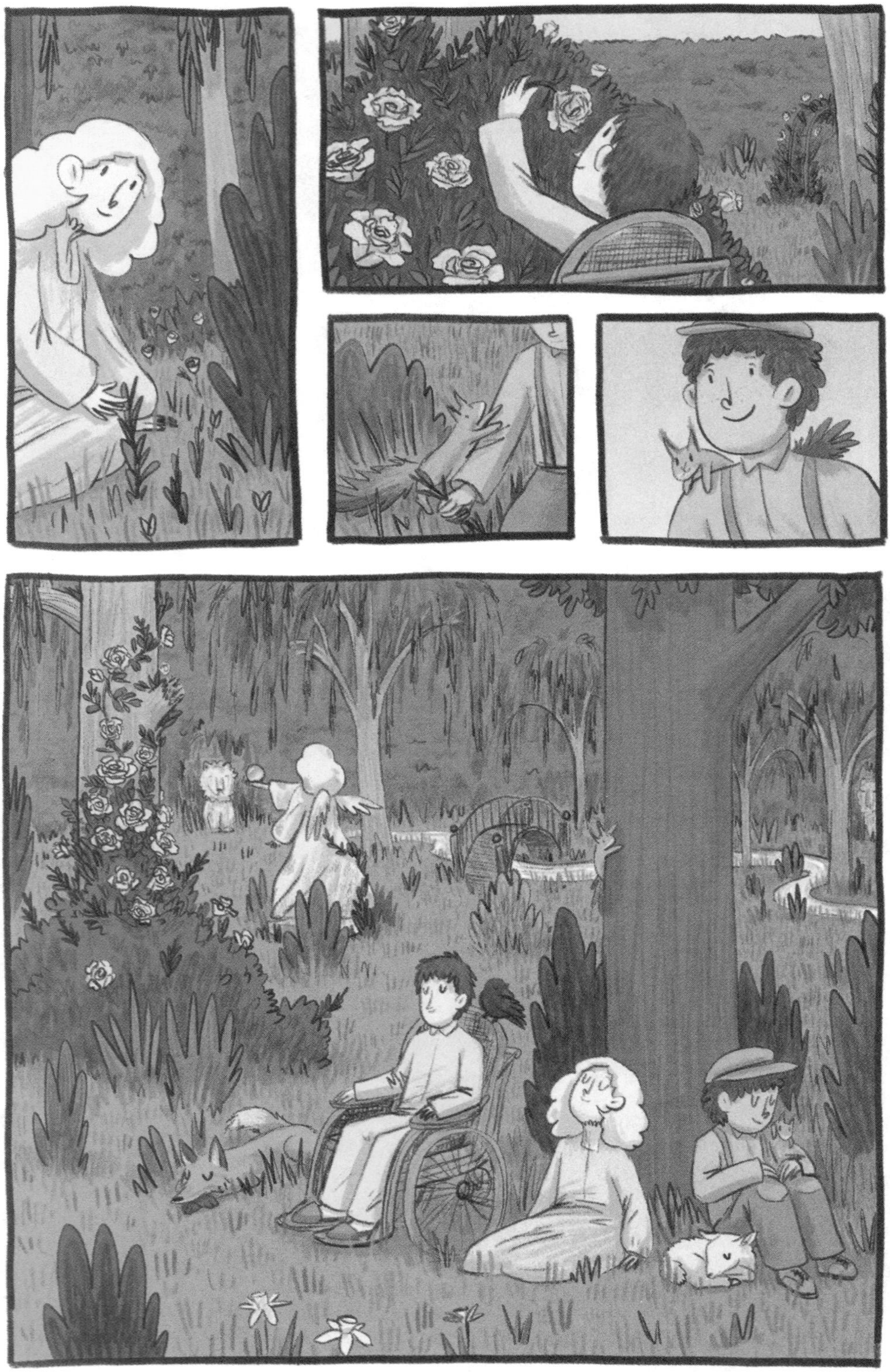

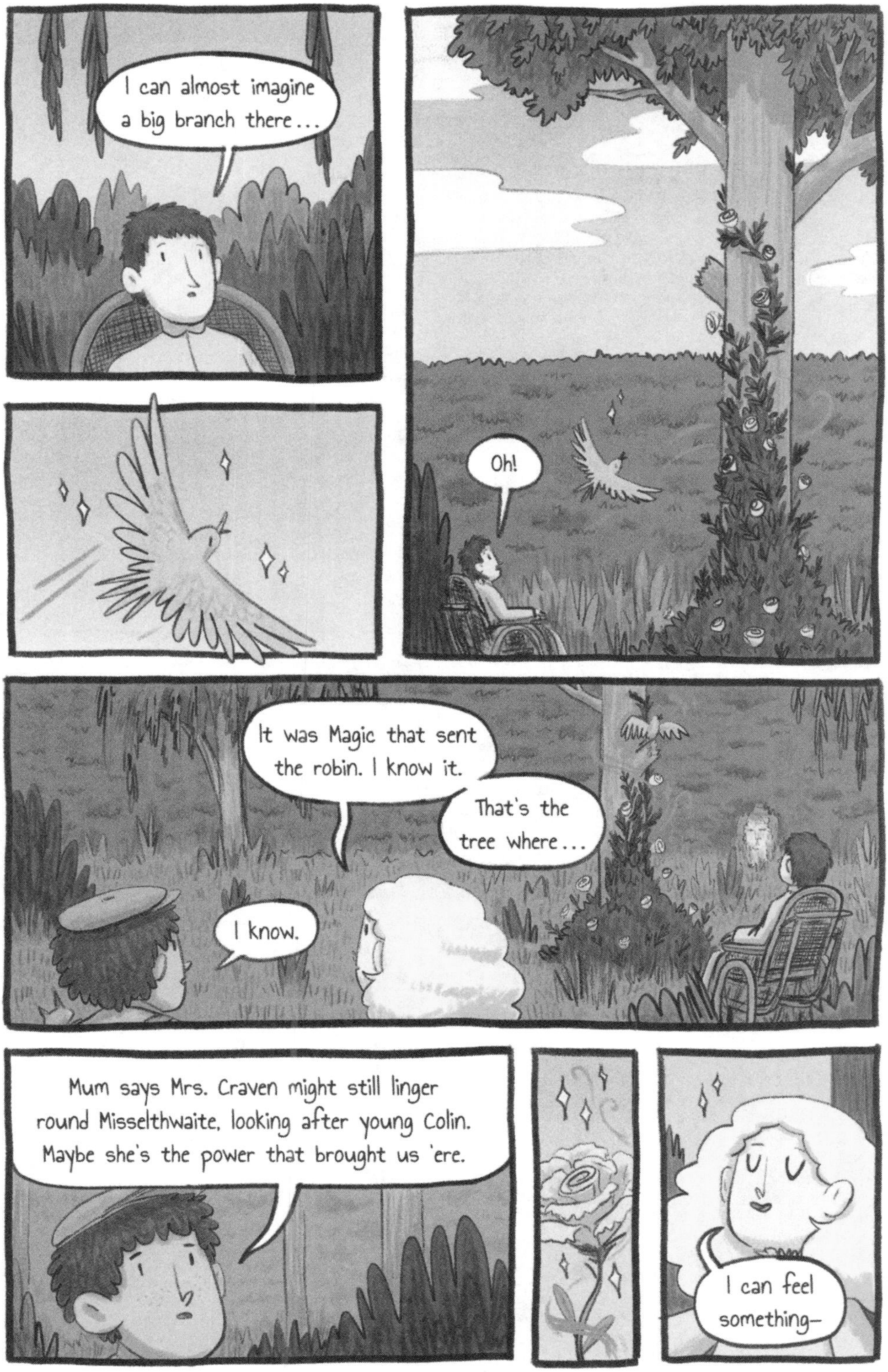
I can almost imagine a big branch there...
Oh!
It was Magic that sent the robin. I know it.
That's the tree where...
I know.
Mum says Mrs. Craven might still linger round Misselthwaite, looking after young Colin. Maybe she's the power that brought us 'ere.
I can feel something—

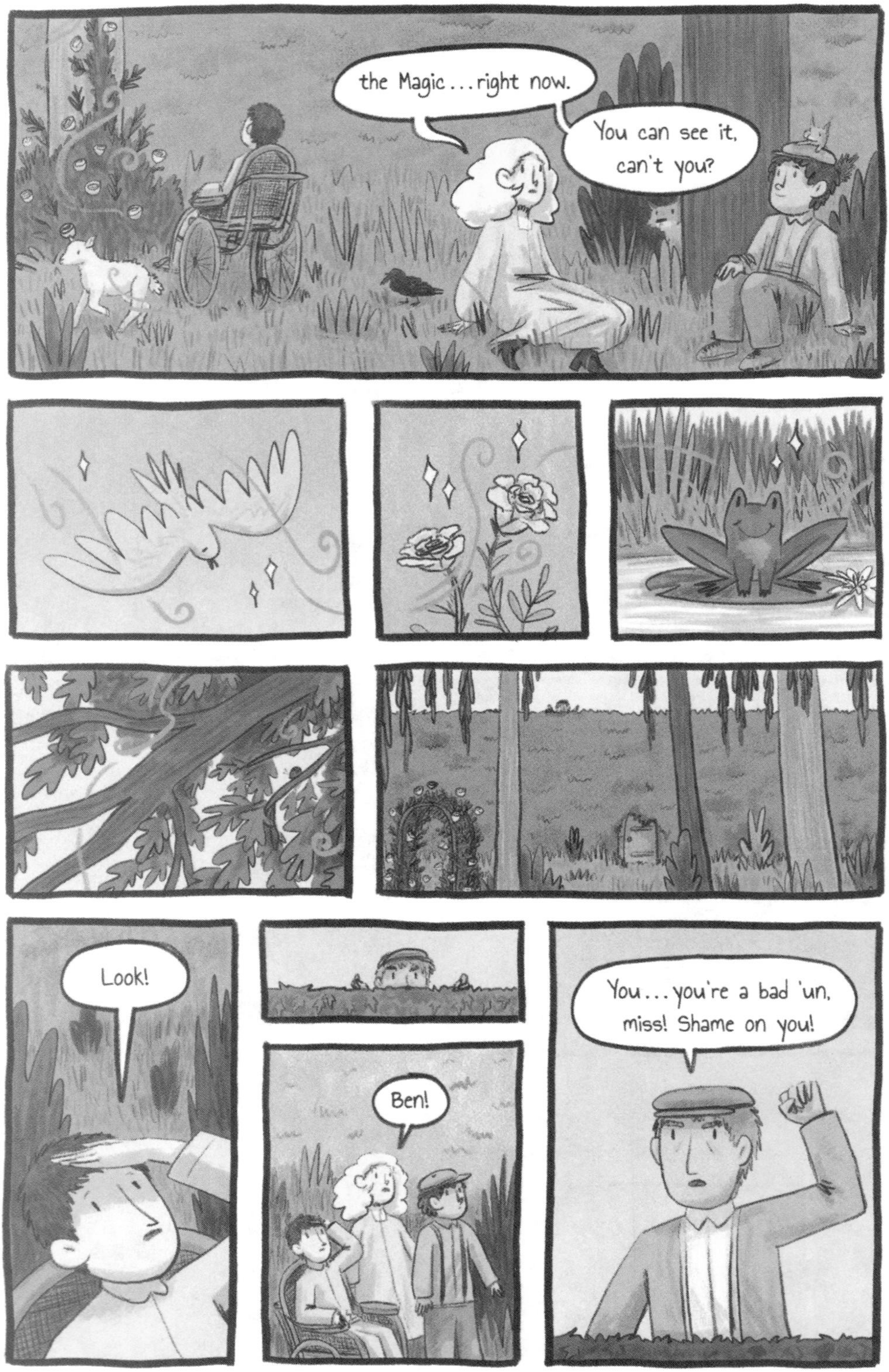
the Magic...right now.
You can see it, can't you?
Look!
Ben!
You...you're a bad 'un, miss! Shame on you!

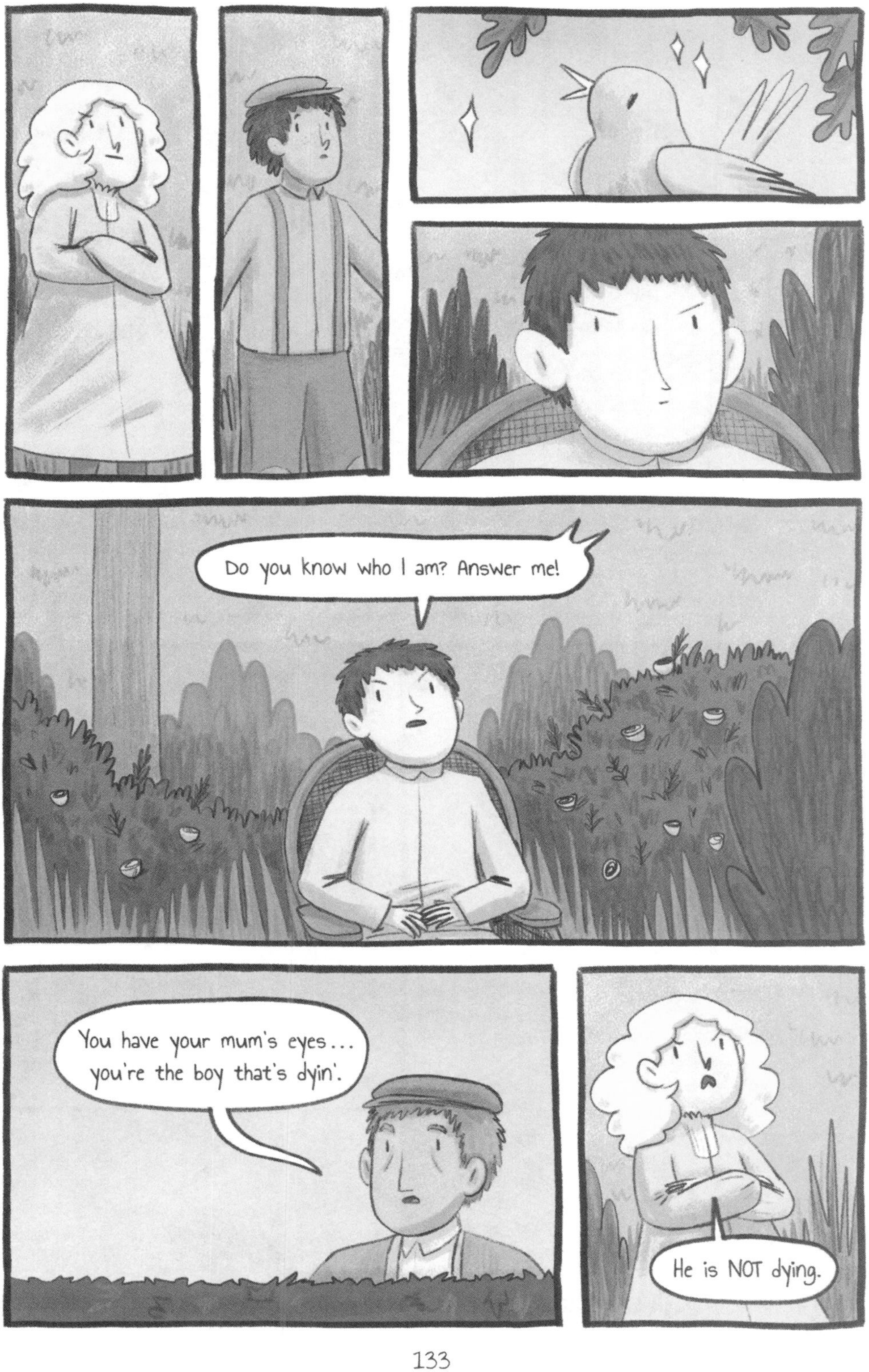
Do you know who I am? Answer me!
You have your mum's eyes... you're the boy that's dyin'.
He is NOT dying.

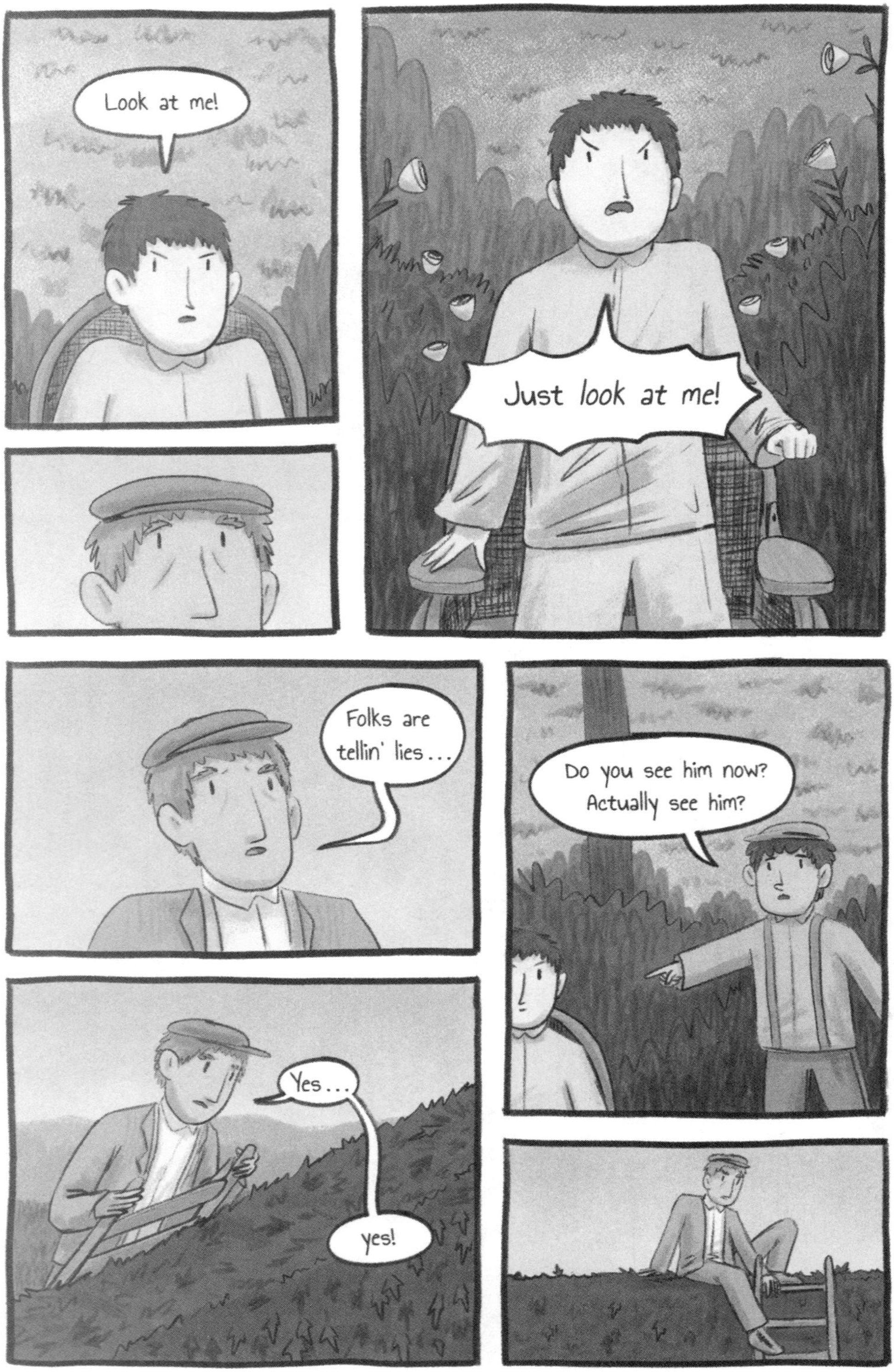
Look at me!
Just look at me!
Folks are tellin' lies...
Do you see him now? Actually see him?
Yes...
yes!

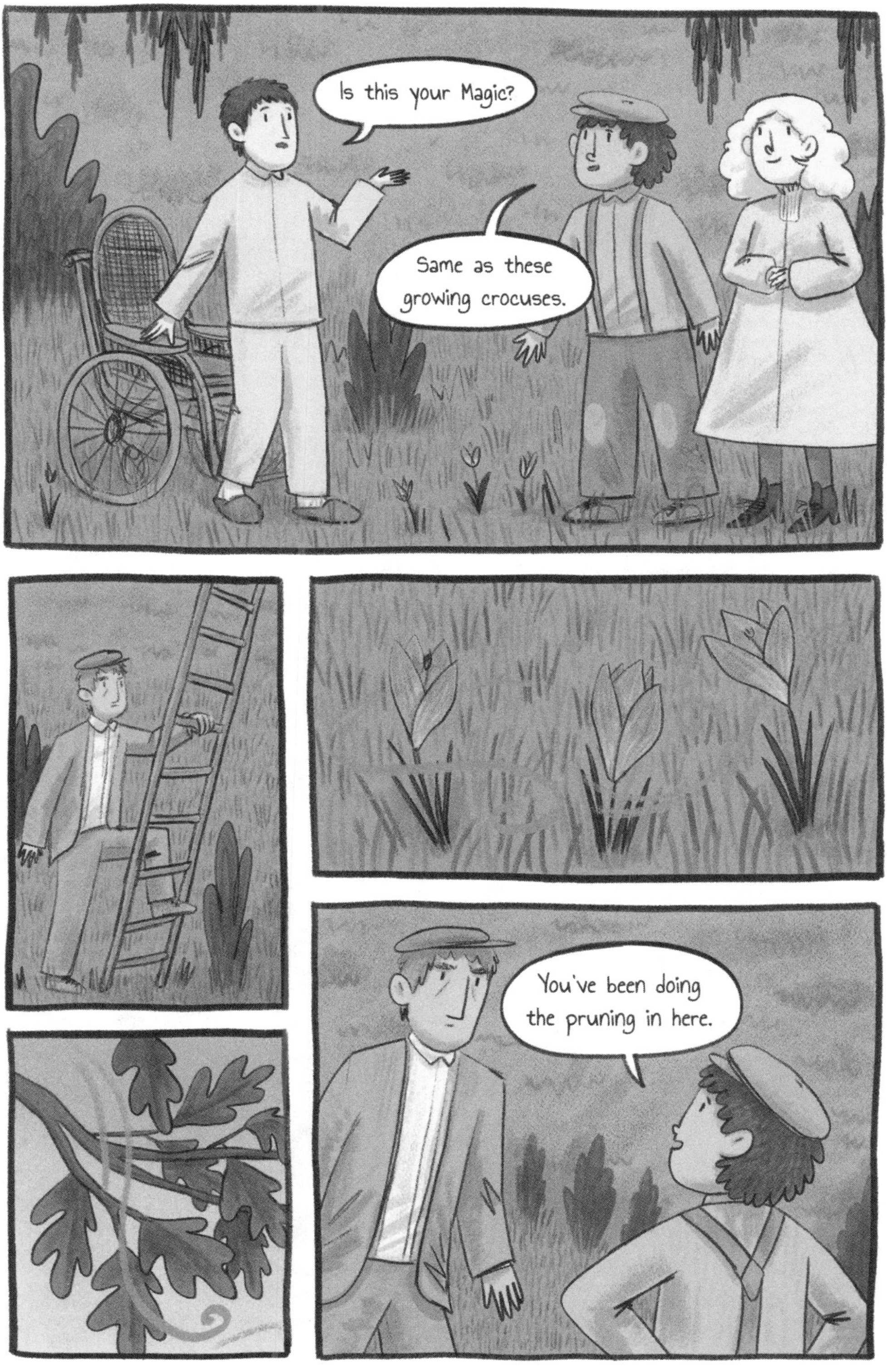
Is this your Magic?
Same as these growing crocuses.
You've been doing the pruning in here.

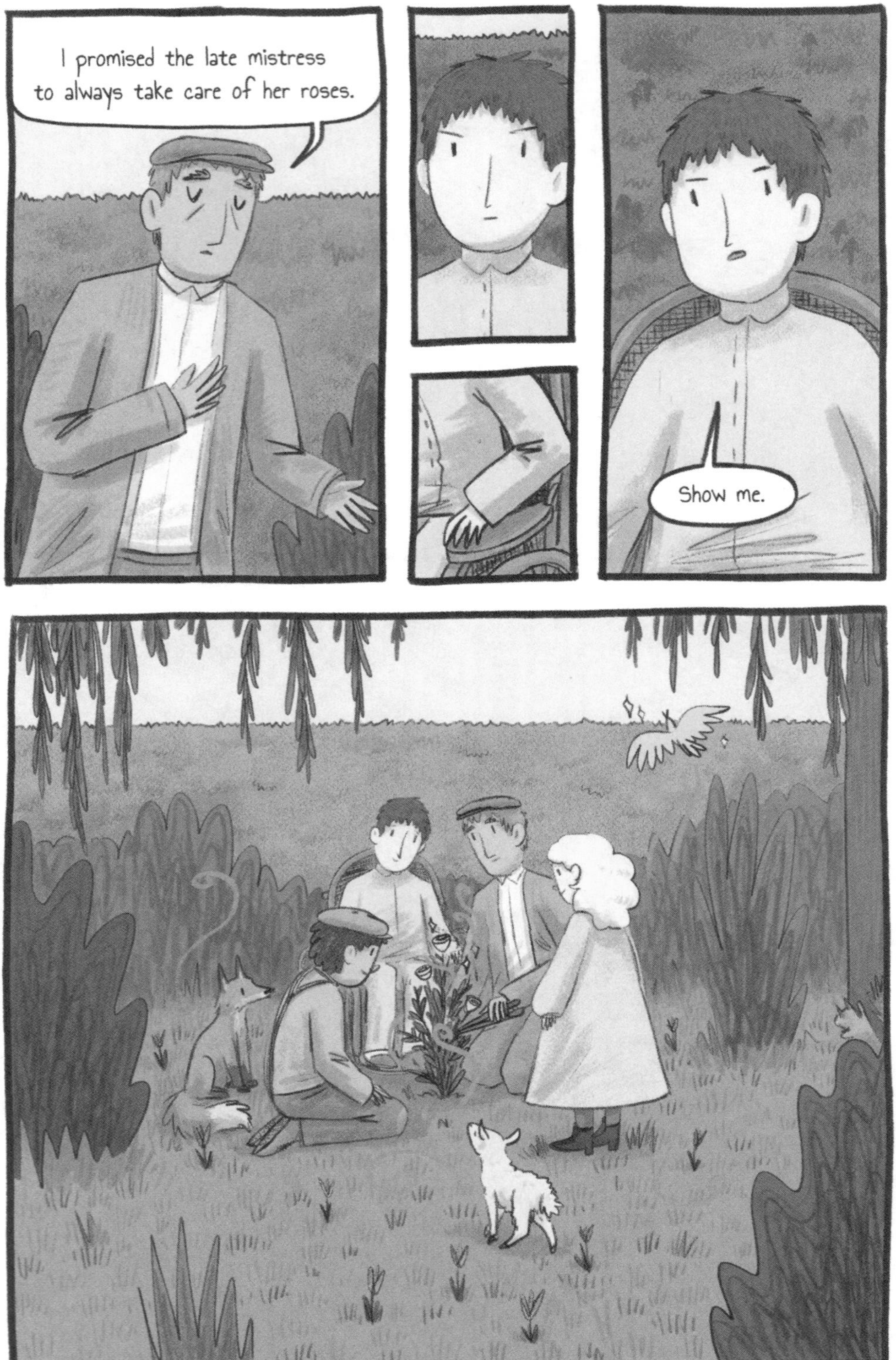
I promised the late mistress
to always take care of her roses.
Show me.

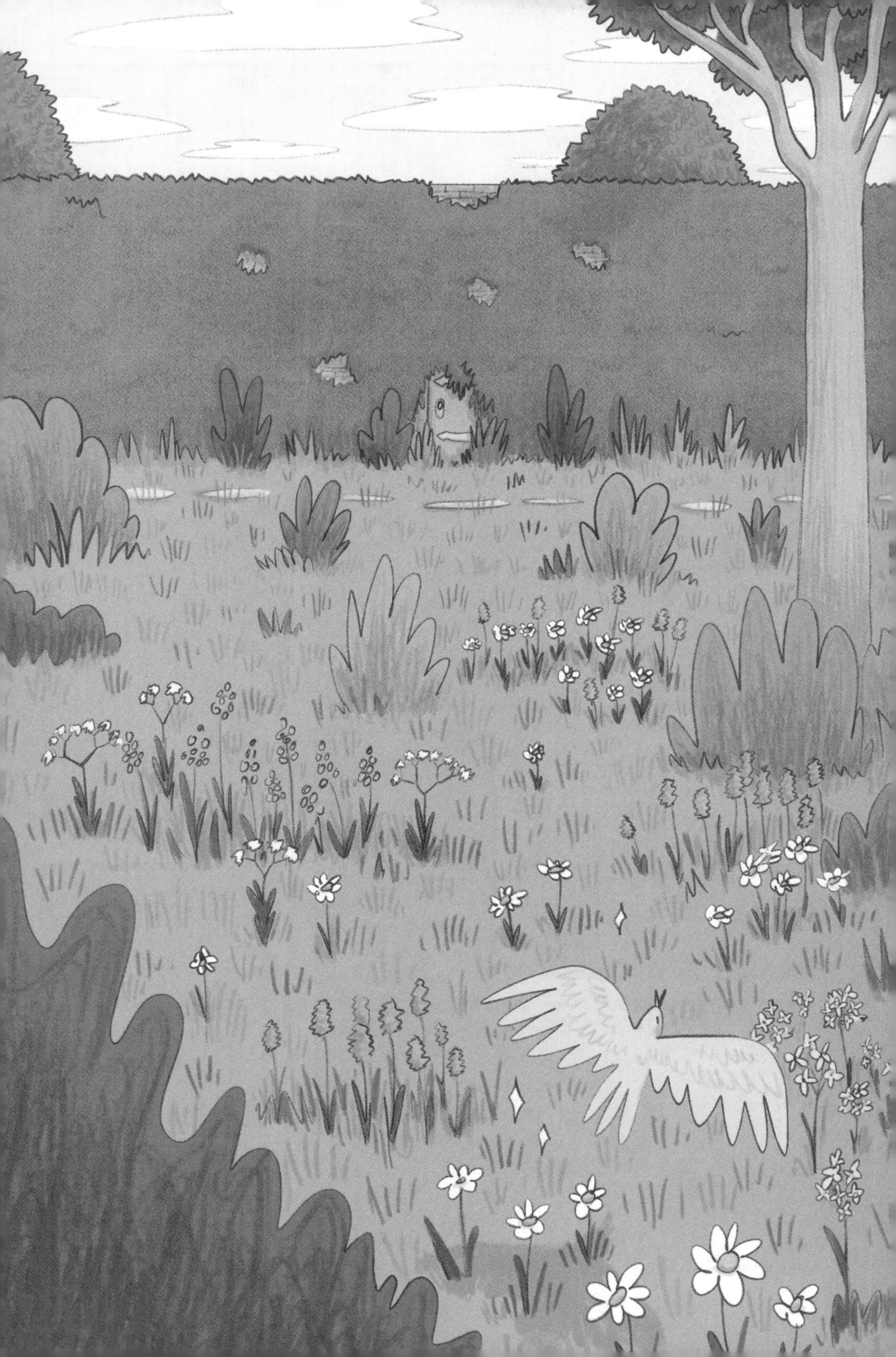

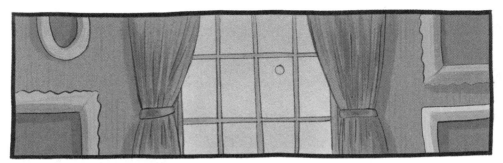

You've stayed out too long.

Today, I'm going out in the morning and afternoon.

I'm not sure I can allow that...

It would not be wise to try to stop me.

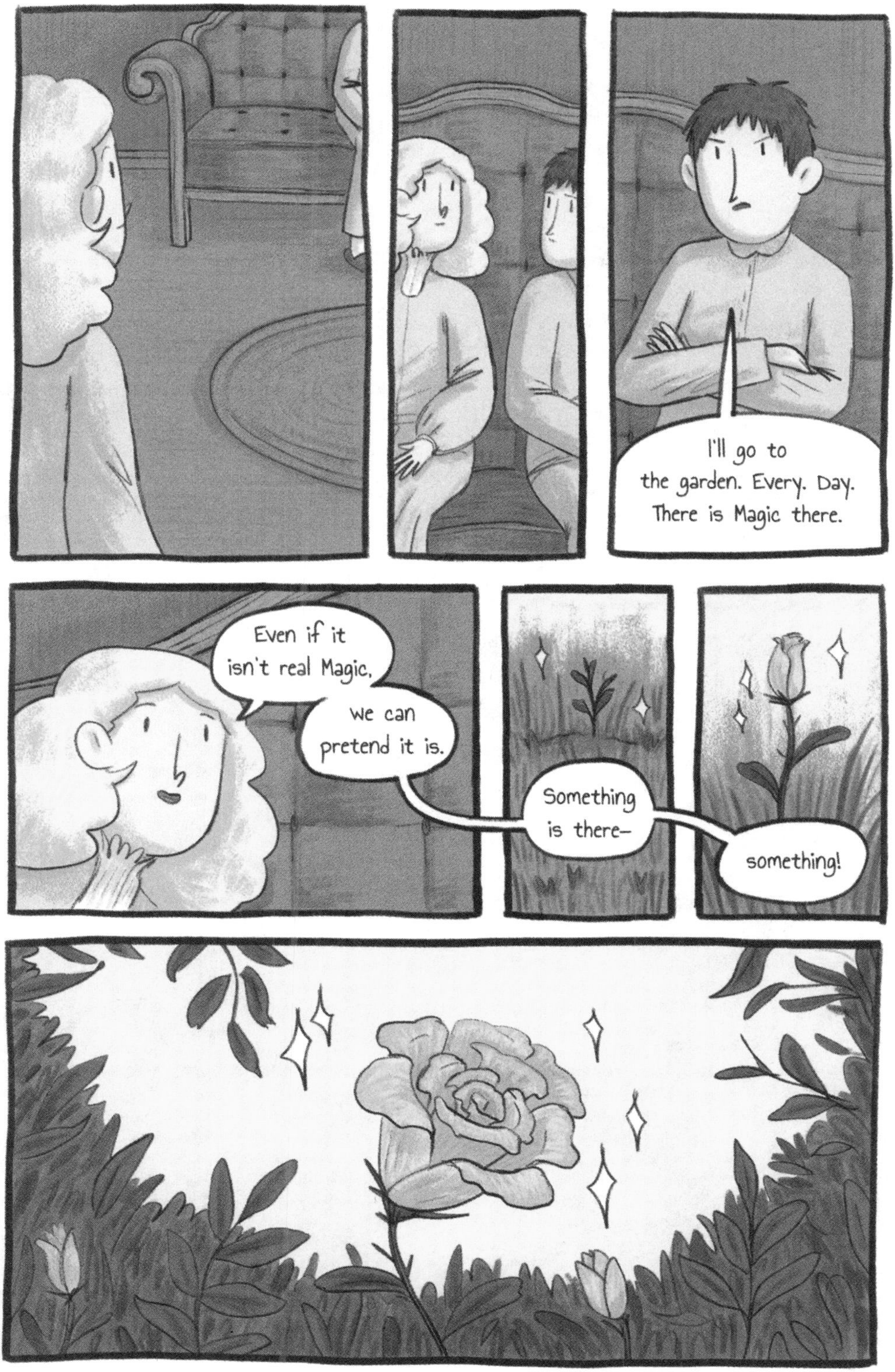
I'll go to
the garden. Every. Day.
There is Magic there.
Even if it
isn't real Magic,
we can
pretend it is.
Something
is there–
something!

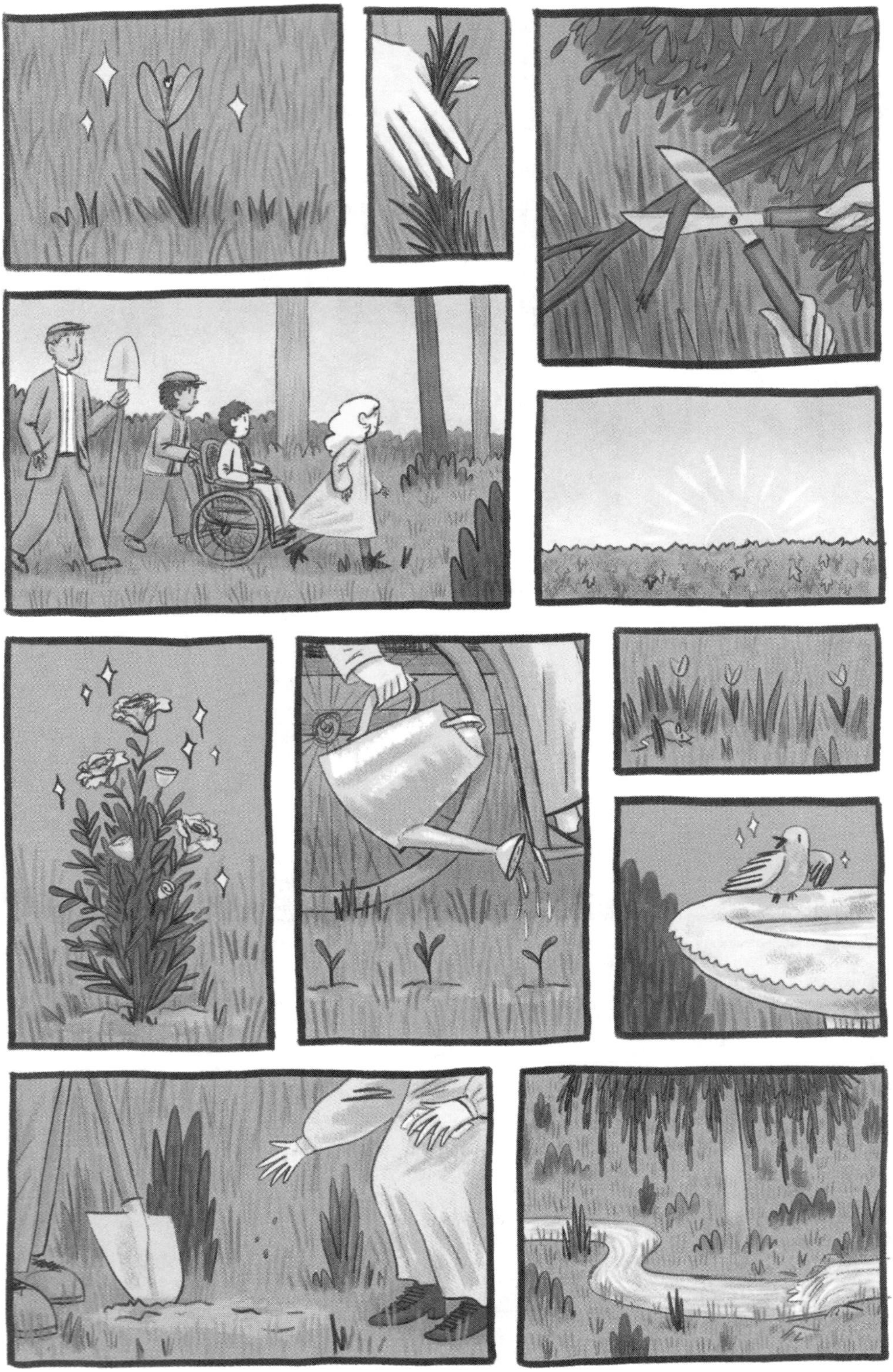

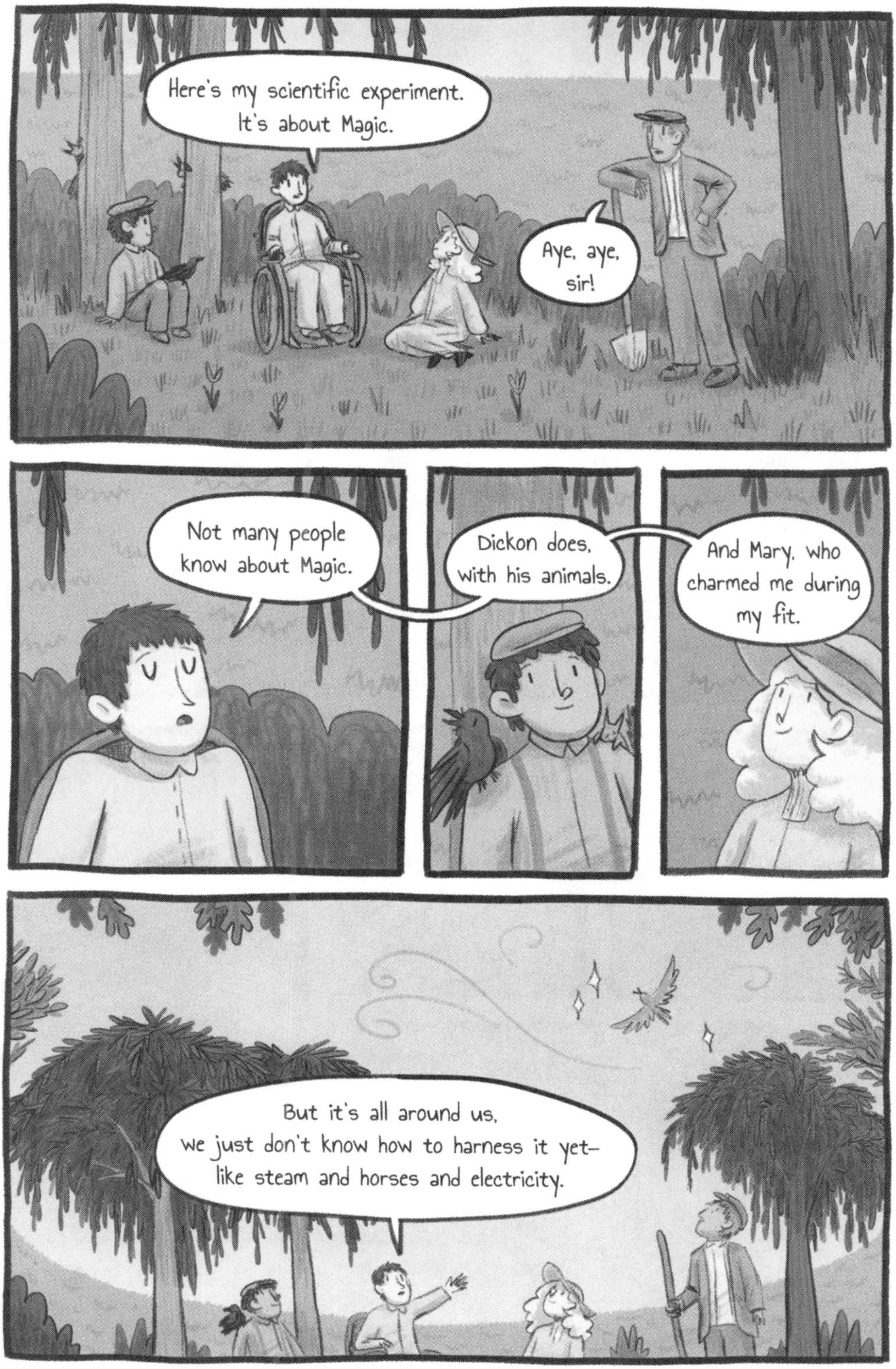
Here's my scientific experiment. It's about Magic.
Aye, aye, sir!
Not many people know about Magic.
Dickon does, with his animals.
And Mary, who charmed me during my fit.
But it's all around us, we just don't know how to harness it yet—like steam and horses and electricity.

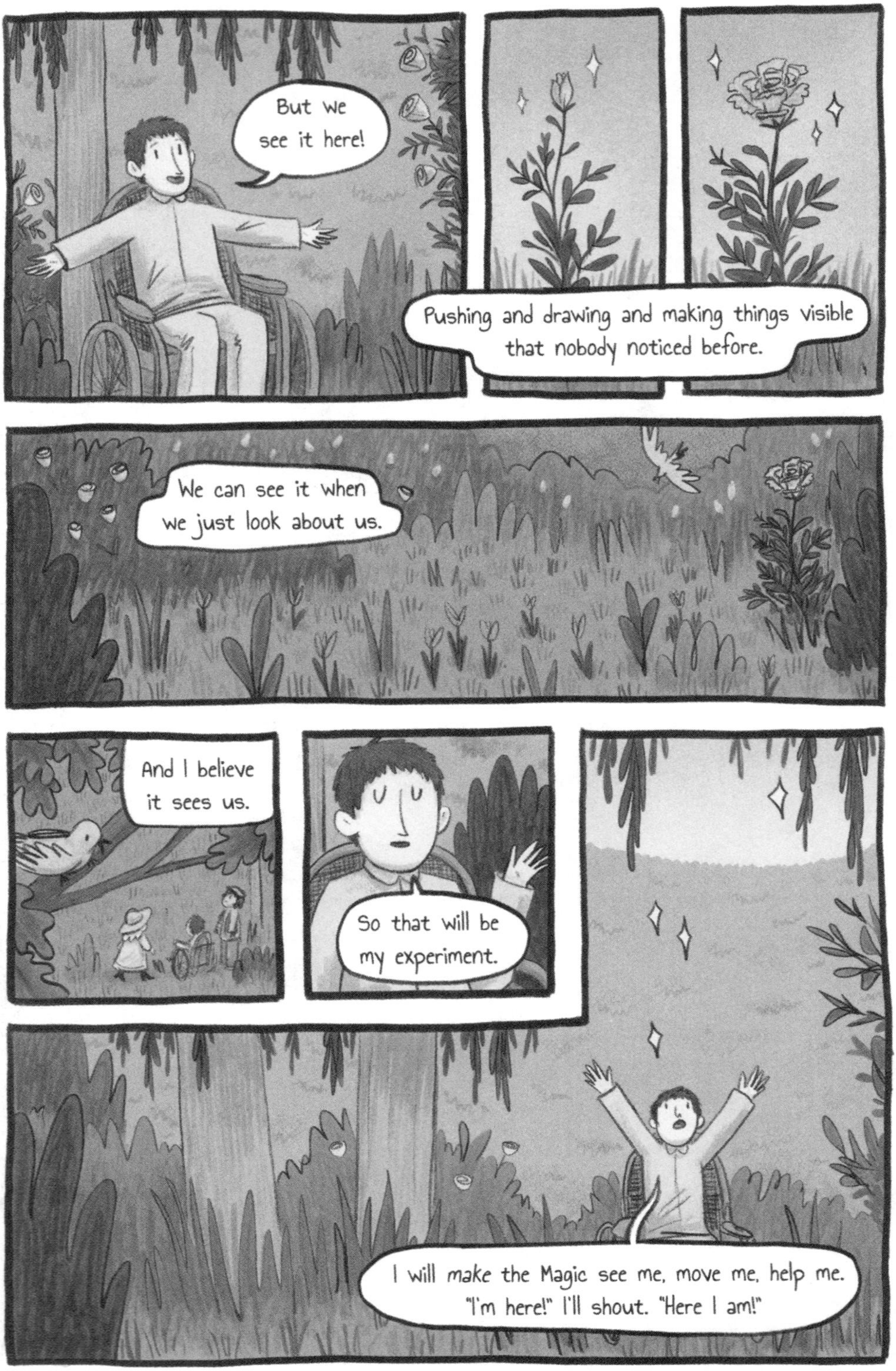
But we see it here!
Pushing and drawing and making things visible that nobody noticed before.
We can see it when we just look about us.
And I believe it sees us.
So that will be my experiment.
I will *make* the Magic see me, move me, help me. "I'm here!" I'll shout. "Here I am!"

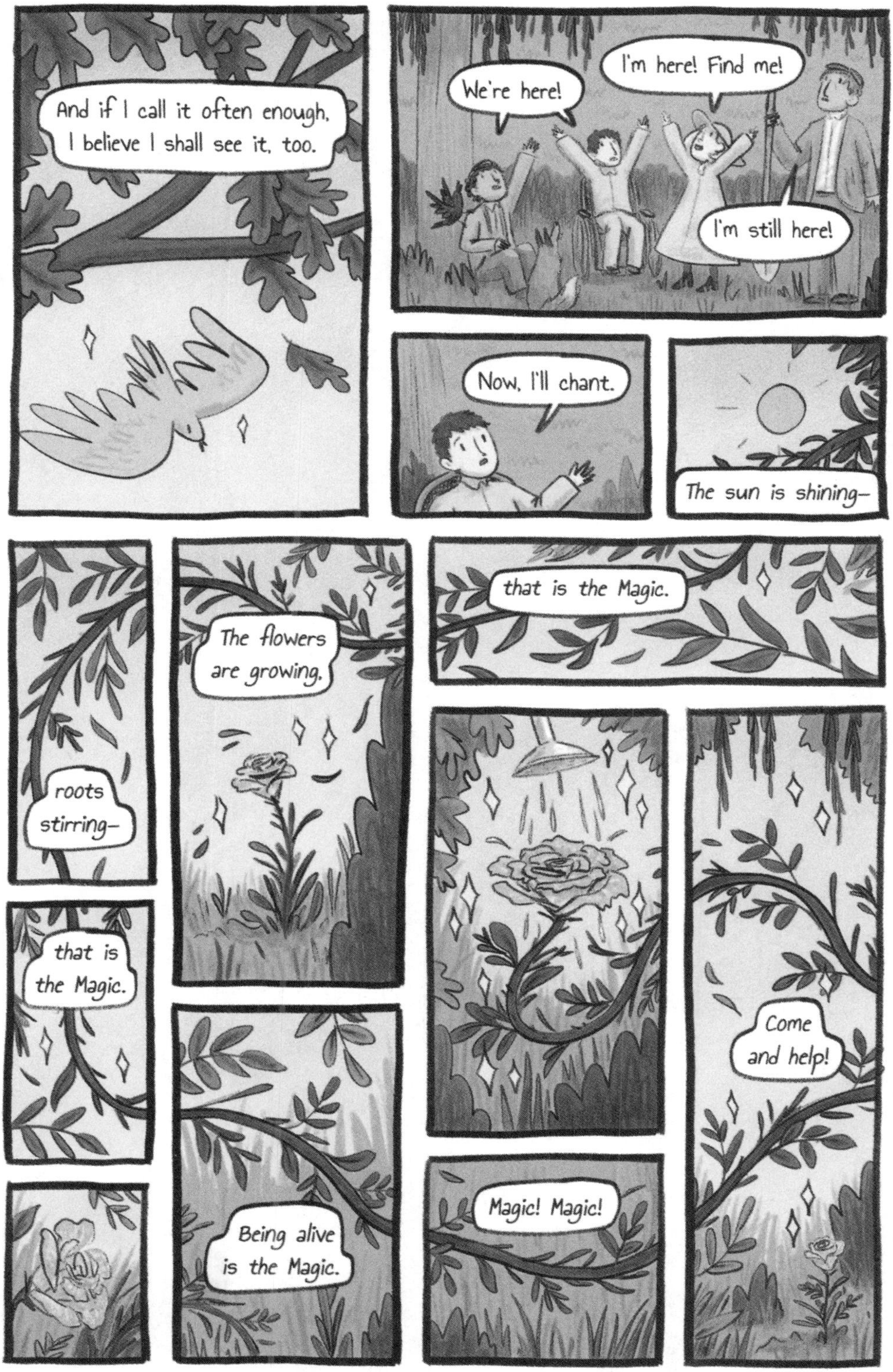
And if I call it often enough, I believe I shall see it, too.
We're here!
I'm here! Find me!
I'm still here!
Now, I'll chant.
The sun is shining—
roots stirring—
The flowers are growing,
that is the Magic.
that is the Magic.
Being alive is the Magic.
Magic! Magic!
Come and help!

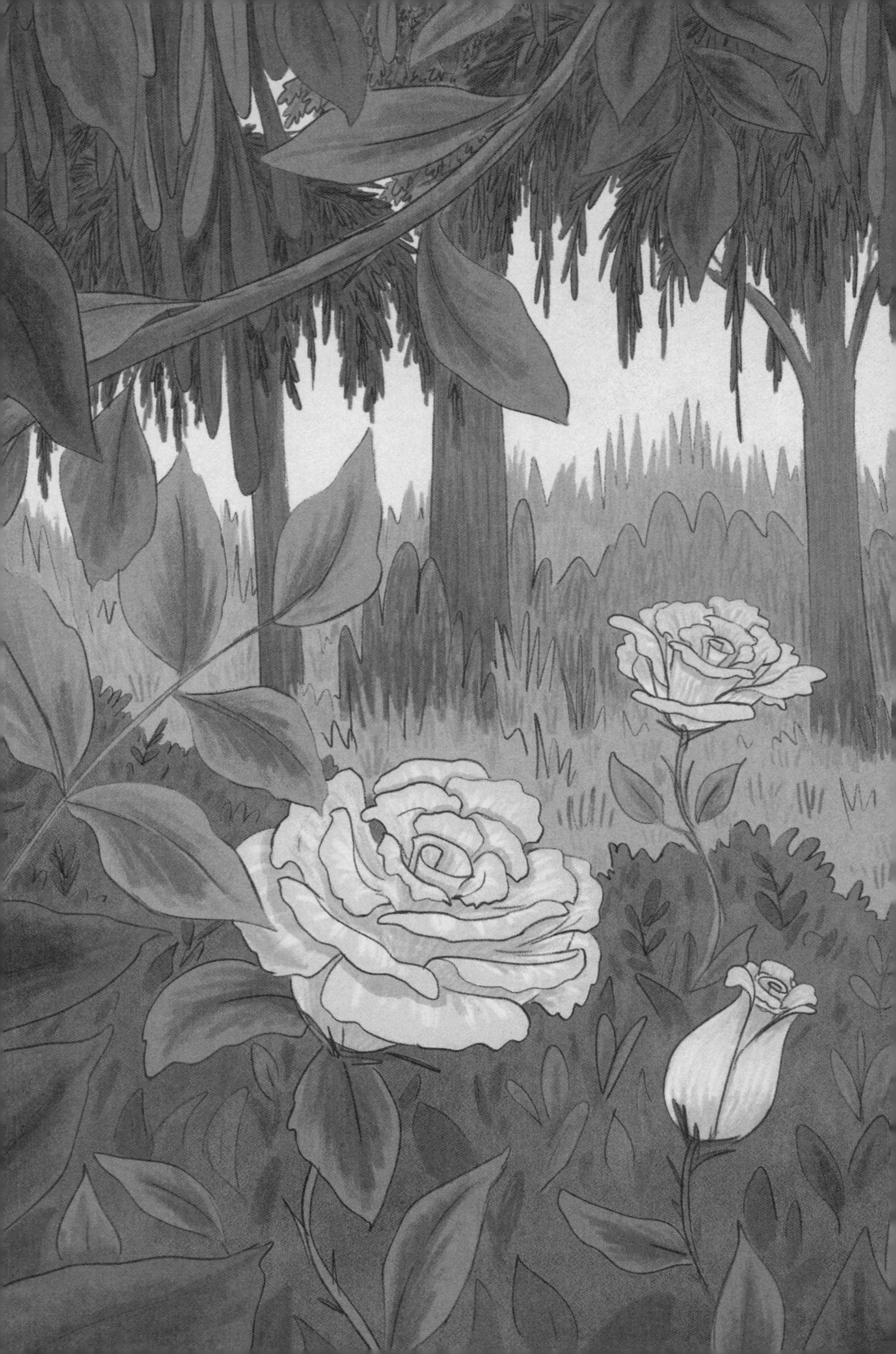

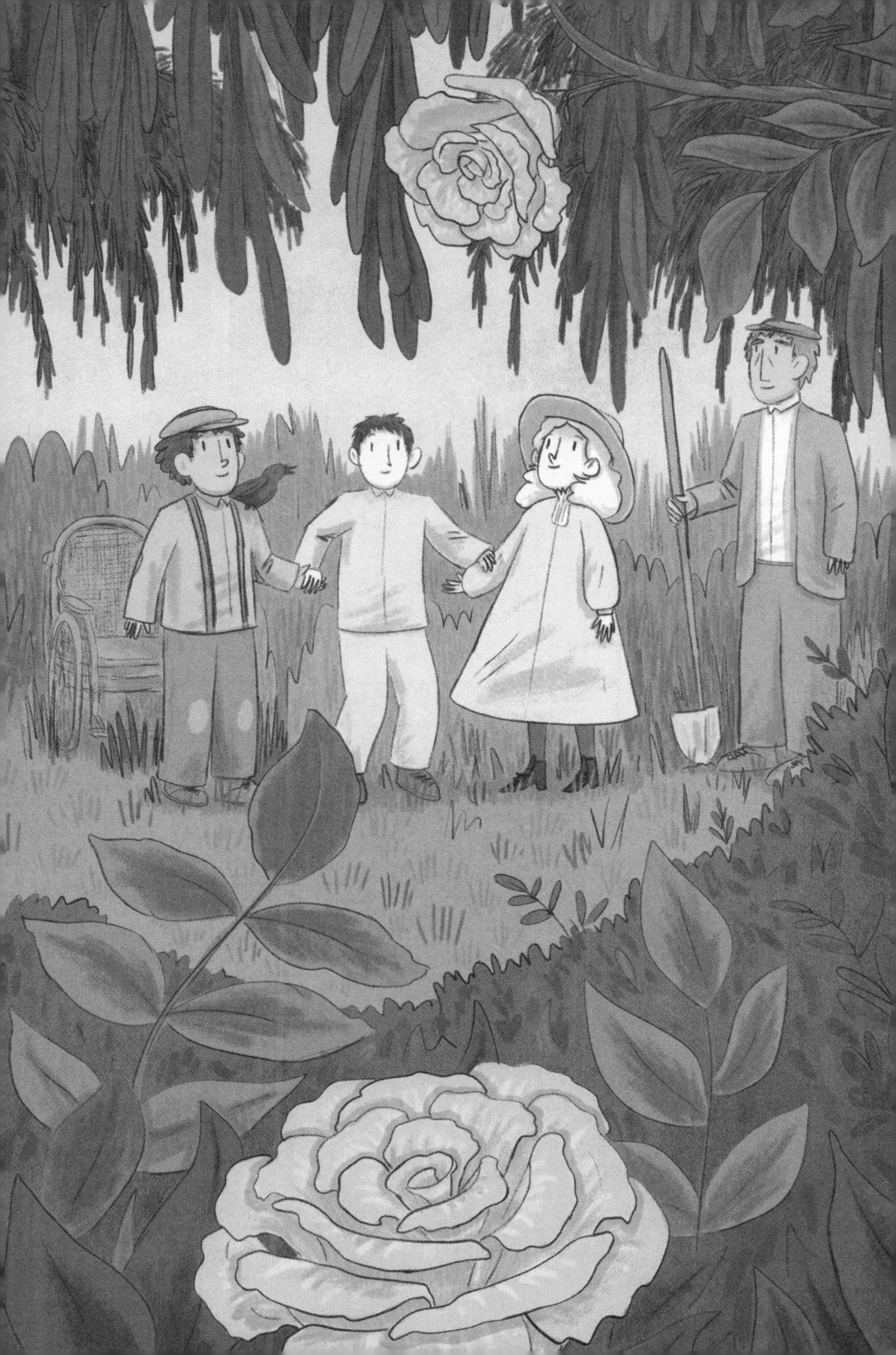

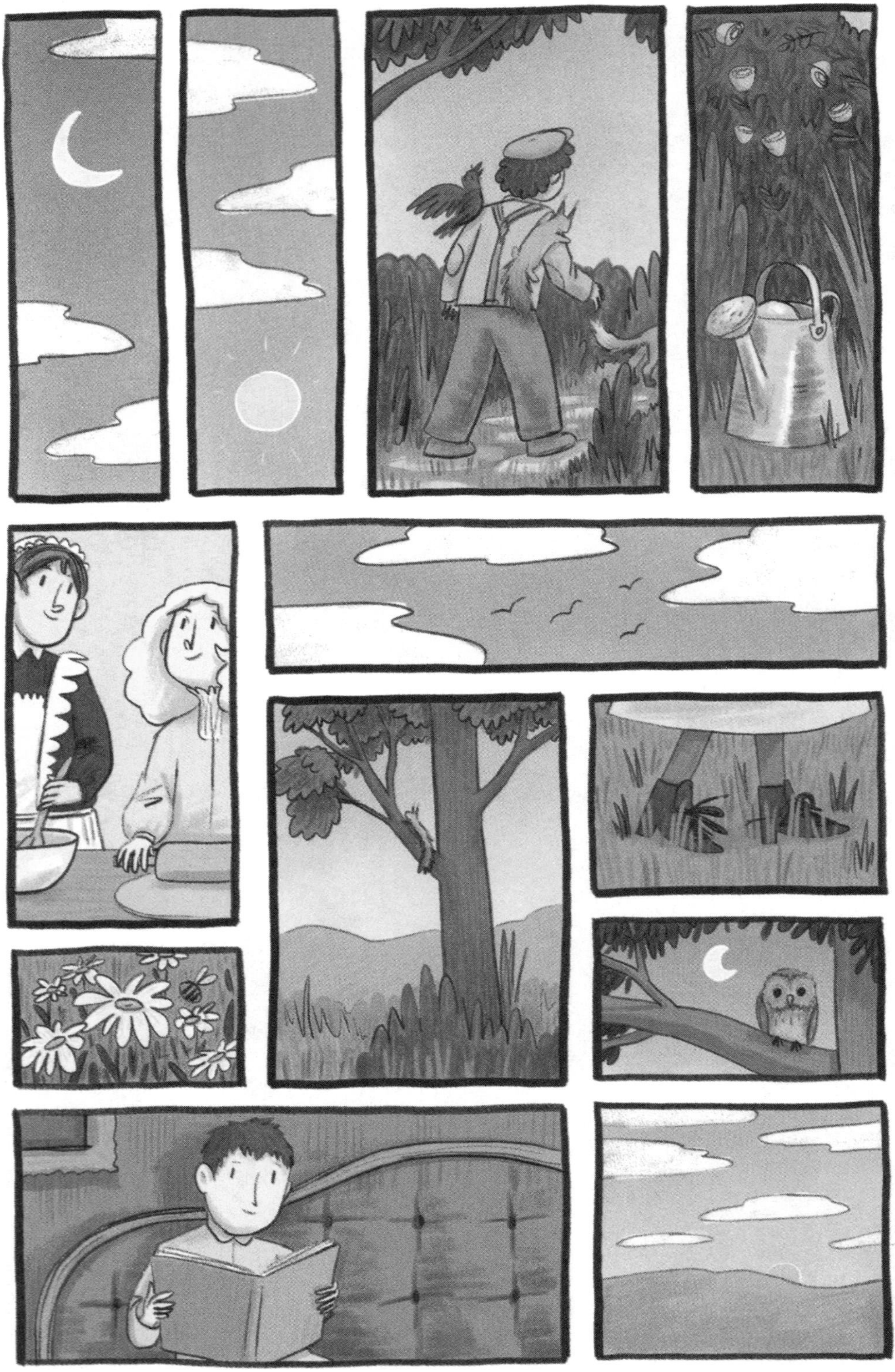

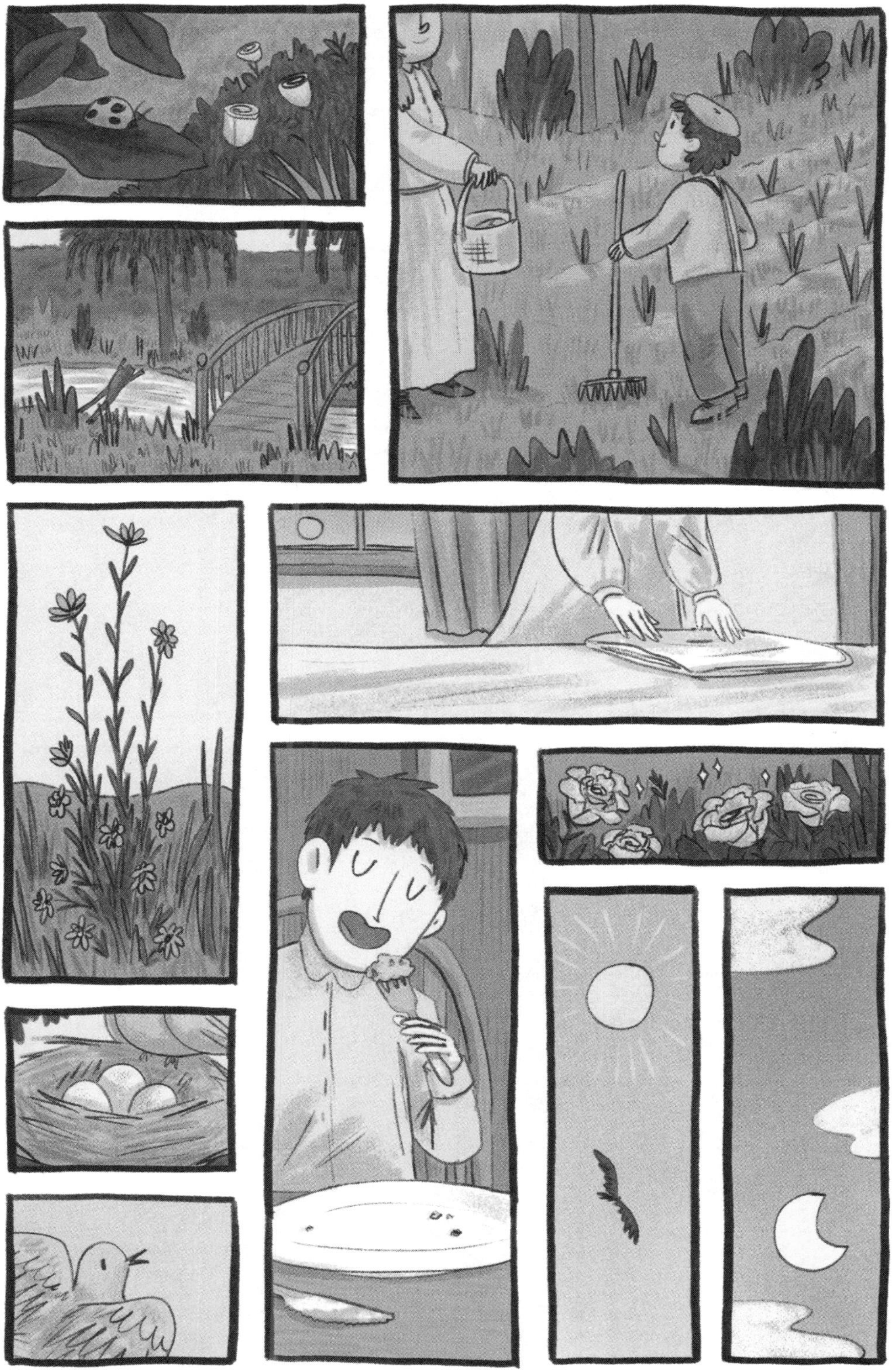

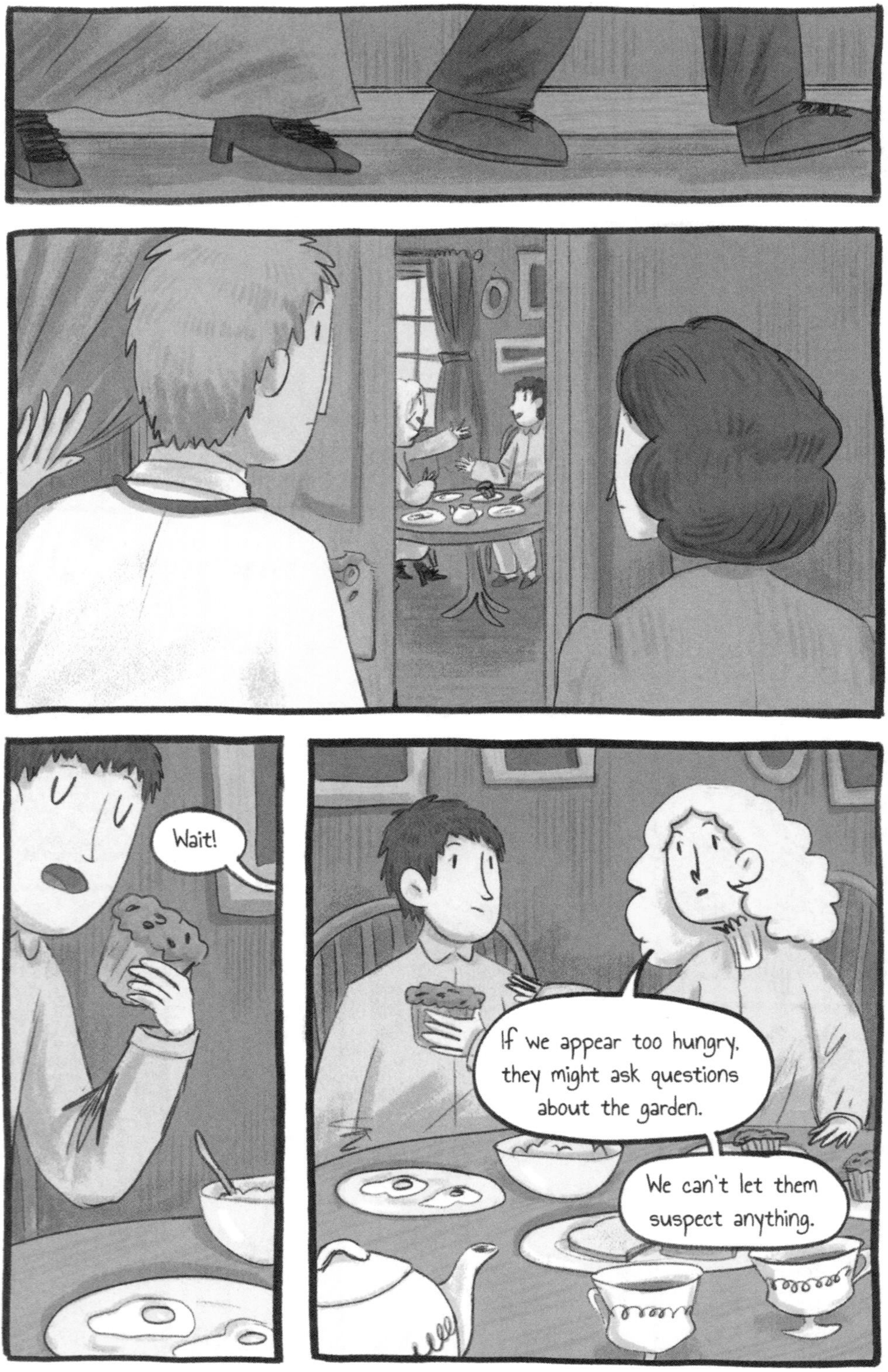

Wait!
If we appear too hungry, they might ask questions about the garden.
We can't let them suspect anything.

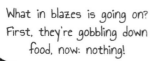
What in blazes is going on? First, they're gobbling down food, now: nothing!

How peculiar...

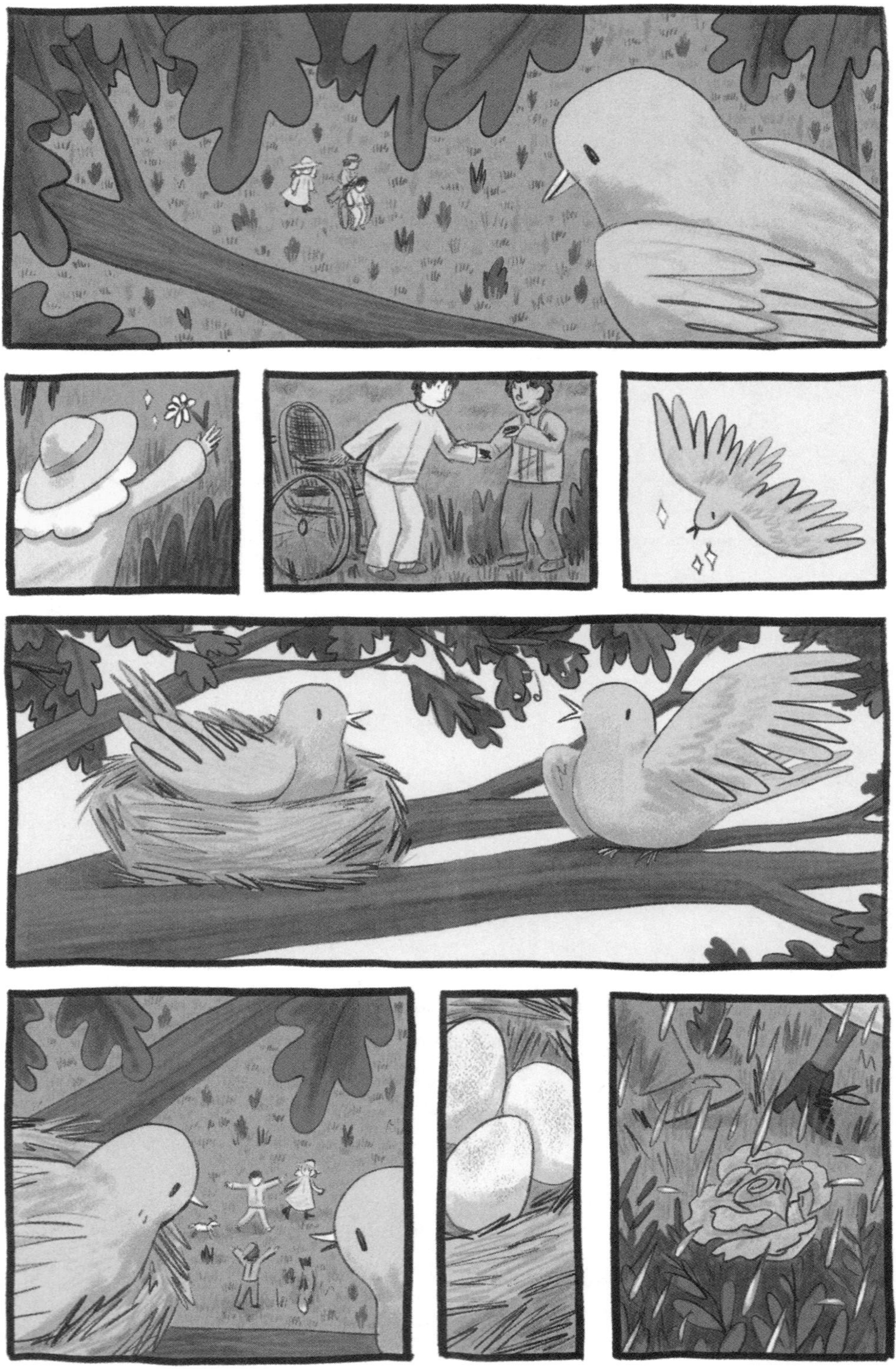

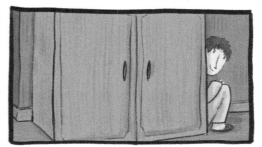

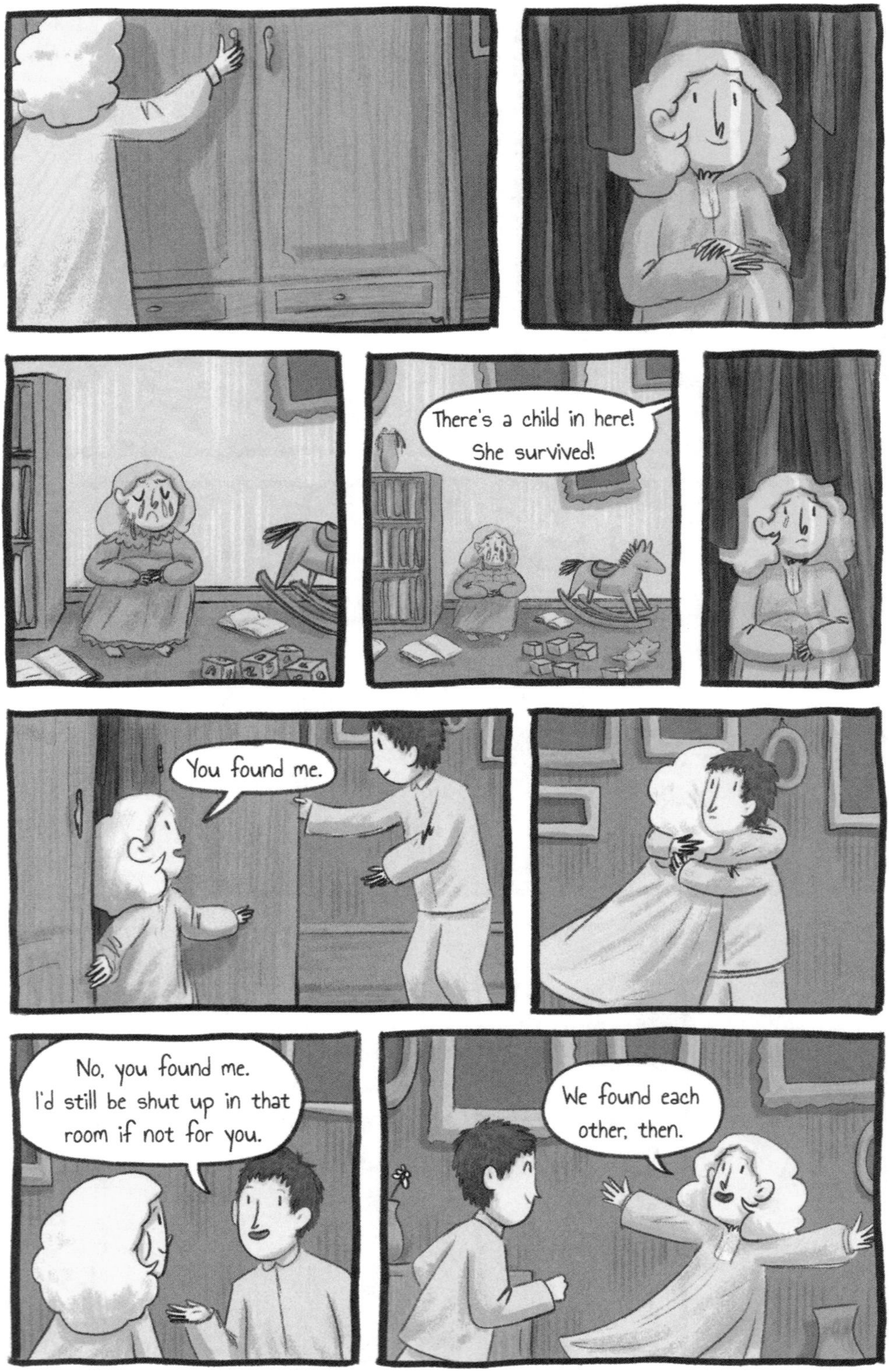
There's a child in here!
She survived!
You found me.
No, you found me.
I'd still be shut up in that
room if not for you.
We found each
other, then.

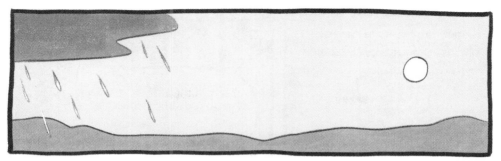

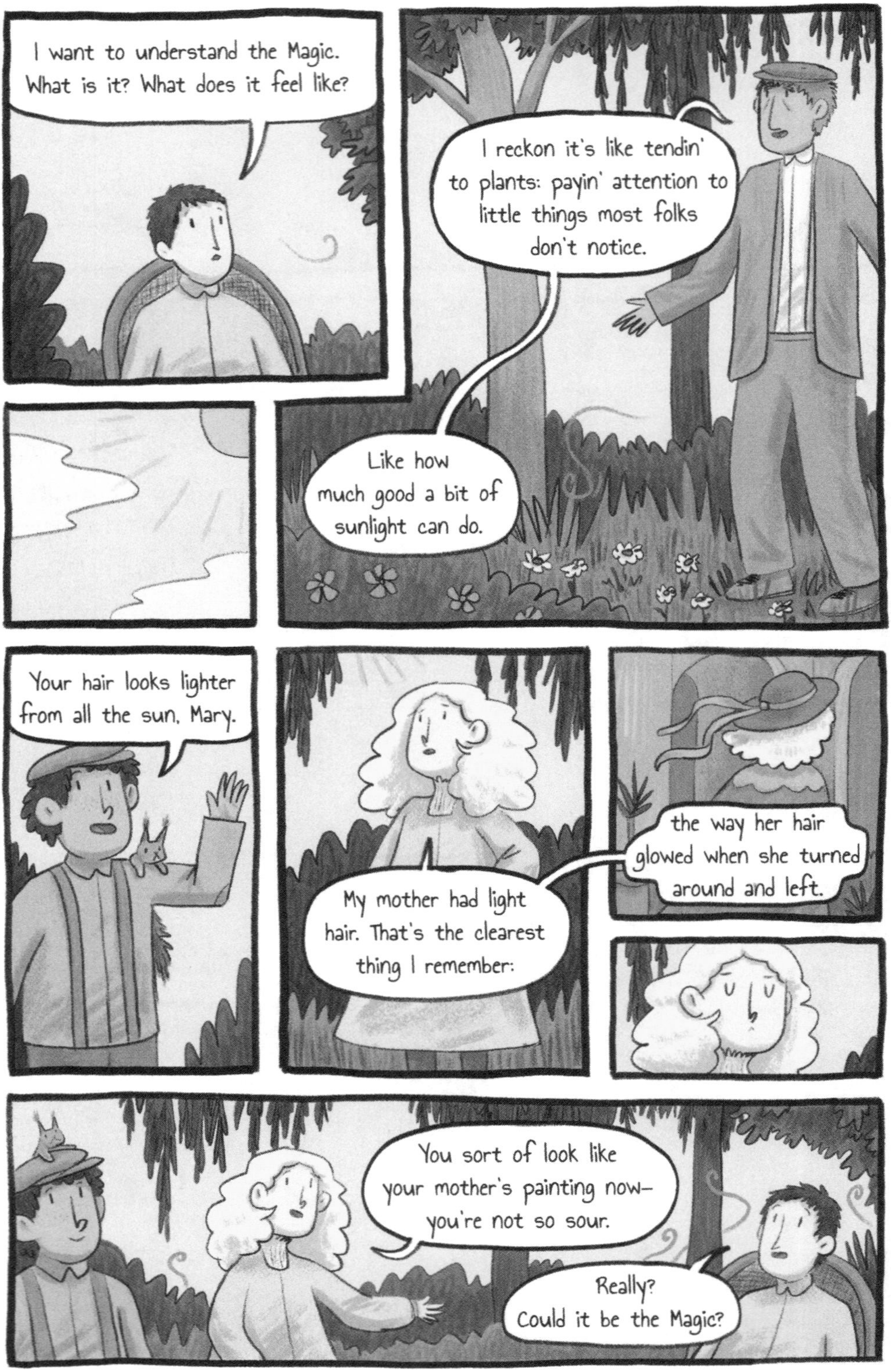
I want to understand the Magic. What is it? What does it feel like?
I reckon it's like tendin' to plants: payin' attention to little things most folks don't notice.
Like how much good a bit of sunlight can do.
Your hair looks lighter from all the sun, Mary.
My mother had light hair. That's the clearest thing I remember:
the way her hair glowed when she turned around and left.
You sort of look like your mother's painting now– you're not so sour.
Really? Could it be the Magic?

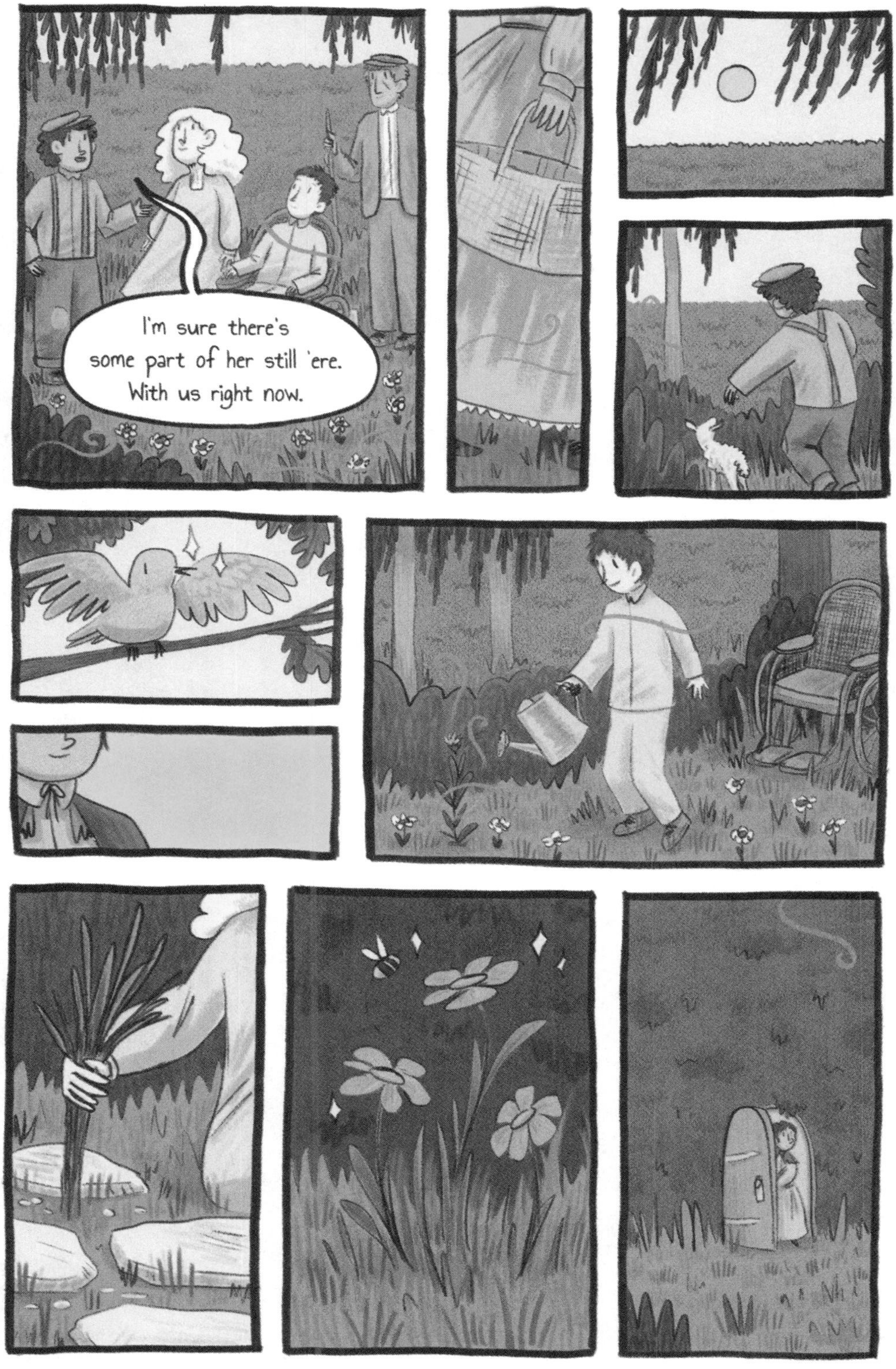
I'm sure there's some part of her still 'ere. With us right now.

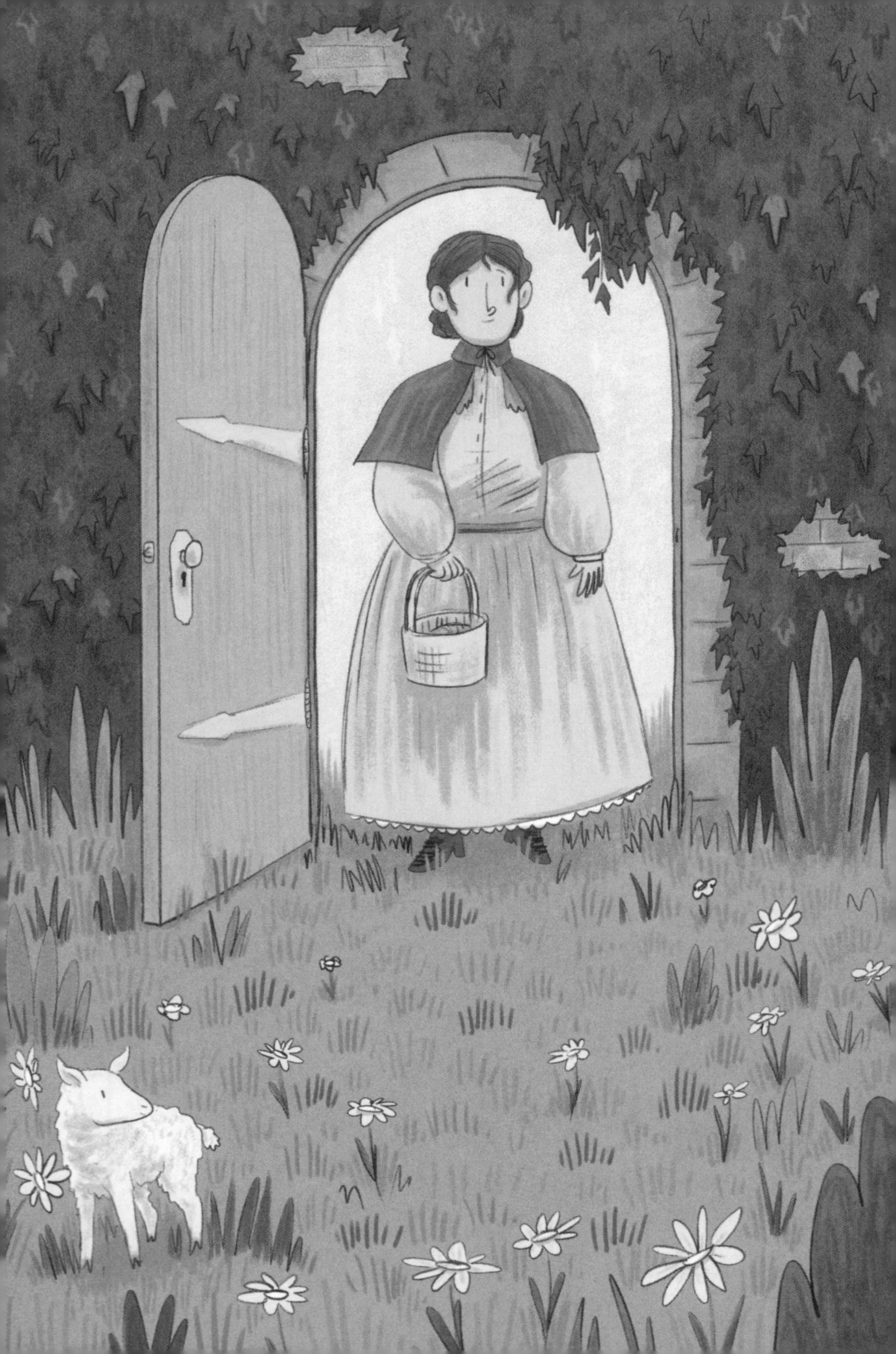

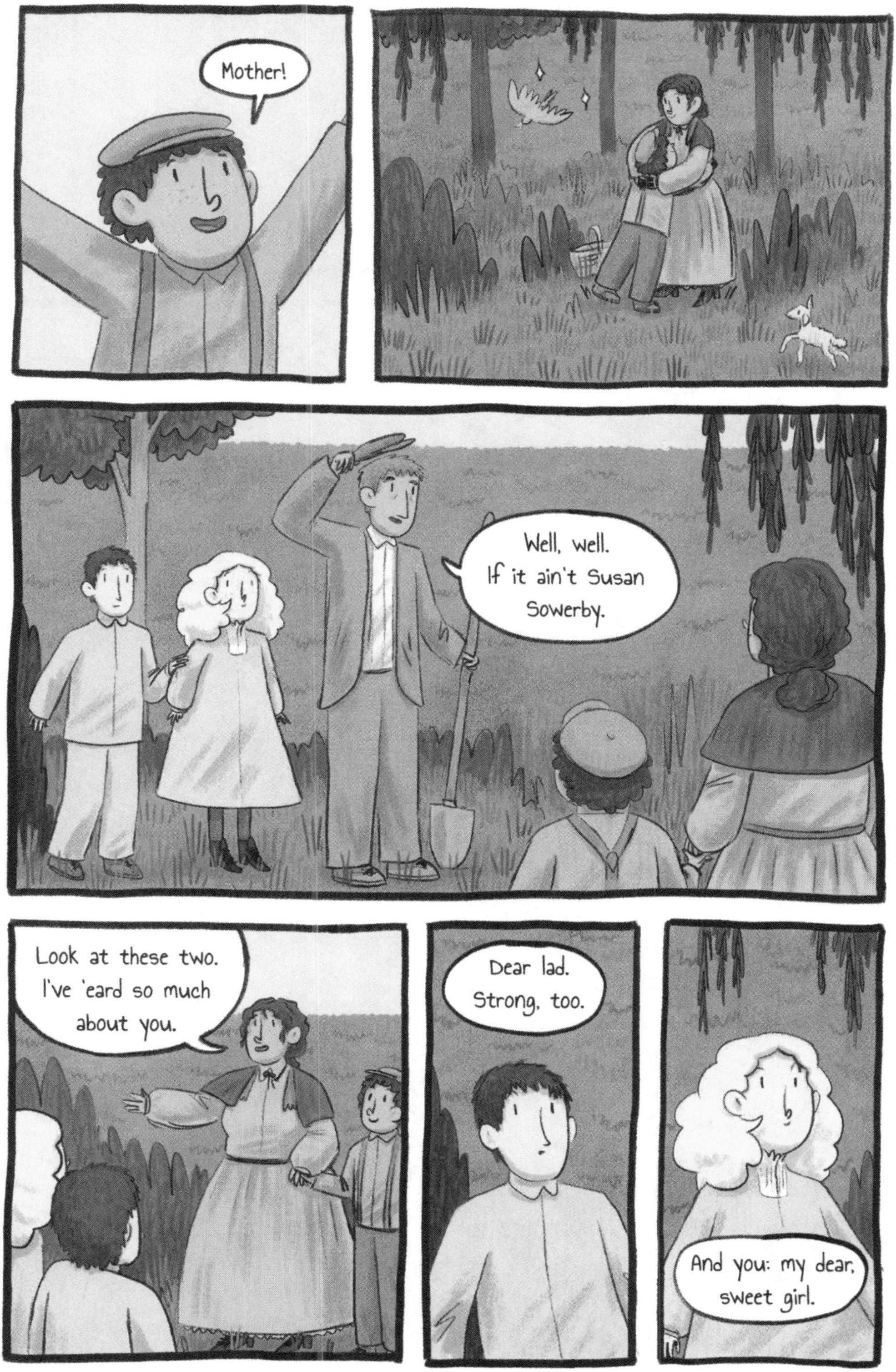
Mother!
Well, well. If it ain't Susan Sowerby.
Look at these two. I've 'eard so much about you.
Dear lad. Strong, too.
And you: my dear, sweet girl.

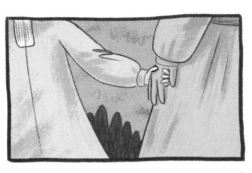

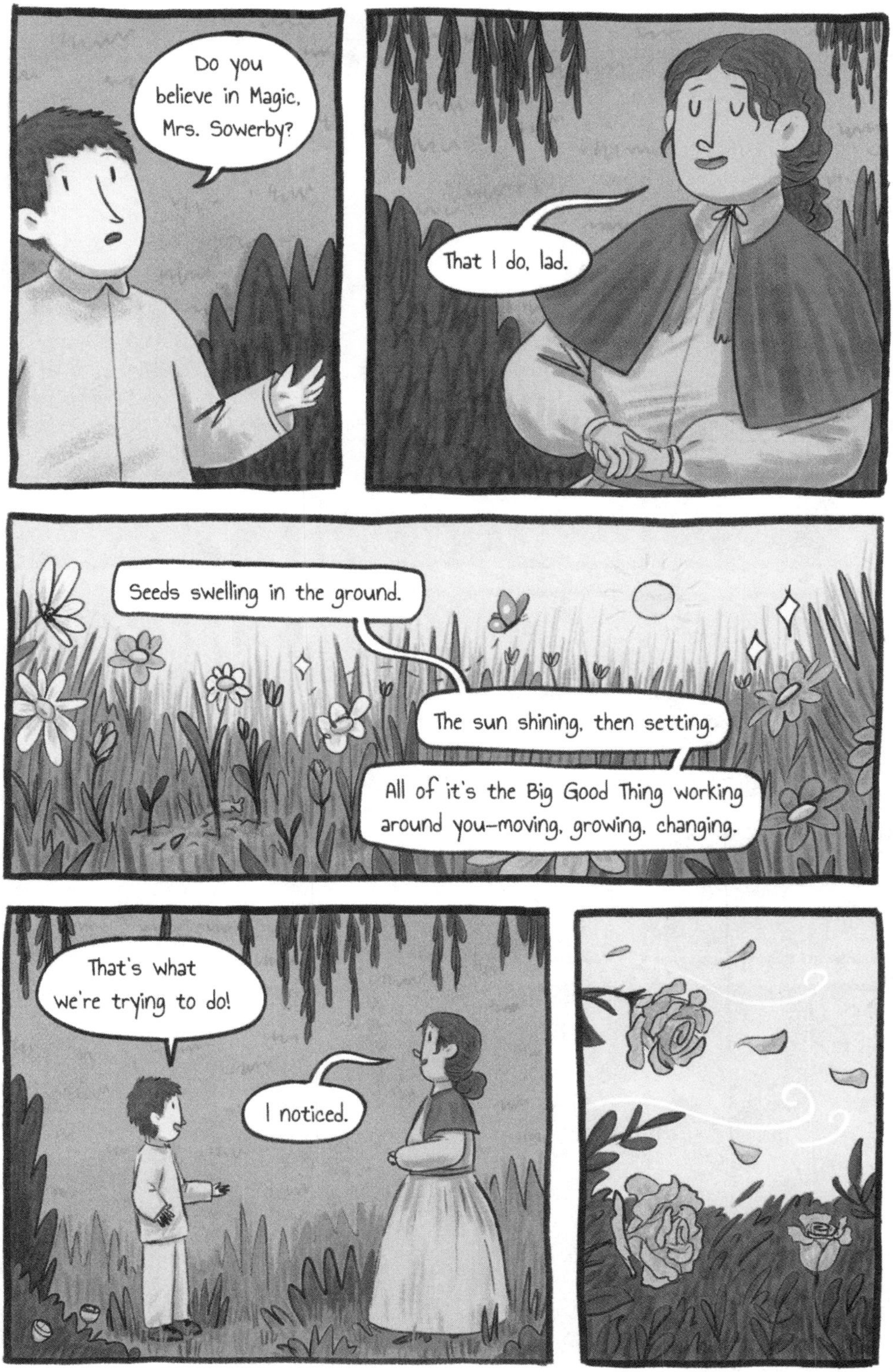
Do you believe in Magic, Mrs. Sowerby?
That I do, lad.
Seeds swelling in the ground.
The sun shining, then setting.
All of it's the Big Good Thing working around you—moving, growing, changing.
That's what we're trying to do!
I noticed.

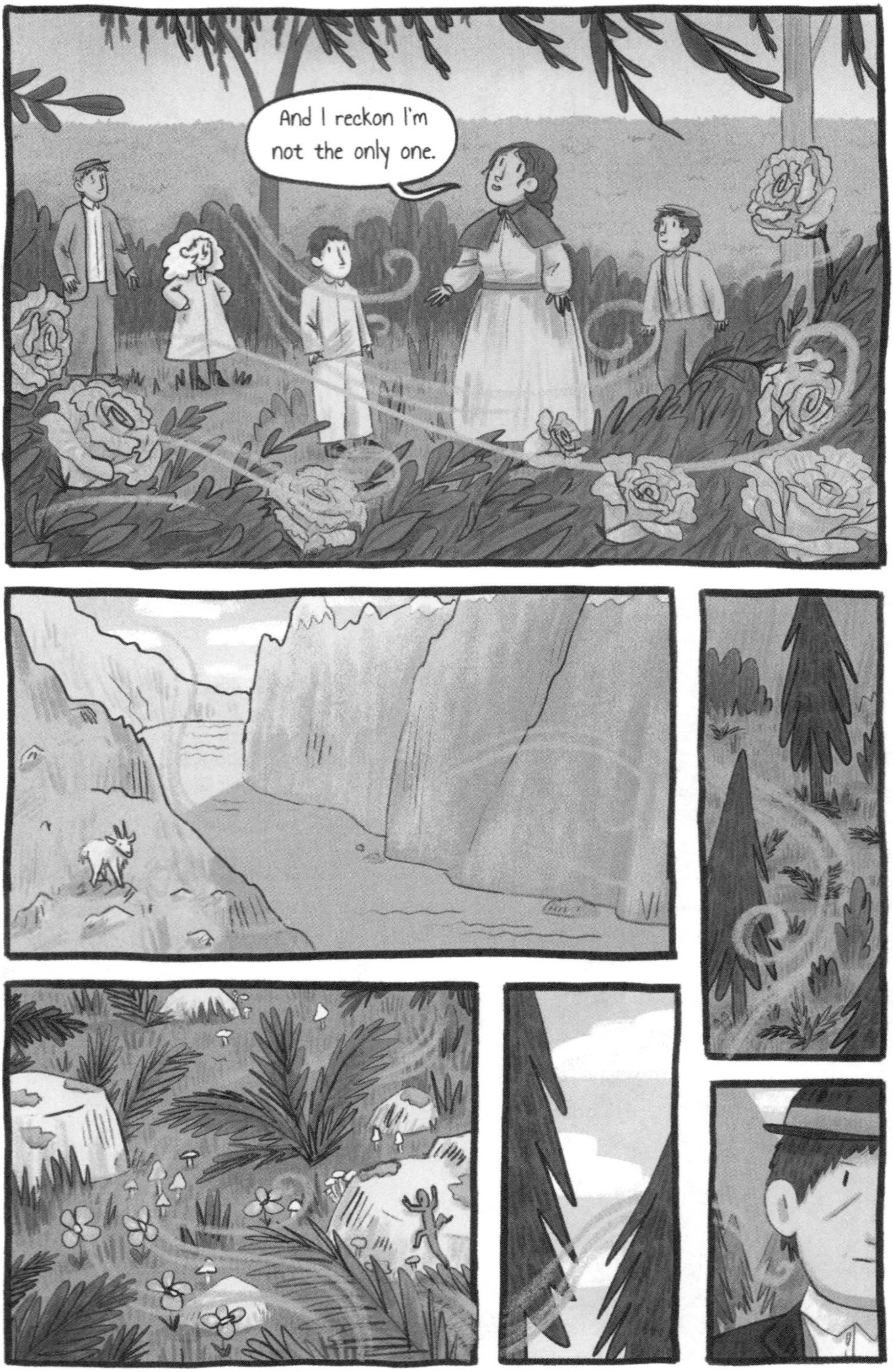
And I reckon I'm not the only one.

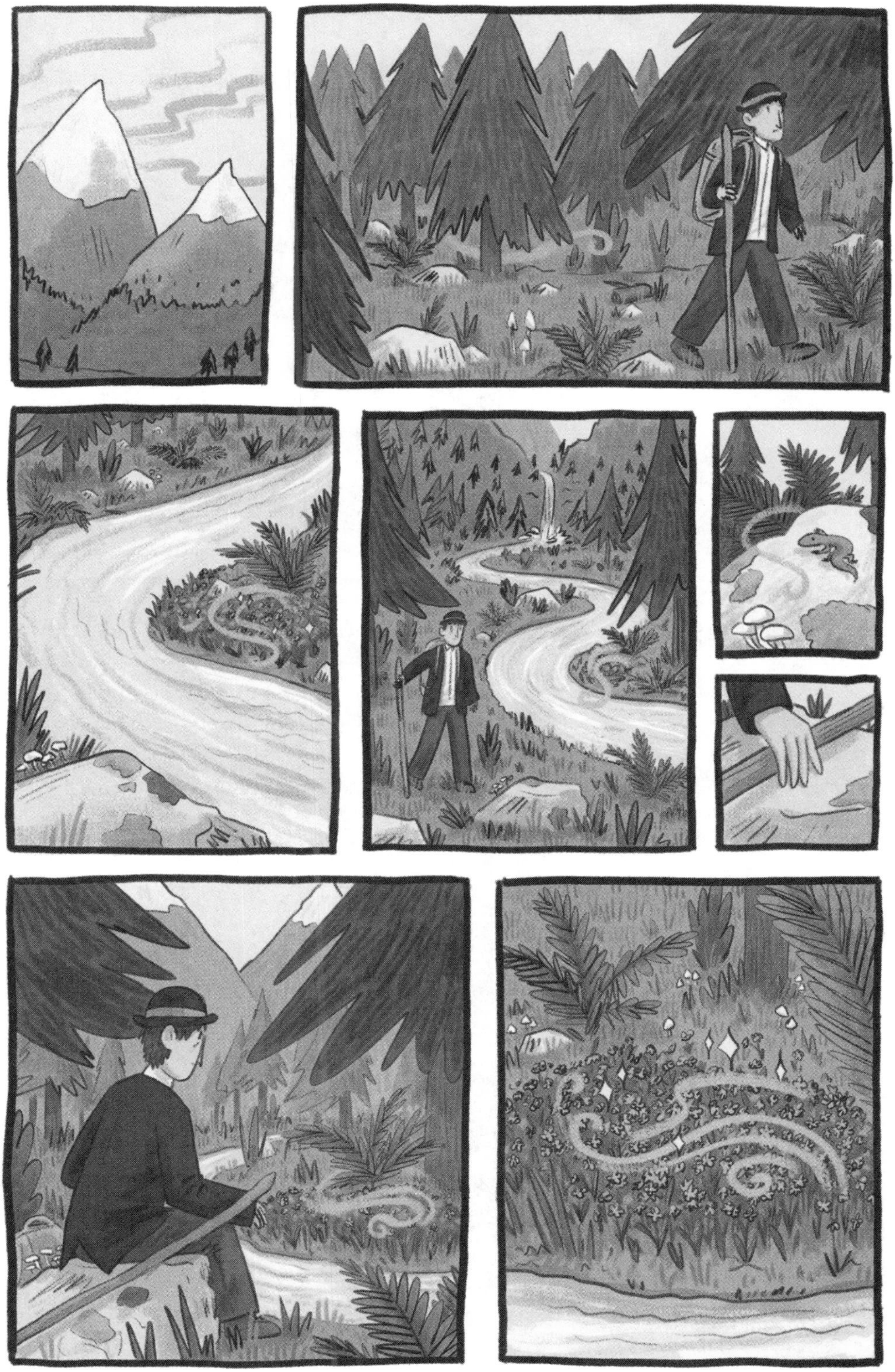

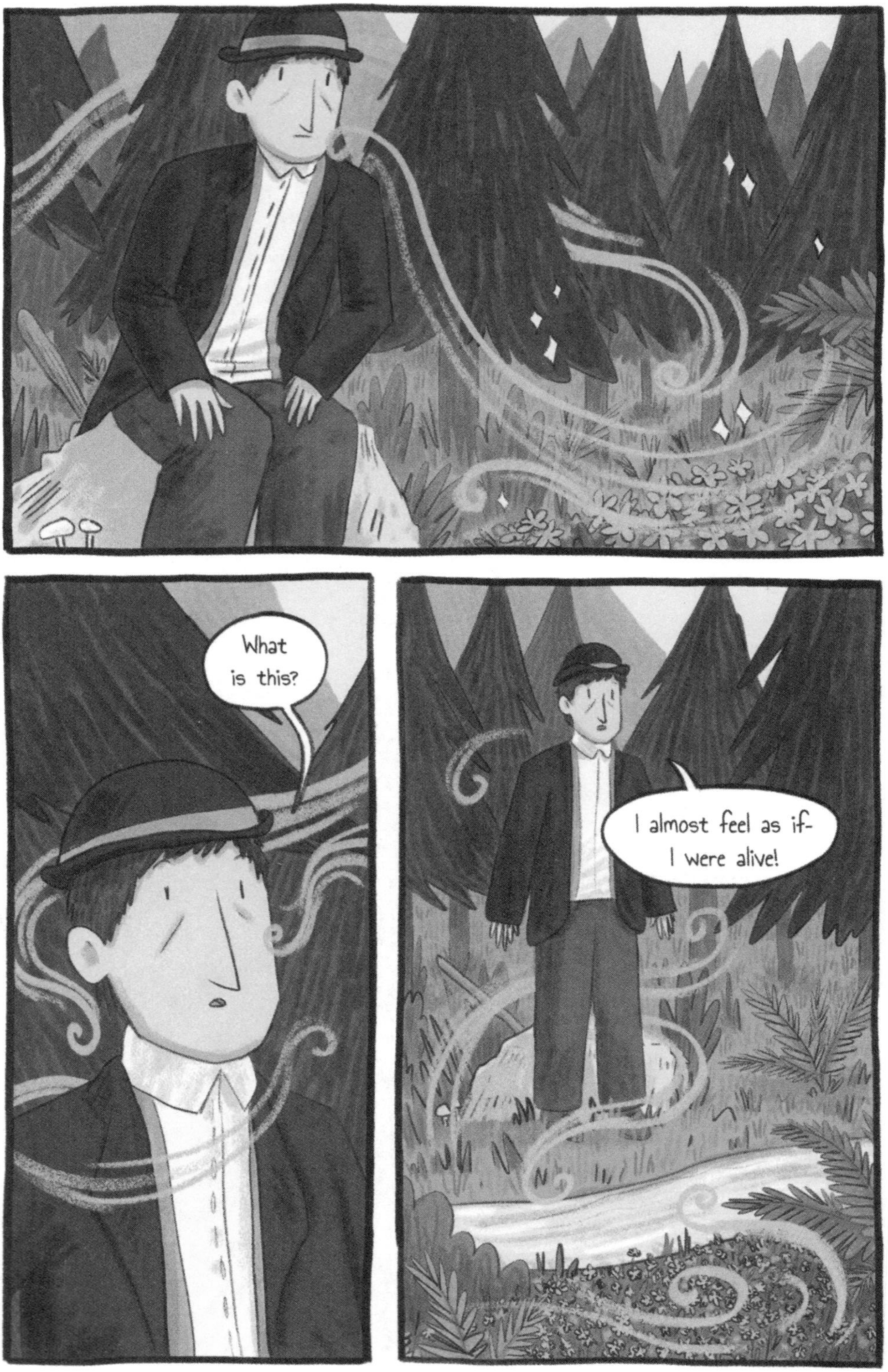
What is this?
I almost feel as if- I were alive!

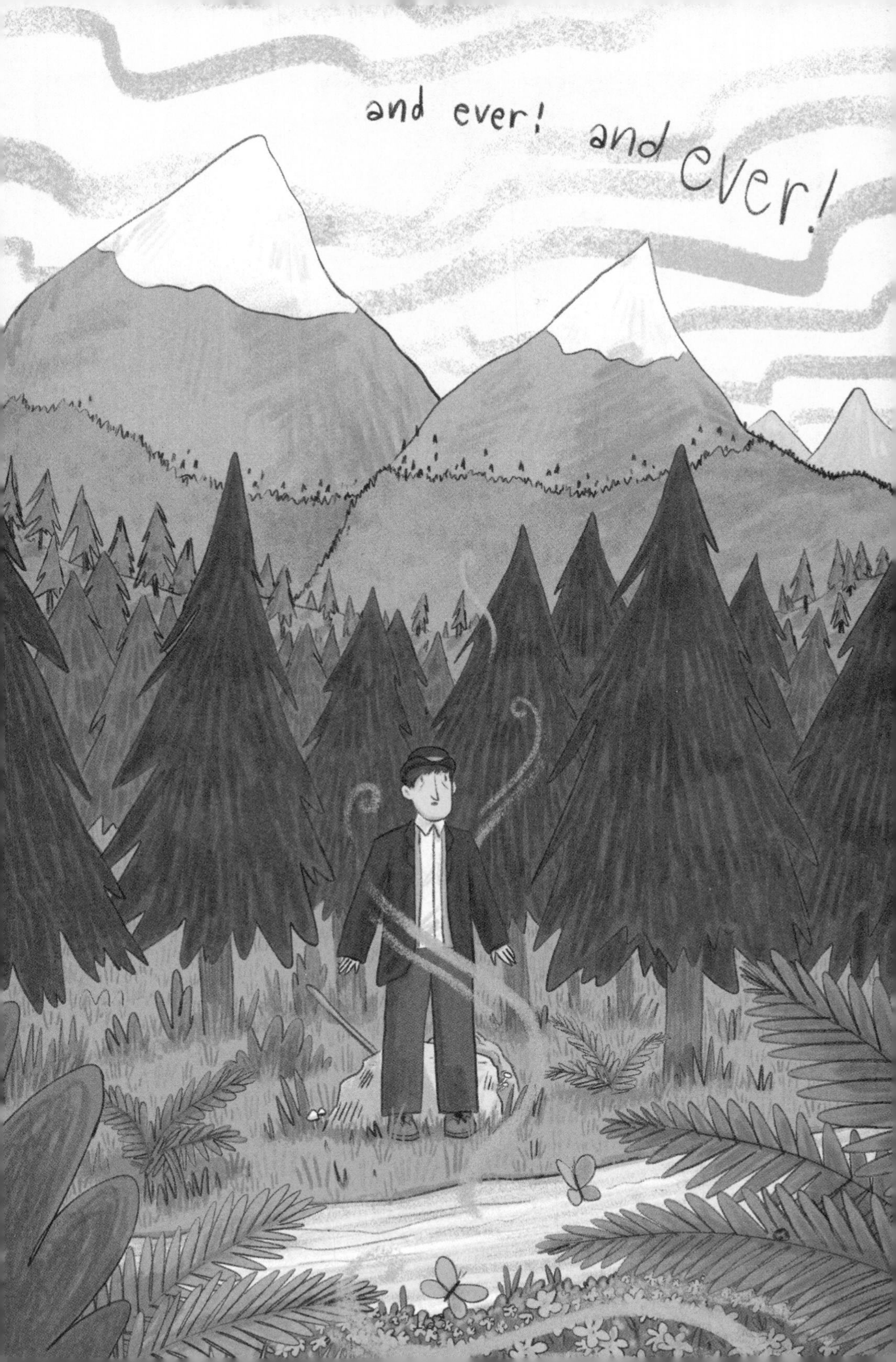
and ever! and ever!

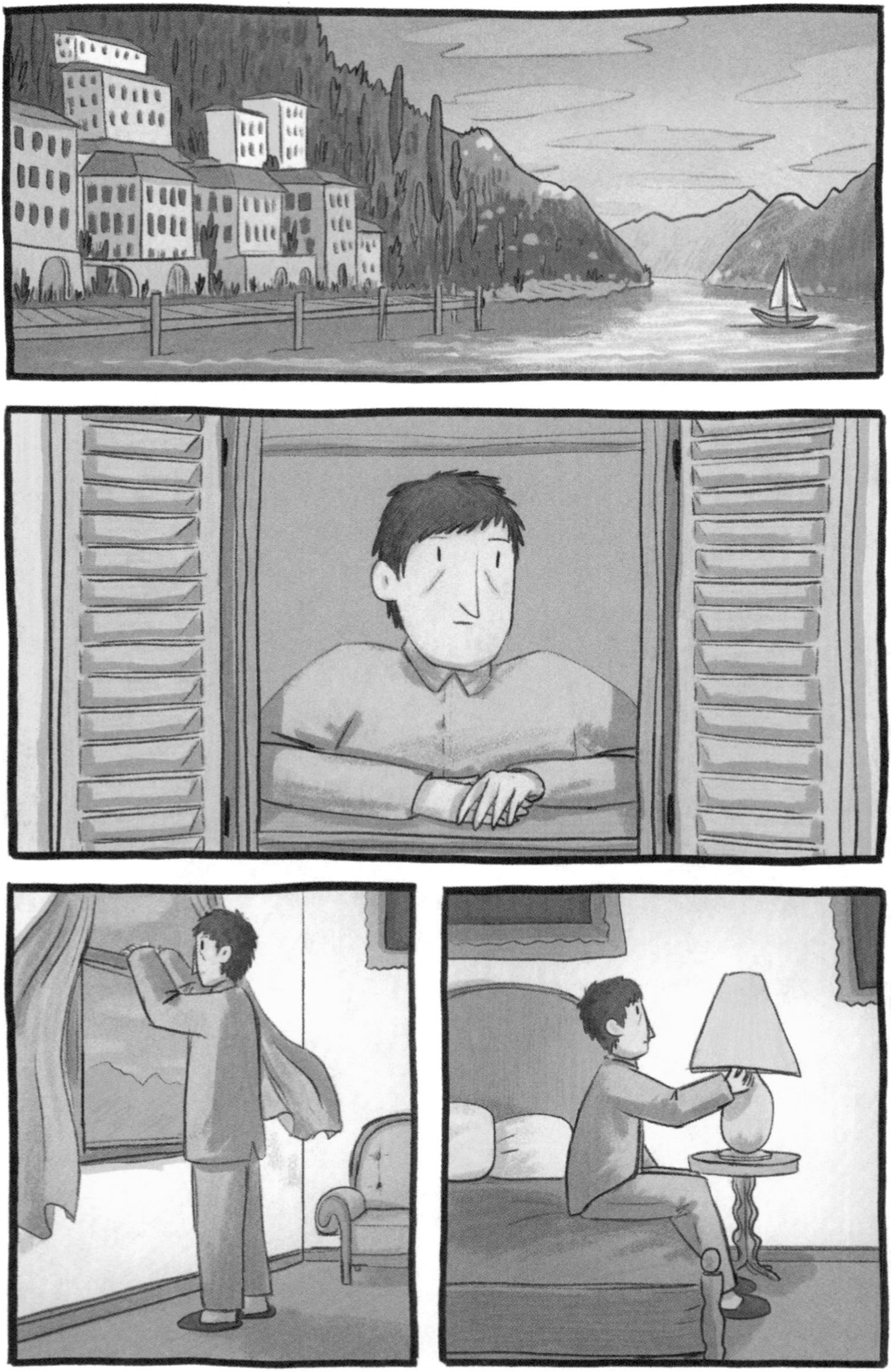

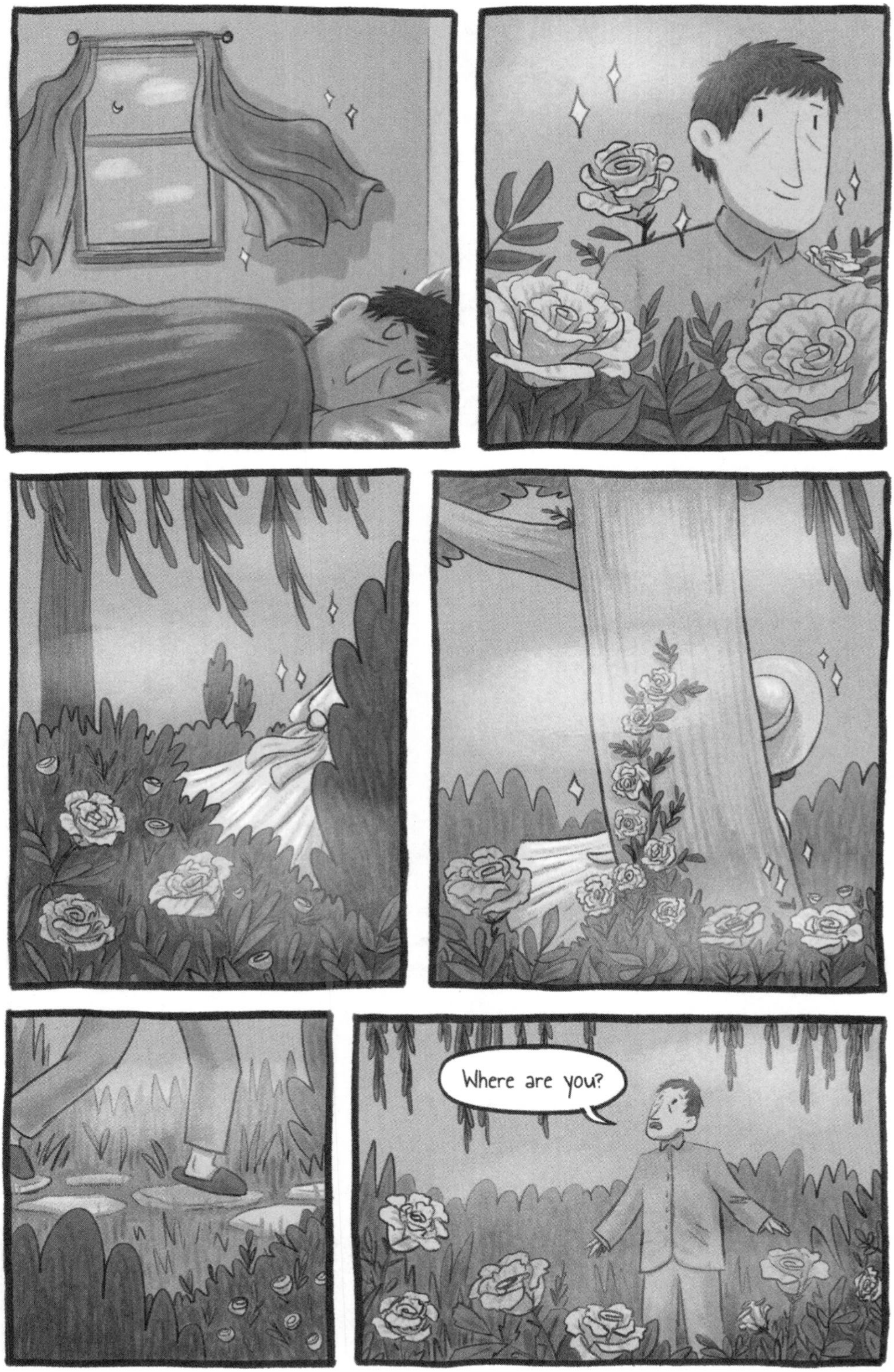
Where are you?

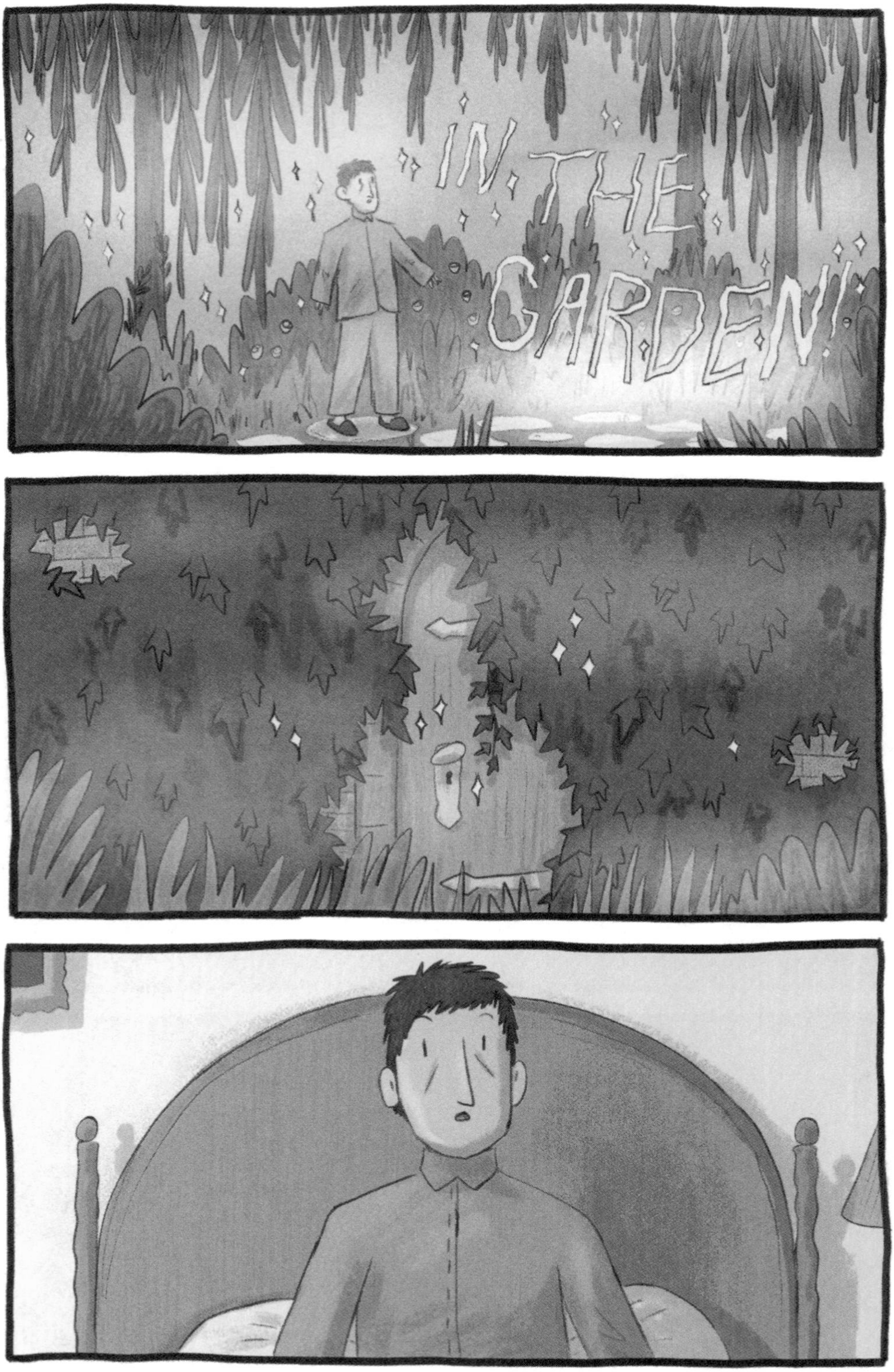
IN THE GARDEN!

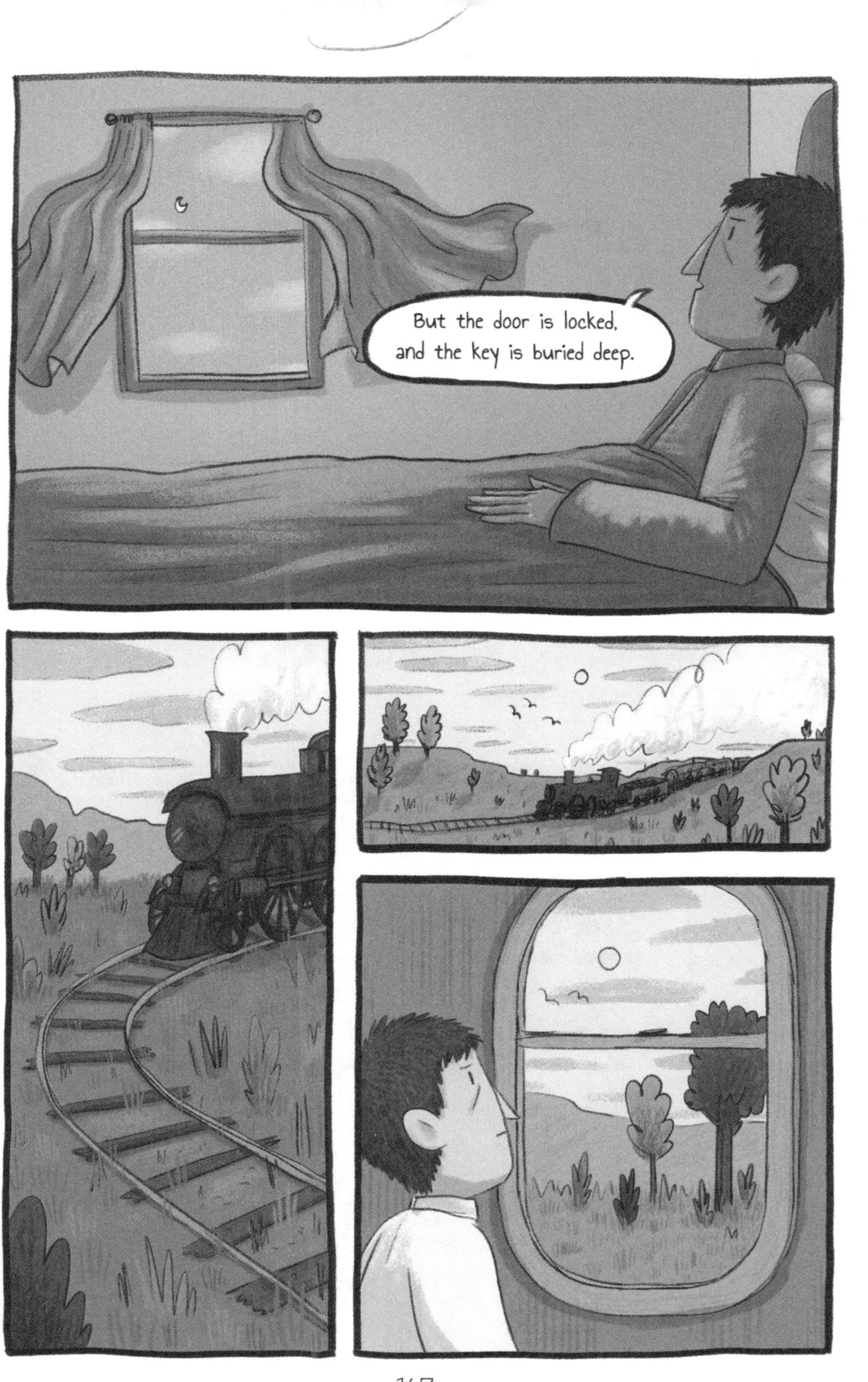
But the door is locked, and the key is buried deep.

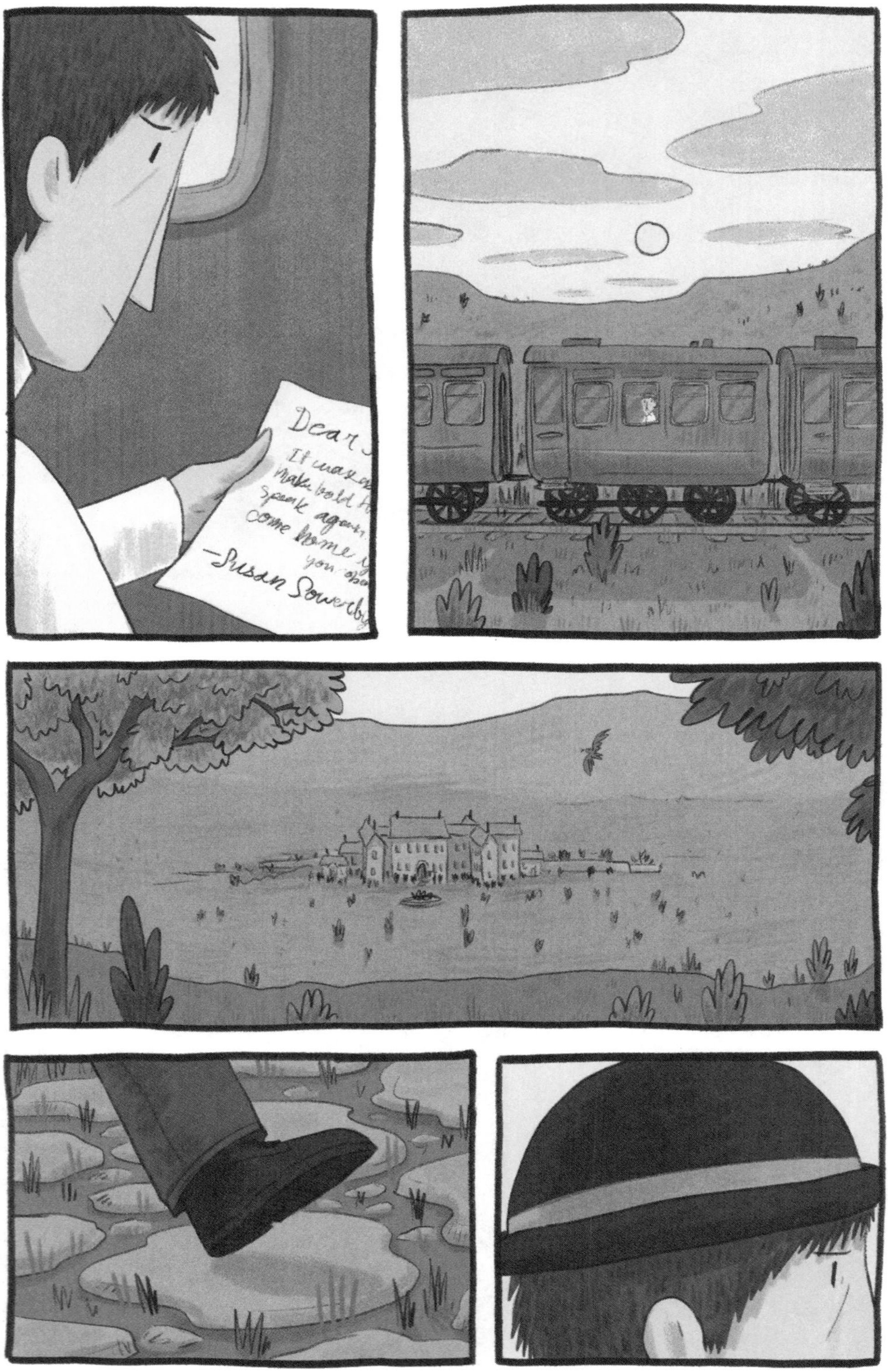
Dear
It
make bold
speak
come home
you
—Susan Sowerby

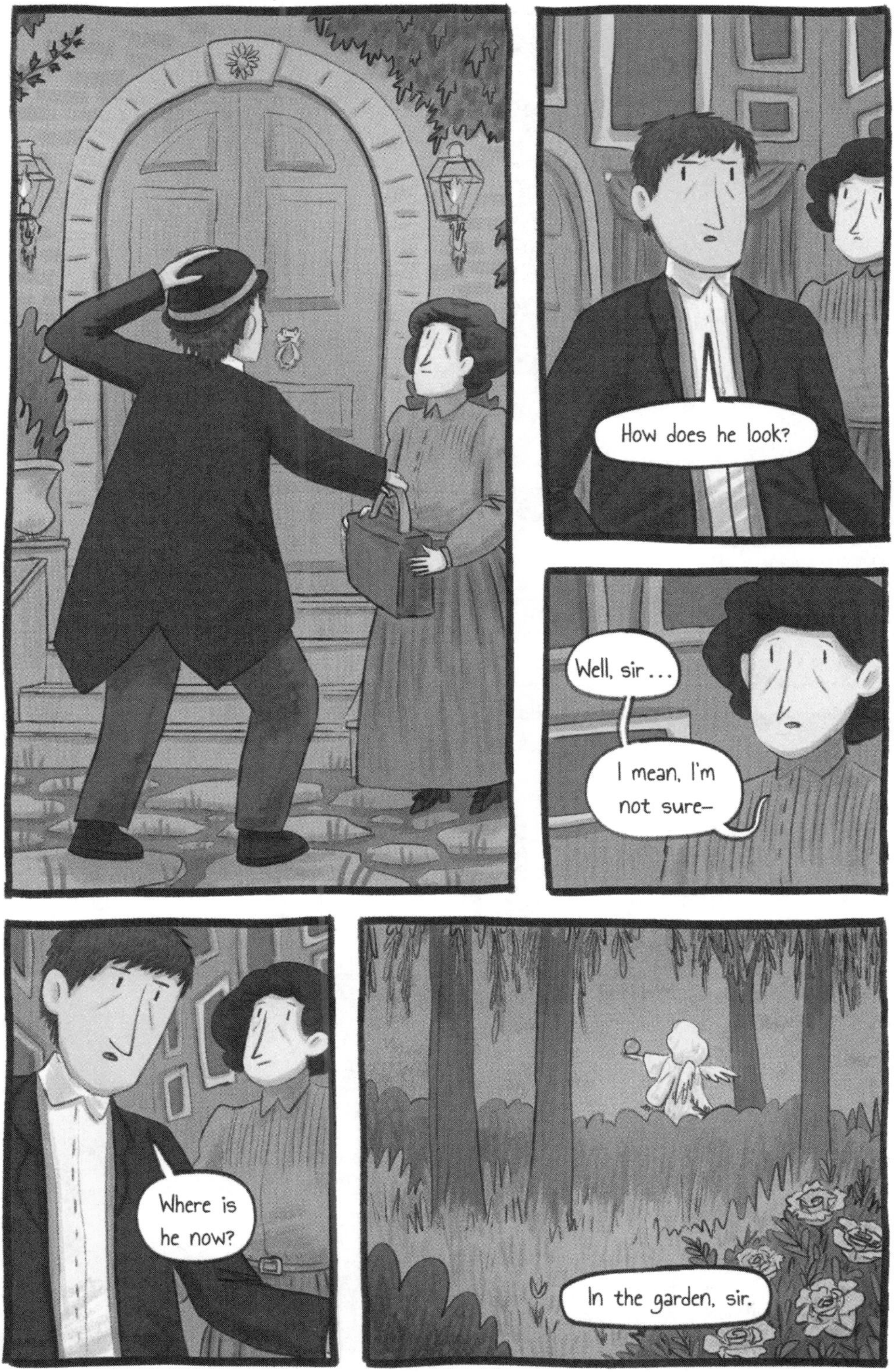
How does he look?
Well, sir…
I mean, I'm not sure–
Where is he now?
In the garden, sir.

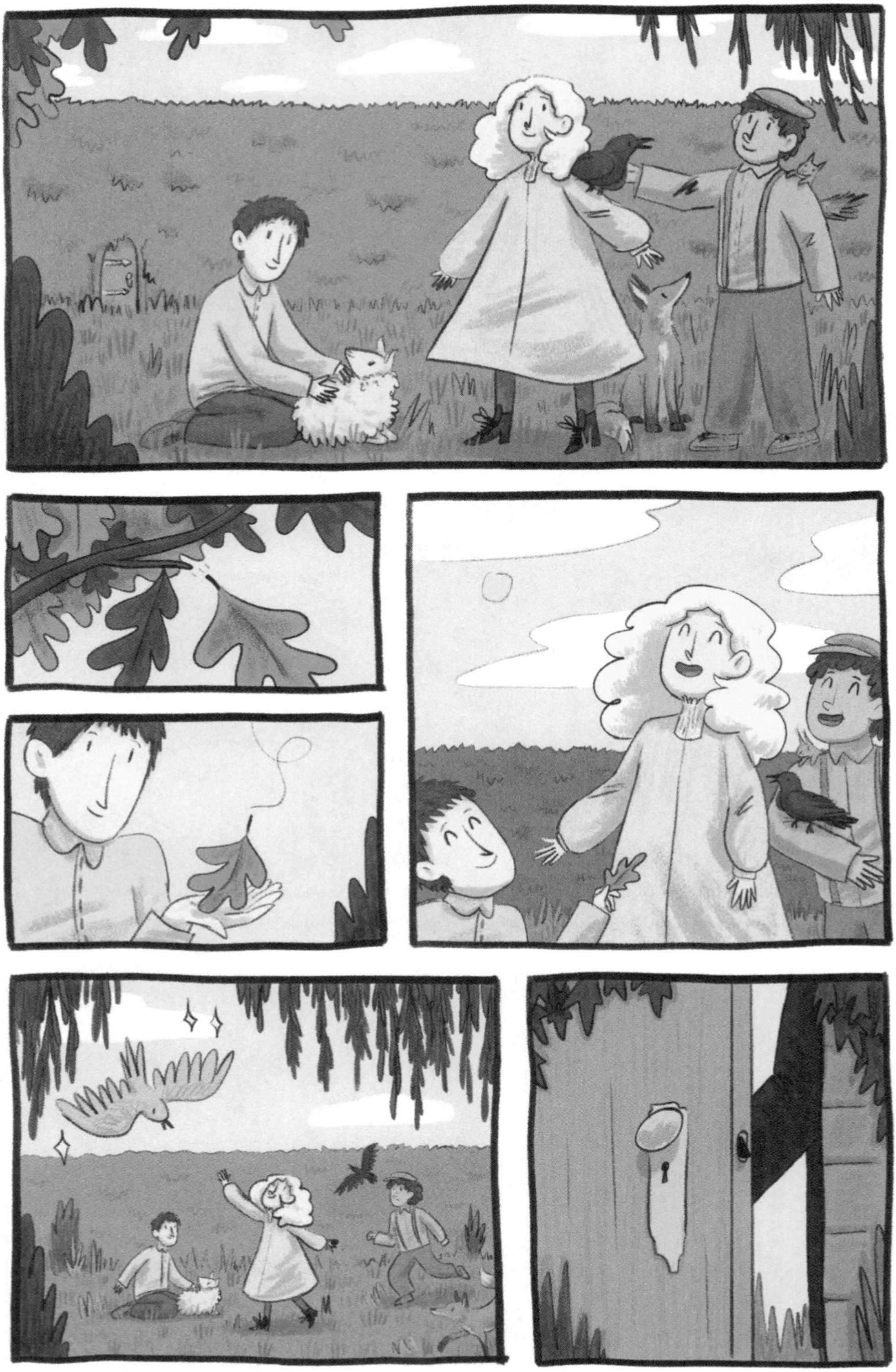

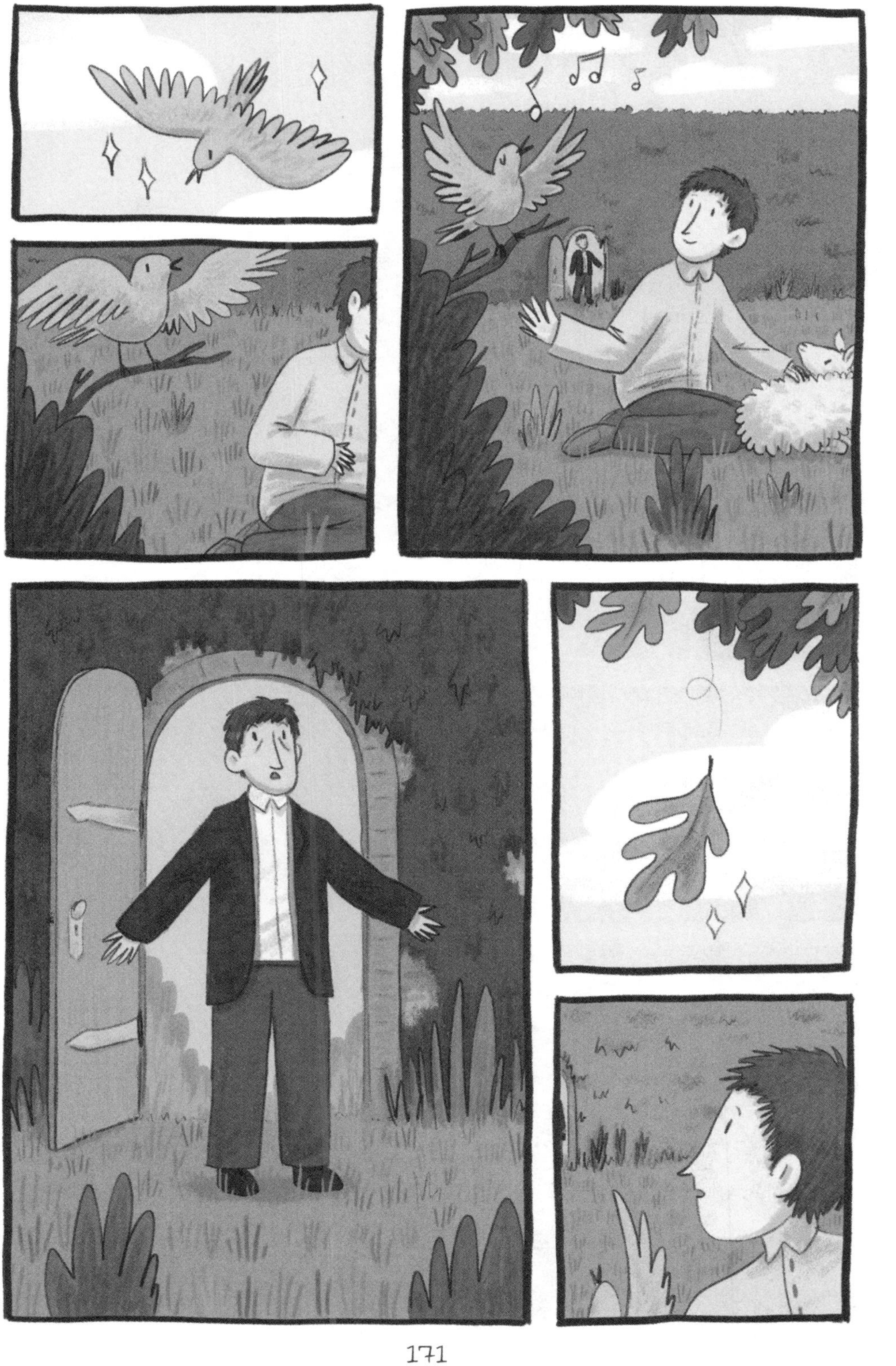

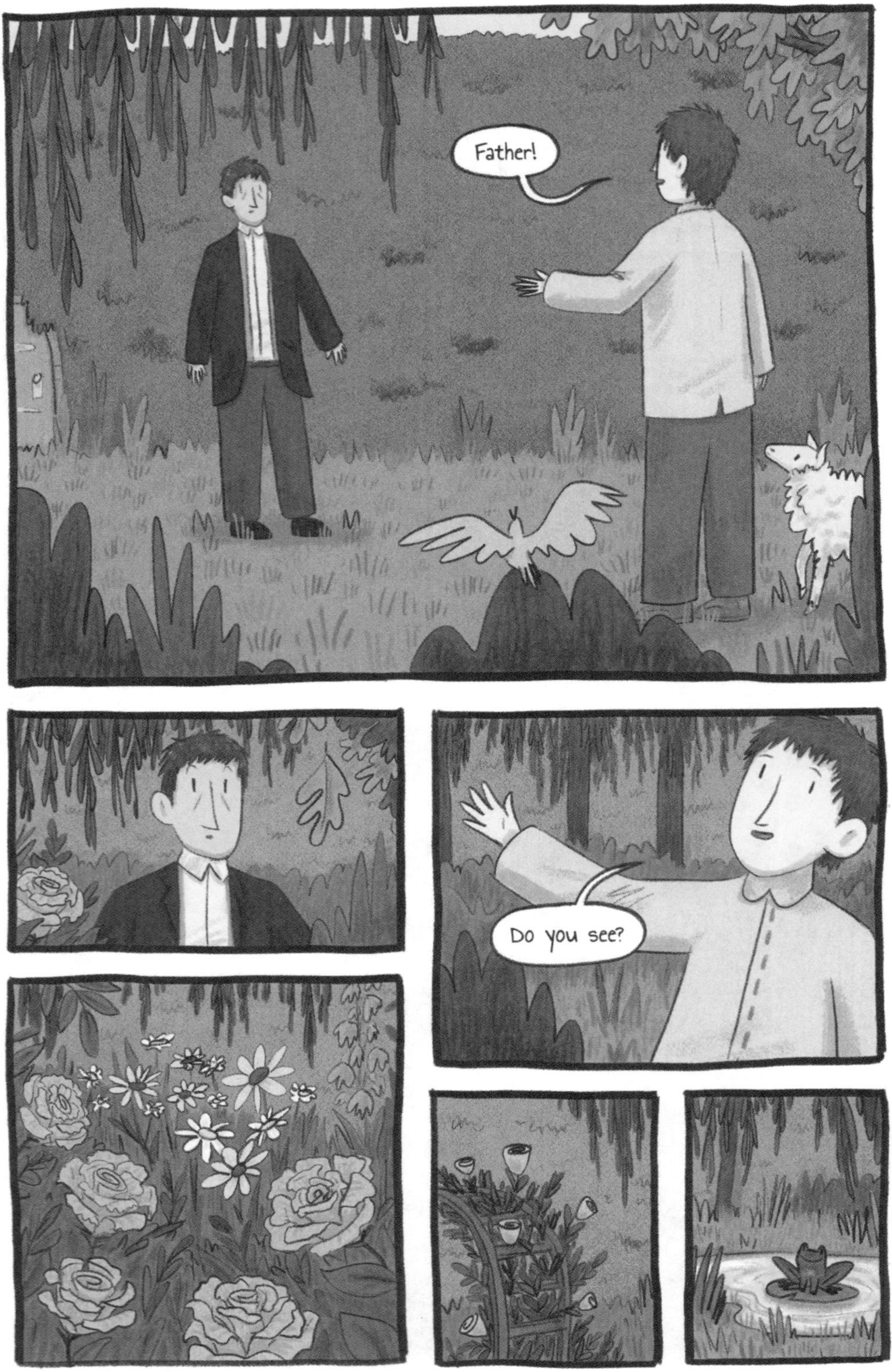
Father!
Do you see?

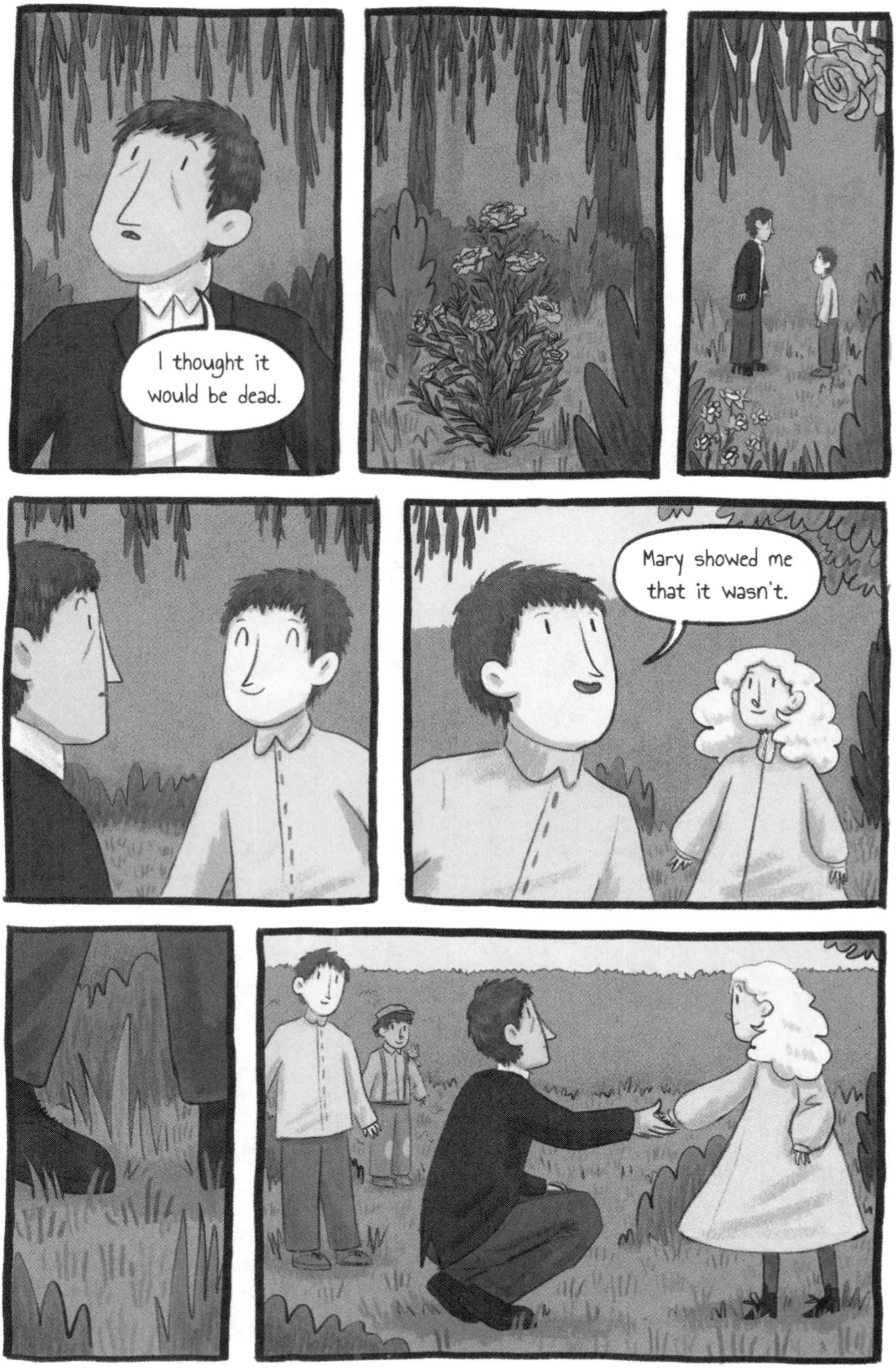
I thought it would be dead.
Mary showed me that it wasn't.

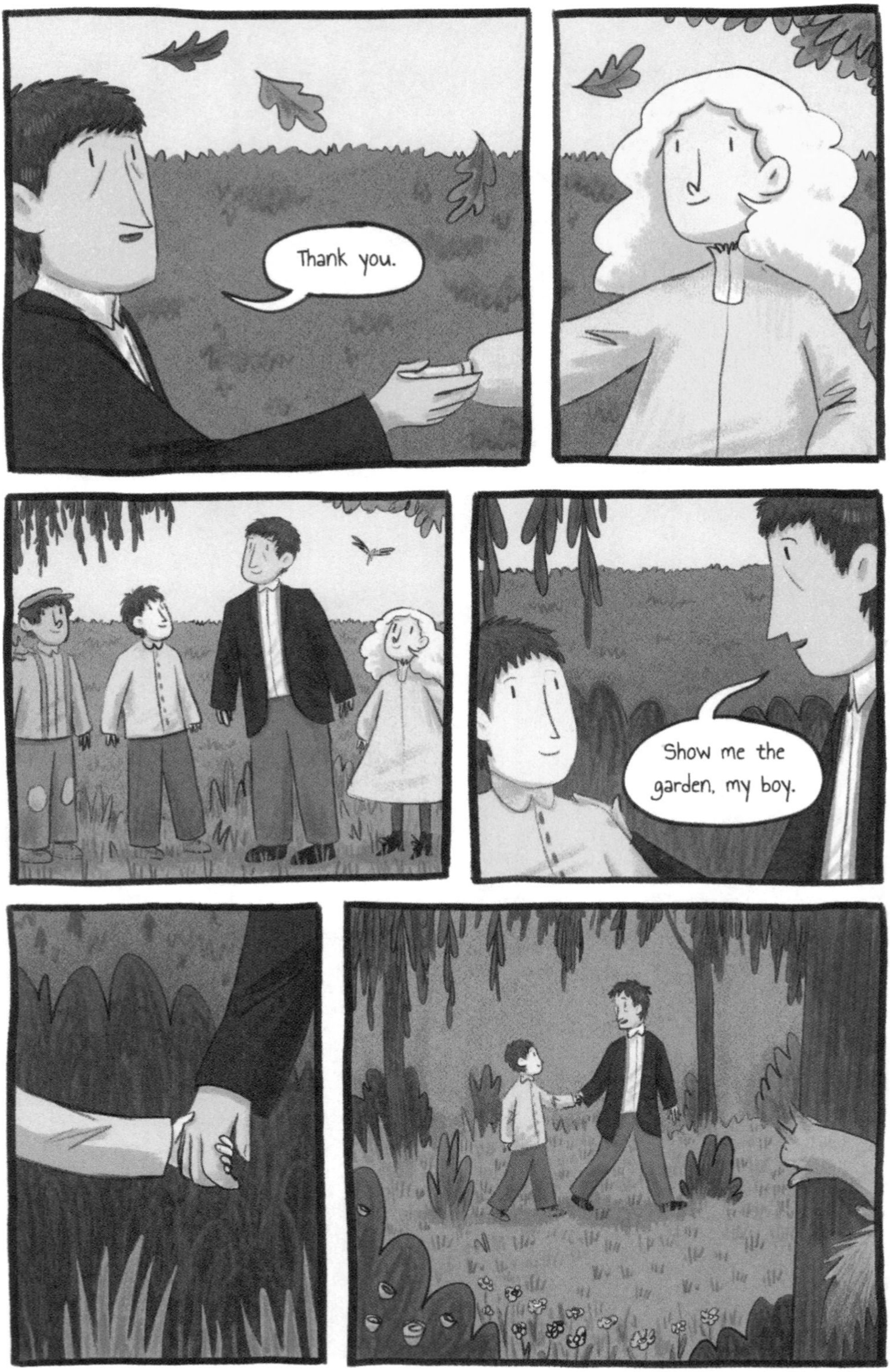
Thank you.
Show me the garden, my boy.

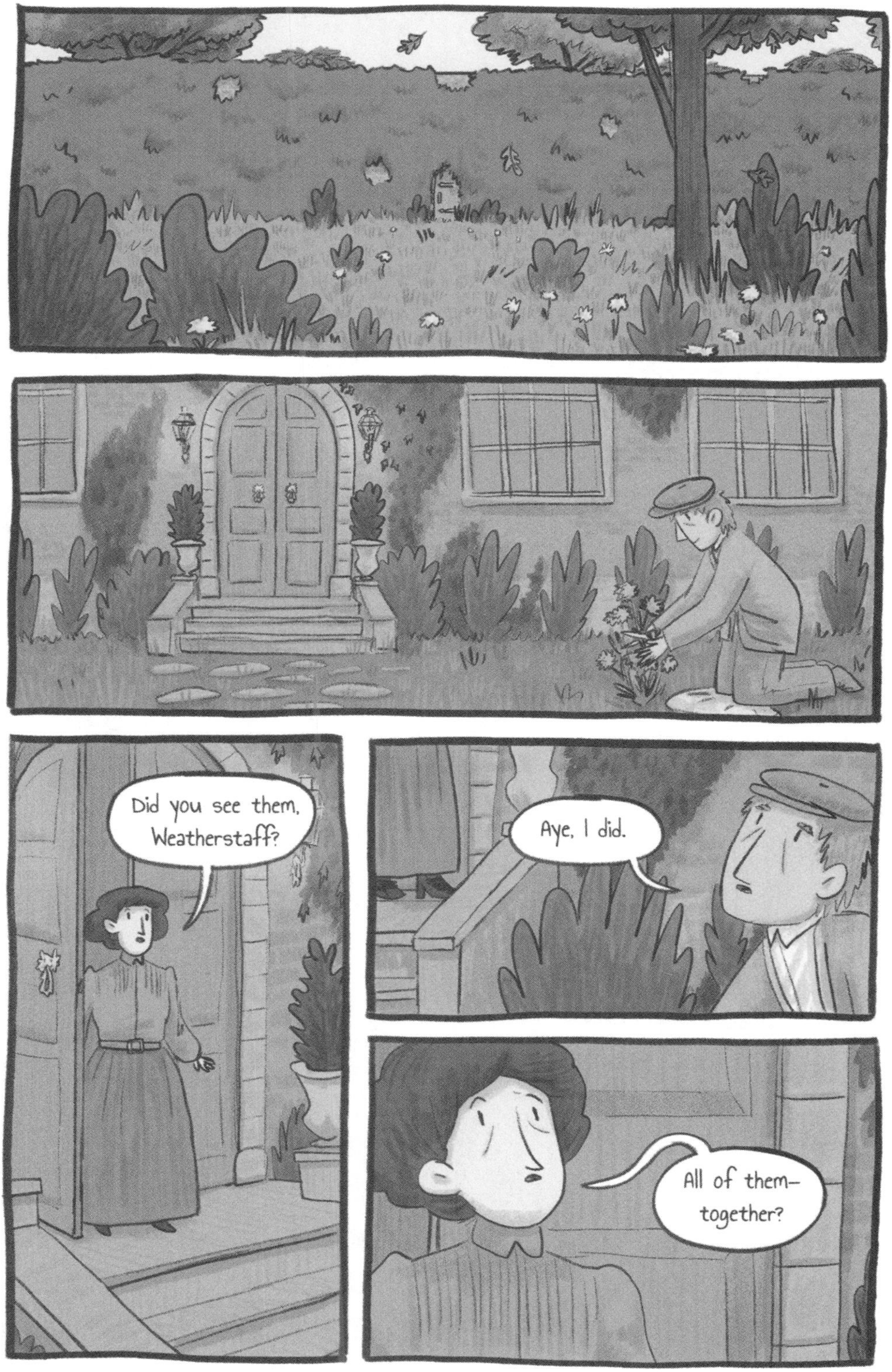
Did you see them, Weatherstaff?
Aye, I did.
All of them—together?

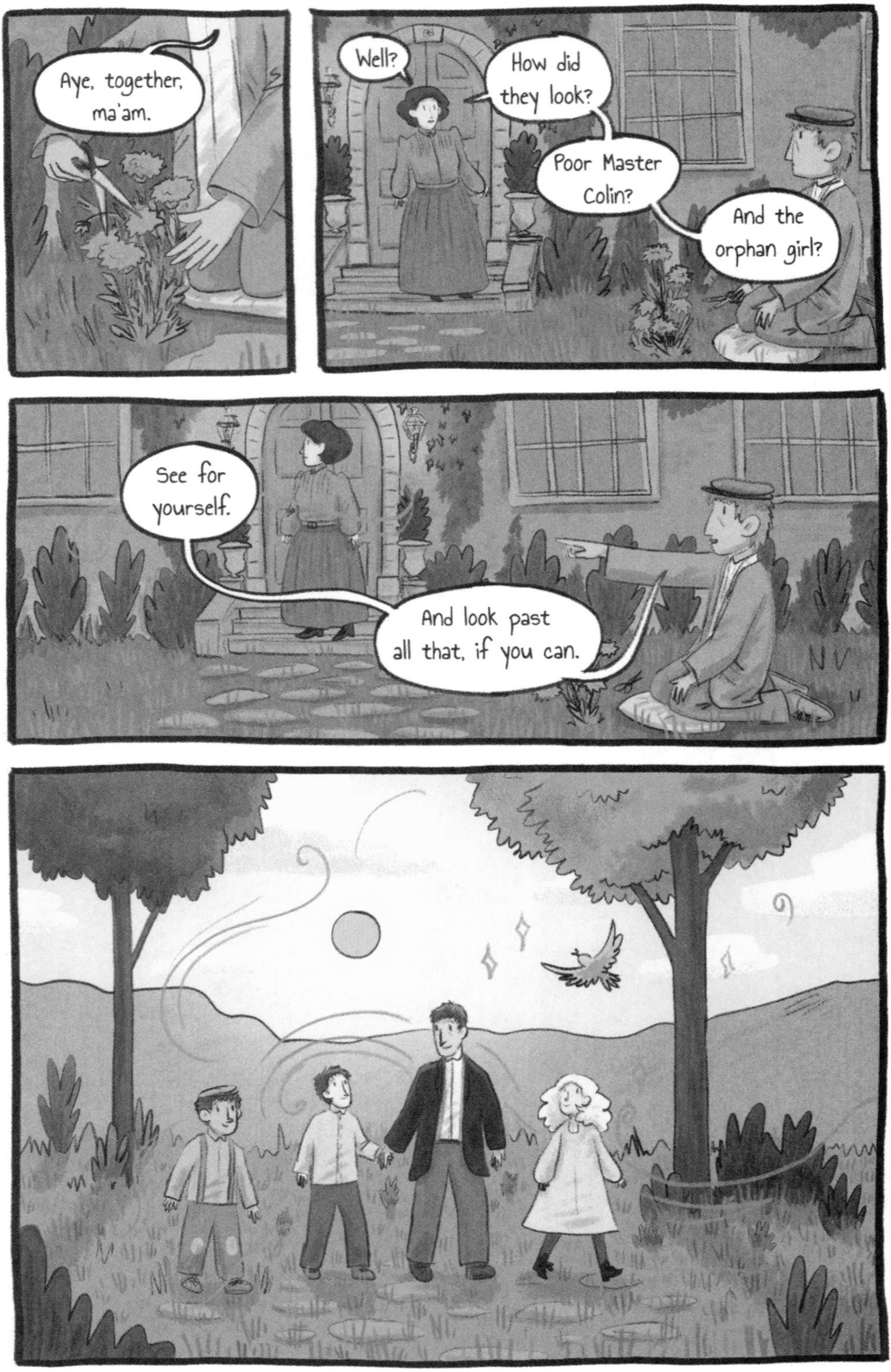
Aye, together, ma'am.
Well?
How did they look?
Poor Master Colin?
And the orphan girl?
See for yourself.
And look past all that, if you can.

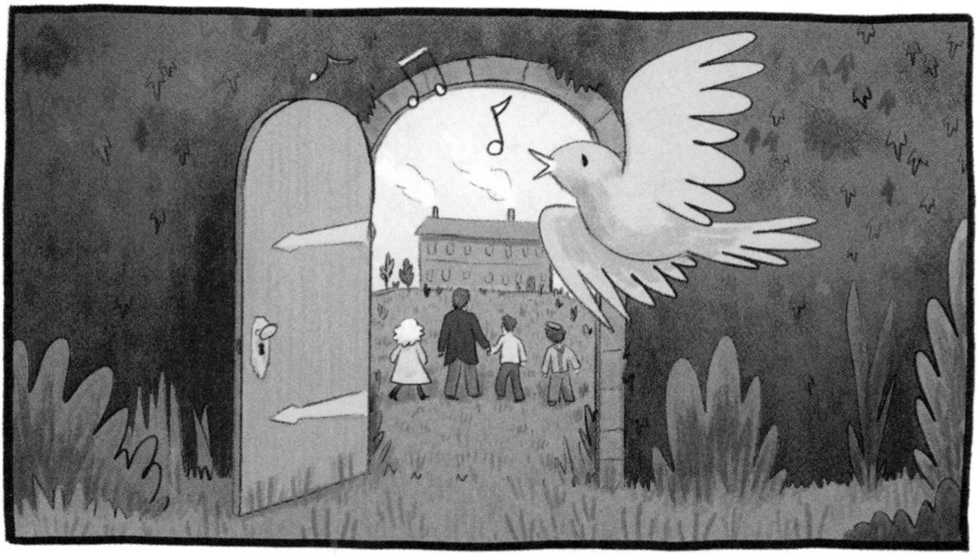

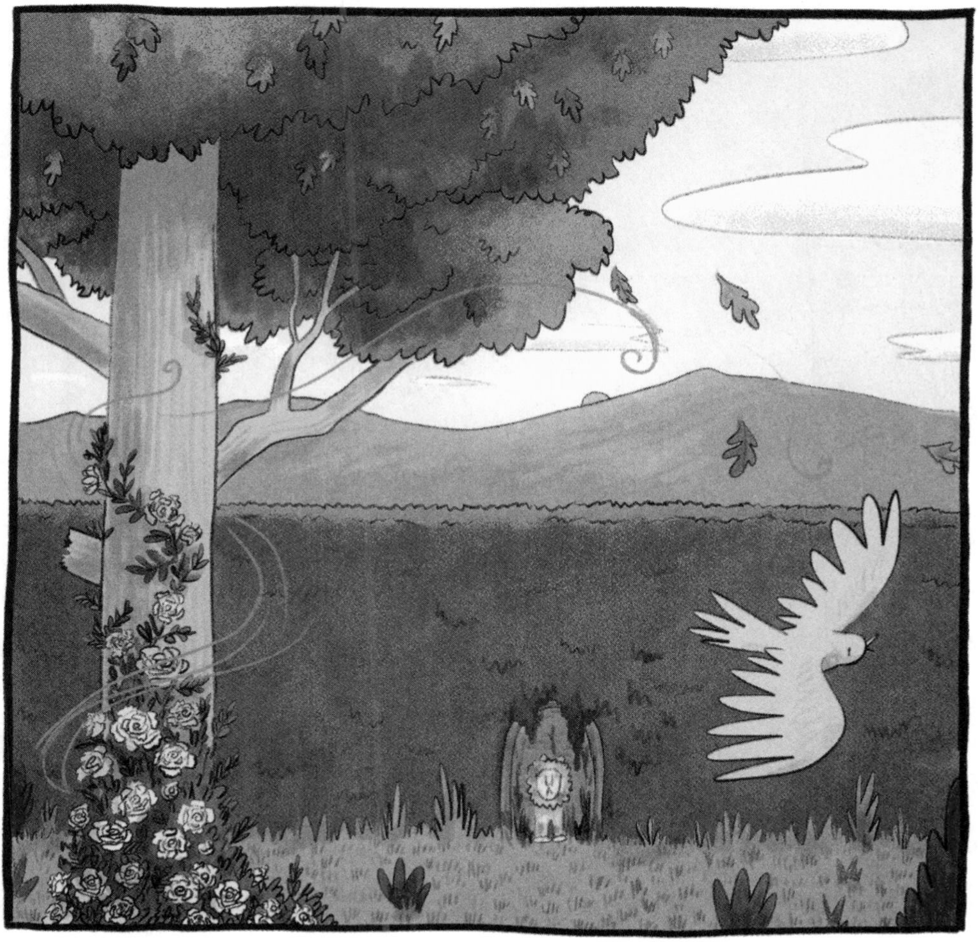

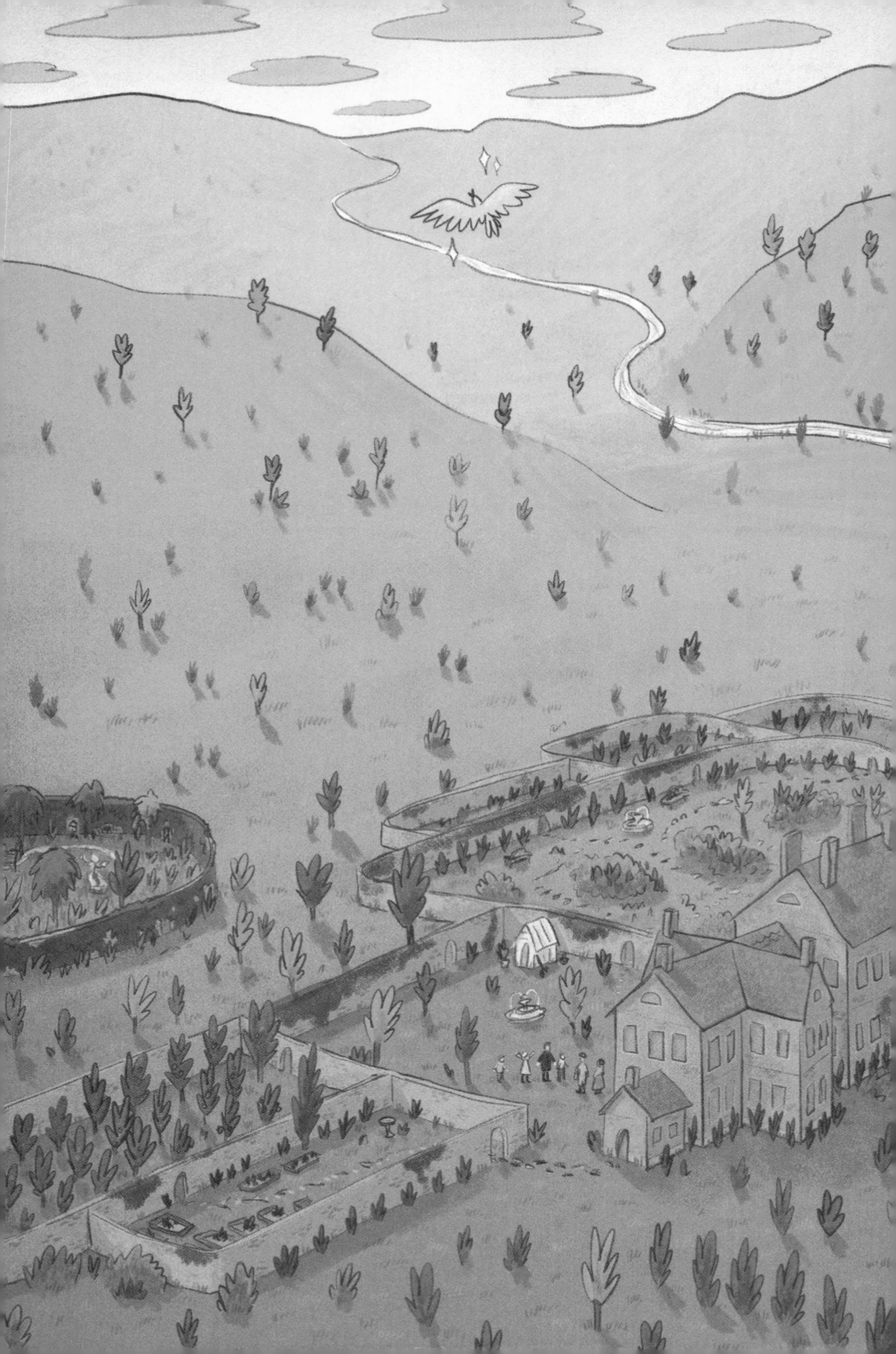

Who Was Frances Hodgson Burnett?

Frances Hodgson Burnett was the original author of *The Secret Garden*. She was born Frances Eliza Hodgson on November 24, 1849, in Manchester, England. Her father died when she was just three years old, leaving her mother to raise five children and run the family's **iron foundry**. To help her mother, Frances lived for a time with her grandmother, who gave her books and encouraged her love of reading. Among Frances' favorites was *The Flower Book*, which contained color illustrations and poetry. Young Frances developed a love of the outdoors—especially flower gardens.

In 1865, the Hodgsons moved from England to Tennessee, where they stayed with relatives in a log cabin. Just as Mary befriends Colin in *The Secret Garden*, Frances befriended a neighbor boy, Swan Burnett, who had suffered a leg injury as a child and was often kept indoors. She shared stories with Swan, introducing him to some of her favorite authors. Many years later, in 1873, Frances and Swan were married. By then, Swan had become a doctor, and Frances was a published writer. The couple had two sons, Lionel and Vivian. They eventually settled in Washington, D.C., where Frances met other authors and began hosting weekly literary **salons** at her home. Her first great success was *Little Lord Fauntleroy*, published in 1886, which was cherished by children and adults alike. In 1888, she published the play *Sara Crewe or What Happened at Miss Minchin's*, which later became the beloved children's novel *A Little Princess* (1905).

After their son Lionel's death from **tuberculosis** in 1890, Frances and Swan grew apart. They divorced in 1898, and Frances began spending most of her time in England, where she lived at Great Maytham Hall in Kent. Much like Misselthwaite, the manor had a system of walled gardens, including a rose garden where Frances spent long hours writing. She wrote *The Secret Garden* during this time, publishing it some years later in 1911.

In 1909, Frances returned permanently to the United States. She built a home in the town of Plandome Manor on Long Island, New York, where she continued to write, publishing books and stories until the end of her life. While *Little Lord Fauntleroy* was Frances' most successful book during her lifetime, *The Secret Garden* has been her most enduring. Embraced by generations to follow and adapted for film several times, it is often cited as one of the best children's books of the twentieth century.

This portrait of Frances Hodgson Burnett was taken by the early American photographer Frances Benjamin Johnston sometime between 1890 and 1910.*

---

*Johnston, Frances Benjamin. *Frances (Hodgson) Burnett, 1849-1924.* [Between 1890 and 1910] Photograph. From Library of Congress: *Johnston, Frances Benjamin, 1864-1952.* https://www.loc.gov/item/2002697460/.

Places and Spaces in *The Secret Garden*

In Colonial India

When *The Secret Garden* was published in 1911, the British Empire covered one-third of the globe, including all of modern-day India and Pakistan. This period of direct British rule over the Indian subcontinent, which lasted from 1858 until 1947, was called the British raj. Today, it is remembered as a time of widespread cultural, social, and economic **oppression**, when Indian people were **discriminated** against by the British and given little to no control over their daily lives.

In Burnett's original novel, Mary's parents are British **colonists** living in India. Her father worked for the English government. Like most colonists of the time, the Lennox family probably lived in a private, isolated camp outside of an Indian city. Racist attitudes among the British led them to avoid interacting with the local people, except those they hired as servants.

In the original book, it's implied that Mary's family had a number of Indian servants, including Mary's nurse, or "āyāh," who looked after her every need. You might have noticed that, in this graphic novel, you don't hear about Mary living in India before coming to Misselthwaite Manor. We chose to leave out those parts of the story because they don't do justice to the history of British oppression in colonial India.

From 1899 to 1923, **cholera** cases spanned the globe in a **pandemic.** Under British control, India was especially hard-hit by the disease. At the time, many Indians worked in coal mines benefiting foreign companies, built railroads that would transport foreign troops, and served in the households of the British people who governed their lives. Those needing support during the pandemic were often left in need as the privileged

British elite retreated to distant estates in the **Himalayan** foothills. In *The Secret Garden*, Mary's family doesn't leave the city in time, and both of Mary's parents, along with her āyāh, die of cholera, leaving Mary an orphan.

On the Yorkshire Moors

After her parents' deaths, Mary is taken into the care of her uncle, Lord Craven, who lives in an old **manor house** on the Yorkshire moors of England. In the 1890s and early 1900s, while she wrote *The Secret Garden*, Frances Hodgson Burnett lived in a similar house in the English countryside. During her time there, she became very fond of the local **flora** and **fauna**.

Today, if you take a spring walk on the Yorkshire moors, you might spot the long, slender beak of a **snipe** as it makes its home in the boggy areas, hear the piping call of the shiny **lapwing**, or follow the flight of a graceful **emperor moth**. The hills are always changing, covered in pink and purple **bell heather** that blooms in summer and ochre **bracken** in autumn.

Do you have a special place, either indoors or outdoors? What kinds of plants and animals do you see in the world around you? What colors do you notice— and do they change throughout the year?

In the Garden

Frances Hodgson Burnett was an avid gardener herself. Having lived through the height of Queen Victoria's reign, she would have been familiar with the Victorian language of flowers or "floriography," which continued to be popular in the twentieth century. Strolling through Burnett's garden at Maytham Hall in England, you might notice some interesting flower combinations with secret meanings. **Pansies** were messages of love. **Gentian** blooms showed gratitude. **Cornflowers** meant riches or hope for the future. **Geraniums**, sincerity. And green **nettles** symbolized defiance—something that might be found in Mary's own garden.

Do you see many flowers where you live? Can you find them inside or outside? What flowers might you choose in your own garden—and what secret messages might you encode?

Glossary

Bell heather (n.): A type of flowering plant with rose-colored or purple blooms.

Bracken (n.): A tall fern with coarse fronds that often grows over large areas.

Cholera (n.): A bacterial disease often spread through water contamination. Symptoms include diarrhea, dehydration, and vomiting.

Colonist (n.): A settler or occupier of a **colony**—a territory belonging to or under the control of a distant nation.

From 1858 until 1947, India was a colony of Great Britain. British rule in the country ended in 1947 with the independence of India and Pakistan.

Contrary (adj.): Engaging in or demonstrating childish misbehavior. (See page 79.)

In the story, some of the children mock Mary by calling her "Mistress Mary, quite contrary" (which is believed to be from an old nursery rhyme about Queen Mary of England) to say that she's stubborn, unruly, or impolite.

Cornflower (n.): A plant similar to a daisy with a head of deep blue, pink, or white flowers.

The blue cornflower is the international awareness symbol of ALS, a disease of the nervous system that affects muscle movement and mobility.

Discriminate (v.): To treat a group or person differently than others without a fair reason, sometimes based on their race, nationality, age, ability, gender, or sexuality.

Emperor moth (n.): A large moth with shapes that look like human eyes on its wings.

Fauna (n.): The animal life of a particular place or environment.

Fledgling (n.): A young bird that has just acquired its feathers for flight. (See page 24.)

Flora (n.): The plants or plant life of a particular place or environment.

Gentian (n.): A type of plant with deep blue, trumpet-shaped flowers.

One variety, the fringed gentian, is the official flower of Yellowstone National Park.

Geranium (n.): A small shrub with purple, red, or pink flowers. They make particularly good houseplants, adapting well to indoor environments.

Governess (n.): Someone who cares for and supervises a child. (See page 49.)

Himalayan (adj.): Relating to the Himalayas—a range of mountains in southern Asia on the Indian border that has some of the tallest mountains in the world.

Iron foundry (n.): A workshop where iron is cast to make tools and other equipment.

Lapwing (n.) A large wading bird known for its slow wingbeat and piercing call.

Manor House or Manor (n.): A large house, usually belonging to a lord. (See page 6.)

In England, during the time when The Secret Garden is set, a manor most often consisted of an estate (a large property) ruled over by a lord. Tenants living on the property would pay the lord to live there in the form of money or labor. In the story, Martha, Dickon, and Mrs. Sowerby are most likely tenants living on Lord Craven's estate.

Missel Thrush or Mistle Thrush (n.): A type of bird found in Europe that has a spotted underbelly and eats mistletoe berries. (See page 80.)

Moor (n.): A hilly habitat of open land, or, a boggy area of land. (See page 5.)

Nettle (n.): A flowering plant with stinging hairs.

According to some folklore sources, stumbling upon these protective plants means that you might find a fairy's home nearby.

Oppression (n.): When people who have power or authority use it in an unfair or cruel way.

Pansy (n.): A type of small, colorful flower with large petals.

In one of Shakespeare's plays titled A Midsummer Night's Dream, *characters used the nectar of this flower to create a love potion.*

Pandemic (n.): An outbreak of disease that occurs over a wide area and affects many people.

Salon (n.): A regular social gathering of writers and artists.

Snipe (n.): A wading bird with brown feathers and a long, straight bill.

Spade (n.): A tool for digging, often used in gardening. (See page 61.)

Spick-an'-span or Spick-and-span (adj.): Clean and orderly; spotless. (See page 78.)

Tuberculosis (n.): A bacterial disease most often affecting the lungs. Symptoms include chest pain and a lasting cough.

Mariah Marsden grew up hunting for faeries amidst the old hills of the Missouri Ozarks. A former children's librarian and co-author of *Anne of Green Gables: A Graphic Novel*, she earned her MFA in Creative Writing & Media Arts from the University of Missouri-Kansas City and is now a PhD candidate in English at The Ohio State University. She writes about the dreams and difficulties of girlhood, the folklore of her region, and the complexities of rural life. She's still on the lookout for faeries.

Hanna Luechtefeld spent the early part of their childhood in New Hampshire, the later part in Missouri, and all of it in the woods. Long afternoons filled with outdoor adventure gave them a flair for the creative and a love of storytelling. They graduated from the University of Central Missouri in 2019 with degrees in graphic design and illustration and a passion for zines and DIY comics. Today, Hanna lives in Kansas City, where they help run a local art gallery and music venue. When not preparing for a zine fest, you can find them outside: mountain biking, rollerblading, or hiking. Someday, they hope to have a backyard "secret garden" of their own.

The Secret Garden: A Graphic Novel

Andrews McMeel Publishing
a division of Andrews McMeel Universal
1130 Walnut Street, Kansas City, Missouri 64106

www.andrewsmcmeel.com

21 22 23 24 25 RR2 10 9 8 7 6 5 4 3 2 1
ISBN: 978-1-5248-5815-5
Library of Congress Control Number: 2021930895

Photo credits:
Page 189: Author photo supplied by Mariah Marsden; Illustrator photo by Collin Cornelison

Based on the novel by Frances Hodgson Burnett

Illustrator: Hanna Luechtefeld
Editor: Melissa Rhodes Zahorsky
Art Director/Designer: Spencer Williams
Production Editor: Jasmine Lim
Production Manager: Chuck Harper
Colorists: Hanna Luechtefeld, Melissa Mallory, Eric Scott,
Sierra Stanton, and Spencer Williams

Also adapted by Mariah Marsden
Anne of Green Gables: A Graphic Novel

Made By:
LSC Communications US, LLC
Address and location of manufacturer:
1009 Sloan Street Crawfordsville, IN 47933
1st Printing – 4/26/21